# Return to Me

## MELISSA MACKINNON

A THISTLE AND OAK PRESS PUBLICATION

*For Daniel.*

# RETURN TO ME

## MELISSA MACKINNON

# Prologue

*Galhaven Manor*
*Winter*

Lady Emmony clutched the bedpost, her birthing gown still wet with blood. Weak, and her vision blurring, she drew a ragged breath and glanced at the sweet babe fussing in a cradle. Her husband, Bertram, Earl of Galhaven, raged opposite her.

His fists clenched the handle of a blade and flexed as his anger consumed him. "You will die for this," he seethed.

Emmony hesitated. Her sweet darling daughter, with her tufts of beautiful golden hair and bright blue eyes, cried for her mother. She yearned to hold her just once more.

But it would not be.

"Magda," she calmly told the nursemaid cowering in the corner. "Take the babe."

The nursemaid shook her head, slinking further into the darkness. "No, my lady."

"You will," Emmony told her. "And you will raise her well. You shall call her Brynn, and you will tell her just how much I loved her."

Magda rushed to the cradle and swooped the newborn into her arms. Then, with stumbling steps, she left the bedchamber.

Bertram lunged for her.

Emmony narrowly escaped his grasp. "I curse you," she spat. "I curse you with age, and sickness, and death."

"Shut your mouth, you witch!"

"I told you she would be born. I warned you. She will possess the power of the winter child, and she will stop this war of yours. I gave her the second sight and she will live to see you die."

He was on her then, her throat in his grasp. "You speak lies."

She laughed, manically, under his hold. "I see the fear in your eyes. You know I speak the truth. Touch one golden hair on her head and you will die from *unspeakable* things. Things you know nothing about. The darkness will come for you. Your sons will die before your eyes, your power will crumble into ruin, and I will dance on your grave from the spirit world."

# Chapter One

## WARRIORS

*Galhaven, Engel*
*Autumn*

Covered in a thick blanket of darkness, Brynn was trapped between the snares of restless sleep and dreaming. Indistinct shouts bounced from wall to wall. The echoes of pounding hooves reverberated through her as horses raced through the courtyard. She searched the space around her for the cause but found nothing. A horse shrieked in the distance, shaping her dreams into a twisted nightmare. A fierce wind blew against her face, roaring as the skies opened in hellish fury. Her older brothers barked orders to one another. Three black ravens circled in the sky, waiting.

Searching the vast emptiness surrounding her, Brynn pawed the air. Desperate to find her brothers, she sought their frantic voices. Something was terribly wrong. She urged herself to move forward, but heavy wind gripped her shoulders, pinning her against the darkness. A strong gust violently shoved her away from the aberrant visions of her brothers.

She fell to the balcony floor with a thud, startling her from restless sleep. She pushed matted hair from her face, realizing the terror was no dream. Men with torches ran beneath her balcony shouting commands. Servants chased after their masters, trying to keep pace. Swollen drops of rain spattered across her face. A storm lingered, encroaching on them with every gust of icy wind. Could her father's men be strapping down the area in preparation? No, there was far too much commotion below. A different kind of storm was brewing.

Making her way to the stairs, Brynn clutched her quilt tight around her chilled body. She reached the spiral stairwell and started her descent, one stone at a time. She paused just as the entrance doors to Galhaven Manor flung open in furor, and Brynn tucked into the shadows. Armed guards burst through escorting four massive men. She spotted her brothers, Michael and Marcus, at the center of the madness. Her betrothed, Julian, followed behind with a sword drawn. Her father, Bertram, waddled not far behind.

The strangers towered above those who confined them. From their sheer size, Brynn knew they outweighed and could easily outmaneuver any Engel in the manor, yet they allowed themselves to be guarded. The absurdity of the situation was briefly comical. They were placating her brothers, and she wasn't the only one thinking so. Engel faces told truths. Underneath the grime, muscle, and leather were the unmistakable sight of pale yellow hair. As dirty and matted as it was, she knew who the intruders were.

Archaeans.

Archaeans in the *manor*.

Her stomach roiled, twisting and curling into tight knots as she fought to keep its contents down. She'd never actually seen an Archaean before, but legends of battles in centuries past flowed through her mind, as did the current wars raging around them. Archaeans were fierce warriors from the north. They spoke no language any civilized citizen from Galhaven understood. Their only purpose was to spill the blood of their enemies — her people, the Engels. They were born and bred for it. There was no reasoning with them, no mercy. The warriors had come to kill them all, and her father allowed them into their home.

*The fool.*

The people of Galhaven feared Archaeans, and for good reason.

Villages caught between the borders had been all but abandoned over the years. The two realms never ceased to be at war.

An Archaean was arguing with her father, but she couldn't make out the muffled words. One of the warriors — a tall beast clad in leather — pointed to the warrior who favored his injured arm. A crudely fashioned bandage immobilized him from forearm to shoulder. The one speaking with her father was tall and broad. A truly wondrous sight. Never had she seen such an abundance of restrained strength in just one man.

"Brynn! Why are you out of your chamber?" hissed a familiar voice from behind.

Brynn clutched her chest, then the wall, to keep from tumbling down the stairs. "By the gods, Magda, you gave me a fright!" She tugged on the nursemaid's sleeve. "What is happening?"

"I overheard Master Michael shouting about an alliance and your father must honor it or face being attacked!"

"Who are they?" Brynn eyed the men with fascination. There were only a handful of people in Galhaven with pale hair and light eyes — herself being one of them. No one ever mentioned her abnormalities — though they were blatant — but rather graciously spared her further humiliation over her years. Her father, Bertram, a wealthy nobleman and Lord of Galhaven, had only wanted sons. Strong, willing, and loyal sons. When his third wife gave birth to the fair-haired Brynn, he ordered the unwanted babe kept out of sight — if alive at all. Bertram dreamt of wealth and higher nobility for his sons and expressed his feelings on the matter frequently. As three of the five sons perished from battle, sickness, and an untimely accident, he'd come to realize his continued wealth very well might fall on his only daughter... the strange, quiet, repulsively towheaded, out of sight Brynn.

Because of her father's hatred for her, Brynn knew she was different. Strange things happened when she was near. Good or bad, she knew naught how to stop it. Something dwelled inside her and sang like no other. Some called her healer; some called her witch. Whatever her truth, people did their best to ignore her.

Magda placed a palm on Brynn's shoulder. "Warriors from the north. Archaeans."

7

"But why are they here?" Archaeans had no business being in peaceful Galhaven unless they were surrendering to the militia.

Magda seemed to have heard her thoughts. "They are free fighters and pledge allegiance to no man. I hear they serve under the command of Brockington, but that cannot be possible since Brockington serves the militia."

Brynn strained to listen to the argument. Curious fascination bit at her.

"I must return you to your chamber," whispered Magda as the altercation escalated. "With strange men in the manor, it is best we keep everyone safe in their rooms. Come." The nursemaid took Brynn by the hand and retreated upstairs. They both melted into the darkness.

Exhausted from the commotion and endless questions about Archaeans, Brynn dozed off to the muted sounds of disorder, ready to dream once more. But peaceful sleep didn't come. Instead, her dreams were haunted by visions of warriors invading the entrance hall, their strange voices echoing in her thoughts between sleep and consciousness. The blended scents of smoke and rain, sweat and leather, lingered in her nostrils, fueling her restless dreams. The three ravens circled once more.

In the wee hours of the morning, Magda jolted Brynn from precious sleep. Her voice was strained and stern — not a Magda Brynn easily recognized. "Your presence has been requested by your father. Get out of bed and dress. Quickly, now."

Brynn rubbed the sleep from her eyes. "What?"

Magda pulled the bed covers down. "You must hurry! Your father insists on it."

"Let me sleep, you daft woman."

A light slap to each cheek pulled Brynn from her daze. "My girl, wake up *now!*" Magda nudged Brynn's shoulder.

She groaned in protest. Remnants of her fitful dreams played fresh in her memory. She reflected on the few rare moments of freedom spent with her brothers. They had played long and hard in a meadow with mock battles and silly games of capturing warring flags on horseback. It was a memory she recollected often — one she tried hard to hold on to, for soon after that joyous day the peace had been broken, treaties severed, and war declared.

Brynn rummaged through her wardrobe. She grabbed a worn shift, a simple skirt, and a belt to hold it all in place. They smelled of horse sweat and hay but would serve well enough for whatever her father needed at such an hour. She made her way to the door, hopping on one foot while slipping a boot on the other. She rushed to the stairs to catch up to the nursemaid. "Magda, wait!" She blindly followed the old woman down two more sets and into the dark depths of the manor. The air was moist and humid and clung to her like a blanket. The strong stench of fouled dirt and mold stung the insides of her nostrils, making her eyes water.

As she turned the last corner, out of breath and damp with sweat, Brynn stumbled into Magda's backside. Righting herself, she peered around the nursemaid. In a dimly lit corner on a long wooden table lay one of the Archaean warriors. Another sat in a rickety chair to his left, which threatened to give way to his size. Two more Archaeans leaned against a back wall, standing guard. Brynn entered the room.

Bertram rose and motioned for her. A nervous twinge took root inside her belly. "Michael tells me you have a steady hand," said her father.

Brynn lowered her head. "Yes, my lord." Panic washed over her.

"And you are knowledgeable with herbs and tinctures. Is this true?"

"Yes," she replied, hesitant. "But only with animals. I have never—"

"Quiet. Come here."

"Yes, my lord," she whispered, obediently stepping forward and taking the basket of rags from Magda.

"This man is injured, and by the treaty, we must see to his needs."

"I have never treated a man before, my lord." A few medicinal tools rested on top of the linens in the basket. Brynn timidly took one and swallowed hard. "Are you sure you wish me to do this?"

"Do it *now*."

Taking a deep breath, Brynn commanded her feet to move. She approached the man on the table. Her legs felt numb as if they weren't her own. Her heart pounded inside her chest and she wondered if the warrior in the chair could hear the loud thumping in his ears as she did. "More light?" she asked, setting the basket beside her patient.

Magda retrieved an oil lamp for her.

"Thank you." Brynn surveyed the wound. A blood and mud-crusted rag covered the man's shoulder. She touched the skin around it, testing for signs of pus and fever. He moaned under the pressure of her fingers when she set to work peeling away the layers of bandage. The rags were fused together, heavily soiled with blood. She did her best to remove them gently, but as she worked at a particularly matted piece, the Archaean groaned in agony and spewed words in a language she couldn't understand.

A tug on her shoulder jerked her from her task. The man spoke angry words at her.

Startled, she turned to face the warrior behind her, eyes narrowed. He looked at her expectantly as though she should understand him, but she did not. "My apologies. I do not mean to pain him, but the bandage... it must be removed. There is something—"

"An arrowhead." The man glanced at her, his eyes flickering with curiosity. He took in her every inch, judging her and unraveling what little composure she had left.

Through grime and sweat covering his face, Brynn could clearly see his intrigue. He understood her babbling. He spoke her language, used her words. Brynn wasn't at all expecting that from an Archaean. *Stay calm. Breathe.* "Will you tell your friend that I—"

"Brother," the Archaean interrupted. "He is my brother."

"Very well, would you tell your brother I need to remove the arrowhead? He will feel the pain, but at least..." Brynn's voice failed her as the warrior's eyes raked over her again. His appraisal burned her skin even in darkness. She wanted to see those eyes — see if they were like hers — but ghostly shadows denied her.

The man muttered a few words to his brother, clasping his hand. "He is ready."

Brynn released a breath between pursed lips and dipped a clean rag into a water bowl. Pressing the cloth against the wound, she squeezed out the water until the bloodied bandage gave way. She struggled with the bulkiness of his muscular build, desperate not to cause more damage as she finagled the cloth from his underarm and shoulder. Somewhere in the back of her mind emerged the realization she had just touched a man for the first time. It wasn't at all what she had expected. Brynn leaned close, taking a good look at the wound. She closed her eyes and turned away in haste, breathing slowly to keep from vomiting. Deep in the muscle were the shattered shards of an arrow tip. The wound oozed pus. The slightest pressure sent the viscous yellow liquid spurting out from the smallest of cracks. The permeating stench caused even the warrior beside her to cover his nose.

"How long has he been like this?" She turned her attention to the thick mass of brawn and muscle hovering nearby, her words infused with a tinge of anger and frustration. How anyone could let a wound get that grotesque without seeking proper care was beyond belief. The man was lucky he hadn't yet lost his arm.

"We have been riding for five days, perhaps six."

Brynn shook her head and clucked her tongue. Any fear she held of these men vanished. Every word seeped with disapproval. "He is severely damaged. He will need close attention for days. This infection is in his blood, and he may yet lose his arm. I do not know if I can mend this. He is a mess."

"You must." The man rose to his full height, towering above her. With one step he was nearly on top of her, and he leaned in so close Brynn could see his face. His voice, husky and raw, penetrated the thickness of the air.

*Blue.*

His eyes were blue — a deep, rich blue, like the sea on a summer's day. Brynn had never before seen such a splendid color. Humbled, she hung her head and whispered, "Yes, sir." Her attitude was quite out of line. She'd overstepped her bounds, letting her mouth run away with her again. The sheer size of the Archaean standing before her unsettled her stomach, but something soft reflected in his eyes. "I shall do what I can. I need more light," she called, transfixed by the unwavering beauty hidden beneath the layers of concern and sadness on the Archaean warrior's face.

Clearing her throat and grasping at composure, Brynn turned to the injured man. She washed the wound's outer edges, wiping away as much pus and blood as she could. "Magda, I need honey and some tea brewed. Also, some blackweed and..." She paused, trying to recollect what she had read in her herbalist books. The immense pressure from the Archaean's gaze flustered her. "And... and some elderflower as well. Yes. And the bark from a pula tree. The brown bark, not the white."

Magda disappeared into the shadows of the corridor.

With little left to do now but wait, Brynn concentrated her efforts on removing arrow fragments. "This will hurt," she told the warrior. She dug her fingers deep into the man's flesh to fish out the largest, deepest piece. The man shrieked and lashed out at her. She stumbled backward, colliding into the body behind her. The Archaean grabbed her by the arms, steadying her steps. His hands burned her like fire. "I'm so sorry," Brynn mumbled, pulling away. "Forgive me."

"No need to apologize." He released her.

Regaining her footing, Brynn checked the man for consciousness. Finding him unaware, she continued her work, dropping each shard she found into a bowl. Brynn wiped a bloody hand over her brow then paused to accept the assortment of herbs and tea from Magda when she returned.

"What is this treatment?" The Archaean hovering over her probed her assortment of healing items.

"It will ward off any decay that may be left in the wound. It will help maintain his vitality, as the infection has spread. I will flush out the wound with the brewed tea," she told him, pouring a bit of the liquid on the wound. "Then I will pack it with the honey and herbs. They must be removed no later than tomorrow's eve, or it will fester." She covered the gash with plenty of honey and an array of herbs before covering the wound with fresh bandages. "Do not let him use the arm when he wakes, and give him the rest of the tea to drink. He requires rest, but you must remove him from this room. This place will hinder his recovery. He needs fresh air." Turning to her father, she said, "I'm finished. May I go?" Bertram nodded. Brynn gathered the remnants of her work and bolted for the door, thankful to be removed from the Archaean's watch.

The sun rose high during her time in the belly of the manor. Birds chirped cheerful tunes while her horses grazed in the pasture. It was too late in the morning to return to the comfort of her bedchamber, so Brynn decided it would be best to continue with her daily activities. After taking a quick bath and changing her soiled clothing, she meandered to the stables to visit with her horses. She trudged up the path to the barn, excited for the respite they gave her. "Good morning," she called to a passing servant.

"Hello, beautiful," she cooed upon reaching the stall of a large brown mare. The horse nickered a cheerful greeting and poked her muzzle over the door, sniffing for a treat. "Silly girl." Brynn pulled open the stall door and slung a lead over the mare's neck. The horse willingly followed through the barn. After tying the mare to a hitching post, Brynn brushed its coat, forgetting the world around her. Lighthearted, she hummed, switching from one tune to another — whatever her heart desired. She sang of love and romance, and of the rain and dancing. Of dreams she knew would never come true for her. She sang until a crouched figure in the shadows caught her attention. Brynn stopped in her tracks, her eyes wide.

The two stared at each other in silence.

Brynn told her body to run, to seek the safety of the manor, but her legs would not budge. Her heart pounded. A scream stuck in her throat. The Archaean. The one with the blue eyes.

In one fluid motion, he rose to his full height. His arms hung at his sides, his fingers splayed away from his body. He eyed her with a wary interest, just as she did him.

---

S he matched each step he took toward her with one step back.

"Stay where you are," she warned. Her shoulders touched the mare's flank. No more room.

"'Tis all right," he said in his language.

Panic-stricken, the golden-haired girl ducked under the mare's belly to place the horse between them. "Stay away from me!" She cried Engel words, throwing the brush at him.

He dodged it with ease and repeated the words, slowly this time. He shook his head in frustration when he realized she could not understand him. The girl didn't understand her *own* language. In recalling her cleansing of his brother's wound, she hadn't attempted speaking to him as the Archaeans did. The girl had been raised in this place.

*Did she not know what she was?*

He paused. "Thank you for helping my brother," he blurted out the Engel words she understood. The girl clung to the mare's front legs, trying to get as much of the horse between them as possible. Tears streaked her

13

dusty face. Fair skin shone through the dirty smears, and eyes as blue as the sky stared wildly back at him.

"You're welcome," she muttered.

***

B rynn wiped away a tear to clear her vision. He stared at her with those deep blue eyes and bestowed a lopsided grin. Clean and shaven, he didn't look as old and mean as Brynn first thought him to be. He was still large as his shadow reflected, but his face hadn't yet begun to wrinkle. There was a softness hiding there. His eyes still twinkled; he couldn't have been much older than her ten and seven years. Certainly, old enough to know better than to sneak up on a girl.

The man peered under the horse's belly. He paused before speaking, clearly translating the words in his mind. "I'll not hurt you." With his fingers, he beckoned her forward. "What are you called?"

"Brynn."

"I am Marek Coinnich of Cinn Tàile. Now that we know each other, you can come out. I mean you no harm. I just wish to thank you properly." He tapped the leather pouch tied to his belt, the coins inside clinking against one another.

Brynn edged her way to her horse's lead. "You have stated your thanks, now leave. I require no coin." The sound of footsteps coaxed her attention from the warrior. Someone was coming. "Quickly, you must not let him find you in here." Her beating heart leaped in her chest. He was coming.

Within moments, her father rounded the corner, his face a deep shade of scarlet upon seeing her. "Where have you been, girl? There was the business of your dowry to attend to, and you were called for. I looked the fool in front of Julian!" Grabbing her by the arm, Bertram pulled Brynn from behind the horse. His fingernails dug deep into her skin and she let out a cry. "Let's go, you ugly wench!" The smell of ale was fresh on his sour breath. "Take care, girl, and learn to obey!" Bertram grabbed her throat with a clenched hand then forced her against the wall so high she could barely touch the floor. "Julian is the richest offer yet, and for some reason, he will still have you. He almost changed his mind when he learned of your disappearance, but I managed to calm him. He required your presence, and, where were you? Not in *this* manor! No, you're out here in the barn consorting with this heathen!"

Desperate to loosen his grip, she clawed at his hand, gasping for a small trickle of air.

"I should have disposed of you when I had the chance, just like your whore of a mother!" Bertram's face twisted in disgust before he dropped her, and she slumped on the floor.

Brynn sucked in a precious gulp of air, filling her lungs and coughing up the burning in her chest. Lacking the strength to run, she staggered to her feet. Her eyes darted toward the Archaean for but a moment, then down toward his clenched fists.

"And what do you think *you* are doing in here?" the earl bellowed at the Archaean.

Marek stood rigid, the blue in his eyes piercing through her. "This is a stable, is it not? Might I tend my own mount, Engel?" Fingers flexed with careful restraint.

Bertram pointed a knobby finger at Brynn. "Get your hide back to the manor. See to your duties."

"Yes, my lord."

"And *never* insult me like that again!"

As Brynn passed her father, Bertram raised his booted foot and kicked her thigh. She stumbled and, losing her footing, careened onto the floor. With her palms scraped and her pride wounded, she picked herself up and scurried from the barn before allowing her tears to fall.

She secluded herself to the balcony, wallowing in self-pity while waiting until it was time to tend to her patient. Her thoughts drifted to the warrior in the barn. Marek. He hadn't seemed as menacing as Archaeans were said to be. To her surprise, he'd treated her as an equal. Perhaps all men were not equal. Sighing, she wondered if Julian had an ill temper likened to her father's.

Julian. Her brother, Michael, had arranged for Julian's transport to Galhaven, along with several other courtiers to stay as guests, a fortnight ago. She had mistakenly lost track of the hour. Had she deserved such treatment? *No.* Her betrothed was a gentleman. He was educated and raised properly in Engel society. He would make a fine husband, and she would try her hardest to be a proper wife. Surely, he would not treat her as abhorrent when she was his wife and free from Galhaven and her father.

There was a knock at the door, but Brynn made no attempt to answer it. The only person to ever visit her was dear Magda, and Brynn knew she would enter whether she opened the door or not.

"Milady, are you in?" Magda called as she cracked open the bedchamber door.

"I'm here," replied Brynn, watching the people go about their day in the courtyard below. Several carriages loaded with wardrobe trunks waited near the gate. Their guests would be leaving soon; for that, Brynn was thankful.

She often wondered about the company her brother, Michael, kept. The group was a sordid bunch, particularly the young ladies. Just last eve, Brynn had heard them gossiping about her when she passed their chamber.

"Who does she think she is, taking our men like that?" the one named Meredith had said.

"Well, she *is* very pretty," another commented. "And she does have a higher title than you."

"Do not say such things," Meredith hissed. "Have you looked at her? She is not like us. That hair can only mean *one* thing. And for Julian to even contemplate a match with her... she must have put some sort of enchantment on him. Her kind is *all* like that. Dabbling in books and plants. I heard she reads *spells* like a *witch*. Everyone who has been introduced into society *knows* Julian is mine. Why would he want her?"

"He only wants the property from her dowry, and he'll most likely use her as his whore," whispered another.

"*I* will be his respectable wife." Meredith cackled. "I have a feeling Julian will not be finding her delightful for much longer. Just you wait."

Magda spoke, bringing Brynn back to the present. "Julian is waiting in the hall. The Archaean is ready for you."

"Thank you, Magda. I shall be down shortly." Brynn rose from her balcony seat and took one last look at the courtyard, wishing she were in a carriage leaving on the wind.

The hall buzzed with a fretful chatter. Whispers of encroaching war and the safety of the guests with Archaeans roaming Bertram's halls floated from wall to wall. Julian conversed with his companions on a nearby settee, sipping wine and looking regal in a short coat and trousers. Flames from the fireplace reflected off polished boots. His feet were crossed at the ankles, relaxed and unaware. Meredith, doting on him like she was already his wife, cast Brynn an evil glare.

Julian turned toward her as Brynn entered, his mouth curling up in a constrained smile. "There she is now. My *betrothed*."

A man snickered beside the hearth. "Awaiting your wedding night, Julian?"

"If it pleases you, I am ready for your escort," said Brynn.

"Another glass of this fabulous wine would please me, but I suppose I will make do with your company, my sweetness." Julian handed Meredith his cup. "Have this filled for my return." He rose, teetering to one side before finding balance. "Damn good wine!" He laughed, took Brynn by the arm, and led her from the hall.

Magda met them at Michael's lodge, carrying the tools Brynn needed. The evening sun seared the sky with tawny reds and pinks. Brynn bid Julian farewell and ducked through the entrance. The wounded Archaean was sitting on a stool when she entered, his shoulder propped against the wall. "You're looking better," Brynn commented, setting down the basket. "Come closer." The man looked to his brother, who translated the words, and the warrior shuffled the stool away from the wall.

She sat in an empty chair near her patient. A closer look showed much of the yellow ooze had retreated from the wound. Her treatment had worked well enough and had most likely saved his arm. She methodically peeled away the soiled bandages, tossing them into a bucket on the floor. Using the tips of her fingers she opened the wound just enough to remove the packing. "It looks grand," she told him, smiling.

Marek translated and the brother grinned back.

Brynn prepared a poultice in a small earthenware mortar, grinding her precious healing herbs with the pestle as the men watched with rapt curiosity. Once finished, she massaged the thick paste into the wound, gentle as a mother's touch. "Tell him this will help it to heal on the inside," she instructed Marek.

Never having sewn up a man before, just animals, she took a long breath to steady her nerves before digging through her goods for her horsehair and bone needle. Her hands shook as she tried to thread the needle and missed once, twice... three times. The injured man watched her uneasily, furthering her nervousness. She gave the needle and hair one last attempt before Magda huffed, took it from Brynn's twitching fingers, and threaded it for her.

Finally, she was ready to begin. The warrior sat quite a bit higher and at an odd angle. She stood to pinch the skin together, but it wouldn't close properly. She rotated him to one side and started again but stopped when she realized her torso blocked what little light she had. Frustrated, Brynn pushed a loose curl from her brow. How could she explain in what position she needed him in if she couldn't decide herself? Unable to communicate, she acted on impulse and tugged the Archaean to her lap so his shoulder was directly in view.

Michael lunged toward Brynn. She briefly turned her attention toward him to shoo him away and an argument ensued behind her but continued her ministrations despite the two warriors stepping from the shadows toward her brother.

With every poke of the needle, the Archaean squeezed his eyes tighter and grit his teeth. She knew it must hurt, so just as she did to comfort her horses, Brynn sang a soft, soothing tune to drown out the sound of needle piercing flesh. The room was quiet when she finished. She'd lulled them all into calmness, especially the warrior laying in her lap. She ran her fingers along his forehead, pushing back the yellow hair that fell there before helping him to sit up. "There," she whispered in his ear. "All done." Brynn turned toward Marek. "He must immobilize the arm for a few days, but he should heal quickly. Pull the stitching out when the skin has fused together. Some clean bandages if it seeps." Brynn handed the cloth to Marek while the patient inspected her work.

Testing his mobility, the man chuckled and spoke to her, rolling his shoulder.

"He says you would be most useful to have after battle," said Marek.

Brynn looked at the imposing figure in the shadows. "Tell him... thank you." She wiped her cheeks with her sleeve before gathering her supplies to leave.

The brothers spoke to each other in the thick brogue of their country, the tone harsh and troublesome. The injured brother pointed at her insistently. Brynn stepped away from her place between the two brothers and sought the door. Their words made her uneasy.

With a definite scowl present, Marek turned to Michael. "He wants to know how much for the slave girl?"

Taking hold of her middle, Michael swung Brynn around. "She is not for sale," he growled. "Get to the manor," he told her. "Now." He shoved Brynn through the door, Magda at her heels.

The door slammed, leaving them in darkness.

The women held hands, following the stony path toward the manor. *Slave girl?* Did they make a habit of selling off their nobility? Uncivilized, just as Julian had warned.

*What beasts.*

# Chapter Two

## UNINVITED GUESTS

Brynn's stomach rumbled, depriving her of much-needed rest. She tried forcing hunger from her mind and concentrating on pleasant thoughts, but still, sleep wouldn't come. She changed positions, rolling away from the fire now dying in the hearth, and tried fluffing her pillow. The most she accomplished was an uncomfortable tangle of limbs and feigned sleep. Images of juicy roasts dripping over the embers refused to depart her thoughts. She should have eaten more at the evening meal instead of smiling at the guests like a fool.

Was it too late to sneak into the kitchen for a snack?

The punishment for being caught out of bed — especially with the sudden disruptions — would be strict, but her hunger outweighed a level head. Brynn kicked back her blankets and rose from the bed. She snatched her night robe from the nearby chaise before sneaking out of her chamber.

Deciding to brave the darkness rather than risk exposure with a lamp, Brynn felt her way along the wall to the staircase. She took the first few steps with caution until she found her footing, and counted… all thirty-six stairs to the bottom. Crossing to the left, she felt her way to the door leading to the next stairwell. A dim glow from below illuminated her path.

The sweet smell of bread tickled her nose, and her stomach rumbled, reminding her why she was out of bed at such a late hour. The glow grew stronger; light spilled over the threshold of the kitchen. A burst of laughter stopped her in her tracks. Brynn approached, edging her head around the corner.

Sitting around a large table were the four Archaean warriors. They drank freely from wine goblets and munched on the bread and meats set aside for breakfast. One leaned in close and spoke several words, causing the others to lean back into their chairs, roaring with laughter. Another tossed a chunk of bread in the jokester's direction, hitting him in the face. The jokester grabbed the bread and stood, reached across the table and attempted to stuff it down the other's throat. The wounded warrior kicked his feet up onto the table, chuckling.

She released a slow breath, contemplating whether this adventure was worth the risk. Lowering to her hands and knees, Brynn crawled through the door and hid behind a counter laden with fruits, vegetables, and cheeses — she needed only to reach up and grab what she could. With one hand in front of the other, she crept along the floor, keeping a wary eye on the men through the counter's legs. She didn't see the errant cart, and when she crashed into it, dishes clattered to the floor. Brynn tangled in the excess fabric of her robe. They had spotted her and would now slice her through or… worse.

The injured one had already expressed interest in wanting her. Fear of what he wanted to *do* to her raced with frantic thoughts. Reaching above, Brynn dug her fingers into the counter and hoisted herself from the floor. She sprinted for the door before the Archaean's had a chance to contemplate the situation. The element of surprise had worked in her favor before. But, as Brynn turned, one of the men was already upon her.

Instead of slipping over the threshold, she collided into the arms of an Archaean warrior. She screamed, somehow wriggled free from his grasp, and bolted for another door. Her fingers grazed the cold metal latch, and she seized it, pulling with all her might, but it would not budge. She tugged again, praying it was simply stuck. The latch popped and she yanked the handle. The door remained firm — locked from the outside. "*No!*" she sobbed, continuing to pull the door.

Giving up, she sought to leave the way she'd came.

Two men chased her, yelling and waving their hands, but she didn't understand their words. As Brynn wheeled around the table, her robe caught on the corner. The sharp edge of the table dug into her flesh as she dodged the reach of an Archaean. She dashed for the door through which she'd first entered, terrified she wouldn't make it the short distance. One of the men intercepted her path and lingered near the opposite end of the table, watching her every move.

Brynn paused and glanced at the man and the doorway to freedom. Before she could react, powerful arms wrapped around her torso, pinning her against the solid chest of a man. She did her best to fight back, kicking and squirming until the Archaean returned her to her feet. She covered her face with her hands, shielding herself from the blow she was sure would follow. The warrior could knock her farther than her old father could. His sheer muscle mass would rip her in two. "Please, I beg of you." She sought the warrior Marek. "Please."

Marek approached his comrade and shoved him away from Brynn.

Released, she recovered her footing and then made her escape over the threshold. Brynn slowed to a fast-paced walk when she was sure no one followed. Drying her cheeks with the sleeve of her robe, she sucked in a deep breath to calm herself. The abrasive stone of the manor walls was cold and familiar against her palms as she slid her hands over the rough surface. The cornerstone beneath her fingers indicated she had reached the stairs to her bedchamber.

Her voice shook as she counted. "One. Two. Three."

She stopped to listen.

Silence.

She took another step. "Four. Five. Six. Seven." Brynn thought she heard the rustling of fabric and paused. Narrowing her eyes, she scanned the stairwell for the disruption. A cool breezed passed through a window and blew a wall hanging. The tapestry flapped with the current. She needed to calm herself before she became sick. Brynn took a step and then another, counting each as her feet touched the cold stone, bringing her closer to the safety of her bed. "Twenty. Twenty-one. Twenty-two…"

On step twenty-three she heard the rustling again, this time very near. Within an instant, Brynn felt a strong pressure against her chest. Flinging her hands to the sides, she struggled to keep her footing. Brynn called out to the shadows. "Show yourself!"

Another direct push.

Brynn scraped her fingernails against the stone and strained to keep upright. She could see herself falling. Strange visions flashed before her eyes — running after her brothers as a child, her mares, large black birds circling her. A yellow-haired man in the darkness. She shrieked, smacking the stairs below. Her head collided with the wall as her legs tumbled over her front. A jagged edge of stone jarred deep into her spine as she toppled. Brynn's shrill scream pierced the darkness as she desperately tried to grab onto something — anything. With one last attempt to stop before facing certain death, she rammed into a man's broad chest.

He grunted on impact and wrapped his arms around her middle, clutching her tight. He, too, was now helplessly falling. The pair tumbled down the rock together, coming to a stop at the end of the stairwell. Brynn's head lay motionless on his chest. His heart raced beneath her ear. A familiar woodsy scent clung to the thin tunic acting as a barrier between them. Marek. Her head moved with the rise and fall of his lungs as he sucked in shallow breaths. She stirred, attempting to roll from his body.

Marek raised an arm and slung it over her, pinning her to his chest. He groaned, muttering incoherently.

Too exhausted to move, Brynn lay still. Her body burned. Every muscle lashed out in protest. A warm trickle of blood reached her trembling lips. Marek cradled her, drawing her closer in his delirium. He mumbled something she couldn't understand. As she listened to his smooth voice, the reverberations of people running through the hall swept through her. Darkness disappeared as torchlight filled the room. Her shrieks and thuds had brought the manor to life.

Brynn shut her eyes as the footsteps came to a halt. She knew exactly who approached by the distinctive clacking of shoes upon the stone.

"By the gods, what have you done?" her father whispered.

Marek still clung to her protectively, her head still propped on his beating heart. Her life had come to an end. One way or another, she would die that very night.

Murmurs and accusations echoed off the walls, making the room seem like a broom closet. Finding her strength, Brynn peeled away from Marek. She stood, faced her father, and watched as his face reddened to a deep scarlet. He scanned her body, noticing the torn garment, her tangled hair, and the Archaean laying on the floor.

Brynn wiped a smear of blood from her cheek and stared at the earl, trying to keep upright. She couldn't stop her swaying long enough to think of a rational explanation.

"You filthy whore!" Bertram spat, approaching. "You unclean, dirty, impure little bitch! And *you*..." He glared at Marek. "How dare you come into my home and lay your hands upon my betrothed daughter! Who are you, Archaean? Get up off my floor! You're *bleeding* all over it!" Bertram balled his fists.

Marek rose, distancing himself from Brynn. "My name is Marek. I am not here under false pretenses. I have told you no lies. Your *daughter*... fell down the stairs, and I merely saved her from an untimely death. I meant no harm, and I assure you she has not been violated in any way."

Brynn stared at the Archaean. Her situation didn't at all look promising. How was he to explain following her to her bedchamber? That in itself was enough to condemn her. She looked to him for help — for safety — but he only stared back.

"You will pay for this, girl. You will never marry from this family, as you are no longer worthy of a dowry! You are a whore, and so you shall be treated like one!" Bertram raised his hand to her cheek, cracking the corner of her lip with the back of his palm.

She didn't weep, though her body screamed to fight back. "I was pushed, Father, I didn't shame you! Please don't disown me. This place is all I have."

"How dare you speak to me? You are no daughter of mine. You never have been!"

Brynn collapsed to her knees and wept.

---

Could he trust his eyes? Was the man she called Father going to beat her senseless in front of everyone?

Like hell he was. "Stop this. She has done nothing wrong!" Marek looked about the room. Surely one of the men would interfere on her behalf, but not a single one stepped forward. How could these people stand idle while this Engel accused his own daughter of such things?

*Cowards.*

Marek reached for his side but realized too late he was unarmed. He'd left his weapons with his men when he chose to go wandering off on a spying mission after his late-night meal had been so very wonderfully interrupted by the beautiful slave girl.

The earl turned to Marek. "Gather your men and get out of my village. I *knew* you would be trouble the moment you arrived. Your kind is all the same. Big and brawny but ill-bred. Never a smart man among you." Bertram motioned to his guards with a flick of his finger. "Take her away."

Marek fumbled over the Engel's words as the room stirred. "What are you going to do with the girl?" he blurted.

"'Tis none of your concern," replied Bertram. Two men approached Brynn and took her by the arms. "Although it should be, as you are the one who made her do this unspeakable act. Perhaps you should be punished together. I could arrange it."

"I told you…" Marek's temper flared. It took all of his inner strength not to strangle the earl where he stood. As much as he wanted to, breaking a treaty would be more damaging to his people.

Her sobs and desperate screams echoed through a distant hallway as she pleaded for mercy. After a few tense moments, the screaming ceased and all was quiet. Marek approached Bertram. He positioned himself as close as he could without touching and leaned toward the earl's ear. "We will meet again, you and I," he growled. Marek turned on his heels and stormed from the entrance hall in search of his men. He would make this right… somehow.

# Chapter Three
## PUNISHMENTS

**M**arek found his men dozing in the stables, content with full bellies. Kicking the nearest boot, he roused them. "Wake up, you dogs."

His brother, Ronan, rolled away. "Let a man sleep, ye bastard."

"Get up. We have a problem."

"You mean *you* have a problem, eh?" Ronan pushed himself up from his makeshift bed in the hay.

"Aye, I'm fecked." Marek stretched his arms over his head and sighed, pacing the floor. "Come on, wake your asses up."

"But we just settled down!" Gavin protested in a drunken whine.

"You can sleep later. Remember that servant girl we were chasing 'round the kitchens?"

"Aye, the delicious tart. How could we forget *her*?" Gavin answered. "A beauty I'd like to find myself between."

The men snickered amongst themselves.

"We've been dreaming of her rump all night." Gavin grinned, winking at Marek. "We took bets while you were gone. The lad to beat down everyone else gets first go at pillaging the servants."

Marek's conscience tugged at his insides. "She is that Engel bastard's daughter, Gavin."

"*Och*," crowed Ronan. "This means we are heading on then, eh?"

"Is that where you've been off to then? Did you get caught indulging on that piece of tart?" Gavin flashed Marek a wide grin, dimples puckering his cheeks.

Marek's jaw twitched as he took a deep breath. Slowly releasing it, he clenched his fists tightly by his sides. "Don't make me flog you, *boy*."

Gavin raised his hands in defense. "'Tis nothing wrong with tarts, Marek. I rather enjoy them from time to time."

"Just shut your mouth for a moment."

"*Fine.*" Gavin sat back with a huff.

"I followed her up some stairs, and she came tumbling down. Someone pushed her, and she landed flat on me in a rather… compromising position. I didn't really make much of it — I was a bit delirious." He rubbed his head with his palm, recalling the scene. "Her father found us on the floor together and said something about her being a whore. My translation is weak when Engels babble on like babies."

Ronan stood, leaning close to Marek's ear. "You really *are* fecked, brother. You have had nothing but girl troubles since we were old enough to chase them. And this time, all on your own."

"As soon as we're gone, she'll be dead. I know it. That Engel has been waiting for the day he had enough cause to rid himself of her."

"Let the rich man take care of his own whore problems," replied Ronan.

"She's not a whore, Ronan. She's just a girl, and I won't have her death on my conscience. You didn't see her eyes." That sullen blue would haunt him the rest of his days. The anguish and fear were unmistakable. She'd sought him — a dangerous stranger — for help, and he'd done nothing but watch as she was beaten and dragged away.

"*Wait.*" Aiden sat in the shadows, listening. "How can an Archaean girl be the daughter of an Engel earl?"

"She cannot," Marek said dryly.

"Are you sure you speak of the same girl? The one from the kitchens? The one who fixed Ronan?"

"She clearly called him father. I know *that* word… and he mentioned her being his betrothed daughter, so I would believe that as her being the same one, yes." *Betrothed.*

Marek understood why the earl overreacted. He lost his marriage profit. Her father should be grateful he caught her, not condemning her to punishment. *Fecking Engels.* The daftest race amongst which he had ever had the displeasure of walking.

"So, what is it you plan on doing, then?" Ronan sighed.

"I need to think, but pack your gear and ready the horses. We'll be leaving in the morning."

---

B rynn curled up in a corner of the room she'd been stuffed in, trying to warm herself. A cool breeze seeped through the cracks of the crumbling stone that imprisoned her. Despite her best efforts to bury them, her thoughts spun out of control. She had hidden behind the truth for too long. She couldn't come to terms with her fate. Her father had been waiting for the chance to rid himself of her for years. He just hadn't been presented with the right opportunity. And now, she'd given him the perfect one. Why ever did the gods curse her so? Why had she not been born a boy? Brynn was the last child; her mother had died shortly after giving birth. Bertram had not taken another wife. Her brothers and Magda had raised her. They had shared their lessons in secret, teaching her various things about the world. They showed her the way of a sword and bow, taught her how to read, write, and count numbers. Her eldest brother, Marcus, had shown her how to ride a horse.

Magda once told her in bitter confidence she suspected foul play surrounding Brynn's birth and her mother's death shortly thereafter. The nursemaid told her Bertram chased her mother in a mad fury one evening after a heated argument, and she never returned. No one spoke of it.

Brynn's head throbbed and a dull ache seared up her spine. Someone had pushed her down those stairs. Pushed her on purpose, she was sure of it. Who would do such a thing? Those stairs were the only set leading to and from the bedchambers, and no one had used them after she had fallen. Whoever pushed her had to be — a lump rose in her throat — in the guest suite. Meredith. She'd been absent during the incident. Only the men had entered the hall, and all too quickly. Surely, the women must

31

have heard her scream. It had awakened the rest of the manor. Why not the guest suite?

The storage room door burst open, abruptly sidetracking her accusations. Michael entered and swiftly shut the door behind him. Lowering himself to one knee, he looked her over in the candlelight, examining her wounds. Michael took her chin in his palm and inspected the bruise on her cheek, clucking his tongue.

Rather unexpectedly, he blurted, "There is no other way to put this, Brynn. Father is in one of his moods and has decided a most terrible fate for you. I haven't been able to convince him otherwise, but I will still try. I will always think of you as my sister, and I do not wish to see more harm befall you. Father declared you must leave the manor to surely freeze when the snow falls, for no one in Galhaven shall be allowed to house or feed you — or you can repent, take your punishment, and continue to stay here... not able to marry for the rest of your days. Of course, you can also dedicate your life to serving the gods, but that would mean a life of solitude at the temple of Eris. I believe you deserve more than what the gods can give you. The choice is yours."

Could she be trapped in some horrid dream? One she hadn't foreseen? What she was hearing couldn't possibly be true. Brynn tried to sort it out. "But I haven't wronged him, Michael. I was pushed, and I believe I know by whom. If only you could speak for me. You could reveal the truth and remedy this. That Archaean, he only caught me. He saved me — does that not count for anything?"

"I believe you, Brynn, but the situation seems terribly suspicious to the others. You were out of bed in your night robe, and this man — who was not even *allowed* in the manor — was underneath you on the entrance hall floor at the bottom of your chamber stairwell. It doesn't look favorable. Why was he on the stairs to the bedchambers?"

"Oh, it doesn't look promising at all, but I honestly did nothing wrong. I didn't even have impure thoughts!" Brynn hid her face in her hands.

"As your brother, I would advise you to repent for your sins and take your punishment. The outcome may be more painful, but at least you will have a shelter over your head. You will save your own life."

"Have I displeased the gods so much that I must suffer like this? I have lived my life chastely and dedicated to Father and his people. I don't understand why this is happening. Do I even dare ask what the punishment is?"

"Thirty lashes."

"*Thirty lashes*! But Marcus didn't receive that many when he stole Father's court horse and sold it at market for a belly full of ale!" Brynn couldn't believe the words. Thirty lashes would tear her to pieces. She was strong of will, not strong of body. "He wants me to die, does he not? He knows full well I could not withstand thirty lashes. He has chosen this punishment so that I might leave by my own doing, not his. I know it to be true."

"My thoughts as well, Brynn," Michael muttered, pushing his dark locks from his brow. "What do you choose?"

"Tell him I shall take the thirty lashes," she answered with defiance.

"Brynn— please consider the options. I will do my best to take care of you, if…"

If she were to leave. She sighed. "What of Julian? I assume Father has told him the lies?"

Michael's eyes wavered from hers. "He has renounced the engagement."

Brynn held back a sob. "And what of your guests?"

"They shall be leaving with him in the morning. The women feel they are no longer safe."

"Might I ask who will be doing the lashing?"

"Father. He believes it will cleanse you properly if he is the one."

She sucked in a breath. "Tell him I will be ready."

---

When daylight broke through the early morning darkness, Marek and his men trudged to the manor to inquire of the girl. Surely by speaking to the calmed earl, Bertram would be ready to hear the truth. When they reached the main entrance, the doorman explained the girl was in the village square for her punishment.

"What *punishment*?" Marek pressed the old man against the door.

"Her repentance. She must be cleansed!"

"How do I get there?" spat Marek, releasing the man.

"Follow the road. It will lead you to the village. But you should hurry if you want a good view!" The doorman scratched his balding head with spindle-like fingers. "'Tis not everyday nobility takes a lashing. The entire village is bound to show for it."

Marek left the old man to mount his horse.

"What are you getting yourself into, brother?" asked Ronan, rechecking the girth on his saddle. "Do you want to do this?"

"I'm in the mood for a fight," was his reply.

The four Archaeans rode into the village, slowing when the crowd grew thick. After dismounting, they tethered their horses to a nearby rail and waded through the people, pressing farther through the commotion. Surprised stares greeted them at every turn, but made no attempt to make room for the beastly warriors.

The people formed a circle around the center square, awaiting the show. A stout man read from a piece of parchment in front of two tall wooden posts. Marek couldn't hear the words over the thrumming of the spectators but assumed the man announced the charges. Strapped between the two posts stood Brynn, her back outward.

Marek threw his elbow up, attempting to fight his way forward. He was pushed back with every step forward. After the man made his proclamation, the earl uncurled a long, leather whip and released its fury. It bit into her flesh like a snake, leaving jagged lines of red across her back. Another lash whipped through the air and found its mark. Too many. He growled his anger, shoving forward through the crowd.

Shrieking out in agony, Brynn pleaded for her life. Another lash dug in. Then another. Her wails did not deter the earl. Her feet gave out from under her.

Marek elbowed his way through the blood-crying mob. With every crack of the whip, he pushed himself farther. He would slice these fools through if it would clear him a path. The girl's screams echoed in his ears, signaling every lash reached its target. The crowd cheered with each crack. Five lashes. Six. He cursed, finally stumbling from the spectators. The girl hung lifeless before him.

The seventh lash cracked through the air, and the earl pulled his arm back to deliver the eighth when Marek charged. He wrenched the leather from Bertram's fist and the Engel tumbled to the ground. Marek tossed the whip aside. Standing over the shocked man, he pulled his sword from its sheath. The edge lingered dangerously close to the earl's throat. Marek wedged the tip under the man's chin, pressing it into the fat.

"Why do your people not rush to protect you, Earl of Galhaven?" Kneeling beside Bertram, Marek chose his words with care. "Touch her again, and I will kill you. I do not make idle threats, Engel."

Bertram stared ahead, his face void of expression.

Marek drew back his weapon before rushing to Brynn's limp body. Swinging hard against the ropes binding her, he freed her with a heavy blow. The girl dropped to the ground, landing in a small puddle of her own blood. After removing the ropes, Marek scooped her up. Blood painted his arms as he pushed his way back through the crowd to his horse. His men stood guard, but he met no resistance. Her lifeless arms dangled to her sides, swaying with his every step. A steady trickle of blood dripped from her fingers to the ground like dark drops of rain. Her heart beat against his chest as he climbed up into the saddle. It was slow but still beating.

With Brynn tucked safely into the crook of his shoulder, Marek turned his horse away from the village. No one followed, not even the earl. No one in Galhaven cared for this wild-eyed, free-spirited girl. It was for the best. She was his now. And they had started their long journey home.

"We are traveling too slowly, Marek. At this rate, we will never make it home in time." Ronan told his brother.

"We have time," he replied. For three days they had traveled at a walking pace, pulling the semiconscious girl behind them on a makeshift pallet built from saplings and a woven quilt. They made frequent stops to give her broth made from bones and to tend her wounds. She battled a raging fever but would live. Marek would make sure of it.

"What are you planning on doing with the girl? The slower we travel, the sooner we might meet resistance." Ronan's voice didn't waver, but Marek could sense his worry.

His brother's injury, and now the girl, sent their plan to a sharp halt.

35

The concerns of his men weighed heavily on his mind. The weather could turn at any moment, snowing them in and forcing them to seek shelter at whatever village happened to be nearest. They had already spent too many winters away from home. "They will not seek out the girl. But they may come for us. As soon as we reach the Crossroads, we'll drop her off somewhere. We will make it home in time, Ronan. Do not worry."

Ronan smiled before trotting ahead to the others. "Gavin, Aiden! Marek says we are to be ridding ourselves of the girl as soon as we reach the Crossroads!"

"I cannot wait to reach home." Aiden sighed, the longing in his voice evident. "*Och*, to eat some real food. I am sick of this Engel *shit*."

"When I get home, I'm going to swive every woman I see," Ronan boasted, a wide grin curling his lips. "What about you, Gavin? Care to join me?"

"*Join* you? Hell, no. I'm going to drink, steal a man's woman, then drink some more, start a fight, and then keep on drinking. And maybe steal another woman. Or two."

Aiden and Ronan nodded in agreement.

"Sounds excellent." Gavin gripped Ronan's shoulder and gave him an excited shake.

---

The smell of cooking meat tingled Brynn's nostrils, rousing her from a wicked dream. She'd been caught between sleep and restlessness, and it was always the same dream. Black ravens waiting. Always waiting.

She rolled to her back, stretching her stiff muscles. Sharp, needle-like pain radiated throughout her as she pushed up on her elbows. Brynn blinked, focusing on her surroundings. A cloth billowed in the wind, surrounding her on three sides. A large boulder blocked the open end. A tree branch jetted across her shelter, leafless and dark, casting strange shadows that seemed to follow even the slightest movements. Someone went through a great deal to see to her comfort. She crept to the cloth and peered through the opening. Seated around a small campfire were the Archaeans. Her hand covered her mouth to stifle a scream. They had taken her. A quick shot of panic quivered up her spine and made the tiny hairs on her arms stand on end. Brynn followed their movements until she connected with those cobalt eyes. A brazen stare met her gaze. There was a want in those eyes — something she had never seen before — and it frightened her.

Impulse told Brynn to move. She crawled from the shelter, scampering to a nearby bush to hide behind what false safety it provided. Even tucked out of sight, she couldn't overcome the alarm rooting itself deep in her belly. She wasn't sure if she should be terrified of this man or forever grateful for saving her life — twice. Brynn stayed huddled in her fortress of shrubbery while the four Archaeans ate their dinner, every last morsel.

Occasionally, Marek would glace her way, seemingly to check on her whereabouts. The sun set well below the trees before she mustered the courage to venture from her hiding place. She ached all over, and her stomach twisted in tight knots. She'd grown weary in the cold, was in desperate need of rest, and she certainly wouldn't get it hiding behind a bush all night. With her luck, she would likely be mauled by some wild beastie in the dark and become dinner.

The small fire popped and crackled, breaking the monotonous silence of the forest. A bitter autumn cold settled over the land and the warmth of the fire beckoned her forward, but her bladder had a higher calling. Surveying her surroundings, she contemplated her actions carefully. Forward? Or backward?

Brynn crept into the darkness. Her eyes wouldn't adjust to night's nocturnal mask. Trees took the form of people, reaching into the night. A rustling too close to her feet startled her and she stepped on a branch, its crack echoing through the trees. Brynn pawed the darkness as she stumbled through the forest, straining to see. Tripping over a tree root, she stepped into a shallow brook. At last. Brynn steadied her legs, lifted her skirts, and sighed in delight as she allowed the contents of her bladder to flow into the stream.

With that ache now gone, Brynn couldn't help but notice what freedom she found under the trees. No one had come for her yet; perhaps they didn't care enough to search. A thorn bush tugged on her skirts, keeping the fabric snug in its grasp until she yanked it free, leaving a swatch still attached to the branches. Quickening her pace, she pushed onward, hoping she was heading toward Galhaven. The tree canopy above hid the directional position of the stars.

The forest only seemed to grow darker with no end in sight. Her mouth was dry, her chest heavy. Her breath formed into tiny little ice crystals as she trudged up a steep hill hoping a clearing in which to rest was at the top. The incline proved difficult. A slick frost covered the terrain, and she slipped several times trying to conquer it.

When she reached the plateau, her toes snagged in the bramble, sending her reeling forward. She fumbled, trying to regain her footing to no avail. She clawed at the ground, reaching for anything to slow her descent, but the wet bracken only accelerated her speed. She groped at the darkness for a root or vine, something to grasp, but all Brynn found were fistfuls of dirt and leaves. Trying to dig her heels into the mess only ripped off her shoes. The ground vanished from beneath her feet.

Brynn extended her arms wide before certain death claimed her. By the grace of the gods, she touched a loose root. She wrapped her fingers around it just as her body slid from the edge of a cliff. She screamed, crashing into the rock wall as the root ripped through the dirt above before coming to an abrupt stop. She dangled in the nothingness surrounding her.

Without a moment's notice, the root gave way into the dark depths. A spatter of dirt rained from above. "Oh, no," she whimpered.

Brynn prayed. "Tyr, god of strength, give me courage." She slipped again. "Lunos, goddess of love, protect my family. Dragus, keeper of the dead, grant me a swift and painless death and safe passage when I cross." Hot tears burned her chilled cheeks as the root slipped through her fingers. Clamping her eyes shut, Brynn waited to tumble to the depths below. She repeated her prayers, mustering what strength she could. There was no sense in delaying the fall — it would only terrify her more. Death was calling, telling her to let go. With a sob, she released one hand. Releasing the other proved to be a bit more difficult. Perhaps, with just a short fall, the ground would not be so far below. She looked down, only to be greeted by the empty nothingness. She would have to pray it would be there.

Uncurling one finger from her slipping grip, Brynn chanted her death prayer. As she let loose the last of her fingers and began to fall, a still calm flowed through her. She was ready. Then a hand curled around her wrist. She dangled in the cavernous void for what seemed like an eternity until another hand circled her arm, pulling her. Fingers dug into her flesh, pulling her from the jaws of death.

Safely retrieved from an early demise, Brynn breathed in heavy silence, exhausted. Her rescuers panted quick words to each other in Archaean before staggering to their feet. The familiar voice wafted through her muddled thoughts. Marek. Her rescuer. Brynn, too weak to stand, was plucked from the ground and flopped over Marek's shoulder.

He gripped her tightly, his arm wrapped across her thighs with a hand resting comfortably on her buttocks.

Brynn didn't object. On the verge of tears, she kept silent. He must be furious with her, what man wouldn't be? She could have pulled him over the cliff with her, but he'd taken the risk... for her. Why had he done so?

Marek stumbled but held his cargo tight, chuckling to his companion. He flexed beneath her, readjusting her weight. She inhaled him deeply. Scents swirled about her, masculine sweat and earth, stirring her insides like nothing she'd ever before experienced.

The men seemed to encounter no difficulties finding their way back to the camp. They trudged through the forest with ease, talking to each other in hushed tones. Brynn's view was limited to mostly the backside of Marek's shirt and the darkness of night, but it didn't take long to realize they weren't far from where they had stopped for the night. Brynn had made a wide circle during her escapade in the forest, and the men must have heard her screams echo not far from camp.

Marek carried Brynn to the makeshift tent then set her down on a pile of blankets with an abrupt pitch. A lit torch with the end shoved into the ground provided light.

Shivering, Brynn pulled the warmth of the wool over her legs. She picked at her hair and tattered clothes matted with mud and debris. Her lip oozed fresh red around the curve of her chin. Brynn watched Marek wet a cloth with a water bladder. He approached her, but Brynn pushed his hand away.

"You are covered in filth," he told her. "Hold still."

"Do not touch me!" she cried out swatting at him.

Marek growled and threw the cloth, hitting her in the face. "If you could stop trying to kill yourself, that would be great."

The cloth fell to her lap, soaking her skirt. She took the rag and tossed it back with a scowl. It smacked his chest, then fell to the grass.

Marek ran his fingers through his golden waves. "You need not be afraid of me, girl."

"You are going to kill me," she replied, hugging her knees. The surety of her voice surprised her.

He sighed, folding his palms over the soft yellow curls lining his nape. "You seem to be doing a fine job of that on your own."

"You have no use for me. I'm better off dead to you."

Marek turned, his eyes cutting through her like a steel blade. "If I was going to kill you, I would have done it by now."

"Then why am I here if not to kill me or to—" Brynn shut her mouth, pushing thoughts of what these men could do to her from her mind. He shot her a menacing glance, and Brynn flinched.

"I give you no reason to fear me. I'm probably the only one right now who can say that." Marek knelt to retrieve the cloth, sighing. "Are you going to let me help you?" His Archaean lilt was thick and rich when irritated.

Braving boldness, Brynn countered, "I can do it myself."

She held out her hand for the rag.

"Oh, *now* you want this?" He squeezed the wet fabric in his fingers.

"Not if you're going to throw it at me." She pouted, tasting the blood with the tip of her tongue.

"Here, have at it." Marek handed her the cloth and the water bladder. "When you need my help, I'll be waiting for your thanks." Busying himself with the torch, Marek let her be.

The process was slow. Every inch of her ached. What she wouldn't give for a bath — a proper one. When she was sure she had scrubbed her face thoroughly, Brynn set to work on her arms and legs. Mud resided in every cranny, making her tattered clothing seem like rags themselves.

"Would you care for help now?" he asked, watching her struggle.

"I'm fine."

"'Tis all right to ask for help."

"I *said* I'm fine," she replied, peeling a section of matted hair from her shoulder. Brynn winced and sucked in a breath through her teeth, trying not to cry out while he was near. "Might I have a bit of privacy, warrior?" She set to work peeling the remnants of her dress from her shoulders.

"My name is Marek," he corrected, "and do not worry — you haven't anything I have not seen before. I've been cleaning those wounds of yours for days now. I've already seen it all."

Brynn's cheeks flushed, and she directed her attention elsewhere, ignoring his shameless stare. She focused on her wounds, keeping her distance.

Near the curtain, Marek unbuckled his belt to remove his tunic. He pulled the fabric over his head and then down his arms. He stood bare-chested and Brynn averted her eyes. Marek let out a rumbling laugh. "You are welcome to look, love."

"I fear the gods will not forgive me if I do," she whispered. How she wanted to. The man standing before her was breathtaking. His skin, kissed by sun and sweat, glimmered in the light of the fire. His muscles constricted with each movement; a taut definition like no other. Never had she seen such a sight. A fist-sized tattoo inked on his chest resembled a knot intertwining within itself, creating a marvelous spiral design. It came to a point at three ends. Her breathing quickened when he closed the gap between them, his tunic in his hand.

Kneeling beside her, he offered it to Brynn.

Brynn lowered her head, humbled and embarrassed by her thoughts. "I cannot do it by myself." She looked up at him.

"Ask me nicely." His eyes flickered over her face.

"Please, will you help me, Marek?"

The corner of his mouth twitched, briefly curling into a soft grin. "Aye, I will."

She whispered, "Thank you."

"Turn around," he told her, taking the cloth and water bladder. Marek wet the fabric and used it to cleanse her wounds, washing away the dirt and caked-on debris from the small of her back. His fingers grazed the curve of her neck, sending a shocking surge of heat reeling down her spine. He pushed her hair to the side, stroking her skin in delicate waves with the cloth.

Closing her eyes, Brynn exhaled, savoring every touch, not wanting them to end. Marek worked with quiet diligence before Brynn broke the uncomfortable silence. "Why did you take me?"

His hand paused near her shoulder. Water trickled down her sides, curving around to seep into the hems of her clothing. "Take you? I thought of it more like a rescue, myself. That Engel was going to kill you."

"The gods would have protected me."

Marek released a brusque laugh. "Your *gods*? Where were your gods on the stairs? Where were they when you were being whipped like a horse? Where were they when you were busy throwing yourself off a cliff? *I* heard your prayers. They did *nothing*." He grasped her arms and turned her to face him. "Any moment might be our last. We should cherish our doomed lives." A heat flickered in his eyes. "You underestimate your beauty, Brynn. I have never seen your equal, and you must protect yourself, even from men like me. You will only grow lovelier by the day. Do not depend on gods to save you. Your gods do not exist."

Brynn bit her bottom lip, brushing a curl from her eyes. "You speak as if you know much... but you do not. You shamed me in front of my people. I deserved my punishment, and I accepted it for dishonoring my father and my betrothed. You should have just let me be."

Marek continued with her bath. "You dishonored no one. You accepted a punishment for a wrong you didn't commit. Your people follow strange beliefs. You must get them from your *gods*. No one in *my* country would be flogged for touching a man."

"You don't understand."

"I do. Your men take many women. They do so for money, not for love or loyalty. Women are treated as property. We Archaeans honor our women. They are not inferior to men. We cherish them, love them, and make babies with them. We do not do as your Engel men do. Now *women... they* are gifts from the gods."

Brynn cracked a smile. "I thought you said there were no gods."

"Do not contradict me, woman."

"Your people attack ours, raiding and taking the women. You have burned villages and killed children for simply being in your path."

"You have heard the stories." Marek smiled. "Grossly exaggerated by Engels, but having a fierce reputation in battle keeps the men on your side. Put your arms up."

Brynn raised her arms, and Marek removed what was left of her sleeves. "This might sting a little," he warned before placing a finger along one of the many gashes in her flesh.

Brynn hissed, arching away from the pain.

"What is that?"

"'Tis a salve for your wounds. You will need it if you want to heal."

"Whatever is in that, I don't need it."

Marek continued, "You of all people should know of treating wounds."

"Don't put that on me. It hurts."

"I've been using it all along and it's healed your wounds immensely, so hush and hold still."

"I'll be all right."

"How long have you been a healer? You saved my brother with knowledge I have never seen before."

She huffed slightly. "I have always been this way. It just comes to me, or I find it in books. Or in dreams. I... see things. Things that come to pass one way or another. My brothers told me my mother had the second sight, too." She turned slightly to gauge his reaction. "Most call me witch, not healer. Does that scare you like it does my father?"

"Hmm." The corner of his mouth twitched slightly. "Turn around so I might finish. I am healer now."

"Just pass me the tunic." A crisp autumn breeze wafted through the gaps in the tent, settling on her dampened skin. Brynn pinned her arm across her chest, covering her breasts from view. She reached behind her, waiting for the clothing to be placed in her hand.

"Those are fine manners for the help I just gave you. You want it, you come and get it." Marek dropped the tunic behind her then crawled to the opposite side of the tent beside a bit of bread and meat. He brought them to Brynn. "Eat."

"Do you enjoy provoking me?" She huffed. "Would you *please* pass me that tunic so I might cover myself? No woman, even your kind, would ever enjoy being subjected to this type of indecency."

"So you say," he grumbled, kicking the tunic closer.

Brynn snatched it before he changed his mind then patiently waited for him to turn around. When he didn't, she scowled at him. "Would you

43

*please* turn around? I don't care if you've already seen me naked. I'm conscious now, and I'd like to preserve what bit of modesty I may have left."

Marek ripped off a large chunk of bread with his teeth and slowly turned his back to her.

When Brynn was sure his view was blocked, she found the neck hole in the tunic and slipped it over her head. The covering hung from her like a dress but was still warm from his body heat, and in one piece. She fumbled with the neck strings of the tunic and managed to tie them before Marek faced her. He pushed the food at her, and Brynn ate until she couldn't stomach any more. She ignored the Archaean while she chewed, wondering why he stared at her so.

Sleepy, Brynn watched the flickering of the torch. A rustling near her head startled her, and she propped up on an elbow to see Marek settling down in front of the curtain. "What is it you think you are doing?"

"Making sure you don't go throwing yourself off another cliff." Marek tucked his arms under his head for a makeshift pillow and sighed.

"Am I your captive?"

"Go to sleep, witch."

# *Chapter Four*

## SPEAK

"Get up."

Still groggy, Brynn forced her eyes open. Marek towered over her, fully dressed in leather armor with his sword strapped across his back. He looked stunning with his sun-bleached locks and defined muscular build. Being a warrior fit him well. Her makeshift tent was tucked away, and the horses saddled and ready for travel. Morning dew littered the ground, and a blanket of fog had settled over the valley. Brynn rose and handed her blanket over to be packed. She wrapped her arms around her middle against the sudden chill. The fog swirled about, coating her skin with a fine mist. The men talked amongst themselves, occasionally pointing in her direction. Brynn approached Marek.

"Where are we going?" she pressed, her heart pounding.

"Heading north, going home." He avoided her eyes and turned his horse from her.

Brynn circled the horse, seeking Marek's face. "You are not leaving me here, are you?"

"You clearly prefer the Engels over your own kind, Brynn, and have nearly succeeded in killing yourself. I have no desire to see you achieve it. And no, I will not leave you here."

"You must take me back!"

"I owe you nothing."

"You must take me home! To Galhaven." Brynn gripped the horse's bridle, preventing the animal from moving.

Marek laughed. "After all that has been done to you there, you want to go back? What makes you think you are still wanted? Women and children will throw stones at you. The earl has disowned you, and you want to go *back*? Do you even hear the words coming from that pretty little mouth of yours? You really do welcome death, girl." He jerked the reins, and his mount stepped to the side, freeing itself from Brynn's grasp with a shake of its head.

"But…" Brynn's bottom lip trembled. "I do not wish to go north."

"By the gods, don't cry," he muttered.

"I only wish to return to my home."

"You are not my problem anymore."

Brynn stomped her foot. "*Your problem*? Why is it I am always somebody's *problem*? I was unconscious when you brought me here. Had I been conscious, I would have demanded you leave me! I have never been outside the walls of my village before now! Take me home." She reached for his horse once more. "Please."

"Let go of my horse."

"My fate is in your hands, Archaean. You decide." Brynn matched her eyes with his as hot tears rolled down her cheeks, but she stood her ground.

---

Marek's eyes locked on hers. There was no time to take her to Galhaven, as too many days had been lost having Ronan mended after the rebels' ambush. They were already months overdue at their highland homes. With war upon them, his people needed their protection. He wanted nothing more than to be home with his wife and young son. Nearly three years had passed since he'd seen their faces. His men were just as anxious to return. They enjoyed the coin the bounties brought, but no man should have to wander aimlessly for another's cause.

Marek sighed. Neither should this girl. "We are at an impasse, Brynn of Galhaven, for I cannot take you with me, and I cannot take you home."

"Then what am I to do?" She looked up at him, those blue eyes burning a hole in his heart."

"Ride with me?" Marek offered his hand.

"I'd rather walk." She huffed in defiance.

"You're still healing."

She crossed her arms in defiance.

Marek's mouth slackened into a frown. "Very well. You better keep up." Gathering the reins, he nudged his horse with his heels and it started forward, leaving Brynn behind.

She kept her distance as she followed. The morning fog lifted, and the remnants of a warm summer played with her hair as she plodded a path behind the Archaeans. Marek frequently glanced back, and when Ronan reprimanded him for turning around so many times, Brynn smiled at him. Marek countered her with a scowl. She sang little tunes of love, and the others seemed content to listen. She even had them humming along after a while.

When Marek dismounted to rest his horse, he fell back from the group to walk with Brynn. "I didn't think you'd make it this far," he told her, casting a lopsided grin.

"I didn't think you were going to stay seated on your horse."

"Just making sure you weren't falling behind." Marek kicked a rock from his path.

"I am able to manage."

"It would seem so." He walked beside her in silence, listening to the patter of her bare feet as she matched his pace.

"How did you learn to speak my language?" she asked, breaking the monotony.

Marek was silent, recalling a distant memory. He was back in his croft, a roaring fire warming him as his wife snuggled beside him, book in her hand, teaching him to read and write. His young son, nearly two at the time, sat cross-legged on the floor next to them, listening intently to the stories. "Someone close taught me." She didn't question him, so he let it be. The less she attached to him, the better for them both.

O
n the bank of a river, the group stopped for water and a bit of rest. Stretching out on the long grasses, Brynn let the warmth of the sun radiate through her aching body. She closed her eyes, wishing she had the time to fit in a nap — a light doze, even — but the sounds of the Archaeans proved distracting. Ronan struggled with his horse, attempting to unpack supplies from the saddlebags. The animal veered in wide arcs, backing away from Ronan's one-armed foraging.

Rising, Brynn strolled in his direction, clicking her tongue at the horse. Its ears perked forward, and she took hold of the bridle to stroke its muzzle with the tips of her fingers. "There, there," she cooed, puckering her lips to give it a kiss. "How may I help?" she asked Ronan.

He rattled off in Archaean, digging several empty water bladders out from the saddlebag. Ronan thrust them in Brynn's direction.

"You want me to fill these with water?" Brynn pointed to the river and flashed him a wide smile when he nodded his head in response.

After hobbling the horse, Ronan gave its neck a swift pat and turned to the river. Brynn scampered after him. Following his lead, she knelt beside him and plunged the bladder in the frigid water. Her hand tingled as the water gushed through her fingers, but she did as Ronan demonstrated and waited for it to fill completely. She picked up a smooth stone and showed it to Ronan. "Rock," she said holding it on her flattened palm.

Ronan stammered out in his thick brogue, "R-r-rock."

"Very good! We will get along, you and I."

A slight blush colored Ronan's cheek, and he muttered in his own words.

He was a handsome man, she decided, with a boyish charm and eyes that twinkled. They taught each other words while filling the rest of the bladders and splashed one another in playful banter. Brynn looked to Ronan for help, having difficulty corking her water bladder, but as he pushed on the cork, Brynn accidentally squeezed the pouch, spurting a gush of icy water down his front. She gasped, covering her mouth with her free hand.

Ronan bellowed out a deep belly laugh and bursts of giggles spewed between her laced fingers as Brynn tried to keep a snort from escaping.

---

Marek scowled from his perch.

Ronan had always been quick to make friends, even with those who could potentially hinder him. Ronan's likability was his downfall; he was entirely too trustful. Put a pretty girl in front of him, and Ronan turned into a drunken sot. This had to stop. Marek couldn't push his men onward with their tongues wagging behind her every step. She was too much of a temptation for them all — himself included — and he couldn't allow it. The girl would have to go, and soon. He was anxious to claim his payment and return home with his spoils. Bounty hunting had finally taken its toll, and walking the entire way home was going to make for a very long journey. This beautiful distraction had to end.

He dragged his palm down the side of his face, cursing himself. How could he be jealous of his brother? What in hell had come over him? Marek tried to picture his wife but instead found himself focusing on his own tunic, the same one covering the most delicious curves he'd ever seen on a woman. His clothing did her delicate body no justice. And by the gods, what he wouldn't give just to see her out of it. Her profound allure still shocked him, even now. He'd never seen blue until he'd lost himself in her eyes.

Those same eyes now looking at his brother with the adoration Marek craved. An ache rooted itself deep within, imploring him to readjust his seat. Those flirtatious smiles should be his, damn it. Watching Ronan push a long curl behind Brynn's ear made Marek's insides explode.

Deciding Ronan had lusted after the girl more than to his liking, Marek determined he'd seen enough. He called out to his men, "Come on, lads, time to go." Helping Ronan with his bags, Marek commented, "You seem to be having fun. Are you enjoying yourself, little brother?"

"What is it you're getting at, Marek?" Ronan tugged on a leather strap to fasten a bag. "Help me up."

Marek held the horse still while Ronan heaved into the saddle. "Just keep away," Marek warned, gathering the reins for his brother.

Ronan cocked an eyebrow. "And why is that? A bit jealous that your little brother has the lady's favor and she prefers me? Miss your wife?" Ronan tugged the reins from Marek's ever-tightening grasp. "It's not my fault I was born with this face," Ronan teased, heckling his brother.

Marek mounted his own horse. "Hold your tongue before you lose it."

"The lads and I have decided." Gavin grinned like a fool, trotting his feisty mount around the brothers.

"Have you, now?" Marek paused.

"We have agreed..." Gavin stroked the patch of hair covering his chin and chuckled, a sinister smile enveloping his mouth. "You should just have a go and get it over with. This tension is driving us mad. Be a man and do it, or let the rest of us. We have been out here a long time and never seen anything so fine and tempting." Gavin's smirk could have spread from ear to ear as he teased. "Your lust for her is too obvious. Just do it already. No one would ever have to know the great Marek fell for an Engel girl." He cantered off laughing before Marek could pull him to the ground and tackle him for his arrogance.

# Chapter Five

## NOTHING WOULD BE EASIER

"Marek, a word?" Ronan approached his brother, testing his temper.

"Is this what I think it is about?"

"Well... aye, it is." Ronan matched his brother's gait, reining in his mount near Marek's. "We are wondering — *I* was wondering... What *are* you going to do with her?" Ronan shifted his weight in the saddle. "Have you had time to gather your thoughts?"

"Take her to the Crossroads," answered Marek.

"Wait... what? Still?" The shock in Ronan's voice made even Marek question his decision.

"A pretty little thing like that?" Ronan shook his head in disbelief. "'Tis shameful."

"She is a distraction to us all, and one more mouth to feed. We don't need her slowing us down."

Ronan cleared his throat and muttered, "What if I buy her from you when we get our money from Brockington? You may take my share."

Marek grunted. "Buy her? She is no one's property. But what would you do with her? Cart her to the highlands, have a cozy little croft together? She is of noble upbringing, Ronan. Brynn wouldn't survive a week in our country without someone to coddle her. What would you do

55

when we get another offer? When war comes? Would you leave her alone in your crumbling home to tend to the fields and care for your babes? How will you explain to her what we do? We murder for a living, brother. Try telling that to a woman you cannot speak to. Would you have her wash your bloodstained hands before she serves you the evening meal? No, she will be better off with some wealthy family where she will have food in her belly and clothing on her back. She will be safe and out of harm's way. They will provide for her. Take her in as their own."

"Perhaps you are right." Ronan sighed, avoiding Marek's eyes.

"You know I am right, Ronan."

"But do you have to sell her? Could we find someone—"

"Selling her will ensure her safety, Ronan. Only the wealthy will be able to afford her." The brothers traveled in silence. Marek couldn't shake their conversation. Would selling her really be for the best? Ronan had planted the seed of doubt, and for the first time in ages, Marek questioned his own actions. If Ronan hadn't taken the hit by that arrow, they would never have stopped in Galhaven. Marek wouldn't be burdened with such guilt and temptation. He would not be burdened with *her*. Yes, he must leave her behind, but would at least make sure she would be well taken care of.

"She could stay with Nya." Ronan's optimism cracked the silence. "Your Nya would be able to communicate — help her to learn our language, just like she did you. She seems to catch on well enough, I bet with some—"

"*Ronan, enough!*" How perfect — the pretty thing he lusted after becoming friends with his wife. Caring for his son. Oh, the stories they could share.

"But I want her," Ronan grumbled.

*So do I.* Marek couldn't say the words.

With every step farther from her homeland, Brynn's legs shook in protest. The last hill had proven difficult, but she trudged on. She had fallen behind the now out-of-sight Archaeans. Brynn estimated herself to be several hundred paces from them. Sucking in a deep breath, she calmed her nerves. The hoof prints remained visible — she wasn't yet lost. She contemplated simply turning around. Trudging back the way she came, but she'd already proven to herself that she had no sense of direction, unlike the members of her traveling party, who seemed to know exactly where they were. With every mile behind them, their pace quickened, most anxious to press onward. Brynn gathered they headed north, as people with their coloring were from there. From the stories she had been told as a child, the Archaeans were a fierce people with fiery spirits and a thirst for blood. They took no prisoners and were bred for fighting. The men were tall and thick and the women just as vicious.

Her time alone had given her much time to contemplate her own life and fate. Indeed, she truly looked like them. Had what her father said been true? Why had Marek taken her? Brynn had a twisted feeling in her gut that told her she wouldn't be meeting any lords and ladies where they journeyed. No chicken pasties, no luxurious baths, and certainly no rose petal soap — only a golden-haired country she knew nothing of. Surely, someone would come for her.

She stumbled as the incline she trudged up steepened sharply. Exhaling long and slow, she closed her eyes to stop her surroundings from twirling in an evil dance around her. She now regretted her decision to walk her own path and her body balked, begging for the torment to stop. Another short rest wouldn't hurt. She needed to regain her strength. Her knees buckled, and she gave in to her body's protest. *Just a bit further,* she told herself, *you must get up.*

A breath hitched in her throat as she fumbled to stay upright, making a feeble attempt to stand when a solid grip wrapped under her arms and pulled her upward. In one fluid movement, she was on horseback, her back pressed firmly against the radiant heat of a body.

Marek had come for her.

Exhausted and strangely relieved, she collapsed against his chest. The familiar scent of smoke and sweat surrounded her, and she nestled deeper into the crevice of his arm as he held the reins. Content, Brynn dozed, lulled by the steady rhythmic beating of his heart.

---

Between the swaying of the horse's pace and the warmth of his body, Marek wasn't at all surprised by how quickly her head slumped to the side in slumber. Hell, even he could sleep for a full day given the chance. A cool breeze picked up from the west, and judging by the upturned leaves on the trees, rain was soon to follow. He looked to the horizon. A golden haze was all that remained of sunset. They needed to make camp within the hour. He'd hoped to clear the approaching forest earlier in the day, but when Brynn disappeared from view, he made his men continue while he set out to retrieve her. The slow pace became a concern when forced to wait out the night once again, falling prey to whatever might be hunting them. They should reach the Crossroads before dusk the next day. If he pushed forward, they might be able to make it by midday. The girl would have to ride — no more independence.

A long lock of golden hair swept across his face, distracting Marek from his thoughts. It fixed itself to several days' worth of growth covering his chin and cheeks, daring him to swipe it away. The tip of the tiny curl flicked in a mischievous wave, lingering by his lips and nose, taunting him with its flowery scent. He let it remain until he could stand the tickling no longer and maneuvered his hand to brush it from his face. Brynn stirred, muttering incoherently, before sighing and turning in toward him, snuggling ever deeper. Glancing down to check her position, the tunic caught his eye. The tie had somehow worked its way undone, exposing the exquisite coloration of womanly curves. The mounds of her breasts pressed against him, inviting Marek to steal a glimpse. Her flesh called to him.

With a finger, he traced the lines on the palm of her splayed hand. Something within him stirred when he touched it. The creamy flesh beckoned him to look, to feel, to taste. "Damn the gods." He exhaled, readjusting his seat to alleviate the uncomfortable arousal growing in his trousers. He wasn't like other free fighters — he took no mistresses. He stayed faithful to his wife on this and every other employment taken. If there was one thing he would keep sacred during his regrettable life, it would be his honor. Resisting this one particular provocation proved more difficult than all others. Noble skin was soft and supple to the touch, not hardened and leathered by endless days of labor, and knowing how his men wanted to get their filthy hands on it made his cheeks burn. He'd been the one to nurse her wounds, to massage the spasms from her muscles when she writhed in pain. If anyone deserved to sample her, it was him.

Marek cursed, forcing his thoughts back to Nya. He tried to picture her lovely smile but all he envisioned were those two silky breasts bouncing in his line of sight. What he wouldn't give to cup them in his hands and suckle her until she screamed his name.

"Marek..." A firm touch to his shoulder roused him from his thoughts.

"Brother." Marek yawned, straightening in the saddle.

"I didn't mean to stir you, but we must make camp. The skies are about to open. Aiden found a small cave near the hills. 'Tis this way."

Marek veered his horse, following Ronan.

---

B rynn awoke with a start. Panicking, she flailed, until a pair of possessive arms pinned her tight, securing her with their strength.

"Shh, you are safe." The whisper was soft and low in her ear.

His voice brought her back from a troublesome dream. She'd seen the ravens again, and not knowing their meaning troubled her. Bits and pieces of visions jumbled together inside her mind. Her brother, Michael, and a strange woman with graying dark hair. She seemed to know them in dreams but they became strangers of the night once she awoke. What message were they trying to deliver? She wished she knew.

Heavy drops of rain splattered against Brynn's face and she turned into him, seeking shelter. The horse jolted under them and she gripped his forearms, steadying herself. The horse leaped across a brook, and Marek brought the security of his arms to her chest, pushing her closer, molding her body under his. Her pulse raced as his heat melted her insides. His thighs pressed against her own as he commanded his mount, igniting a spark in her belly. A quick breath collided with the shell of her ear, hot and moist against the coolness of her skin. Then the sky fully opened, releasing a torrent of cold mind-numbing rain.

They were fully drenched when they reached the shelter. Marek slung her to the ground and she scurried inside the cave while the men tended the horses, tossing their gear and saddles out of the rain, shouting to one another above the claps of roaring thunder.

The cave was small and shallow but served its purpose. What little protection it offered was sufficient against the storm raging outside. Shrubs and fallen tree limbs covered the mouth of the shelter — perfect for hiding. Brynn moved to the back while the Archaeans rushed about gathering wood for a fire and spreading their blankets before darkness consumed the land. After struggling for a flame for a few tense moments, a fire crackled, infusing the air with its raw perfume. The men chatted amongst themselves, all but one sparing no attention to Brynn, huddled against the rock. Every so often Marek would shift his eyes in her direction, a constant reminder he hadn't forgotten about her.

After stoking the fire, the men stripped their clothing and laid them out to dry before bounding into the rain. Their sleek silhouettes were perfect in every way.

A shame she'd never felt before enveloped her body and Brynn diverted her eyes by covering them with her palm. But soon she found herself splaying her fingers, peering between the cracks, unable to resist the intense desire to indulge in the view. A steady gush of water rolled from the lip of the cave, and the men took turns plunging their heads under it. She spotted Ronan by the way he favored his arm. His profile, long and robust, left her in awe until the flames flickered along the sinewy lines of the figure standing next to him — Marek.

Marek's back was to the fire, his head hung low. A steady light glimmered along the shadows of his muscular thighs and the sinuous curves of his backside. Flames traced the rigid edges of his lean form, revealing a teasing taste of his power. Tiny droplets gathered in small crevasses of muscle until the pools spilled down his back, following the paths carved by the twisting musculature of his frame. A wondrous sight to see, and despite her best efforts, she could not look away.

The godlike statues stepped from the water, speaking in hushed tones as they dressed. Marek slipped his tunic over his head, his eyes wandering in her direction and lingered there. He spoke so eloquently to her without words. His eyes told her much. Brynn swallowed the knot in her throat. Something was amiss.

Ronan squeezed Marek's shoulder, and the warrior's face creased into a full scowl. A decision had been made, and the cold truth sliced through her. The sliver of hope she clung to faded into memory. No one would be coming for her. She was truly alone in this all-consuming darkness. Alone with strangers who cared naught about what would become of her. Hot tears burned her cheeks. Smearing them away, she devised her own plan. She must stay strong and survive. She would make her way home by herself and beg for forgiveness. There could be no other option.

The men lounged near the fire, drinking from their water bladders and snacking on their rations. Her stomach grumbled, but she dared not move closer. Brynn settled down into a shadow, hoping to disappear. A shiver ruptured from her body and she hugged her knees, longing to bask in the heat of the inviting fire. Her plan to melt into the walls faded quickly. Ronan approached with a bladder and a chunk of bread in hand, beckoning her to eat. Even in shadows, Brynn could sense his smile was radiant and kind. She was hesitant to accept the food, but she needed her strength. Her belly urged her to take it.

A horse's shrill whinny diverted Ronan's attention, and he turned from her. Marek called for him, and Ronan thrust the bread and bladder at Brynn before disappearing into obscurity. In the commotion, Brynn heard a light tinkling — metal against rock. With the men preoccupied with the horses, she crept from her spot, exploring the cave floor with her fingers. She found the object not far from her. A dagger. Squinting through the haze of smoke she peered at it, thumbing it with a hesitant caution for its shape and size. It was an oddly-shaped dagger — not one she readily recognized — but small enough for her to hide without notice. She stuffed it into her hem and secured it in the ties of her skirt. A dagger would prove useful when it was time to make her escape. A little self-protection gave her the confidence boost she needed. For once, she was thankful for the lessons her brothers had included her in.

Hearing voices, Brynn scrambled back to the cave wall and stuffed the bread in her mouth. As she chewed, the men stumbled back inside, bringing with them wafts of damp earth and the freshness of clean water. They shook the excess drops from their hair as if beasts escaping the rain. They returned to the fire, stoking the embers for a flame, muttering amongst themselves in hushed, warning tones. The words were in their Archaean tongue, and she knew they spoke it purposefully. Such weakness was language.

Without hesitation, Marek's eyes searched for her. He hadn't forgotten. The fiery blue eyes raked over her, and Brynn questioned her thoughts. Did he know she'd stolen the dagger? Had Ronan reported it missing? She took a long gulp of water from the bladder, wetting her parched palette. When the men bedded down, she would make her escape, slip into the night, never to be found. Her plan had to work.

There was no other way.

---

"Here, cover yourself." Marek stood above her, a blanket in hand. The girl shivered in her restless sleep, clutching her knees to her chest. Her eyes fluttered at the sound of his voice, and she roused to take the blanket from his outstretched hand. "Thank you."

"There's still a small fire. You may warm yourself if you like." Brynn retreated deeper into her little corner, shaking her head in defiance.

Marek released a heavy sigh, lowering his frame against the wall opposite her. "Very well, but I would much rather be near the fire. I don't relish freezing this night as you do."

"You don't plan on... sleeping there?"

"As I said, I would much rather be closer to the fire."

"So, go then," she countered.

"So you can run out foolishly into the night? No." Marek placed his arms behind his head, feigning relaxation. "And you seem to have my only dry blanket."

She shoved the covering at him. "Take it."

"Might we share it?" he offered, amusing no one but himself.

Brynn snorted a distrustful laugh. "As if I would ever allow that, Archaean."

"I merely offer warmth on this bitter night. You seemed to enjoy my company on horseback not too long ago, I recall. The sooner you accept this, the easier it will be for everyone."

"What is it you plan on doing with me? If you won't take me home, and I cannot leave your sight, what exactly are your intentions?" Brynn looked at him with expectant eyes.

Deep conversation was far from his thoughts; he much preferred silence — and sleep. He rubbed his brow with his fingers, reluctant to reply. "We are taking you to the Crossroads, and then my men and I are going home." He needed to remain calm, to stay in control. This girl had a way of taking over his mind as if she'd cast some sort of spell over him. It was unnerving.

"What is the Crossroads? What are you not telling me?" The quivering of her words as they slipped off her tongue outweighed the hint of anger in her voice.

*Damn it*, he should have kept his mouth shut. Now the questions and the tears would flow, and he'd be forced to deal with her womanly emotions. By the gods... women and their crying, they turned him into a bumbling fool.

Brynn sucked in a shaky breath, a clear sign of tears.

"The Crossroads is where our two lands meet. It's the safest place for you to be with war about. We will find you a home, head to our own lands, and be done with you. You are a liability to me and my men."

"Surely you jest," she protested. "You cannot be serious; I am of noble birth."

"Oh, I am more than serious, *milady*."

"How dare you mock me!" she shouted "Never more than now have I wished you dead! I could have you hanged!"

"*Me* dead? Why, *my lady*, you would be the one *dead* if it were not for *me* saving your life. Living the life of a nursemaid or a healer will be far more beneficial than living under the rein of that man you call your *father*!"

"My father is an Engel ruler! He would love nothing more than to snap the neck of an Archaean!"

"You defend him? Still? After all he has done for you, you rush to protect him. When was the last time you took a good look at yourself, *Engel?*" Marek found himself creeping ever closer to her seething little body, those taught breasts heaving and those deliciously tempting full lips taunting him with a pout. "What little I was taught about people, love, is that Engels have not been born with *yellow* hair for hundreds of years. If my memory serves me well, the entire reason your Engel army has been attacking our villages for a lifetime is because of that same yellow hair that adorns *your* pretty little head! Engel? *Horse shit.*"

He was close to her now, so close that her breath was hot against his own, clinging to every little bead of moisture coating his skin. Marek curled a long tendril of her hair around his finger and rubbed it with his thumb. "Trust me, *Archaean*," he whispered, releasing the curl, "your Engel father has disowned you — if he ever claimed you at all — and life as you once knew it is no more. You never have been, nor will you ever be, an Engel."

"No…" The word barely escaped on a breath as she shook her head in weak disagreement.

Marek reined in his temper. "The life of a nursemaid is a good life. It is money in your purse and a roof over your head. Forgo trying to live as an Engel — you will never *be* an Engel. Marry an Archaean, one that will love *you*, not some piece of land and a bit of coin. Have a family… children. Do not submit to your father, he doesn't want you. Find someone who does."

Her heart shattered before his eyes — he watched it crumble into irreparable pieces. Her anger for him bubbled over into her face, flushing her dampened cheeks, and she turned from him, hiding her emotion in the shadows. He watched as the realization of her fate became final in her mind as she attempted to rationalize the situation.

"Never will I be a servant to any man. You make a grave mistake with your words."

"Then you will die alone. You are just a little girl. You do not know what is best for you." Marek's voice grew unsteady with frustration. The more she spoke, the more he wanted to shut her mouth for her with his. By the gods, she made his blood boil.

"I am *not* a little girl!" Brynn edged herself upright.

64

Harsh shadows contorted her movements, jutting across the cave wall like ocean waves. Countering his advancements to match hers, Marek questioned her actions. "Going somewhere, Brynn?"

"I won't be sold to the highest bidder, Marek." Her voice, low and smooth, dripped with determination. She had made up her mind about something, but Marek couldn't decipher what. And that made him extremely nervous. He had no idea what this tiny girl was capable of.

She circled behind him, molding into the curvature of the rock. Before he could differentiate her from stone, she was on top of him, rolling him to his back. Marek scrambled to snag what he could of her as she viciously clawed at him, beating his chest with bunched fists, writhing under his control.

He stilled, his hold on her slackening when the familiar texture of cold steel bore down against his throat. So, the little she-devil had found a dagger. *Ronan*, he realized.

His thoughts raced in circles.

How much had he gathered about her? *Not enough.*

Did she have the strength and courage to do it? *Possibly.*

Had she used a weapon before? From the way the blade was shaking, shaving off tiny bits of skin with each quiver of her hand, it was hard to tell. She seemed comfortable with it, but anyone with her determination could wield a blade given the right opportunity. Several tactics crossed his mind before deciding which path to follow. He knew what he must do — he'd found himself in worse situations before, but did he want out of this one? A ravishing creature with a dagger sat raving mad on his chest, and strangely, he rather liked it. His heartbeat quickened with each breath. "Do it," he told her, growling the words. "Nothing would be easier."

Hot thighs constricted his torso, clenching tighter with each rise and fall of his chest. Marek studied her, his eyes unwavering. The dagger on his throat pressed deeper, and he swallowed hard against it, unsure of her next move. Countering any man, instincts would have taken over, and he would have gutted his opponent by now with the very blade they held, but never before had he been pinned by a mere woman.

Yet, there he was — rendered powerless against a captivating girl who simply held a blade to his throat, and a small one at that. He could easily toss her with one arm, but every time he looked at her, his thoughts contorted into utter distraction. She intoxicated him like rare wine and drove him mad for more.

His fingers found her ankles, encircling them in one smooth caress. She caught a breath in her mouth and the dagger shifted. The silent warning, however, didn't deter his intentions of exploring her calves with his palms. Marek stared up at her, never shifting his gaze. A torturous ache gushed through him, tingling with gluttonous pleasure. He lingered along her calves, exploring every new curve in thorough adoration. In deliberate disregard of her feeble objection, Marek hooked his thumbs under the hem of her skirt and manipulated the fabric to her waist. His hands arched around the fullness of her thighs and squeezed tight, kneading her flesh with a demanding urgency.

He jerked her forward onto his chest.

"*Do it,*" he commanded.

"*I will do it.*" Brynn could barely breathe. What had he done to her? She wanted to touch him, to quench her thirst for him. With every passing moment, he took her deeper into oblivion. She placed her hand on his chest to steady herself. She needed to see the fear in his eyes, to know she was still in control. But as she leaned into him, what looked back at her wasn't fear. She saw something she had never before seen in a man's eyes... hunger.

She didn't resist when his wandering embrace somehow found its way to her middle, up her torso to graze the swell of her breasts, and over to her shoulders to the delicate length of her neck. Marek brought his face to hers, the dagger still pinned against his throat. With one hand on her nape and the other possessively on her waist, he pushed her lips to his and parted them with his tongue.

Her body betrayed her, and she collapsed against him.

In one swift movement, he locked his arms around her, rolling her body to the ground beside his. His fists tangled in her hair. Marek pulled her close and tasted her. She lay helpless in his arms, fully welcoming his exploration of her mouth. She moaned, edging closer to the verge of losing herself in his embrace.

He teased her tongue, nipping at her lip while muttering fervently in his lyrical lilt and hungrily devouring her kisses. Lost in the moment, Brynn released the blade. The dagger clinked to the ground, ripping her back to the present. He had enchanted her, made her lose focus. He took advantage of her innocence to free himself from death. The tips of her fingers found a loose rock and she clasped it in her fist, brought it up from her side, and cracked it against Marek's skull.

He dropped her with a painful shout, covering the wound with his hands. Brynn scrambled away from him and staggered to her feet. She leaped for the mouth of the cave, still reeling from her very first kiss.

# Chapter Six

## TAKE MY HAND

Marek roared.

Brynn veered toward freedom by leaping over a saddle blocking her exit. She took the next barrier in stride, but Gavin caught her in midair, and Brynn crashed into his chest. Kicking and screaming, she knew she must escape. The rain poured from the skies with a constant drumming overhead, and she could lose herself in it if only she could break free from his tight hold. With a swift kick between his legs and a bite to the arm nearest her face, Brynn wriggled from Gavin's hold. She bolted from the cave and into the downpour.

Her heart didn't slow until she was a great distance from the cave. The Archaeans must have chosen not to follow, as there was no sign of them. The rain receded with the rising of the sun, and only then did she drop her guard. But she would not make the same mistake twice. She had taken the bit of freedom for granted the last time she headed for home, and she would not do it again. Brynn took care to cover her tracks and keep her skirts tucked, as to not leave a bit of evidence behind. She kept a watchful eye and kept to the trees where being on horseback would prove difficult. When she stopped by a stream for a bit of water, Brynn touched her bottom lip with her tongue, still able to taste Marek on her mouth.

The sound of water splashing on rocks sang to her while she sat upon its back for a light rest. Her thoughts clouded in her mind. She felt ashamed of what she'd done. It had been wrong to act in such a way... but it has procured her freedom. She missed home. She thought of Magda and hoped her father would not turn her out now that Brynn was no longer in the manor. The poor woman would have nowhere to turn. She missed her brothers.

With eyes closed, she imagined herself on a breezy hill tumbling with her brothers. For an instant — just a small one — she saw her mother's glowing face. How beautiful she must have been. Then, a certain lopsided grin flashed through her mind just before she returned to the present. Brynn stood, unnerved that the Archaean's face had appeared in her thoughts so suddenly. What had possessed her so?

B efore daybreak, Marek set out on his horse to find Brynn. He couldn't push her from his thoughts. Her face lingered fresh in memory as he picked his way through the woodlands. He'd lost control — how had that happened? He'd kissed her fully and thoroughly, and he liked it. Hell, he still craved it and, given the chance, he'd do it again. He cursed, knowing full well his conscience would eat at his soul until he was safely home in the arms of his Nya.

The best thing for him would be to get as far away from the girl as possible. His body had taken over in the cave. He couldn't let it happen again. He would transport Brynn to the Crossroads, see to her safety, then be on his way and forget all about her.

If only he could.

Small footprints along the edge of a puddle caught his eye. Perhaps she was still close. A light breeze toyed with his wavy locks, bringing with it sweet smells of wildflowers and the faint sound of... singing? He followed the footprints along the tree line until he spotted her, there by the water, running her fingers through the mass of thick curls over her shoulder. A goddess if none other. If a war were to wage on behind him, he never would have noticed. A branch cracked under his horse's hooves as it shifted its weight.

She turned to face him, the color draining from her face.

"Please, don't run," he warned. "I'm not up for a chase today." He towered over her from atop his large black mount, arm extended. "Just take my hand."

---

T hose eyes. They stared at her with such earnest honesty.
How could she do anything but accept his offer? Despite her best efforts, he still had found her. Marek grasped her wrist and lifted her to the saddle. For a moment she sat facing him with her legs wrapped around him, straddling so close she could feel his breath against her cheek. She wanted to touch him, to trace the lines of his roughhewn jaw — wanted to feel his lips against hers once more. She yearned for him to brush his fingers against her skin, to make her body quiver the way it had the night he'd first touched her when he so gently tended to her wounds. How could she have such sinful feelings about the man who sealed her fate? Why did the gods curse her so?

The horse jerked its head high, flaring its nostrils and snorting. Wrapping her arms tightly around Marek to remain steady, all thoughts of sin drifted from her mind when a familiar voice floated by on a breeze.

"*Marek!*"

Pulling the reins taught, Marek swung Brynn to the back of his saddle. With a kick, the horse whipped around then burst forward. They darted between trees, over rocks and roots with effortless skill as Ronan's urgent call filled the air.

Upon finding Marek, Ronan leaped from his horse.

Words spewed from his mouth. "Marek! Riders... from the south. They have found us."

"How many?" Marek asked.

"Twenty... maybe more. Engels."

The brothers switched their words to Archaean and Brynn could understand them no longer, but she did understand the only word that mattered. *Engels.* She could sense the nervousness and severity of the situation by the low tone of Marek's voice. Her heart quickened with every strange word they spoke. "What's happening?" she whispered.

71

Marek hushed her with a wave of his hand, then cinched an arm around her middle and dropped her to the ground before dismounting.

"*Ouch!*" she cried, landing on a rock. Brynn staggered to her feet. What was wrong? "*Marek...*" She grasped him by his shoulder. He was too busy digging through the leather satchels on his saddle and talking with his brother to pay her any attention. Not getting a response, she tugged again.

This time he turned toward her. "What in hell do you need, woman?" He withdrew a long sword from the saddle's blanket roll. He spun it full circle with a flick of his wrist, parting the air with ease.

Brynn stumbled backward, tripping over her skirts and unleashing a frightened scream. He was going to kill her. Terrified, she buried her face in the moss-covered ground and trembled, but the fatal deathblow didn't come. Peering between the crevasse of her arm and the ground, she watched Marek busily buckling his back scabbard across his chest.

He smiled down at her and winked, adjusting it to its proper place. Marek pulled the sword from the scabbard and gave the blade another full swing before sliding it back into its sheath and pulling more leather from his bags. While strapping a baldric across his chest, he muttered a few words to her. Not receiving an answer, he turned to her with eyes narrowed.

"I don't understand what you are saying!" She pouted, returning to her feet with a frustrating sigh. "You speak to me as if I should know, but I do not!"

"It would be wise to learn." Marek shoved his dagger under his belt and continued to dig through another satchel.

"When would that be? In my leisure time?" she quipped, placing a hand on her hip. As Brynn brushed stray hairs from her face, she realized Ronan, too, had donned his armor and weaponry. A battle was about to begin. And she was going to be in the middle of it.

M arek turned to his brother, addressing him in their native
tongue. "How much time, Ronan?" he pressed.

Ronan wiped his brow. "If we don't find a way out of this valley we will be slaughtered for sure."

"And the others?"

"They will be here. They must have tracked us, Marek."

"How is your arm?" Marek asked his brother.

"Still attached." Ronan winced while sliding his wounded arm through the hole of his leather brigantine. Strapping the vest tight on the sides, he pounded his chest with his fist.

"Can you fight?"

"We'll find out soon enough." Ronan checked the clasp on his greaves.

As Marek buckled a leather arm guard, his thoughts turned to Brynn. He had to hide her somehow, keep her out of reach of the riders. But how? There were no walls, no strongholds — just trees and sticks. And certainly no time. They would take one look at that yellow hair and kill her, too. Frustrated, he rubbed his palm over his head. He winced slightly as he brushed over the fresh bruise from the rock she'd stuck him with. He looked at Brynn. "That really hurt."

She averted her eyes, toeing the dirt. "Not sorry I did it," she muttered.

In all honesty, he was left with a sore head and a bruised ego — nothing everlasting. How foolish he was to let her run off in the rain. Damn his stupid pride. Now they faced a nightmare of a battle because of his haughty arrogance. Marek closed his eyes, gathering his wits. To survive he needed to focus — absolute concentration. He couldn't possibly fight well with her safety consuming his thoughts. Hoofbeats in the distance grew louder. He paused, counting the thrumming. His men were approaching.

The battle would soon begin.

# Chapter Seven

## A GREAT WARRIOR

"The only way out is to the east. It will bring us into the open, but it will give us the high ground advantage. Their horses grow tired, and if we stay centered, we'll have a better chance."

"Can we outrun them?" Marek asked his scout.

Aiden shook his head. "They are mercenary. It seems to be that bloody bastard we dispatched was well-liked."

Marek huddled with his men, devising a course of action to keep them all alive. It wasn't often they were confronted after completing a bounty. They'd always been stealthy. In and out with the night. Marek sighed. He had no idea if they were retaliation or from Galhaven, but he would find out soon enough. "We're outnumbered, we know that much."

"Let us not forget our tart," Gavin added.

Marek glanced at Brynn. "You know I never back down from a fight, but—" His words were cut short by a whinny in the distance.

"They are close."

"Well, somebody bloody well come up with a plan." Gavin smiled, slapping Marek on the back. "I don't feel much like dying today."

The party headed east, finding an advantage point near a row of trees to ready for battle. Marek galloped to the farthest tree possible. It would have to do, for he had no other option to keep her safe from the sword.

"You must hurry." He told Brynn, hoisting her up the tree to the nearest branch. Marek searched the distance for the riders. "Climb high, and don't come down no matter what you hear, do you understand me?"

"I... I..."

He reached up to cup her flushed face in his hands, searching her eyes. "Soldiers are coming from the south." Brynn's eyes lit, but Marek seemed to know exactly what she was thinking. "Listen to me. These men will not care who you are or where you are from. They are riding for one purpose and one purpose alone — to kill anything in sight, and that includes a little yellow-haired girl from the south lands. They are not coming to chat over tea. *These men will kill you.* Stay in the tree, Brynn."

Fear reflected in her wide eyes. She nodded.

"No matter what you hear, climb high… and stay there." And then he kissed her, hard and fast, stealing one more bit of pleasure that damn well could be his last.

"I will," she told him.

"I will come for you." Marek gave Brynn to the tree, where she began to climb, one limb at a time. With a shout from his men, Marek galloped away, leaving her in the safety of the wooded canopy.

T he fierce howl of steel grinding against steel pierced through the thick fog. Murderous cries — cries of unbearable pain and certain death — echoed through the trees like ghosts carrying the sickening smell of blood and sweat.

Men were dying.

Her men.

The screams and grunts edged closer to her as the battle raged on, the familiar language of Engels among the shouts. Perhaps they *were* coming to her rescue, but from the sound of the death screams, Brynn didn't believe they would be at all successful.

Engel pleas of mercy met an abrupt end.

A sickening wave of nausea lingered precariously high in her throat as she envisioned the ruthless slaughter. Archaeans didn't show mercy. The carrion birds circled above, waiting.

A horse shrieked far too close to her hiding place. It was nearly beneath her. Frightened, Brynn let go of the tree branch she had steadfastly clung to. She covered her ears and clamped her eyes shut. It was all just a nightmare, and if she could only wake, she'd be back at the manor picking wildflowers. Raindrops splattered against her, and she huddled closer to the tree, picturing the vivid image of home.

A powerful gust crashed over her and Brynn heard her name ambling in its wake. The call of her rescuer? Her bothers, perhaps? They had found her at last. She must be ready. If they were searching for her, they would never see her hidden in the clouds. Descending to a lower branch in hopes of catching a glimpse of them, Brynn readied to signal them if the opportunity arose. She wanted to be sure her brothers would hear her call when she recognized them.

The devastation took her breath away. Bodies littered the clearing, most severely damaged to the point of being unrecognizable. Brynn scoured the horizon for familiar faces. Desperate, she sought Marek, but couldn't locate him. They were faceless bodies in a sea of men.

Perhaps if she lowered herself a bit more, she could assure herself he still lived. Bryn left the safety of her tree nook. As she lowered her frame to a rickety branch, a horse and rider bolted from the right, slamming into her perch and knocking her loose. She scrambled to keep her footing and regain her grip on the branch above, but the tree was wet and the bark slippery. With a shrill scream and a solid thump, she was on the ground.

"Well, well, what have we here?"

Brynn turned toward the snarling voice. A large man with a devious smirk stalked toward her. She turned to run.

"A little sparrow, fallen from the tree." He laughed, reaching out for her. His hand caught her by the hair and pulled her to the ground.

"Let go of me!" she screeched, clawing for his eyes.

Despite her effort, he hunched over her — dagger in one hand, her neck in the other.

"Never have I encountered such a prize during battle," the Engel growled, rubbing the gray stubble on his chin against her cheek. He inhaled deeply, edging the blade under her chin.

"Please, no," she begged, trembling beneath him.

The soldier laughed, his lips pressed tightly against his rotting teeth. "Please, yes," he corrected, jerking up her skirt.

"Beast!" she spat, raking her fingers along his cheek.

"You little bitch!" The blade pushed deeper. A stinging warmth fanned along her skin.

His mass was too much for her to maneuver, even when he moved to spread her legs with his. Brynn let out a blood-curdling scream as she brought her hands to his, trying to pry them from her body.

He raised the dagger above her chest.

I t was the scream that caught his attention. A woman's ultimate terror — he'd heard it many a time throughout his hardened life. For a quick moment, Marek's eyes shifted in search of the tree line instead of the soldier he battled. The swing of a sword narrowly missed his shoulder and sent him staggering backward on his heels. He barely escaped the bone-crushing blow from the Engel on horseback. Regaining his stance, Marek blocked the next blow with only seconds to spare. He couldn't focus — he worried for her safety. *Damn woman.* He was going to get himself killed.

Marek found himself torn between two battles. Did he attempt to fight the man he engaged, praying Brynn could fend off her attacker until he could reach her, or did he make a run for her, hoping to surpass his own battle? Given another few minutes, Marek would slay his opponent.

Another scream sent him reeling. The Engel held a blade high above her. *Damn, she won't be afforded another few minutes.* He was out of time, and no risk was greater than that of her life. Narrowing his eyes, Marek charged his opponent and wrenched him to the ground. The soldier, caught off guard, slid from the saddle, dropping his weapon. With one swift jerk, Marek's sword slid along the man's throat, severing it.

A wild fray of blood spurted at the sky as the body slumped to the ground. Marek spun on his heels to race across the field. Losing his footing to the slick mud, he skidded to his knees, realizing he'd never make it to her side in time. The soldier would have the dagger in her chest before he could intercept. Marek fumbled for the protruding handle of the knife still wedged in his boot. Finding it, he pulled the blade from its sheath. With his heart racing and his hand oddly trembling, he whirled the knife into the back of the soldier's skull.

———

T he soldier froze mid-plunge, his mouth agape in a bellow that didn't come. A sickening gurgle erupted from his throat as blood flowed from his nose and mouth. The soldier's beady eyes rolled back behind saggy eyelids just before he slumped forward, pinning her against the tree.

His weight crushed against her. Every breath was a struggle. Brynn shoved his chest to no avail. His body only slumped further. She pushed on his shoulders trying to slide out from beneath him, but the massive man's head snapped to the side. His lifeless white eyes stared back at her, his grim expression of death only accelerating her terror.

A mixed cry of sobbing and screams welled in her chest as thick, sticky warmth dripped from her palms. *Blood.* A fearful cry left her lips when the weight ascended from her chest. Two hands gripped her shoulders, and Brynn thrashed aimlessly, too exhausted to continue to fight.

"Brynn." A voice echoed through her.

She opened her eyes. Kneeling before her was her warrior, her rescuer. At the sight of his familiar face, she rose to fling her arms around his neck, crushing him with all her might. "He's dead!" she cried, in hysterics. Brynn pulled Marek to her chest in a fitful embrace, trembling in his arms.

He peeled her clinging frame from his to brush the hair from her face. "Aye, I know, I know," he breathed. "I killed him."

Anguish overtook her, and she buried her face in the crook of his neck, weeping uncontrollably against him. She wove her fingers through the waves of hair at his nape, never wanting to let go, to be separated from the safety she found in his arms.

Drawing her tight against him, he knelt with her, letting her sob. He didn't speak nor try to hush her weeping — he simply wrapped his warmth around her lithe body when she pulled him close. He placed tender kisses on her eyelids, attempting to staunch her tears. He could do nothing to console her but surround her trembling frame as the rain fell upon them, washing away the screams of battle, the smell of freshly spilt blood, and the hot tears of fear.

Only when her crying slowed and her breathing calmed did he break away. Tilting up her chin with his thumb, he looked into her eyes and murmured, "Come, we must leave this place."

Her voice quivered. "You..." Brynn's gaze lingered on the soldier with the small knife still protruding from his skull. The body lay motionless, submerged in a reddened puddle, still and stone-like. She dared not believe the ease and accuracy with which Marek had ended him. Her mind drifted back to when she had held the dagger to his throat. He could have killed her one-handed. "You're injured," she gasped, spying the large crimson stain on his left side.

"'Tis not mine," he reassured her, rising. "Come. We must find the others." Marek helped Brynn to her feet then crossed over to the corpse and placed a muddied boot in the center of the Engel's shoulders.

Brynn averted her eyes when Marek retrieved his boot knife from the man's skull. A quick sucking sound was followed by fresh crimson that oozed and gurgled from the open wound.

He wiped the knife on the man's tunic before tucking it back inside his boot. "*Fecking Engels,*" he cursed low under his breath.

The Archaeans were busy searching the bodies of their opponents and recovering weapons when Brynn and Marek reached the center of the clearing. Ronan sat on the ground, inspecting his injured shoulder. Gavin was busy looting the dead soldiers, taking anything that could be of value.

"Ronan, where is Aiden?" Marek inquired, approaching his brother.

"He's gathering the horses." With an exhausted sigh, Ronan fell to his back in the grass.

"Are you hurt?"

"Eh, nothing that won't heal." Ronan chuckled, fingering a fresh gash on his thigh.

"Need anything sewn back on?"

"*Och*, no, I'm well."

"Brynn, make sure his stitches have not let loose, would you?" Marek turned to Brynn, his eyes expectant.

A shout from Gavin turned everyone's head.

"What did he say?" asked Brynn.

"He says a few are still alive," answered Marek.

Brynn's lips formed a circle, but she made no sound.

"Kill them all," Marek purposefully replied to Gavin.

Brynn watched from a distance as Gavin grinned with delight, drew his sword, and plunged it into the chest of a barely living Engel soldier. The bone-crunching noise reverberated through her body, and she let out a small cry, horrified by the brusqueness and ferocity of it all. These men cared nothing for the lives of others. She watched as Marek found another and ended the man's life with a quick slit of the throat. So many. There were so many. A small army had fought against a mere four men, and they had lost. The ferocity of it all was maddening.

The last man alive caught her attention. Oddly, the soldier looked familiar. "Wait!" Brynn commanded.

Marek cocked his head inquisitively, lowering his arm when she approached the sputtering soldier. "Who sent you?" he asked the soldier. "With what army do you ride?"

The dying soldier spat blood at him.

The Engel was just a boy, sent to do the bidding of some nobleman. Brynn stepped closer and kneeled beside the mortally-wounded man. With the corner of her skirt, she wiped the blood from his face. "William? Oh, William… what have you done?" she whispered, shaking her head in disbelief. Just days before, he had been a strapping young lad with a bright future under the command of her betrothed. They'd dined together in the great hall. But now, he lay broken and dying.

She wanted to comfort him, see to his wounds, but he was badly damaged. His body was a mangled mess, even with the armor he wore. He'd been slashed as if his attacker toyed with him — used him as target practice — and he bled heavily from his nose and mouth. His insides were outside. Death was imminent.

William struggled to breathe. When attempting to speak, blood, not words, spilled from his mouth. Brynn placed his head in her lap and stroked his matted hair as tear droplets fell onto his distorted face. "I am so sorry, William. I cannot mend this." She caressed his cheek as his chest gurgled.

"The militia called out… Lord Dugray murdered… by… Archaeans."

Stunned, Brynn paused to put his words together. "W-what?" Everything that had happened suddenly seemed to piece itself together. The Engel arrowhead, the alliance, Archaeans deep in Engel lands. They had murdered Lord Dugray. Slowly, Brynn raised her eyes to meet Marek's.

That fiery blue told her everything.

***

She knew. Marek had never been ashamed of what he had done until that very moment, with that look she gave him. He wanted to thrust his sword into this boy called William for spilling his secret, but the tones of Brynn's hushed weeping told him the boy was already dead. Marek fetched the boy's sword and placed it vertically on his chest, crossing his arms over it ceremoniously. "It is an honor to die in battle," he told Brynn. "Even as an enemy." He placed a gentle palm on her shoulder, but she pushed him away.

"An *honor*?" Brynn was furious. "He was just a boy, barely older than me! And you slaughtered him like an animal!" Despite her temper, Brynn lowered William to the ground with the gentleness befitting a friend. She kissed his bloodied forehead in farewell before standing to confront Marek. "You honored this man, but did you even glance at the others?"

"If I took the time to honor every man I have *slaughtered*, I would be long dead by now! Aye, he was just a boy, but there are hundreds more just like him that will fall. War is upon us, and he will not be the last to die. As long as Engels continue to wage war against us, we *will* fight back. Until the very last breath. War *is* coming, Brynn, hell, it's already here, and there's nothing you or I can do to stop it. This is just the beginning. I'm thankful it was him and not one of my men! You should be thankful he's dead — he could have killed you! And this Lord Dugray? A main conspirator engaging these battles. He had to die!" Marek turned from her, feigning interest in his armor to avoid her hateful glare. While his words were true, he could not look at her.

"Tell me, Marek," she persisted, "why were you in Galhaven? Why my father's door? That arrowhead was Engel. Even a girl like me knows the difference."

"Don't try me, woman. You have no idea what I'm capable of." Marek gritted his teeth, trying to hold his tongue. She was beautiful when angry.

"I know you're capable of murder!" Brynn snagged him by the arm. "Tell me! *Why* were you in Galhaven that night? To murder *my* father? He is no rich nobleman like Dugray was, but I'm sure you could get a hefty price for *his* head!"

"I suggest you hold your tongue." She drove him to the brink of madness, and there was nothing left to distract himself with but her.

"Why? Are you going to kill me now, too? I mean nothing to you — why will you not slit *my* throat and be done with it? I have no purpose to you other than your own personal amusement!"

With three paces he was in front of her, eyes narrowed and clenching the pommel of his dagger so tight his knuckles bore white.

She countered his steps backward, searching her surroundings in uncomfortable silence.

Marek paced toward her until she could back away no further.

She stood rigid against the trunk of a large tree when he finally reached her. The color drained from her face. "I am not afraid of you," she whispered.

His lips touched the shell of her ear. "You should be," he muttered, his voice husky, as his finger grazed over the curve of her cheek. When his thumb reached her chin, he trailed a finger the length of her neck, feeling her swallow hard beneath the hollow of her collarbone. "Never trust a man," he warned her, his Archaean lilt thick and guttural. "Especially one like me."

"Why do you touch me so? Do you think me beautiful, Marek?" she asked, her eyes rising to meet his. "Is this why?"

His fingers lowered to her breast, and he traced its outline. "I would cut down any man who dared speak differently." He cupped her shoulder, pushing the tunic to the side with his fingers to expose delicate skin. His lips burned hot as he tasted her cooled flesh, nipping at her collarbone. A small moan escaped on a breath, but she made no attempt to stop him. Marek placed four lingering kisses, each growing higher, with the last finding her eagerly awaiting mouth before he garnered the courage to push himself away. Frustrated by his willingness to give in to temptation, Marek cursed himself before turning his anger on Brynn. "Why do you have to taste so good? *Damn you*, girl!" He ran his fingers through his hair. "Damn you and your... *ugh!*" He could not even find the words. What was this power she held over him?

"I have done you no wrong. I am not here by my own doing. *You* are the one who brought me here, remember? If I recall, you plucked me from my home without even asking if I cared to join you on your little romp back to the Archaean highlands. I have seen you butcher my people. You have... taken your own familiarities with me and I unashamedly let you." She blushed. "Why must you treat me like this? Why are you so bitter toward me? I don't understand! One moment you treat me with hatred and the next you're tasting my mouth." Her fingers absentmindedly brushed against her lips.

He could see her desire for him. Her body pleaded for more, as did his. "Why? Why am I bitter? Why can I not make up my mind about you? Not tell you the things I want to do to you? Because you are making it nearly impossible to stay faithful to my wife!" His truth had been told. Aggravated and upset with his own actions, Marek snapped at her without choosing his words wisely. "You don't realize just how... damned *tempting* you are! And not just to me — no — to every fecking one of us! Hell, if I didn't have her waiting on me, you would be *mine* by now! Mine!" Marek pounded a fist against his chest, spitting his frustration. "You have cast some sort of... *spell* on me and I am powerless against it!"

B rynn could feel the life drain from her body, and she stood dumbfounded in front of him, not sure if she should stay or run away in shame. She was a fool. How stupid she had been to think there was meaning behind those kisses. He'd given her a taste of passion, and she'd welcomed it, new to the wonderful feelings he stirred in her. She had fallen for his tactics, completely and entirely — and she chose to say nothing... she couldn't find the strength. Tears carved a trail down her cheeks while she nodded in acceptance. Now, she understood.

Marek stormed away, cursing. He didn't glance back at her; he did not return to comfort her. His touches had ended.

Strangely, her heart was heavy with emptiness. He was married. He had a wife. Somewhere there was a lonely woman eagerly waiting for her warrior to return, not knowing if he was still alive or rotting in the ground on some distant battlefield, and all the while he had been lusting after her. No, she was fooling herself. Marek was just a man, and no man was worth such heartache. Straightening her skirts and wiping her cheeks, Brynn walked toward the group in the clearing, wishing her lips didn't still burn for him.

---

He trotted his horse in circles around her, but Brynn focused on the path in front of her toes as she walked. "You may ride, we have extra horses."

"And bring me that much closer to my fate? I'm quite fine with walking, thank you." How her feet ached. The rain had chilled her to the core, but there was no way she would continue to accommodate the man. She was, after all, his captive — a piece of property to be bartered for profit. She would keep telling herself that, no matter how dashing he looked dressed in his armor perched on his impressive black mount.

"Just a stubborn little girl," Marek hissed through his teeth.

"Stubborn I may be, but at least I'm not a heartless beast that preys on innocent little Engel girls."

"You liked it just as much as I," he told her.

"Do not speak of what you know nothing about." Brynn bit her lip, hoping the pain would keep her mouth from turning into a telling smile.

"What I know nothing about? What I know is that if you keep up your prissy little attitude, I may just pull you up on this horse and smack that curvy little bottom of yours."

Her hands went to her hips. "You'd like that, wouldn't you?"

"Very much so!"

Brynn closed her eyes and drew in a calming breath. "Tell me, Marek, why did you choose this life?"

"What life?"

"To be a warrior. To be a part of this war."

"I did not choose this life. I was born, and this is what I am."

"Every soul has the opportunity to choose his or her fate. You do not have to fight."

"So you chose to marry a man to please your father, to be beaten, and pay for the sins of your mother?"

Brynn opened her mouth to speak but quickly closed it at the realization of her contradiction. Arguing would get her nowhere.

"We shall arrive soon." Marek grabbed her arm, effortlessly pulling her into the saddle.

She rode in silence, pondering what had become of her in days past. How quickly one's fate could change. With each step, the forest path changed to a trodden mix of pebbles and dirt. Reaching the Crossroads finally became a reality. The horses snorted and pawed at the ground, alerting her they were close.

The men were home again, back on Archaean soil.

# Chapter Eight

## THE CROSSROADS

The Crossroads was a large village centrally located to all areas of the highlands and purposefully used as a trading post. Merchants with large wagons peddled their goods, shouting at anyone who would pause long enough to listen. A blacksmith hammered horseshoes in front of a large forge with smoke billowing to the sky. Taverns filled with drunkards were bustling with activity, while scantily clad women haunted the doors, trying to earn a few coins.

A dreadful unease crept its way into her stomach and chest. It tightened its hold on her with each breath she took. She noticed every head was covered with the same golden hair; very few people had darker locks like her brothers. These Archaeans were like nothing she had ever seen. Their words were like beautiful songs, just as Marek spoke to his men. The women wore brilliantly patterned woolens with full skirts — not a gown in sight.

They rode through the village streets until they reached a small stable. Marek took a firm grasp on Brynn's arm, pulling her close to his side whenever a man passed or glanced in her direction.

Irritated, she lashed out at him. "Leave me be! I am not a dog to be tethered."

"Not a chance," he replied as he unsaddled his horse. He scratched

Arran's neck firmly, gave it a pat, and turned the animal loose to graze in a small fenced in area with the other horses.

"Clearly, my safety is not on your list of priorities, since you are *selling* me to a stranger, so stop treating me as if you care."

"I am not *selling* you. Merely requiring coin to ensure your safety. There's a difference."

"I see no difference, beast."

---

M arek turned to Ronan. "I'm leaving her in your charge, brother. Do not let her out of your sight."

"You have my word." Ronan nodded.

"I'm trusting you. No more sympathies."

Ronan sighed. "Aye, Marek. I understand."

"Gavin, Aiden. Gather as much as you can sell and get what you can for it. Sell the lame horses, keep the coin for yourselves. I will meet you later at the tavern." Donning a sword, Marek turned once more to his brother. "Wait here for me. I shall not be long." Marek stepped out onto the street, his head clear, in search of the trade master. He had done business with him before — never for this, but he had bartered for weapons and horses. He had no reason to distrust Daman. The merchant always treated Marek's pocket well. He found the heavy-set man in the marketplace. "Daman," Marek called, approaching the trade master.

A wide smile crept across the old man's weathered face. "Marek, my friend, it is good to see you."

"Aye, it has been a few years." Daman clasped Marek's forearm in greeting. "Listen, Daman, I have a proposition for you, not one you would usually barter for. I have a girl, she… she needs to be taken care of."

"You wish to be rid of her? I know a man who would gladly chop off her head for just five silver." Daman wrung his hands together in delight.

"She is the result of an unfortunate circumstance. She is to live."

"And you wish to sell her?"

"Aye, I do, on one condition."

"Conditions for barter, Marek? You humor me." Daman let out a hearty laugh. "And what might those be, boy?"

"She is not to be branded a slave. She is a good girl, Daman, and so should be treated as such. I will not have her spoiled. She is to be sold to a family, a wealthy one, as a nursemaid or tutor, or the like. She is *not* to be touched. She needs a family to care for her. Take her in as one of their own until she can find a good husband." His words were firm as he stared Daman in the eyes. Marek knew all too well what Daman thought of beautiful young women. Many Archaeans thought that way as of late. Traditions had been rapidly fading into the past as the Engel ways crept into those of the once segregated Archaeans. With war raging, now more so than ever.

"Well, I am not in the service of bartering people," he replied smoothly. "You have to understand they require upkeep. They need to be fed, housed, clothed... protected."

Marek took hold of the man's tunic with one hand and started to draw his sword with the other. "I do not think you understand, Daman."

"B-but," the man stuttered, "there is a very rich man in the village seeking help, I believe. He has several children and an ailing wife. They seek a young girl, one who will be taken in as one of their own to help with the children. I believe I can negotiate a deal for, say... twenty silver?"

Marek's grip tightened, this time around the man's airway. "*Not* good enough." The more Daman had to spend, the more likely he would be to protect his investment, and the higher the purchase price.

"Forty," replied Daman.

"Fifty."

"Fifty silver and I swear she will be well cared for."

"Swear it." Marek shoved the man back a few steps with his grip still firm upon him.

"I swear it on my own life," the merchant replied. "The utmost care."

Satisfied, Marek released the man's chubby neck.

"Give me the coin and I will bring her."

"I will give you half and give you the other when you deliver the girl."

"Agreed."

Darkness had fallen when Marek returned for Brynn.

"Did you find someone?" Ronan inquired in Archaean.

"Aye, there is a man seeking care for his children."

"Ahh, that would explain the fancy horses the lads were eyeing earlier. I had to convince them they weren't worth stealing." Ronan chuckled.

Handing his brother a pouch full of coins, Marek instructed Ronan to buy a few drinks. "I'll be around later. Come," he told Brynn, taking her by the wrist.

"Where are we going? Stop pulling me!"

Marek's grip grew increasingly tighter as he led her out into the moonlight.

"Stop!" Yanking her arm free, she stepped away from him. "So this is it? This is where we part? You have bartered me away and in doing so condemned me to death? Why could you not have just let me take my punishment and let me be?"

"To have left you there would have been to condemn you to death! Why can you not see that?"

"At least I would have had a chance. You took that chance from me when you felt the need to rescue me. It doesn't have to be like this, you know. If you would only take your eyes from me for but a brief moment, you would be rid of me for good. Why rescue me to only condemn me now? Whatever it is you feel you must do, please, do not do it."

He shook her shoulders, wanting to make her understand. "From the moment I first set eyes on you, you have tortured my soul. I would have spent the rest of my days wondering if you lived or died, and I will not have your death on my conscience. Letting you go off by yourself would only reassure your death. You know *nothing*, Brynn. You would only be feeding some very hungry wolves. There are no sheltered manors here. I am doing the best I can for you." Conflicted, Marek raised his hands to his head and paced a few steps away from her. He wanted to tell her everything would be all right and take her in his arms and never let her go, but he knew that was never meant to be. *It could not be.*

"But what am I to do?" she whimpered. "You are right... I know nothing."

Marek gritted his teeth. The girl never had to lift a finger in her years of life. If she wanted food, she ate. If she wanted to soak in a bath, she bade her servants draw her one. She dined with nobles. Even when taken from her home in Galhaven, Marek had seen to her wellbeing. How would she ever survive on her own? She knew not where to begin. Even he could not offer her these things. "There is a wealthy man here seeking a companion for his children. He is more than likely from an affluent Engel line and you will stay with them, here on Archaean lands. You will have food in your belly and clothing on your back. You shall be able to marry, to have children of your own. You will have a good life, Brynn." How he wished she would turn to face him. "It may not be with the luxuries you are accustomed to, but—"

"A good life?" she scoffed. "A life without my brothers, without my home… A life without…" She sighed, releasing the choking in her throat.

"I have spent most of my life away. My men, they are my family out here. They are my brothers. I do it so that one day my family may live in peace, away from the fighting, away from these *bastards* that call themselves *nobility*. I have not seen my wife in three years. *Three damn years*! My son was just a wee little thing when I last saw him. Life is one big torturous pain in the ass, so get used to disappointment!"

"I wanted children, you know, many of them, and a fine husband that would cherish me. I was engaged to be married before you came barging into my home and took away all hopes of that ever happening. He was a fine man that actually *wanted* to marry me, until you… ruined everything." Her voice was thick with spite.

Yes, he had ruined her life, tarnished her reputation, but was trying his damnedest to fix it the only way he knew how. He had kept his hands mostly off her — her virginity was still intact at least.

"In a few days' time, I should be a bride, not… *here*." Brynn turned from him. "You said you have a son? I bet he looks just like his father. A fine warrior he will be someday."

Kicking a rock from his path, Marek shuffled his way beside her, picturing his little boy as a strapping young lad.

"Aye, a fine one." Ewan looked more like his mother, tall and lean with angelic eyes and fine straight hair. His Nya, she was draped in sunlight when he was near. A smile breached his lips. The things he would teach Ewan — how to wield a sword and aim a bow. How to set a snare and skin his catch, just like his father had taught him.

He turned back toward Brynn. His mind was distracted for only a moment, but it was all the time she needed. Brynn was gone. "The gods help you, woman, when I find you," he muttered, scanning a corner for his missing Engel. He would never live this down if his men were to hear of it. He hadn't even noticed her leave. Instead, he'd kept right on walking like a blundering fool. Never in his life had a simple woman done this to him before. Marek, the mighty warrior, had somehow been reduced to a smitten boy. No sooner had he rounded the next corner did he find her, hissing like a wildcat and surrounded by a mixed group of men looking for something to play with.

"Get your hands off me!" she screeched, pulling her skirts from the toying grasp of the man circling her.

The Engel tossed his head back and laughed. "Oh, come now, sweetling, just one little kiss?"

"Never!"

"Oh, well do ye fancy a feck, then? I could do wondrous things between those legs, darling." He paced toward her and she counter-paced his steps. The Engel cornered her against a wall. "If not, then I will just have to come and get it myself," he snarled, reaching out for her. "I'm sure the others would like some as well, eh, boys?"

They cheered behind him, snickering and taunting her with a mixed jeering of words.

Brynn cuffed him across the cheek. "If you touch me, I swear I—"

"You'll what?" The man raised his hand to strike.

Marek caught the Engel's fist mid-swing. The force of the jerk spun the man around to face his attacker. In one swift motion, Marek brought his clenched fist back then set it loose. Bone crunched beneath the crushing blow. Blood spattered in all directions as the Engel's body twirled unconscious to the ground at Brynn's feet. Another approached, drawing a blade and wildly swung for Marek's chest. He dodged it easily, flitting to the side and tripping the assailant to the ground beside his unmoving friend. Marek stomped on the dagger. It released from the Engel's grip. He picked it up and held it to the man's throat. "Give me a reason," Marek growled, pushing the blade deeper.

The man barely shook his head, but it was enough to make Marek understand he wasn't ready to die. He withdrew the blade and tucked it beneath his belt. He gave the others surrounding him a glare, seized Brynn by her arm, and pulled her back down the alley. When she tried to pull away, he yanked her body to his, wrapped an arm around her waist, and slung her over his shoulder.

"Marek!" she screeched, kicking in a mad battle against herself. "I hate you, you... gluttonous dog!" She clawed at the arm pinning her. "I wish I'd never met you!"

"Good!" A toe dug deep into his ribs. He slapped her backside with his palm in warning, wishing he were touching it under different circumstances. She squealed in objection and demanded release. When her fit got her nowhere other than higher upon his shoulder, she reiterated just how much she hated him as he made his way to Daman's.

Marek returned Brynn to her feet before a rickety wooden door.

"Please, Marek, I beg of you. Please do not do this. *Please...*"

"I am so sorry." He could only whisper. "But I cannot take you with me. As much as I want to — I cannot."

"Then let me go before you make the biggest mistake of your life. Look at me, Marek."

He could not. If he looked at those beautiful pleading eyes once more, he would surely split into irreparable pieces.

He bent down and untied the boot knife and its scabbard from his calf, then reached his hands under Brynn's skirt and trailed his fingers up to her lower thigh. "Here," he told her, securing the straps around her leg. "Always keep this with you. Do not let anyone know you have it. Protect yourself if you must, and always remember where it came from." Returning

her skirts to their proper place, Marek stood and cleared his throat. "Do not be afraid to live."

Brynn searched between the ties of her skirts. Upon finding an object, she untied the securing knots and pulled out a charm. "It belonged to my mother," she told him, running the pad of her thumb over the design. "My brother, Michael, told me it had been blessed and would always protect me — that it contained my destiny — but it has brought me nothing but sorrow. My mother is dead, Michael is gone, and now you are leaving me. I have kept it with me every day since I was six years old. Take it. Perhaps it is only my curse. May it bring you better luck than it has brought me." Her fingers lingered on his for a moment as he took it from her palm.

Round in shape, a never-ending star was etched on its surface. Though a bit dull and smooth from years of wear, the etching still caught the light of the moon and reflected the glow like the constant star in a winter's night sky. He looked at it curiously before tucking it away.

The rickety door swung open, nearly flapping into Marek's side. "Is 'is 'er?" A very drunk Daman burst through the door. "'Outa my way, girl, let a man piss."

"The rest of the money, Daman, or did you drink it all away?"

"I got yer money, Highlander, so do'n go gettin' yer skirts in a bunch." When he finished, Daman turned to Brynn while fixing his belt. "A pretty little thing, aye? What's you called?" he slurred. When she didn't reply, he stomped closer to her and grabbed a fistful of hair, yanking her into the torchlight and closer to his beady eyes. "I asked what you was called!"

Marek pushed Daman to the side, causing him to lose balance. As soon as the man let go of her hair, Brynn scurried to safety behind Marek's frame and he slung a protective arm around her. "She doesn't understand you," he growled.

"Is she a dumb girl? Your rich man won't take no girl like that! What you mean she don't understand me? She's Archaean in't she?"

"Only by blood."

"How's she supposed to—?"

"She will learn," Marek interrupted. "She only speaks Engel. Now go get my money."

Daman returned with a small pouch containing the extra coins. As soon as he handed over the pouch, Marek grabbed Daman by the shirt collar and pulled the man up to his towering eye level.

"She is not to be touched," Marek told Daman, snarling in his ear.

"I... I... She will not be touched," Daman sputtered.

"And the rich man? Where is he?"

"He's comin' in the mornin'. I already have it worked out. Quit yer fretting. And put me down."

Marek released his hold on Daman. He gave Brynn one last long glance, burning her image into his memory before Daman pulled her to the door.

"Marek!" She screamed for him, struggling through the archway. Daman tightened his grip around her arm and jerked her free of the threshold, pulling her deeper into the darkness. "Please, I am begging you, do not leave me! Take me with you, Marek, I promise to behave. I'm sorry for what I said! You are making a mistake!"

"You would not be the first!" A deep scowl hardened his mouth. A flash of panic shuttered through him. Marek had never been one to second-guess himself, but he found himself suddenly lacking. He twisted his steps, but all that stood before him was an empty black hole. "*Feck!*" He bellowed in frustration. "The gods be damned to hell!" He kicked at the dirt, continuing his cursing tirade as he made his way to the tavern to drink away his aggravation and disappointment.

# Chapter Nine

## ABIGAIL

Brynn's eyes adjusted to the absence of light. Staring back at her were at least ten pairs of tired eyes.

"Get up," Daman called to one of them, slowly making his way through the room. Immediately, the frail girl he addressed exited her bed and rushed over to him, head hung low. "Clean her up," Damon ordered. "I want to see her in the morning."

The girl nodded and stood with feet planted. She was dressed in a long, tattered chemise dotted with several holes with her hair neatly pinned back in tight plaits. She was scared, just as those surrounding her seemed to be.

Daman's footsteps thudded back up the stairwell, and a lock clicked.

A dark-haired woman revealed herself in the light, carrying a small oil lamp. She was an older woman, worn by the world and hardened by life. Her appraisal swept over Brynn and her muddy, blood-stained clothes. Her eyes met Brynn's when the small lamp's light passed over her face. They were dark and deep, like earthy caverns. A few wrinkles had taken up residence under her heavy eyes. She spoke with hastened words, expectant.

Brynn had no understanding of the Archaean words.

The woman pointed to her chest and smiled. "Abigail."

"I am Brynn," she told the woman, recognizing the Engel name.

"Ah, I see. From Engel, I assume?" Abigail spoke familiar words.

"Galhaven."

"Galhaven, eh? Did ye serve there? I lived in Kirkwood once. How in bloody hell did you get *here*?"

"I am to be a nursemaid for a rich man's family. I will not be here long."

Abigail shrugged, chuckling. "That is what we were all told, silly girl. Come, let us get you cleaned up. You look as though you were dragged through a swamp." The woman held out her palm.

Abigail led her to a small washtub in the corner of the room where the women set to work finding Brynn fresh clothing, a comb, and a few parcels of food. Abigail promptly stripped Brynn of her clothing. "What is this, now?" she questioned, spying the boot knife strapped to Brynn's thigh. She looked closer and followed with more questions. "What is an Engel servant doing with an Archaean warrior blade? How did you get this?"

"I am no servant. 'Tis very valuable to me. Please don't take it."

"And let you kill us all in our beds?"

"No, I would never!" Brynn gasped, shaking her head. "It was the last thing that… it was a very special gift. Do not take it away. 'Tis all I have left of him."

Abigail allowed her to keep it after giving Brynn strict instructions to keep it out of sight and away from Daman, revealing she secretly had one of her own hidden and tucked away. While Brynn bathed, Abigail chatted away in Engel, asking for news of the towns, about the wars, and if the raids had made their way east.

The bath was bitter cold, but Brynn paid it no mind. Her thoughts fluttered about. She hadn't realized Abigail was still chatting or that another woman was busy trying to get a comb through the snarls in her hair. Brynn simply stared at the dark wall in front of her, wondering if Marek would burst through the door to rescue her. But as the women dressed her and plaited her hair, the door stayed firmly shut and locked while the hours rolled late into the night.

"You will sleep here. Rest, as tomorrow will be a long day."

"What happens tomorrow, Abigail?" asked Brynn as she climbed into a straw-filled bed, trying not to disturb the girls she was to share it with.

"Just call me Abby. Your new life begins tomorrow, and I shall answer any questions you may have while we are in the fields in the morn. Now go to sleep." Abby blew out the lamp and all was quiet.

Brynn found sleeping on a straw bed quite uncomfortable. The sharp needle-like twigs poked her through both the blanket and her chemise. Sighing, she wrapped her thin blanket around her shoulders and crept to the fireplace where a few coals still glowed and twisted in their fire dance with one another. They brought her back to the cave where Marek first kissed her. How she wished he was still with her to rock her to sleep on the back of his horse. Leaning her head against the wall, she closed her eyes, welcoming a bit of restless sleep, wondering if this strange dark-haired woman was the one from her seeing dreams.

Sleep did not last. It seemed mere moments passed before she was disturbed.

"Quickly now, 'tis almost daybreak. You don't want to keep him waiting." The words, sounding strangely familiar, coaxed her to further wakefulness. The fire had long since died, and her blanket hung loosely around her shoulders.

Abby was dressed and ready for the day's work. A hand on her hip, she tapped her booted foot impatiently. "He will want to see you in the light. Now don't worry, I will not let him touch you."

"Who?" For a brief moment, Brynn forgot she was locked in the tiny, stuffy underground room.

"Daman, of course. Here, put these on. They should fit." Tucked under one arm, Abby held several articles of clothing. "They were Nel's, but she... is not with us any longer. She was about your size — these shall do just fine."

Abby plopped them in Brynn's lap and continued to wake the others.

Brynn held up the long pieces of fabric, not quite sure what to do. Everything was so unfamiliar and strange. Even though Abby spoke Engel words, her voice was still thick with that of the Archaean brogue. And the clothing... she missed Marek's tunic. That little piece of him close to her body was gone — his woodsy, smoky scent — nevermore. As she eyed the pieces, a pair of worn leather ankle boots fell to the floor. *Shoes.* Brynn

101

smiled, slipping them over her chilly toes and latched the toggles tight. They were a bit snug, but they were warm. Rising from the floor, she pulled off the nightgown and slipped on the chemise from the pile. It was heavy and awkward with its billowy sleeves and immodest, low-cut neckline. She felt as though her breasts would spill out if she bent over. She cinched the strings tighter around her neck. It would have to do.

"What are you waiting for — me to die? Come on, now." Abby took up the overgarments and dark blue skirt from the remaining pile and slipped them over Brynn's head. "My, one would think you have never seen clothes before."

"Not like this," she replied, sucking in a breath.

"Do not worry — you can tuck up the skirts later. I need you to breathe or you'll keel over on me." Abby laughed while tending to the rest of the garments. "You are a pretty one, you are. You will fit in just fine."

"What is this?" Brynn questioned as Abby draped a long, green fabric about her shoulders. It was a pattern she had never seen before. It was quite beautiful — the color of the rolling hills in spring with a bit of blue added to match the summer sky.

"An arisaid. It took me a while to get used to it at first, but it comes in handy during the cold weather we've been having. You will learn to like it. Here, put it over your head. Like this." Abby took a piece from the back and draped it over Brynn like a hooded cape. "I was not as lucky as you to have someone show me how to wear the latest in Archaean fashion," Abby teased. "Stay close to me and I will keep you safe. I know how to handle that poor excuse of a man."

Brynn smiled. Abby was a lovely woman and was thankful to have her. She followed close behind as they made their way up the steep set of wooden stairs. The room above reeked of stale ale and smoke but was not a tavern. It was a one-room home with a small hearth, much like the ones she had seen in villages in Galhaven. It was empty of drunken men now, leaving only traces of their festivities from the night before.

The morning air left a sharp chill on Brynn's bones as they rounded the building. The other girls were busy eating a bit of bread and sipping from a bowl of water when she approached. A large man on horseback eyed them as they ate.

"Abby!"

"Daman, here she is. Take a good look — we have work to do." Abby puffed out her chest and stood her ground, squaring her shoulders.

Daman circled Brynn, taking in every inch of her frame as she stood awkwardly before him. She could feel his eyes burning over the exposed skin around her chest, but she kept her chin down and waited for it to end.

Grunting, he gave Brynn's chin a little push with his finger. He muttered words briefly to Abby then stomped his way back into the shack.

"Is... is it done?" she asked Abby.

"Aye. Best you eat some breakfast, girl. It's going to be a long day."

After eating, Brynn blindly followed Abby. "Where are we going?" Brynn asked, trying to keep up. She carried a large woven basket, keeping a sharp eye open for any Archaeans she happened to know.

"To the fields. We harvest Daman's crops so he can sell them for ale."

"Every day?"

"Shh... do not speak so loud. Engel is not a very favorable language to be speaking around this village."

"But I know nothing else."

"I will teach you."

Upon reaching the field, Abby turned sharply to the right, hastening her pace. "We will be picking the rest of the beans. The harvest is nearly gone. You shall come with me." Abby proved amazing with her speed and steady hands, while Brynn fumbled about with very few beans actually reaching the basket without first falling to the dirt. She could sense how frustrated Abby was growing when she nearly ripped a plant from the soil.

"I'm sorry, Abby, I must tell you that I'm not used to doing this work."

"Well, what sort of work are you used to doing, then?" Abby stood, wiping her brow with the sleeve of her chemise.

Brynn hung her head. "Well... none."

Abby scoffed. "You have never done a day's work?"

"No, I have not."

"What kind of parents raised a child who does not do work?" Abby pushed her basket to the side with her foot as she moved on to the next bean plant.

"Well, my father is Bertram, Earl of Galhaven. I am... was, his only daughter."

Abby's eyes widened. "What a little liar you are."

"I assure you, madam, I am no liar."

"Heh. *Madam*..."

"My father was trying to marry me off when a group of Archaeans ended up in our manor house. A misunderstanding ensued and so here I am, picking beans in a land I have no familiarity with, alongside another Engel, who I would never have guessed it so if it were not for that dark hair on top of her head." Brynn tossed a handful of beans into her basket and returned to find the ones that had fallen.

"How could *you* be the daughter of an earl? Look at you! If you *are* Engel, you look far from it."

"Perhaps I look like my mother? I never knew her — she died shortly after I was born. My brothers, they all have dark hair."

"You poor thing. You are Archaean and do not even know it. At least you will not have any trouble blending in like this old goat does."

"I am *not* Archaean."

"Where else would that hair come from? Perhaps your dear mother dabbled a bit with the locals." Abby chuckled.

"Do not say such things." Brynn sat on a patch of browning grass. "My mother was an honest woman." The thought of her precious mother carrying on affairs made her heart pound with grief. Although, her father did leave much to be desired. "So how did you come to be here?"

"That is a long story I do not like telling."

"We have the time," urged Brynn as she shelled a bean and popped it in her mouth.

"You best be careful. You could lose an arm for that."

Brynn quickly spat out the bean and covered it with loose soil.

Abby let out a hearty laugh and shook her head. "Oh, to be young again."

"Please tell me. It is nice to have someone to talk to."

"Well, if you come over here and help me with some beans, I shall tell you."

Brynn reluctantly returned to bean picking.

"Well, when I was young — about your age, maybe a bit older — I fell in love with a traveler before the Great Wars. He was the most handsome golden-haired man I ever set eyes on and we made our home in Dunlogh, a village deep in the highlands. It was the most beautiful place I had ever seen, with rolling hills and a view of the sea with rich soil and plenty of food. Oh, how lovely life was." She sighed. "When the Engels invaded, our village was pillaged, the men killed, and the women and children were taken and sold as slaves here in the Crossroads. They may tell you the slave trade doesn't exist, but my dear, here we are. My husband, bless his soul, tried to stop them from taking me, but..." Abby's eyes grew wet with tears. "It has been quite some time since I thought of him, and I have been here ever since. Daman has never been able to get rid of me."

"Why did you not just escape and go back home?"

"There was nothing left for me there."

"I mean to Kirkwood, back to your *home!*"

"My home was Dunlogh. I left Kirkwood long ago. I gave up that life. Being an Engel is a far worse life than this. You will see. 'Tis not all that bad. We are not always locked in that awful room, only when Daman does his bartering in the house. He doesn't want the men getting too friendly — or the other way around." Abby winked at Brynn. "Come, we are finished with the beans. We need to move on to the herbs. Daman needs them to sell in the market tomorrow."

"After you," Brynn teased, lifting her basket in the same manner as Abby. She struggled to balance it on her hip, and the extra bulk from the unfamiliar clothing made her steps a bit awkward. But after a few stumbles and only one big spill of harvested beans, she caught up. "Oh, sedge weed and blessed thistle!" Brynn grew excited when she spied a few herbs she recognized and had used readily in her healing. She dropped to her knees to thoroughly inspect them.

"Aye, start pickin' it. There are gloves in my basket."

"I had such a hard time finding it at the manor. It didn't grow well." Brynn couldn't believe its abundance in just one little spot. "I once read that blessed thistle mixed with calendula and ancient water can bring a man back from the dead. I'm certain it included a few other things, but I do not recall them. I am going to make it one day, though, and it is going to work. I just need to find the book. I know it to be true, as it came to me as a dream when I was a child."

"Are you an herbalist as well as a lady, then?"

"I'm not trained in it, but I can cure most wounds and poisons."

"A healer, aye? I suppose you can read and write, being a lady and all?"

Brynn laughed. "Of course."

"I noticed those lashes on your back — they look fresh. What would the daughter of an earl be doing with lashes across her back?"

"My punishment for disobeying my father." Brynn uprooted a sedge weed instead of breaking it off at its stem. She buried the root, hoping Abby didn't see the mutilation.

The guard on horseback kept his distance as the women ate bread and rested under the unusually warm autumn sun. Brynn was very thankful the day brought with it warmth instead of rain. She had seen her fair share of water as of late and welcomed the dryness as she stretched herself on a patch of grass. Abby had taken on the task of translator for the women, who asked question after question.

Brynn made many of them laugh and smile as she excitedly chatted with Abby, who tried to keep up in Engel and in Archaean. She finally had gotten herself so flustered that she picked up her half-full basket and headed back to the fields, mumbling something about overeducated nobles.

There was still much work to be done after the women made the trek back to Daman's home. The remains of the crops needed to be divided, the herbs sorted, and the loot made ready to sell in the morning. That evening, Brynn settled down next to the fire to stare at its entwining flames, imagining herself elsewhere. She envisioned playing a game of sticks with Michael in the courtyard, a treat they'd loved as children. How simple life had been.

"Would you like to go to the village market with me in the morn?" Abby, who must have spotted Brynn's longing look into the fire, knelt beside her.

"Oh, that would be lovely," Brynn replied, turning her attention from the flames hungrily licking a chunk of wood.

"People will speak with you, and you must know what they are saying."

"But—"

"Just sit with me and we will go over some names of the herbs and of some coins. You will understand soon enough. I learned fairly quickly.

Now, let us go over the herbs. You already know those, so I will tell you what they are in Archaean."

Soon Brynn was calling out items in Archaean as easily as she could in Engel. The lilt gave her a bit of trouble — Brynn's sounded more as though she was losing her dinner than the lyrical brogue of Abby. Brynn giggled, covering a hiccup. "I'm afraid I'm terrible at this."

"You are doing fine. We will practice more tomorrow."

Exhausted, Brynn fell fast asleep in her bed. Dreams brought with them visions of blood and knives, of rain, hot skin, and lustful kisses, awakening her startled and in a cold sweat. He had called out her name, his voice lingering in her sleep. Not able to shake the dream, Brynn rose from bed to ready for the day. She wanted to master the clothing for herself this time. She stoked the coals for light then placed each article of clothing out on the floor separately so she could see them all at once. The dark blue skirt was the first to go on over her chemise. Brynn strapped the leather belt around the large amounts of fabric making the arisaid. The last bit was her boot knife, hidden and secured safely under her skirts.

Abby joined her up the stairs. Outside sat a plain wooden wagon with several baskets of goods being loaded onto its flat bed.

"Do you remember the words?"

"Oh, yes," Brynn replied, pulling her arisaid around her shoulders and neck to block the frigid morning air. "Most of them." The day was dreary and dark; winter was fast approaching.

The center of the village was noisy and busy with passersby and Brynn looked about for a familiar face. Every head looked the same. How was she to spot the difference between one yellow head and another?

"What do you keep looking for?" Abby asked Brynn.

"No one," she quickly answered.

"I did not say who, I said what." Abby grinned. "Come, here we are."

For the rest of the afternoon, Abby and Brynn peddled their herbs and autumn vegetables. Brynn, finding it very difficult to keep up with the language, flustered easily and cursed several times before kicking the small table they stood behind in frustration, jamming her toe against a table leg.

Abby laughed aloud with her big, boisterous laugh, commenting on Brynn's entertainment value. Before packing up the remains of the day's sale, Abby disappeared, leaving Brynn to fend for herself before returning with a package hidden under her arisaid.

"Here, hide these well. Don't let Daman find them, or he'll have your hide for sure. These should occupy that head of yours for a while." Abby passed Brynn a few small, tattered books and parchments when the guard wasn't looking.

"Oh, Abby, thank you," Brynn whispered, hopping on the tips of her toes, eager to see what each contained. She couldn't walk fast enough. The wagon she trotted beside seemed to crawl the short distance back to Daman's. When safe in the depths of the underground room, Brynn ran to rekindle the fireplace. After adding a log, she sat cross-legged in the corner with her books, eager to feel the pages between her fingers.

One was written in Engel, seemingly a translation of words into Archaean. The writing was strange, but within time she would have it mastered. Another book was written entirely in Archaean, but drawings next to the words told Brynn it was a book of herbs. The third book was also in Archaean, and Brynn had yet to reveal its secrets. There were no pictures to give her clues so she set it aside. She would have to wait until her skills had improved to read it. She read late into the night until she could keep her eyes open no longer, excited to tell Abby what she had learned.

# Chapter Ten

## THE BARMAID

*The Crossroads*
*Archaean Highlands*
*Winter*

Hours turned into days, days were followed by weeks, weeks blurred into hopelessness. Brynn was finally able to exchange words with the women and tried to be friendly, but many of them simply ignored her. Her newness had long worn off, and she supposed Abby's particular fondness for her sparked a tinge of resentment. Abigail, however, had taken Brynn under her wing during her transition from Lady Brynn of Galhaven to nonexistence. Nights were spent next to the fire reading her books and staring into the flames, envisioning Marek. Her warrior hadn't returned for her. He only appeared in dreams now, haunting every thought and moment of quietness. Often, she envisioned their time spent together, wondering if she had only done something different — said the right words — she might not be banished as a slave. Perhaps if she hadn't been so defiant and childish with all that running away nonsense, perhaps… No news of a family taking her in as a nursemaid had come to fruition, but she still clung to hope, despite Abby's gloomy truths. Daman breathed lies.

Some nights Brynn would forgo her studies and meticulous note taking and sing a few childhood lullabies in that sweet, soothing voice everyone hushed to hear. The room seemed extra quiet at present, as Brigid, the youngest of the group, had been sold and torn from the clutches of her friends earlier in the evening. Their numbers grew fewer as the ground froze over, the snow piling higher around the doorframes and fences. The women took to baking bread and making stews to sell at market now that the crops had long passed. When the bitter cold forced them behind closed doors, several women worked in the tavern for Daman's brother, Godric. He owned a large brick oven so they would spend much of their time in the kitchen of the tavern, servicing the pub and cooking.

Brynn caught on quickly with the baking and helped Allina, the head barmaid, tend bar. It kept her busy and passed the time, and most of all, it kept her mind from wandering back to her warrior. Every tall man with curly gold locks seemed to have his face and sea blue eyes, but after a few skeptical blinks, the features would morph into nothing but that of a stranger.

Men came and went from the tavern and with every swing of the entrance door, Brynn raised her head with slim hopes one day it might be him, stopping by on one of his many travels. She frequently had to remind herself that he would not be passing through this tavern. He was at last home safe with his wife and his son. After all, he had chosen them over her.

An easy, thoughtless choice.

Brynn forced herself to smile while her heart felt differently. She missed his voice, and their foolish, petty arguments. She missed his stubbornness and she missed… his kiss. Oh, what she would give to taste his kiss, just once more.

"Abby, the handsome gentlemen in the corner are asking for another pint of ale!" The tavern was busy. Warriors traveling from the east had taken refuge in the Crossroads to ride out the raging winter storm brewing above them. Warriors returning from battle licked their wounds in the rooms above during the days and drank away their nights.

"Another? Any more ale and they will be long dead before they ever get their chance to fight!" Abby called from the back room. She was busy stocking barrels of ale with Owen, the part-time barkeep.

"Men with blood on their mind have nothing better to do than to drink themselves into a fight, Abby, you should know this by now," Brynn teased while waiting for Abby to bring her an order of ale.

"Hello, Brynn, you seem to be in good spirits today."

Instead of Abby, it was Owen who brought her the mugs. He was an Archaean man, thoughtful and kind to her, and Brynn certainly couldn't deny she had a fondness for his handsome qualities. Owen had no interest in wars or spilling blood and kept to himself and his books. They had much in common.

"Hello, Owen," she replied, practicing her Archaean words. She flashed him a sweet smile, playfully fluttering her eyes. "I learned a few new words last night," she told him, anxious to share her newfound knowledge.

"Ah, and what might those be?"

"Handsome… and lovely, and what was the other one?" She pointed her finger to her cheek and innocently turned her gaze upward. "I forget."

After swiftly kissing the indicated cheek, Owen asked, "Was it 'kiss'?"

"Hmmm, perhaps." Brynn blushed. A coy smile creased her lips as she took the overflowing mugs from the bar.

He ran a palm over his fiery red hair, then sighed, coming to rest on his elbows. He laughed as she walked away from him, her hips swaying with each step.

"Put your tongue back in your mouth," snickered Abby in passing.

"Here you go, lads," Brynn greeted, setting three mugs of ale in front of her customers. "A coin apiece, now." The men slapped a coin each on the table and Brynn swept them up and dropped them in her pouch. As she crossed back to the bar, the regulars shouted her name.

"Brynn, sing us a song! Sing to us of home!"

"No, lads, I'm not in the mood to be singing today. Later?"

"Oh, just a short one! Remind us of what is still good in this world."

Brynn sighed. She must keep the paying customers happy. It took her a few moments to remember the translation, but she began to sing a village favorite. Most missed their families and their homelands — she understood their heartache. "Land of our people, land that gave us home and hearth…" Silence surrounded her when she sang. "Hear our voices, hear our prayers," she continued. "Lead us home and bless our dear ones. We pray to you now and forevermore."

"To home!" a man cheered, raising his mug of ale in the quiet room. Others joined in as they all took a drink and toasted to wherever their home might be.

Brynn returned to the bar, fetching a few empty mugs on her way.

"Why such a sad face?"

Startled, Brynn turned toward Owen. "Oh, no reason." She halfheartedly laughed, trying her best to replicate a genuine smile.

"Why do I not believe you?"

"I have never been a good liar."

"I have something for you I think might cheer you up. Can you stop by my father's workshop tomorrow?"

Brynn beamed into his emerald-colored eyes. "I might sneak away. What is it? You know I love your surprises." His latest surprise was a beautiful and delicate seashell bracelet.

"Just come by."

"We will be baking bread in the afternoon. I'll stop in while it rises."

"'Tis settled then. Tomorrow."


Brynn worked the dough with her palms, kneading it into small rolls and setting them aside on the large counter in the kitchen. She minded her own, while the other women gossiped around her. She hummed a tune to pass the time, to transport to a far better place where winter's cold embrace couldn't touch her. She sang of love, and of her warrior, wishing she was in his arms under a warm autumn sun. Happiness flowed through her as she envisioned his smile. "Come, my love, come quickly to me. Come to my door and away we will flee. I wish in vain, I wish I had my heart again. But now my love has gone I fear, has gone away and left me here. Come love, come quickly to me, and away we will flee."

Abby slammed a pot on the counter. "All right, girl, tell me who it is you be singin' about. Who is this lover of yours you lament over day in and day out? Every day it is the same — he's left me here, he's left me here, please come back. Whine, whine, whine. Poor me." She tossed up her hands and walked to the other side of the table to tend to her baking.

"There is no one. It is just a song, 'tis all, and I like to sing it."

"And I am the Queen of Engel!" Abby laughed. "Who are you trying to fool? We can see right through your songs."

"There is someone behind those words," a woman in the kitchen commented, stifling a giggle.

"Who may it be?" asked another.

"There is no one!" replied Brynn, punching a fist into freshly risen dough. Brushing back a curl that had somehow worked its way loose, she muttered, "Not anymore."

"Ahh, so there *is* someone. Who is he now? You must tell us all."

"It's Owen, is it not?" Allina crossed the room, immersed in the conversation.

"No!" scoffed Brynn. "Definitely not."

"Why not? He is a handsome lad."

"And he fancies you," chimed another.

"He doesn't hold my heart," Brynn pined.

"Then who does?" They all seemed to ask her in unison.

Brynn couldn't divulge her secret. Surely, they would laugh at her for the mixed feelings she had for the tall *married* warrior she had only known for a handful of days.

"No one. He doesn't exist to me anymore."

"He's the heaven and the earth to you, love. I see it in your eyes. Do not shut out love, for a life without love is a lifetime without the sun — an ocean without water. A life without love is a life unlived. You remember that." Abigail poked Brynn's chest with her flour-covered finger.

Abby's words rang fresh in Brynn's ears as she shuffled her way through the slush-covered alley toward the blacksmith shop. Perhaps Owen *was* the one for her. He was a very nice man — educated and certainly smart — but when she looked at him, her heart didn't skip and her knees didn't grow weak. Only one man had ever made her feel like that... the one she could never have.

115

"Hello? Owen, are you here?" Brynn entered the front door to the shop.

"Aye, he is in the back, lass."

"Thank you, Alec. How is your arm?" Nearly a fortnight before, Owen's father burned himself on hot steel. Brynn had made him a poultice from dried blackberries and calendula for the wound. His condition seemed to have improved greatly as he was working again.

"Quite well, thank you. Go on, now, he is in the back." Alec pointed to a door and continued his work sharpening a steel blade on a spinning whetstone.

Brynn greeted Owen with a wide smile as she rounded the corner. "Hello, Owen!"

"How is your bread baking?" He laughed, pointing to the contrasting flour adorning her skirts.

"Oh, enough chatter, what do you have for me?" Brynn was eager with anticipation like a child just given sweets.

"Right on point today." He chuckled as he crossed the room to find his satchel.

"Aye," she giggled. "As always."

"Close your eyes."

Brynn clamped her eyes shut, holding out her palms. "This better be good, Owen. I snuck out for this."

"Aye, it is," he told her, digging in the depths of a satchel. He placed a small worn book in her awaiting hands.

Upon feeling the leather binding, she clutched it to her chest. She inhaled its musty scent deeply before opening her eyes to see what prize she held. Further inspection concluded she held no ordinary book. Her heart jumped into her throat.

"I found it in the great library while delivering some of my father's swords several weeks ago. It being so far from home, I shoved it in my bag and I stole it. It is written by the ancients," he blurted before she could ask. "I think it might contain something you have been looking for."

"You little thief." But a thrill of elation raced through her veins as she thumbed through the pages. It would need translating, but she would soon have it mastered. She wouldn't stop until she had its entirety decoded. As if reading her mind, Owen passed her another book. "You spoil me." She cracked the cover of the new book. It contained the ancient symbols and letters roughly translated into Archaean. She rose on the tips of her toes to kiss Owen's cheek and thanked him several times before pulling the arisaid over her head and shoulders. "I must get back. Thank you again, Owen. You have no idea how much this means to me. I am forever in your debt." She blew him a kiss before ducking through the door.

Her feet couldn't fly fast enough to the tavern. She nearly dropped the books as she leaped over the puddle at the entrance that never seemed to dry. "Abby?" she called out as she entered. "Abby, look!" Brynn raced to the kitchen and pulled her friend aside to show her the books. "It's the one I told you about, remember? He found it! I cannot believe he found it for me." Brynn huffed out of breath. "Look, it's filled with all the ancient herbs and medicines. It's in here, I know it."

"What are you talking about, girl?" questioned Abby as she took one of the books from Brynn. "What is this now?"

"Remember when I told you about the ancient water bringing a man back from the dead? Well, this is the only book in which it is written. I have been searching for it since I was a child. I just... I cannot believe I hold it in my hands even now!"

"Shh," Abby heaved Brynn aside. "Do not speak so loudly. They'll brand you a witch if they catch wind of your musings."

"Methinks Owen is a bit sweet on our dear Brynn," one of the girls teased, pulling loaves from the oven. A few others laughed as Brynn's cheeks grew hot. "Why else would a man bribe a woman with expensive gifts?"

"He is my friend," Brynn replied, tucking the books away. Abby placed a large bowl of dough in front of her. "He understands me."

Moments later Daman burst through the kitchen door, a half-consumed mug of ale in his hand. "You," he slurred, pointing a stubby finger at them.

Not sure which person he was pointing to, they looked at each other uneasily. More often than not, special requests weren't for ale delivery.

"What is it that you want, Daman?" From the back of the kitchen, Abby stepped into view, distracting him from the others. Her hands were placed firmly on her hips and she tapped her foot as she often did when irritated by his disturbance.

"Godric needs extra help tonight. He wants her." He pointed in the direction of Brynn.

"She is helping *me* tonight," replied Abby, standing firm. "We agreed, or does that thick head of yours not remember?"

"Are you arguing with me? You know what happens when slaves argue," spat Daman. After taking a long gulp of his remaining ale, he then wiped his mouth with his sleeve, threw the mug against a nearby wall, and stomped in Abby's direction.

As he reached out to strike, Brynn leaped in front of him. "It is all right, I will stay. There is no need for that." She placed a hand on his forearm, beckoning him to lower it.

"She is not staying without me," huffed Abby.

"Fine, but she is serving."

Long after the sun had set, a steady stream of men wandered through the doors of Godric's tavern. Brynn could sense something was different about this night. The men seemed anxious — on edge. There was blood in the air, she was certain of it. She remained guarded for the entirety of the evening until she could safely retreat to the warmth of the hearth in the kitchen.

Abby joined Brynn shortly thereafter, pulling up a wooden stool next to the fire. Wiping her brow on her sleeve, she sighed. "There are Engels in the tavern this night, and they are not to be provoked. I must warn you of one. I knew of him from my husband. He carries a self-proclaimed noble title of Lord Westmore. He has made his way to the Crossroads and takes what he wants whenever he wants it, and there is not a soul alive who can stop him. Stay away from him at all costs."

Brynn's eyes widened at the horror Abby instilled inside her. "This man is here, in the tavern?"

"Aye, I saw him earlier — tall, with hair as dark as night. If you catch his eye, go and hide. Seek out Owen, or run to Daman's. I will lie for you."

Brynn listened intently as Abby described evil. Rumors of his cruelty and black heart flamed like wildfires throughout the highlands, and villages prayed for solace from his wrath. Westmore had taken it upon himself to rid the Engel lands of Archaeans, and was a key player in the game of war so many years ago. And now, with new wars waging, he'd taken up his position again as master and executioner.

For nights on end, various men, Archaean warriors and Engel alike, passed through the tavern doors, speaking of great battles and plots to invade bordering villages. Brynn kept her head lowered and stuck to the shadows the best she could, but couldn't completely ignore those she must serve. Her existence was at stake. Defy Godric and Damon, and a beating would soon follow. The Engel, Westmore, used the far corner table as a meeting station, laying out various maps and markers most evenings. His emotionless eyes and lingering stares grew increasingly worrisome for Brynn. She hadn't spoken a word to the man, yet somehow, he'd taken notice. Brynn wanted nothing more than to fade into obscurity.

Having cleared the last of the tables, Brynn set a tray of cups on a nearby counter and joined Abby near the hearth for their nightly sit. Brynn rubbed her temples with her fingers. "I cannot wait to sleep." She yawned, stretching her arms above her head.

"A bit of sleep would do me good as well," Abby replied.

"My thoughts are not where they should be. I nearly dropped my tray when that Engel walked to the bar. I thought he was going to grab me, Abby." Brynn swallowed the lump in her throat, still rattled by the evening's events. "To be honest, I was relieved when he took Allina and not me. I thought I was next. I would sooner kill myself rather than allow such evil to touch me. If you find me dead one morning, you'll have your reason why."

The kitchen door creaked, and both women turned toward the audible intrusion. Owen lingered in the threshold, his face ashen and eyes wide with fear.

Brynn stood to face him. "What is wrong, Owen?"

He sucked in a deep breath. "He wants you."

Brynn's hands crossed her middle, hoping she could somehow keep her heart from bursting from her chest. She shook her head, unwilling to believe it. She lightly touched her thigh, regretting her decision to hide the boot knife Marek had given her so long ago. She wanted to keep it safe, she'd told herself. And now, she couldn't even keep herself safe.

"I've been ordered to fetch you. You must come now." Owen reached his hand out for her.

Glancing back at Abby, Brynn sought reassurance. She didn't find it. Taking a hesitant step forward, and then another, she clasped Owen's hand when she reached him. She squeezed it tight.

"Stay strong," Owen whispered as he entered the main room of the tavern with Brynn clinging to his side.

Two men were upon her then, taking her about the arms. She was ripped from Owen's grasp and left to put up a useless battle she wouldn't win.

---

T he doors closed behind her and all was silent.

"He has her now." Abby wrung her hands. "I should have known better. I should have kept her hidden."

"It's not your fault, Abby. He would have been propositioned by Daman sooner or later."

"That man is pure evil." Weary, Abby lowered herself into a nearby chair and buried her face in her hands.

Under the rule of Westmore, there would be no escape.

# Chapter Eleven

## LORD WESTMORE

B rynn huddled in a corner when Lord Westmore entered the room. He politely offered her a chair but she declined, defiant.

Shrugging, the Engel lowered into the seat, crossing his feet at the ankles. "Have you ever been with a man?" He spoke in Archaean. He had no lilt, nor the proper pronunciation that Brynn had worked so hard to learn. He was educated, undoubtedly smart, but lacked a certain something. Compassion, perhaps? Empathy? "No," she seethed, scowling at him. "I'm not married."

"I've not met a barmaid who was," he replied. He was tall and thin with hair as dark as night, with a strikingly handsome face, and a straight nose offsetting his deep green eyes. His tightly cropped hair was a stark contrast to his fair skin, complimenting his willowy features more than it should have. He was a meticulous groomer — everything had its place, right down to the shiny buckle on his belt, matching those on his remarkably clean shoes. "Do you know who I am?" He sniffed, picked a piece of something from his tailored jacket and shifted his weight in the chair, angling his head to one side, awaiting a reply.

"I know you are a filthy Engel." She spoke to him with a sharp tongue in her former language.

"Ahh, a smart one you are. What gave it away? My handsome good looks or the fairly bad tongue I don't care enough to replicate?"

"The hideous clothing you wear, *My Lord*, and that atrocious dark hair on top of your fat head gave you away."

In two strides he was at her side, jerking her upright enough to plant his palm across her cheek. Her head snapped back at the blow but she did not cry.

"I shall enjoy taking you, whore. I enjoy a feisty tart now and then... especially one who fights back."

At his release, Brynn placed her palm to her cheek, rubbing away the sting. "I'm not a whore. You have no right to assume so." She had heard of Westmore during her time spent in the tavern, although none had spoken his name. Some said he'd strategically set his sights on the Cross-roads to use as a military outpost between the two neighboring countries, while others argued he only raided the villages to strengthen his army. He promised good Archaean men lands and wealth if they joined him. Defy him, and he killed anyone in his warpath who didn't accept his sover-eignty. He had been the sole cause of the many uprisings throughout the highlands, striking fear into the hearts of those not able to defend them-selves. Westmore had arrived in the Crossroads not to rule it, but to take from it what he wanted — traveling soldiers looking for work and women to satisfy them.

"Tell me, where did a slave learn to speak such forthright Engel?"

Brynn spat at his face.

Infuriated, Westmore snagged a fistful of hair, pulling her close so that she would have no choice but to look him in the eye. "You are mine now, Archaean, do you understand that? It would be wise to treat your master with respect!"

Fighting back tears, Brynn tunneled her anger into her words. "You may have bought me, but I will *never* be yours. You may try to lay claim to my body, but my heart and soul belong to another. And the gods help you should you ever decide to touch me — I will slit your throat while you sleep. You have been warned, Lord Westmore."

"Such bold words for someone in your position."

"I have been in worse," she muttered.

Westmore tossed his head back in a laugh. "Worse? Tell me, when was the last time a man raped you for nothing more than the pleasure of hearing you scream?" Her gasp only fueled him. He forced her against the closest wall, allowing no escape. Tracing her jawline with a long, slender finger he seemed to soak up her features, memorizing each line and curve, the color of her eyes and the fury that lay behind them. He clamped a palm to her breast, and squeezed it, assessing the validity of the flesh. "Let us see if your words ring true," he snarled, reaching for the hem of her skirts.

Brynn swung at him, throwing her weight behind her attack.

He overpowered her, his fingernails tearing the tender tissue of her inner thigh. "Ah, see how you yearn for me already." Westmore released her, his fingers lingering on her fleshy thigh before she clamped them shut. "Yes, I shall enjoy you immensely. You will work at my residence when I call for you, and you will learn your place. And when I am finished with my campaigns, I will send for you. A pure virgin shall be my reward for a perfectly played out war."

Brynn drew a ragged breath. "Remove your hands, My Lord."

"Learn your place, whore." His attention turned to his two guards. "Watch her. I have business to attend to."

A small ray of light flickered over swollen eyes from a night's worth of tears. Rising, Brynn paced the empty floor. She hadn't slept much, between the dreams and the fear. The ravens had visited her during the nice. The three of them—circling in the sky above, except this time, one bore his face. The raven had his eyes, and instead of feathers, Westmore's dark hair on its head. *Kill...* it had croaked. *Kill.*

As she stood near a window contemplating whether or not she could wriggle through it, the locked door clicked and in walked Lord Westmore, bringing with him a cold gust of winter's air. Wrapping her arms around her chest, she backed away from the window.

A strange man followed Westmore through the door. A thick beard and mustache covered most of his facial features, leaving only round bulbous eyes and a thin nose poking out from his bushy face. He carried a bag over his shoulder with stains matching those on his hands.

"You… take her arms." Westmore pointed to a guard, who obediently rushed at Brynn to pin her arms behind her back.

She balked, twisting and turning, but was no match for the man's wrenching grip.

"Must I teach you another lesson? There is no use in fighting me. Bare my brand so all will know you belong to me or slit your own throat. The choice is yours." Lord Westmore tossed a dagger to the floor.

Brynn watched the blade clink across the stone, stopping only inches from her feet. She chose the dagger, without hesitation. She would gladly plunge the blade into her chest rather than be subject to another assault. But before she had a chance to declare her answer and reach for the dagger, a light breeze from the open door entangled itself through her skirts. It wrapped around her waist to play with her golden hair before settling in her nostrils. His face flashed before her eyes, and for a moment, she could have sworn he was standing there beside her, lovingly caressing her cheek. "Marek?" she whispered to the air, closing her eyes to absorb the touch.

"What is your choice?"

"So be it." Brynn chose life. The gods had given her a sign to trust them. They told her Marek was coming.

She was held against the floor, her arm askew, while the branding man inscribed Lord Westmore's symbol of choice deep beneath her skin. The chosen spot was inconspicuous enough — hidden on the underside of her wrist, but noticeable in dark black ink. With each jab of the bone needle, her thoughts drifted to Marek — his kisses had left their own brand on her skin. Brynn thought of his overwhelming desire to taste her, to love her. She reveled in it, losing her mind to the pleasure he'd given her to drown out the pain.

Soon her branding was finished, her wrist wrapped in a cloth, and Brynn was sent on her way. A guard followed close behind, watching her every step. As the days blurred by her scars healed, leaving the curving emblem of Lord Westmore for all to see. Most knew of its existence as word spread throughout the village, and no one dared speak to her anymore. She had returned an outcast and unrecognizable, gruesomely maimed by the gods themselves.

. . .

Brynn spent her evenings working in the tavern while her mornings and afternoons were occupied by Daman's fields, tilling the softening spring soil and sowing seeds for his crops. Whenever Westmore would arrive in the Crossroads, she was carted off to his residence to serve as his maid where she would do as he bid of her. Meals, bathing him, even helping him to dress.

Brynn's body had strengthened and filled out with the daily extra meal she received per Westmore's instructions, but her spirit faded with the passing of the seasons.

"Oh, I am getting too old for this, I fear." Abby stumbled behind the tiller.

"Just wiser, is all." Brynn gave Abby a half-felt smile, wiping her neck with a dusty hand.

"That sweetness doesn't fool me, girl. Help an old woman up." Abby reached out to Brynn, who helped Abby to her feet. "The sun is setting. Get the horse, will you?"

Brynn unlatched the straps of the harness. "Here, you should ride." Brynn steadied the horse, helping Abby to mount.

"What are *you* looking at?" Brynn stuck out her tongue at her guard she affectionately referred to as "Brute". She quickly learned how to deal with him by fueling his ale addiction until he could no longer stand. Brynn would pay one of the other women to flaunt at him until he vanished with the whore, not to be seen for a better part of the night.

"Owen tells me there will be a wedding during the full moon," Abby stated, trying to fill the silence with useless blather as they traveled.

"I heard rumors. Owen doesn't speak with me much anymore." Brynn missed her friend. Before her branding, there had been talk of him buying her freedom and perhaps asking her to be his wife — she heard the women chat about her when they didn't know she was listening. But now… he barely had the courage to look at her.

"Horse shit. Go ahead and speak to Owen. He misses you, I'm sure of it."

"He is afraid, Abby. Everyone is." She was.

"They are afraid of his madness, not of you. Don't confuse the two, my dear."

"We must leave this place," whispered Brynn.

"Shhh!" Abby scolded, turning to see if the guard listened to their conversation. "Don't let the brute hear you speak of such things. He will report it."

"Oh, but we will," Brynn countered. "We will be free of this place, I know it."

# Chapter Twelve

## WE WILL GO HOME

*Daman's*
*Late Autumn*
*Seven months earlier*

"Marek!" She screamed for him, struggling through the archway. Daman tightened his grip around her arm and jerked her free of the threshold, pulling her deeper into the darkness. "Please, I am begging you, don't leave me! Take me with you, Marek, I promise to behave. I'm sorry for what I said! You're making a mistake!"

"You wouldn't be the first!" A deep scowl hardened his mouth. Marek had never been one to second-guess himself.

He twisted his steps, but all that stood before him was an empty black hole. He bellowed in frustration, tossing his hands to his face, rubbing his eyes with his palms. "The gods be damned to hell!" He kicked at the dirt, continuing his cursing tirade as he made his way to the tavern to drink away his aggravation and disappointment.

Marek downed several mugs of ale at the bar before joining his men at their table. He listened to their prattle and stories until he could stand it no longer. "Come on, lads, let us leave this place."

"But we have just settled in! Come on, Marek, have some fun." Gavin beckoned another pitcher to be brought to his table.

"Come, join us, brother. Take your frustrations out in the ale. Wallow in your own self-pity if you like, but don't take it out on us... especially because of a *woman*." Ronan clutched Marek's shoulder, then slid a frothy mug to his brother.

"I would like to get the money I am owed, aye?"

"*Och*, tomorrow, lad." Gavin downed the rest of his ale as the barmaid approached. "Fill it up," he told her, hiccupping. "What a good lass." Gavin strained around Aiden to watch her sway away. "Did you see that?" He took a long gulp, wiped his mouth, and grinned at her from across the room. "She smiled at me." He rose from his chair, a bit tipsy, and chuckled as he stumbled sharply to the side. He pawed the air for balance, and finding nothing, careened headfirst to the floor.

Ronan kicked Gavin slightly with his toe. "She's not smiling now, you drunkard."

"He cannot ride like that." Aiden took a swig of ale to keep from laughing.

Marek finished his drink then stood. "Then tie him to the damned horse. Come on, pay your tab and let us be gone."

"You need to find yourself under a woman before your cock explodes. A simple fix for your foul mood. Go find the one smiling after Gavin. She was willing enough for him, and well, you seem like a better prize right about now." Ronan laughed, jabbing his brother in the gut with his elbow.

The journey home without the girl tagging behind did indeed prove to be quicker, but he missed her. Her eyes haunted his sleepless nights. Dreams left him restless and cold from sweat. Many nights he imagined she was beneath him, but would awake to find only darkness. The men pushed forward for days on end. The only detour during their travels was stopping briefly near one of Brockington's outposts to collect their fee for disposing of Lord Dugray. A hacked off lock of the man's scalp and a personal effect proved death and they were rewarded with their share of coins. Spirits lifted and their pace quickened as they passed familiar territory. Marek could taste the sea salt when a misty breeze forced him to pull his cloak tighter. Snow would fall soon. Digging in his heels, Marek spurred his mount ever faster.

Five days later, the group reached the mouth of the valley hugging their homes. Their tiny ocean village awaited their return just over the peak of one last hill. To Marek's dismay, there was no welcoming party, no children running to greet them at their sighting. Instead only the scorched remains mingled in between a few new crofts scattered across the dull horizon.

"What in hell?" Ronan's bewildered gaze matched his brother's.

Urging their mounts onward, the men cantered toward the seemingly abandoned village.

Every scenario possible ran through Marek's mind as he paced his horse through the village. Recognizing the largest of the remains as what was once the meeting hall, Marek dismounted and worked his way through fallen timbers to the entrance. The door was missing and fire had scorched most of the walls, but the structure was still relatively sound and standing. "Hello?" he called, half expecting someone to jump from behind the rubble to greet him. His voice only echoed off the walls. Frustrated, Marek kicked a chunk of ash. It crumbled on impact.

"What happened here, brother?" questioned Ronan.

"The proper question would be, 'Where is everyone?'" Marek's growing concern turned to his own wife and child.

Ronan tried to comfort him. "Perhaps they escaped the raid. Maybe there was just a fire that took wind and latched on to thatch. There are rebuilt crofts here. Someone had to build them."

Marek returned to his mount. "Let us take a look around, aye?"

The men spread out to search the entire village, leaving no cranny overlooked. Shortly after Marek began his search, he heard his brother's excited shout riding on the gust of a sea breeze.

"Lads! Over here!"

The urgency in Ronan's voice made the hairs on the back of Marek's neck stand tall. A shiver ran up his spine and he veered his horse toward the voice, intercepted by Gavin and Aiden. The four met on the crest of a hill overlooking the shoreline with mouths agape at the sight of two funerals below.

The villagers faced the sea, watching two bodies burn on a raised ceremonial platform. Marek recognized many faces but realized many were missing. He practically fell from his saddle in dismount, scanning the small crowd for his family. There in the back with head hung low, a weathered woman caught his eye. "Mother?"

At his voice, the head perked, turning in recognition.

At the sight of her two sons, Murron gathered her skirts and rushed toward them, disbelief radiating from her face. Her arms wrapped around them both as she wept tears of joy. "And all this time I thought you were dead. Oh, my sons…" Pulling their heads down to hers, she kissed them both before beginning her motherly prodding, searching for injuries and missing limbs. She raised their arms, turned them in circles, and clucked after Ronan for allowing such a serious injury.

"Mother, we are fine, and in one piece. All are accounted for."

"Praise the gods!" Murron raised her face to the sky briefly before her palm connected with Ronan's scruffy cheek. "That is for leaving us." Next, she cuffed Marek and chided, "And that is for my suffering."

Marek rubbed his stinging cheek, examining faces. "Where is everyone?" he asked. "What has happened?"

"Our numbers are few. We were attacked by an Engel raiding party many seasons ago. Men are swearing fealty to that Lord Westmore along the coast. He promises land and riches, but—" Her words were cut short as Marek left her side. "Marek." She reached out for him. "She is not there, my son!" Murron grunted as she shifted her weight from one hip to the other, following her eldest son.

Marek's home graced the shoreline. It wasn't much, but it provided shelter for his family. He raced for it now. Every imaginable thought flooded through his mind as he galloped the overgrown trail. Heavy stones seemed to have been placed on his chest — trying to catch his breath was impossible as he rounded the last hill before setting eyes on what was once his home. Nestled quietly in the shadows was a charred building overrun with weeds and the remains of summer's growth. Autumn's leaves huddled in crevices, ready for a long winter. The wooden fence he had spent so many summer days constructing had fallen into disrepair. Marek pushed aside what his gut was screaming and swallowed the burning sensation in his throat.

"Nya?" he choked. Hearing no reply, he hastened his steps ever closer.

A shard of pottery crunched beneath his boot as he approached the entrance. "Ewan? Da is home." Hesitant, he took a deep breath and entered the remains. A floorboard cracked under his weight and Marek took a leap back, stumbling into a scorched wall. It fell to the ground, spewing dust and ashes into the air. His breathing quickened, his heart settling at a steady pace. "Nya, answer me!"

"They are gone, son," said Murron.

"What?" Marek didn't want to listen as he pawed his way through the debris, searching for his family. "Where is my son?"

"We burned their bodies and buried the ashes on the hill overlooking the sea. The spot that Nya loved so much seemed appropriate."

Marek shook his head, pursing his lips. "No." He refused to hear the words. He had asked her to be his wife on that very spot. "*No.*"

"I am so sorry, Marek…" His mother couldn't comfort him. Hell, he couldn't comfort himself. Everything he fought so hard for was gone.

Anger and heartache consumed him. Marek picked up a nearby rock and hurled it into the rubble.

He screamed.

He cursed the gods.

A gut-wrenching sickness overwhelmed him, bringing him to his knees. Crumpling to the ground, Marek covered his head with his hands and cried out in anguish. A tortuous wail escaped from deep within him. If only he had been there, his little boy would be running into his arms at that very moment. He would be kissing his wife — the celebration long overdue.

If only.

# Chapter Thirteen
## BROKEN

Waves of emerald and blue crashed against jagged rock as high tide ascended toward the highlands. For days, Marek had grieved over the grave of his wife and son on the hill overlooking the sea. When the sun would rest below the horizon, he would drink away the memories and images that haunted his dreams around the fire. Never before had he felt so alone and without purpose.

Marek pulled his dagger from its sheath and twirled it in his fingers. He sat against the large stone marking the burial site of his loved ones, contemplating whether or not he should just plunge it deep into his chest and end the aching of his heart or continue with his grieving rituals. A quick thrust would be so much easier, but revenge had crossed the depths of his mind in between swigs of lager.

Sighing, he grasped the handle firmly and placed the cold steel against the back of his neck. Slow and smooth, he dragged the blade flush against his scalp. The golden curls fluttered to the fading grass of season's end. As he carefully shaved his head, he breathed a quiet prayer to the gods, hoping they would carry his words to his wife and son so their souls might rest in peace. When finished, he replaced the knife to its sheath and stared out to sea once more.

Murron, cloaked heavily in her woolens, made her way toward him. "Oh, my son, whatever shall I do with you? You have been out here for too many days a drunken old sod. You will catch your death on this hill, I am afraid." Marek's mother braced her weight on his shoulder and lowered herself to sit beside her son.

He made no acknowledgment of her presence. Marek focused on the dimming horizon as his thumb and finger lightly traced the design on the round metal charm in his palm.

"We need to have a talk, you and I," Murron huffed, pulling her arisaid over her shoulders. "I know the village is hesitant to welcome you back, but I am overjoyed that you are alive. You, my son, are alive." She took his face in her hands and cupped his cheeks, rubbing a knotting finger over his hollowing cheekbones. "Ronan told me of your travels and how he was saved. I know how your heart aches. There has been talk of moving the village east — our numbers dwindle with each passing season. I fear there is no one left to make new babes…"

Marek stared into the nothingness before him and took a sip from his flagon.

"No amount of good highland whisky can take away that empty ache in your heart, Marek."

"Tell me what happened."

"Ahh, so he does speak. Come with me, I will show you. I was hoping you were ready. Ronan is waiting."

Rising to his feet, Marek tucked the silver charm back into its hiding spot beneath his tunic before helping his mother stand.

"Oh, this weather sets my bones to aching," Murron groaned as she stumbled over her first few steps. She forced a smile. "I see you have started your mourning period." Murron's eyes shifted to Marek's shaven head. "Curls suit you better."

"Would you like me to carry you, Mother?" poked Marek.

"There's my boy," smiled Murron, showing a wide, toothy grin. "I have missed him."

As they walked through the old village, Murron explained to Marek how the raiding party swept down the valley and through the village, taking the women and children captive while the men stood helpless. The raiders demanded the men pledge allegiance to Lord Westmore, and when they refused, he slit the women's throats in retaliation. After the highlanders recanted, the raiding party strung the children together and hanged them all from the rafters of the meeting hall. When the men fought back, those caught were hacked to pieces, too old to defend themselves without armor and proper weaponry. I have never seen such wickedness in one man, Marek. Those who could escape made their way to the shore and hid beneath the trees and in the watery caves, as did I. That is when they started to burn everything. They made sure to flush everyone out." Murron's hands shook as she recalled that frightful night. "She fought hard, Marek. You would have been proud."

Marek kept his distance from the haunted place, not wanting to approach the remains in fear of perhaps seeing things he knew had long since passed, so he stood in the cold with his arms folded across his chest. Ronan wandered the remains but stayed close to their mother.

"I recall five. She killed three before they got to us. After they — well, I ran — there was nothing I could do. She told me to run, to take Ewan and run, but I couldn't find him. We found the bodies of the attackers littered with arrows after the fire. It rained that night."

"Good girl," Marek whispered, picking up a blackened wooden object. As he dusted it off with his sleeve, his heart broke into a thousand tiny pieces. In his palm was the toy horse he had carved for his son. Marek wiped his eye with the back of his hand, fighting back the tears. He'd been mistaken. He was not ready for her words. Try as he might, he couldn't drown out his mother's voice. Grieving properly was proving to be difficult when he was filled with pure, unfaltering, hate. He would hunt down this Lord Westmore and tear out his heart. He would hunt this Engel until his last dying breath.

"We found Nya first, run through." Her voice choked, frail and hollow. "Ewan," she continued with a catch in her throat. "He was found some distance from the croft... running, I suppose. The boy had two arrows in his back. He never had a fighting chance... such a small boy."

A wave of sickness spread throughout Marek's body and he tried to keep his footing. Unable to handle the gruesome details, he tumbled to the ground to wretch. He sucked in a breath and looked to Ronan. "I am going to kill him. Brother, come with me."

"I have seen enough battle to last me a lifetime, Marek. This fight is yours, and I do not fault you for it. I mourn your loss. I truly cannot imagine your pain, but I will not leave again. I'm done." Ronan took his mother's arm to lead her from the shambles, leaving Marek to his own vices.

As she passed, Murron leaned over his trembling body and whispered, "At least wait until spring, love." She gave his shoulder a tight squeeze.

Marek clutched her hand in return.

He lingered by the destroyed croft, gathering his thoughts before returning to his mother's fire. A bowl of stew had been set aside for him, and he picked at it; his appetite had left him. Losing himself in his drink was much more satisfying.

For days on end, his mind slipped beneath reality. Marek found himself sitting on the burial hill staring blankly at the sea, drinking himself into a stupor in order to find sleep without torturous dreams. His life no longer had reason. He was broken — a restless, wandering soul without purpose. His only comfort lay in the small little charm he kept tucked away, hoping it may comfort his aching heart while he slept off his ale, but he awoke only to find his heart yearned for something else entirely.

Marek stopped flipping the charm between his fingers to brush a snowflake from his eyelashes. Winter's first storm had been steadily falling for several hours, it's cold only numbing his extremities instead of his mind. Snow crunching from footfalls pulled his attention from tracing the lines on the charm and he turned to see who dared approach his roost.

"Might I sit a while with you?"

"Mother, you don't favor the chill. Please go back."

"Not until you listen to me." Murron had brought with her a thick fur to sit on, unlike her son, whose clothing had grown stiff from the freezing snow. They sat together in silence. Marek continued to gaze at the silver piece, avoiding his mother's weary face.

"She wouldn't want you to be like this," Murron stated, breaking the tension. "The worst is over now."

"It has only just begun," he replied, turning his face toward the horizon once more.

"Your brother, Gavin, and Aiden have all been helping to rebuild. The others could use your skillful hand."

"I have no interest in rebuilding."

Her eyes fell on his hands, and she pointed at the silver charm. "What is that? What is this thing you will never let leave your sight? You are obsessed with this piece of silver. Give it here." She held out her palm.

"'Tis just a medallion. It is of no value to me." Coolly, he placed it on his mother's waiting palm.

"If it were of no value, you would not be carrying it so close to your heart." Murron traced the engravings and designs on the silver trinket. "Where did you get this, Marek?" she questioned.

"Along one of my travels. I don't remember," he blatantly lied.

"Liar. Do you not know what this is? This is a birth charm. It can only be given to a child who is born under the brightest winter star. A child born on this day is said to possess mysterious energies considered close to those of the ancients. The purest of souls, indeed. I have heard tales about the few being born, but they have all been just stories of murdered babes and scared men. I have never seen a forged charm still in existence."

"Well, that explains a great deal." Marek chuckled, taking the charm. He ran his thumb over the lines once more, needing its comfort to release the tightness creeping up into his chest. Doing so seemed to calm his restlessness.

"So, who is she?" blurted his mother. "This winter child of yours?"

Caught off guard, Marek could only stare. "What?"

"Little baby Archaean boys are not given birth charms, no matter what they possess. Only someone with plenty of silver could have had this forged — it's very pure. Who was the woman that gave you this? You must have done something remarkable in order for her to fall so completely and hopelessly for you. She gave you her most valuable possession."

Marek frowned as all the tiny little pieces finally fell into place. She told the truth. What he thought to be just foolish talk had been her truths. And she'd trusted him with it. Witch, healer, seer.

She had given him the charm so he would never forget what he had done to her. She had inched her way into his heart, no matter how hard he'd tried to keep her out of it. His intentions with her had been so clear, why had he gone and done something so stupid as to show her affection? Because he'd wanted her touch upon him, that was why. He'd wanted her in more ways than one, and had shown his weakness to all.

That first moment their eyes had connected, those fiery ocean eyes, she'd reached deep inside him and ripped out his heart. He'd left her severely lacking for that manner, selling her off when all along his heart was screaming at him to do otherwise. The gods had shown him his path, but he'd chosen not to see. Marek shook his head in disbelief that his mother had figured it out before he had himself. "I sold her, that's what I did."

"You *what*? Since when does my son partake in slave trading? If your father were alive, he would skin your backside."

Groaning, Marek proceeded to tell his mother of his last journey home. "We were deep in Engel territory when Ronan took a hit by an arrow. I did what I could for him, but the tip shattered against his bone. We sought refuge at the manor of an earl close to Engel and Archaean borders. Ronan was not faring well at all. He was a mess, Mother, he needed help. A... misunderstanding occurred. Someone tried to kill the earl's daughter, and I somehow got the blame of spoiling her — which I did *not* do," he was quick to add, spying the incredulous look on his mother's face. "You know me better than that, Mother. Well, this girl, she was a healer. She repaired Ronan and brought him back from the edge of death like nothing I'd ever seen before, and I... I *took* her. I took her from her bastard father and I took her for..."

"Go on," Murron urged.

"I took her for myself. I wanted her for my own. Damn the gods! I don't know what came over me. She was just a girl, oblivious to the world and just... perfect, with eyes the deepest blue I have ever seen." Marek softly smiled, recalling her angelic features.

"What Engel would ever have blue eyes?" Murron asked.

"Aye, therein lays the confusion. I thought she was an Archaean slave. Clearly, she was not." He recalled to his mother how stunned he had been when he learned Brynn was that Engel's daughter. "Golden hair, golden skin, and definite Archaean eyes. I was such a fool. I left her at the Crossroads. I found a rich man to take her. She will be well provided for in a family who deserves her. I just couldn't bring her home to—"

"Nya," finished his mother.

"Aye. I took an oath. But it is of no consequence now. You have no idea how many nights I contemplated keeping her, but I couldn't do that to Nya. She was a strong and dutiful wife and bringing home another woman I had lusted over would have killed her. There was just something... different about that girl. I was drawn to it."

"And you are still in love with her."

"Mother, how could you say such a thing?"

"You stupid boy." She sighed grievously, clucking her tongue at her son. "The gods wouldn't let you love again if your wife were not already dead. They breathed you new life and you tossed it aside."

"The gods do not exist. Nya and Ewan's deaths prove that."

"Horse shit. The gods gave you a sign. The gods couldn't prevent their deaths, but they put your new woman in your very arms and you sold her out of them. Death is a part of life. You know this. You may mourn — keep them in your heart — but you must move on. You were given the gift of a new life. How a son of mine could be so blind I will never understand."

"Nya has my heart."

"Never give all your heart, son, for love will hardly be worth thinking of when the one who has your heart is gone, and your heart has gone with them."

"I am not in love with some... *silly* little girl who I transported for a while."

"Keep telling yourself that, Marek, for you are the only one who believes it. Ronan has already told me about her. Corrine, was not it?"

"Brynn," he corrected. Pursing his lips together, he frowned. Once again, his mother had bested him. The snow had begun to settle on his clothes, cooling his core. His hands were shaking — strange, he hadn't noticed before now. "Enough of this chatter, Mother. Let us get you next to the fire. You'll catch your death sitting up here."

"Better here with you than alone," she replied, shifting her weight forward to stand.

"I will be leaving once the snow is dormant." Standing, Marek took his mother's arm in his.

"Only you can slay your demons, my son. I fear in my heart that once you leave me, you will not be returning."

Marek shrugged. "Perhaps."

Perhaps she was right, and they both knew it.

# Chapter Fourteen

## CAIRN

*Archaean Highlands*
*Late Spring*

"Pass me that last bit of thatch, will you?" Marek asked Ronan, busy repairing leaks in the roof of Murron's croft.

Ronan scaled the ladder two rungs at a time to toss an armful of thatch to Marek. Tucking in a few stray strands, Ronan lingered on the ladder. "There has been talk of moving the village. Have you heard this, brother?"

"Aye, I have," Marek replied, indifferent.

"Well, what are your thoughts?"

"Honestly, I think it unwise. Combining forces — now *that* would be a wise decision. Leaving a village that has already been raided and taking it to a village due for one is not. I have been meaning to talk to you and the lads about riding over to Cairn to see about putting an end to these raids. I've heard about its vulnerability." Wiping the sweat from his brow, Marek finished the roof and descended the ladder after his brother. "What say you?"

"Marek, I don't think we should leave our people unprotected."

"It will be three days, four at the most. They have soldiers — strong men ready to fight. Come with me. We can end this. I need you on my right, Ronan."

"I'll talk to the lads — see what news has been roaming the village."

Marek clasped his brother tight. "I'll find you later. I have something I must do."

Strolling under a rare spring sun, Marek let out a shrill whistle, calling the only one happy to see his face as of late — his faithful friend and battle comrade, Arran. Within moments, his mount cantered from the far end of the fenced-in pasture with ears perked. Inquisitive eyes peered over the railing. Swatting away a pesky fly, Marek apologized for not visiting as much as he should have. "I'm sorry, my friend. I've been troubled lately."

Arran nickered, nuzzling his nose beneath his master's cloak, seeking a treat.

Marek playfully pushed the insistent mouth aside. "What did you find?"

Arran persistently investigated a certain spot on Marek's chest. A glint of sunlight reflected off the silver charm. The horse took it lightly in his lips, decided it wasn't food, and released it with a snort.

"You miss her, eh? I do, too." Marek continued his guilty conversation with his faithful steed. "I know I told you no more battles, but what do you say to one more? For Ewan and Nya. You were her favorite, you know," he teased. "One last fight and I promise you can live out your days making many more little Arrans." The animal gave up his search then turned to rejoin the herd at the far end of the pasture. "I'll take that as you care nothing for me and my thoughts." Marek fastened his cloak. "It seems nobody gives a damn these days."

As word spread about Marek's pending plans to head to Cairn to seek out a handful of willful warriors, a meeting was called by the elders. Marek sat beside his brother in the shadows, quietly taking in his environment.

"If we go, the village is left to fend for itself. We are small in numbers as it is. Take away our best warriors, and we will be annihilated for sure this time!" one man argued, raising his voice above the chatter.

"Aye!" another agreed. "We have done our share. We need to continue rebuilding, not fight someone else's battle!"

"Until they come back, looking for more," called Marek. "How long are we to wait before this Engel is tired of his women and wants fresh bodies? How many more of our sons have to die trying to defend their mothers? How many times are we going to rebuild while that Engel parades up and down our lands looking to take whatever he can get his filthy hands on? Are we supposed to sit idly by while he preys on our own? If so, then why do we not just give ourselves to him? Let him cut our throats? Hell, I will let him use my own knife!"

"Marek is right, lads," added Ronan. "We need to show this Lord Westmore that we are not going to let him take our people and destroy our homes any longer."

"I say we gather some fighters and intercept the Engel... show him what Archaeans are *really* made of, and that he will not win against warriors blessed by the gods! He may be able to defeat a village filled with women and children only because he has yet to face true Archaean warriors!"

With much convincing, the villagers finally allowed Marek to take a group of warriors and ride to Cairn to speak with their elders.

The very next morning, eleven men rode against the rising sun to the coastal stronghold of Cairn. After a long and hard ride, they arrived as the sun descended. Villagers paused only momentarily at the sight of their arrival before hurrying to finish the day's work. Cairn seemed to be in a steady decline. The village elder, Connell, cared more for his stronghold than he did his own people. He was glorified in battle as a young man, adopting the mindset of being impenetrable, slaughtering his enemy with the power of the gods. Marek wondered how such a man could be so ignorant as he passed the crumbling wall surrounding the stronghold.

Marek and his men were directed to the common room where they were greeted with food and wine. Many chatted about current events and old pastimes, it having been many years since the two clans had mingled. But still, they kept a wary distance and a watchful eye. Marek and his men had been greeted with smiling faces, but the tension could be felt by all.

It was Connell who finally spoke above the thick curtain of unease.

"You are a man now, my boy. If I didn't believe my eyes, I would swear on my soul your father sat before me. A great man, your father. It was my honor to fight beside him in the battle where he fell." Connell embraced Marek like an old friend and poured him a mug of wine. "Tell me what this is all about, lad. Why have you brought so many fine warriors into my home at such a late hour?"

"I'm not going to pitter around the reason I am here. I want command of your warriors, Connell."

Connell sputtered on his wine. "What would a boy like you do with my warriors? I suppose lead them into some great battle?" He gulped from his mug, still chuckling.

"I know you have word of these raids. My village was burned to the ground by Westmore, and I aim to put an end to it — to him — but I need men. Strong men. Men willing to fight. Our village is on the verge of decimation as we speak."

"I have no quarrel with this Engel. I am saddened to hear of your village, but my—"

"Enough!" Anger filled Marek. "Do not tell me how invincible you are. I have seen what destruction this man brings, and I have seen your crumbling walls. Your people won't stand a chance against his army. He recruits Archaeans to fight for him, promising those who join him lands and more women than their arms can hold. Promises like that are quite hard to refuse. And those who don't follow…" His voice quieted as his mind uncontrollably drifted to his wife and son.

"This army does not pose a threat to us. Taking *this*—" Connell boisterously grinned, outstretching his arms to show off the wealth that surrounded him. "—would be quite impossible."

Marek slammed his fist on the table. "You are not listening, Connell! I beg you, give me some men — any men. We will ride out and intercept this Engel before he has the opportunity to spill more Archaean blood. Our people needlessly die because of men like you, who won't stand up and fight for his own people!"

"Now listen here, boy." Connell's voice turned sour.

Rising to his feet with his fists clenched, Marek gritted his teeth and addressed the rest of the men. "How many more tears must be shed over the graves of too many who have died? How many more of our children have to fall? Listen to me, brothers. I know ruin lies before you. There is nothing but bloodshed if you don't act now, while there is still a fighting chance!"

"Sit down, Marek! There will be no warriors and there will be no raiding party! I will offer you and your men shelter this night, but there will be not a word more spoken about this nonsense. Is that understood?"

With a quick side glance to his brother, who nodded in approval, Marek snapped, "Aye."

"I shall have someone escort you to the lodgings. Eat what you like, lads, for I am off to bed." Connell gave Marek a firm pat on his shoulder and muttered, "I like your spirit. You remind me so much of your father. Save that fight in you for another day. We won't be needing it here."

Marek couldn't settle in the terribly small lodging that he, Ronan, Aiden, and Gavin shared for the night. The one-room shelter was lit with a single lantern and devious shadows danced along the walls. While his men entertained themselves with stories and a rowdy game of dice, Marek traced his finger along the lines of Brynn's charm, trying to envision her radiant smile to warm his chilling body and calm his ill-fated temper. A memory of her laughing at one of his Engel-speaking mistakes came to mind and he smiled, imagining it over and over again, clinging to it as if his very existence depended on it. He wondered if she ever recalled his face just as he so often did hers. Alone, his mind was as restless as it had ever been. What a wandering soul he had become.

"Marek..." Ronan's hushed voice stirred him, bringing him back to the present dark hour. In barely more than a whisper, Ronan breathed, "Did you hear that?"

Tucking away the charm, Marek cocked his head to the side and listened to the stillness of night. Under the thick blanket of darkness, a sharp whistling flitted over the thatched roof. "Night arrows." Of all nights to pick, the night they were actually in Cairn to warn them of impending doom, an attack was occurring. What bloody luck.

The men gathered their gear and armor as another shower of arrows flew over their dilapidated shelter. A few landed in the thinning thatch above their heads, the arrows lodging dangerously close in the rafters above them. "And the bastard wouldn't listen," Marek grumbled as shouts from neighboring buildings rose at an alarming rate. "If that fool gets me killed, there will be hell to pay!" he roared while jutting through the door-frame to survey his surroundings. "Stay hidden for a while, lads, let them waste their arrows. Gavin and Ronan, gather the others. Aiden, you and I need to find a fire."

The men split up, going their separate ways to accomplish their tasks. Marek and Aiden searched for an extinguished fire pit. Finding one relatively close by, they risked themselves to the naked open to scoop up as much soot and coals as they could hold before the next round of arrows fell.

An arrow cut through the air pummeling into the soft soil only inches from Aiden's boot, spitting small rocks and debris onto his exposed skin. "Holy hell," he gasped. He had narrowly missed death. "That will wake a man up."

Marek exhaled, staring at the arrow.

"Let's get the hell out of here, aye?" Aiden dug his hand in the fire pit for one last bit of ash as another shower of arrows sliced through the sky.

"Don't have to ask me twice." Marek followed Aiden back to the lodg-ing, crouching low in the long grasses. That was all he needed — to be picked off like a mangy wolf near the sheep's field. "Here, lads, cover yourselves." Marek passed the ash to Aiden. "Let Connell take care of the foot soldiers. Spare as many Archaeans as you can, slaughter any Engels, but most importantly…" A smile lingered on his lips. "Don't get dead."

Marek found it difficult to ignore the screams of innocents as they dashed past him, intent on reaching the stronghold for safety. Women clutched babes to their breasts as they wailed to the gods to spare them, terrified for their lives. Those blood-curdling screams — the ones that never left a warrior's mind — they were the worst kind of all.

They edged their way to the tree line and watched as the raiding party descended from the darkness swarming over the land like wild beasts, devouring anything in their path. Marek encoun-tered minimal resistance along the way, keeping to the shadows. The warriors crept up beside unsuspecting guards, slashing their throats in one swift movement. Body after body slumped to the ground as Marek forged his own path closer to Westmore.

He hit a snag before reaching his intended target, his position spotted by a wounded Engel before being thoroughly silenced. Within moments, a horde of fighters was upon them, hurling swords and death blows in their direction. Realizing his chance to reach Lord Westmore was slipping through his grasp, Marek jumped at the chance to battle him. With his protectors engaged, Westmore was alone. Vulnerable. Marek sprinted between battling warriors, using his sword to clear his way when possible. Ignoring the burning in his legs, he jumped the corpse of a fallen comrade and drove himself faster up a small grassy incline. Two arrows snapped dirt at his feet.

He was close.

Marek gritted his teeth, readjusted his sword, and pressed forward across the raging battlefield. From his left, he heard Ronan's shouts of encouragement. His breath burst from his lungs. Another arrow cut the air near his head. Pain slashed across his neck, bluntly knocking him back. His palm rose to cover the sting. A warm gush oozed through his fingers. He was still breathing — it couldn't be that bad. Shrugging off the injury, Marek regained his footing and darted to the side to avoid a charging horse. Veering back on course, he wiped his neck, ignoring the alarming amount of blood, and scanned the area for the Engel. The scene that lay before him was of absolute chaos and he stood in its midst for a moment, trying to rationalize it. Soaring fires stretched toward the opalescent moon. Arrows set aflame arched over thatched roofs, their flames drowning out the screams of those caught in the slaughter.

So many people... so much death.

When would it end?

Rage consumed him and he funneled his hatred into his sword. Hidden by a cloak of soot, Marek charged Westmore's mount and rendered it useless with one swift upstroke of his blade. As the horse shrieked and reared, Westmore fell beside it, narrowly escaping the crushing weight of the animal. "To your feet!" Marek demanded, eager to begin the battle.

"My my, a gentleman to his enemy even though you have so brutally slain his horse?" Slow to rise, Westmore drew the thin sword hanging by his side. Glancing back at his twitching mount, he frowned. "I rather liked that horse. Choose your enemies wisely, for you have a chance to live this night."

Marek circled his opponent. "I wish I could offer you the same." The shrill scream of a woman was silenced close by, momentarily drawing his attention.

"Your village doesn't have to burn. Join me, and the rest of your people will be saved."

"You have already burned *my* village!" Raising his sword, Marek swung at the Engel, testing him. Westmore easily blocked the blow and thrust back with precision. Clearly, this Engel wasn't the opponent he'd expected. Trained military — there was no doubt about it. Marek swung low, fully engaging himself in the duel. Steel scraped against steel. White sparks danced from one heated blade to the other as the men circled, playing an eerie death song in tune with the rage surging around them.

"You aim to kill me, boy?"

"Aye, I do."

"And why might that be? Other than the obvious reason that I am... well, *me*." Westmore gave a small courtly bow.

"You above all deserve death, not the poor women and children you have slaughtered!" Marek swung with unparalleled speed. The blade connected with Westmore's thigh, forcing the Engel to the ground.

Westmore roared in pain, falling to his knees. His palm covered the wound as he scrambled for his discarded sword.

"Pick it up!" spat Marek, kicking the weapon closer to his opponent.

"You really do wish me dead, Archaean." Reaching for his sword with caution, Westmore moved as if he would grasp it and rise.

Marek gripped his own sword and eagerly waited in his battle stance for the duel to continue. He would fight this Engel with honor.

Westmore shuffled his feet attempting to stand and drifted his concealed hand to his middle, clutching the handle of a dagger as Marek raised his sword to strike. In an instant, the blade flew from Westmore's trembling fingers, missing its intended target and planting deep inside the shoulder of Marek's strongest arm, too close to his ferociously beating heart.

With a thud, Marek's blade dropped to the ground.

The impact of metal striking bone whipped his body violently against the side of a wooden structure. The thatch burned bright, lighting the night sky above them. Unable to withstand the shocking pain, Marek slumped. The wall collapsed under his weight sending a support beam crashing down, pinning him.

*Feck.*

That was all that came to mind. Leave it to his bloody pride to get him in this unbelievable situation.

*Fecking Engels. Never could fight fair.* His body screamed out, furious the blade was still embedded deep in his flesh. The beam had trapped him well — even shoving with what little strength he had left wouldn't budge it. Marek bared his teeth and heaved one last time, roaring out the madness consuming his thoughts. Nothing moved, except for the flowing stream of blood etching its own erratic path from his shoulder. Sobering realities edged their way to the forefront of his thoughts. He was defenseless, unarmed and unable to fight — definitely not the way he wanted to join the gods in the afterlife.

Westmore limped forward. "It is a shame such a fine fighter as yourself should die alone and in such a manner. Such a waste. I could have done great things with you in my army."

"I welcome death rather than fight for you." A metallic tasting ooze lingered on his lips. "So finish it!" He was dying. There was no sense in prolonging it. Rather than swallow the blood, Marek spat it at the Engel. He furiously kicked his legs, shocked to realize they wouldn't move. He must accept the fate that lay unwelcome before him.

Westmore stood to tower above Marek. Reaching down, he gripped the handle of his dagger and wrenched it from the highlander's body, lengthening the gash before wiping the blade on Marek's tunic. "You're bleeding, you know." Westmore chuckled. "You should see to that." Then the Engel left Marek to die.

Warmth oozed from Marek's wounds, trickling to the softening mud below. He wouldn't allow himself to die this morning, not when that man still lived and breathed. He refused it. He would not die. He sighed. If only he had the choice.

He sat alone, left to suffer a slow, agonizing death as his wounds refused to clot. His legs grew numb from the heavy weight staunching the blood flow to the lower half of his body. Thankfully, the burning building behind him had fizzled out long before it had the chance to claim him. Marek focused on memories he could recall in his scattered thoughts, but soon his vision grew too weak to focus any longer and the world around him tunneled into blackness.

# Chapter Fifteen

## FALLEN ANGELS

Ronan paced the ground. The sun had risen well above the horizon before the people of Cairn started retrieving the bodies of their dead. Those that made it to safety before the attack returned to their homes only to find those who resisted were missing or hanging from rafters. The death toll in Cairn was high, but for reasons unknown, the Engel raiding party retreated.

Six Highland warriors herded together near the tree line, waiting for their leader and further instruction. Marek had always returned victorious; how could he not have shown himself by now? The Archaeans voiced their concerns — had he been defeated by the Engel?

Trudging up the hill were Aiden and Gavin, dragging several bundles of weapons and armor. "What?" Gavin shrugged, dropping his cargo at Ronan's feet. "They won't be needing it again."

"Aiden, have you seen Marek?" Ronan questioned.

Aiden paused, wiping his brow. "I lost him after the Engels charged last night. I assumed he was with you."

A lump rose in Ronan's throat. "Did he... fall?"

"I cannot be sure. We parted ways."

"Marek would not fall to an *Engel*," Gavin scoffed. "It is unthinkable."

"Let us spread out, leave nothing unturned. We must find him."

"**M**arek." She smiled, gently caressing his soiled cheek with her palm. "Marek…" She whispered his name time and time again.

His eyes fluttered and he tried to focus, but the bright morning sun made it impossible to see her shadowed face.

"Stay with me, Marek. The gods do not need you yet." Her voice was the sweet music his lonely heart longed for. "*Marek,*" she called to him, rousing him from the cusp of unconsciousness. "They do not need you — *I* do, Marek. Stay alive. Find me. Find me."

He muttered her name incoherently, desperately trying to gaze upon her beautiful face.

"Shh… I'm here," she comforted. "Stay with me, Marek." The woman leaned over his battered body to kiss his forehead before disappearing in between two passing shadows.

A gust of wind cooled his burning skin, carrying with it the hint of heather and lilac, arousing his senses. He heard voices — they were deep and Archaean. Had he finally passed over? Was his Brynn dead as well? Would he now spend his afterlife in a continuous search for her? No, the voices were drawing closer and speaking of Cairn. He was still alive. How, then, had he seen a spirit?

"Found another one. Doesn't look promising, lads," said a man as he passed Marek. "Such a shame, is not it? If only we were warned of this. Give me a hand, will you?" The Cairn warrior sighed deeply before fishing out another casualty. As Marek's body was cleared from the rubble, the warrior paused. "Ronan…" he called. "I found your brother."

"Let me pass!" Ronan thrust his fingers to Marek's chest, searching for his heartbeat. Not finding one, Ronan promptly hushed the others and pressed his ear over Marek's heart. "Come on," he muttered, changing positions.

Marek groaned.

"Marek?" Ronan gave his brother's face a light slap. He winced, and Ronan sighed with relief. "By the gods, the son of a bitch is breathing! Help me get him up!"

With utmost care, the men lifted Marek from his would-be grave and carried him to the infirmary, not far from the walls of Cairn. It was there Marek would spend the next five days, fighting high fevers and body chills as his wounds were irrigated and treated. Many of the women had taken it upon themselves to care for those who had survived the battle.

Several, in fact, had taken a liking to Marek, taking turns nursing him back to health. As soon as he had regained consciousness, Marek quickly learned flashing them his roguish smile could get him far with extra food and fresh water. He had even overheard two younger girls fighting over whose turn it was to change his bandages.

His men kept Marek informed of every detail during their visits. He'd learned a large funeral ceremony occurred several days after the attack. Connell, when approached, denied he ever received a warning from the riders and gloried in his triumph over the Engels. Ronan told him of rumors circulating throughout the village that Lord Westmore had fled with his nobility to the Crossroads to recover. Some insisted he was dead, that he had fallen not far from Cairn after fleeing, too mortally wounded to continue. Still, four days later his body had yet to be found, so his death couldn't be proven. Learning that Westmore could possibly still walk the lands angered Marek the most.

Ronan rarely left his brother's side. He chided those who tended to him like a callous old woman with nothing better to do than order them to find herbs to pack in Marek's wounds. "You're quiet, brother. What bothers you?" he asked during a moment of silence.

"'Tis nothing, really. Don't worry about me, Ronan, although I thank you for all you have done. I couldn't have had a better nursemaid looking out for me."

"If you weren't battered like a rag doll, I would cuff you."

"There's nothing bothering me, Ronan. Nothing of importance and nothing a few drinks cannot cure." Marek shrugged off his brother's concern, filling his mouth with a piece of bread so he wouldn't have to continue with the conversation.

"We leave in the morning. You should rest." Ronan nodded in farewell.

As he made his way to leave, Marek called out behind him. "I saw her, you know… there, in the village."

"What?" Ronan stopped to turn toward his brother, his brow furrowed with confusion. "Saw who?"

"In the rubble. She kept me alive."

"Who?"

"Brynn." Saying her name aloud sent shivers up his spine as if he spoke of the dead. Perhaps he was. Maybe that was why she appeared before him. She was singing with the gods and had been able to protect him in spirit form.

"That is impossible."

"I saw a spirit; of that I am sure." Maybe it hadn't been her, but someone had comforted him during his struggle for life. Perhaps only in the afterlife would they be together again.

"You were on the edge of death, Marek. There was no one."

"I'm sure of it," Marek snapped. How else could he still be breathing if it weren't for her? He sighed deeply, pinching the bridge of his nose. "Thank you for the visit," he added, changing the subject. "Forget what I said, Ronan. It must have been the fever. Sleep well."

"Goodnight, Marek. I will fetch you at dawn." Ronan ducked into the darkness.

Marek collapsed on his pallet. Perhaps he had more injuries that weren't so visible to the eye. He stretched the tightness in his shoulder, seeking a comfortable position for the long night ahead. Sleep never came easily for him, now less than ever. Endless thoughts were a constant river flowing through his mind. He thought of Brynn, of her infectious smile and the delicious taste of her kiss. He mulled over the idea of Lord Westmore presumably dead, and immediately pushed the thought aside. Perhaps Westmore thought *him* dead at this very moment. Rolling, Marek shifted his weight, relieving the pressure in his chest. The cold shock of metal touching warm skin diverted his attention to the charm still strung around his neck. It had been the first thing he had checked for, even before limbs, when he had regained consciousness. Marek pulled the cord over his head to hold the charm in his palm. He brushed his thumb over the engravings before drifting off to dream of her.

Morning welcomed daylight all too soon. A chill numbed his weakened muscles, making an early rise a struggle. His shoulder throbbed from overuse and a dull ache enveloped his chest.

"Out of bed early, are we?" a sweet voice echoed from just inside the threshold. One of the women who favored Marek perhaps a bit too much had arrived to see to his wounds.

"My men and I ride for home this morning. We've been gone far too long." Marek foraged his surroundings for his boots.

"Your wife must be missin' a handsome thing like you, eh?" she teased, dipping her cloth in the bowl of water she carried. "Come now, sit up so I might take a look at you."

Deciding to hold his tongue, Marek helped the woman remove his tunic. The water felt like chunks of winter ice as she pressed the rag to his shoulder, scrubbing flakes of dried blood from his tender skin. His muscles seized, sending a wave of nausea through his weary body. "Damn it, woman!" he cursed, pulling away from her coarse touch.

She apologized, continuing with the cleansing before wrapping a bandage around his wound, across his sculpted shoulder, and down his middle. "Some of us have heard you are heading to the Crossroads to find Lord Westmore."

"Where have you heard this?" Marek asked, stunned from the bit of news. The idea hadn't yet come to mind.

"Everyone is speaking of it — the warrior who gave Lord Westmore that nasty cut is going to challenge him to the death for control of Archaean territory. I assume that great warrior is you." The woman fluttered her sultry eyes.

Her fingers lingered on his bicep until Marek removed her hand. "Stay on task, woman, I cannot stress this enough. Hurry and dress the wounds. I must leave soon."

"Oh." The woman pouted, arching her plump lips like a child. "There's no harm in waiting a few more days. The others and I were hoping we might be able to... once you were healed enough, I mean... join us for..." She giggled, a seemingly sudden embarrassment overcoming her words.

"Trust me." Marek rolled his eyes. "What you want is *never* going to happen. You would be disappointed, especially with a man like me."

"Oh, I find that hard to believe." The woman plopped down the extra bandages and trudged away.

Standing to wriggle his way back into his tunic, Marek heard horses.

Ronan plodded through the doorway. "Are you ready?"

"In a moment, just let a man fetch his boots, will you?" The thick leather slid on easily, hugging his feet and calves like warm winter gloves. After latching them tightly, Marek rose and slid the scabbard Ronan handed him in place. He hissed as the leather conformed to his body, tightening over his wounds.

"We found your sword not far from where you fell, but…" Ronan lingered behind Marek.

"Where the hell is my horse?" Marek bellowed from outside the infirmary.

"Marek, most of the mounts were taken when the Engels left. I'm sorry, I know how much—"

"That son of a bitch!" Arran was just an old battle-driven horse of no consequence to anyone. "He stole my horse — that bastard stole my horse! I'm going to cut his heart out, I swear it to the gods I am!" Marek kicked a nearby rock out of frustration, nearly tripping himself. For the next few tense moments, Marek proceeded to curse every vile word imaginable until he could no longer think of any more that would describe just how angry he was.

His men snickered but waited until his tantrum was through before helping him up on a spirited young filly for the journey home. Nothing felt right about the horse. Her paces were off. He couldn't find his seat as the saddle didn't fit her properly. The replacement just couldn't measure up to his old friend, Arran. He scolded the filly throughout his long trek homeward, asking her what he was going to do with such an untrained horse if a battle arose and caught him unawares. Would she know the correct action to take? "*No*," he informed her. She was terribly small and thin and he reminded her of that fact whenever they crested a hill. "*You are not fit for battle,*" he would growl. The filly snorted and swished her cream tail, swatting a fly from her flanks as she trotted alongside the others, oblivious of his maddened tirades.

"Are you sure he didn't take a hit to the head?" Gavin questioned Ronan, riding up alongside his mount. Glancing over his shoulder, he spied Marek, deep in conversation with his unresponsive horse. "He's not right."

164

Ronan could only laugh. "He's been through much — perhaps it's the fever?"

"Perhaps he's just gone mad," corrected Gavin.

"Aye, methinks you are right."

"We both know he's going after that Engel shit." Gavin arched an eyebrow.

"He'll want to get his precious horse back, I know that much." Ronan turned to glance at Marek.

"He's gonna' get his wee self slaughtered if we let him go off by his lonesome. Well, he has gone mad, to be sure. I've seen mad — and Marek is far beyond that." Ronan sighed, running his palm across the back of his neck.

"And you know he's damn well going to do it…" hinted Gavin.

"I know, and that's why we're going with him," replied Ronan. "Let's just let him recover a bit before we go putting ideas in his head."

"That's what I wanted to hear! The crazy bastard needs us!" Gavin's loud laugh echoed through the trees. Birds took flight at the disruption, disappearing into the horizon.

# Chapter Sixteen

## THE HUNTED

Only seven Archaeans returned home just before the most beautiful sunset of the season nestled down to bed below the trees. Too many tears were shed from grief for those who didn't return. Murron gripped her sons tight, overjoyed they were safe. After slapping Marek for causing her so much worry, Murron coddled her son and saw to his wounds as any concerned mother would do. She fed him hot stew and fetched him blankets when she believed he might have a chill. Before long, Marek couldn't keep her away. She woke him several times during the cool nights to make sure he wasn't hungry or that he was warm enough or still breathing if she could not hear him turning in his bed.

When Marek could no longer stomach another moment of her pampering, he ventured outside to bide his time elsewhere. He needed to work his arm before his muscles grew too weak, but no one would spar for fear of injuring him. Going mad from boredom, Marek convinced his men into exchanging blows with him after a good deal of deliberate coaxing and monetary bribes. At first, he tired easily with even a wooden sparring sword, but after much-needed practice and a few too many ales to numb the pain, Marek was finally able to pin Ronan. They cheered and celebrated over his personal victory, jumping and tackling each other like young boys.

"Well done, Marek. I think you need to rest." Ronan wiped his brow, winded by his brother's match. "I almost had you, though."

"I think he needs to get pissed." A devious smile formed on Gavin's lips as he swung his arm over Marek's shoulder. "Our boy is back, lads."

"A nice, thick lager sounds mighty fine right now."

Marek forced himself to smile, trying his best to hide the pain welling under Gavin's grip.

---

"Mother, you should have seen Marek this afternoon. He was amazing." Ronan praised his brother's accomplishments while helping Murron tidy the kitchen after the evening meal.

"I suppose this means the lot of you will be leaving me here again." Murron heaved a sad sigh, peeking outside at Marek through an open window. He sat quietly in a wooden chair resting its back against the croft, rocking on the hind legs while staring blankly at the sea.

"That is entirely up to Marek. We have all agreed to ride with him."

"Keep him alive, you mean?"

"More or less." Ronan had never seen his brother so lost. With Nya and Ewan gone, there was nothing left for him to live for. Marek's day to day activities varied from ale drinking contests to sitting on that little wooden chair gazing with glazed eyes toward the sea as if he was expecting something or someone. "He has no purpose, mother. He was born a great warrior — he was a father and husband. Now all of that has been taken from him. What has he left to do but sit outside and drink?"

"He hasn't been the same since you returned. His demons haunt him more than ever, I fear. Take him, Ronan. Take your brother to kill this Engel. Only then will the gods give him peace."

"He's weak. And drinks too much. He has grown weary, and his spirit is clouded by a woman. Pretty little thing, though. Almost took her for myself."

"The one who mended your arm?"

"Aye, but I fear you already know this. Therefore, this conversation is going nowhere," Ronan teased Murron, giving her a wink.

"Oh, let an old woman amuse herself."

"A matchmaker are you, Mother? I don't believe your tricks will work on your son this time as well as they did the last."

"What? Me? Play tricks on my own sons? Whatever put that idea in your head, my boy?" Taking a broom from a corner, she swept the floor in lazy circles.

"Why will you not spread your charms this way?" poked Ronan as he finished tidying the area he diligently scrubbed.

"Oh, I'm just waiting for the right lass for you, my son. Do you not know you are my favorite?"

"As it should be." Ronan smiled, cradling his mother's head with his palms to kiss her forehead.

"What are you two chatting about in here? Mother, help me with this, will you?" Marek struggled to remove his tunic.

Murron helped pull it from his arms. "Does it still bother you?"

"Aye, a bit," he replied.

"Look, Marek." Ronan removed his own tunic. "We have matching scars. That should amuse the ladies, eh?"

"I don't need disfigurements to amuse a few tarts," Marek shot back, flexing his chest muscles at his mother.

"Oh, you two — always in competition. First, it was over strength and swords, then women. All I ask for is a few grandchildren before I wither away and die, is that too much to ask?" As soon as words were spoken, Murron covered her mouth with her hands and glanced at Marek. "I'm so sorry. I did not—"

"'Tis all right, Mother. You meant no harm." Marek touched her furrowed brow with his lips and kissed her goodnight. "Go to bed. I have business with your favorite son." He winked at her and smiled.

Murron gathered a few items that needed replacing to their proper spots. "Goodnight, my sons," she called out behind her. "Blessed be the gods that keep watch this night."

"Blessed be the gods," they repeated. The childhood prayer slipped off their tongues without thought and their mother disappeared through a curtained threshold to her bed.

M arek climbed the wooden rungs of the ladder to the loft. Two beds they had used as children were nestled under the rafters. "Do you remember when Father first put these beds up here? They seemed bigger than we would ever be. Now look at us... two grown men still sleeping in our boyhood beds with our legs hanging over the ends like giants."

Ronan laughed, following Marek up the ladder. "The gods forbid that any woman should see where we do our bidding. I remember when you broke your arm chasing that horse of yours and Father and I had to hoist you up the ladder with a rope because you could not climb up yourself. You kept—" Ronan let out a loud belly laugh as he recalled the memory.

"I kept falling down the ladder, I remember," interrupted Marek. "And you were of no help, always pushing me off the rungs."

"Mother feared you were going to break your other arm, and you ended up sleeping with her instead. Father was none too pleased."

Marek kept silent, reminiscing of the past and how less complicated everything seemed back then.

"What is it that you wanted to talk about, Marek? Heading to the Crossroads?"

"How did you..."

Ronan relaxed on his bed, tucking a pillow beneath his head. "You are my brother. I know you better than you know yourself. What is this plan you have been brooding over for... oh, all season now?"

Marek stared at the beams above. "Well, I'm not sure exactly what to do. On one hand, I want to storm in with swords flying and kill them all in one giant rush, but on the other hand..."

"You want him to die a slow death and rot in hell for what he did?"

"Aye, that's about right."

"The lads and I think we should take just a few men and ambush the son of a bitch before his army grows again. If our people don't start standing up to him, all the clans are going to join in arms with him. We cannot let that happen. Of course, we have just a bit more motive than some others, but it will be fun either way. What do you say?"

"I would say it sounds as though you have already thought this through."

"Do you feel you are ready?"

"Enough."

"We'll get together with the lads tomorrow and make plans. Now let us discuss what we are going to do about your woman problem." Ronan cleared his throat.

"What woman problem? I have no woman to have a problem with."

"And therein lies the problem. We need to get you one. And under one."

"I don't need any more headaches, so I respectfully decline." Marek sighed, rubbing the sleep from his eyes.

A snicker broke the awkward silence. "Oh, but they are so much fun, dear brother."

"You've been running with Gavin for too long, Ronan."

"Well, who else was I supposed to get on with while you were drunk and mad?"

"Goodnight, Ronan."

"Sleep well. Dream of me," Ronan goaded, his voice playful like a young maid.

Marek leaned out of his bed and punched Ronan in the thigh.

Finalizing his belongings, Marek checked his armor and weapons one last time with his fellow warriors before the long journey to the Crossroads.

"Keep a watchful eye, my son," warned Murron, embracing her eldest. "Not all Archaeans pursue victory with honor."

Marek wrapped the frail woman in his arms. "Be well, Mother. I will come back to you, I swear it."

"Promises, promises." A soft smile formed on her lips. "Take care of your brother."

"I will."

"Fight with courage and uphold your honor."

"I always do."

"I know." Murron wiped a tear before turning to say her goodbyes to

Ronan. "Take care of your brother, Ronan," she told him. "His heart is weak — weakness will get him killed."

"I promise it."

"And so it begins," Marek told his men with backs turned toward the village. "Let us hunt some Engel!" For days on end they rode hard, keeping to the hidden paths within the trees, rivers, and caves. They met no confrontation along their way. The only problem Marek encountered was with the strong-willed filly he'd named Luri, after the goddess of hellfire. He resorted to letting her fly like an out of control wind down slopes and through the shallows. She was a fine traveling horse for she made her own path over rocky terrain and eager to please by being headstrong, but how would she fare in battle? Marek hadn't made his mind up about her just yet, although he certainly was entertained by their outright mad dashes across the plains together. His spirit ran wild alongside her.

The men headed south, gathering as much information as they could about Engel uprisings, recent battles, and formations where they could. Returning from his scouting mission at the Crossroads, Aiden brought news of Westmore's whereabouts. "He's there, I'm sure of it."

"At least the rumors were true," said Ronan.

"But there are other details."

"Like what?"

"I've never before seen so many people at the Crossroads. Sorting out one Engel from another may be difficult. A battle we would surely lose."

"Can we not separate them from the others?" an accompanying warrior asked.

"We're too small in numbers to strike head-on. We must lay low for a while — find out where he goes, where he frequents, where he sleeps, and when he is alone... strike."

The group turned to Marek for direction.

He paused for a moment, taking in all of Aiden's report. The conditions were not at all favorable, to say the least, and certainly not what he'd been expecting. Westmore would never be alone. There would always be someone—a guard, soldiers, watching. "We will wait until the cover of darkness and walk our way in. The less noticeable we are the better." Their skillful bounty hunting efforts had given them notoriety in years past. The threat of being recognized could prove detrimental.

"Aye," the men agreed, dismounting to rest until sunset.

The men snacked on what little food they had left and tossed a few games of dice while waiting for darkness to cover the valley. When the hour approached, Marek gave the order to head to the village. "All right, let us go, aye? We shall make base camp here to hide the horses. Split up and try not to make a scene. I know that's asking a lot from some of you…" Marek glared at Gavin. "…but the less visible, the less likely Westmore is to know something is amiss. If you have the opportunity, take it. It will not offend. His death is all that matters. Is that understood?"

"Marek?"

He turned toward Gavin and raised an inquisitive eyebrow.

"Can we at least get a drink? 'Tis early yet. The gods know we won't be finding the Engel tonight anyway."

"I will meet you in the tavern after I take a look around."

"That's a good lad!" Gavin smacked Marek on the shoulder. "I will save you a pitcher… and a woman."

"I prefer the pitcher." Rummaging through his belongings, Marek found his cape and flung it over his shoulders, pulling up the hood to hide his face. People roamed the streets with mugs in their hands, gambling and trading stories at every corner. Engel and Archaean alike crowded every street vendor for food and ale. Wine flowed like water and before long, Marek found himself in the midst of a celebration dance. Pipers bellowed to the beat of drums while young maids twirled around each other, toeing the ground in perfect synchronization. Marek caught the collar of a passing child and pulled him taut to his side. "Boy, what celebration is this?"

"A wedding, sir. People have arrived from all ends of the world!" The boy soon broke free and returned to chasing after his companion.

A wedding. Three days of celebration and festivities and strangers abound. He would fit right in. Marek wandered the streets and welcomed whatever was thrust in his hand by an intoxicated partygoer. But soon he grew tired of being shoved around by sopping fools and sought out the tavern to inform the others of what he had learned.

# Chapter Seventeen

## REVELATIONS

*The Crossroads*
*Early Summer*

"Abby, I don't know how much more I can bear." Exhausted, Brynn plopped down on a stool in the kitchen of Godric's tavern. Pulling up her skirts to cool her ankles, Brynn fanned herself with her hand as she took deep breaths to calm her racing heart. Daman's brother, Godric, had demanded Brynn work the wedding knowing his tavern would be filled with attendees searching for ale and beautiful women.

"Have some water, dear." Abby poured a small cup and handed it to Brynn.

"If another one of those *heathens* cuffs my backside, I swear I will slit their throats!" Brynn declared, sipping her water.

"They've been traveling, Brynn. Give them a day or two to get it all out. Here, take these pitchers out to the table in the back corner. They are calling for you."

Brynn moaned and rose from her chair, reluctant. "A day or two, eh? How long do these weddings usually last?"

"A day or two." Abby laughed, taking a ball of dough from a large bowl and tossing it onto a wooden baking sheet. "Just please the customers and make sure to hide your coin. We shall be released soon enough. They are bound to collapse sometime..." Abby's voice trailed off as she turned her attention to the bread.

Sighing, Brynn pushed the kitchen door open with her hip and returned to the bustle of the spirited group crowding every inch of the tavern and bar area. Surveying the room as she often did, Brynn searched for her brute. He was missing from his usual post — a side table in the front corner of the room. Lord Westmore had arrived the day before, so her brute was more than likely preoccupied. Brynn kept out of sight as much as possible, staying deep in the early summer fields during the morning and afternoon hours and only returning to the tavern when she was needed. Word spread that Westmore was in need of foot soldiers to carry on his raids against those not willing to partake in a "treaty" between the Engels and Archaeans. He hadn't fared well during his last raid, and many of his troops had abandoned the cause. Rumors were told that Westmore had been injured. Brynn wished the wound had proven fatal.

Squeezing her way past a sea of overcrowded tables, she reached the far corner in time to refill the mugs before rowdiness overcame the men.

"Will you sing for us later?" one asked, staring at her chest, attempting to get a peek down her revealing bodice.

"Perhaps if you don't stiff me on coin this time, lads," she remarked, her voice thick with disapproval. A few coins clinked to the table, and she scooped them up before Godric's ever-watchful eye locked on her.

"Brynn!" Godric called from the bar. "We're out of lager! Go tell the lads I need some help bringing over a few barrels!"

"Yes, sir," she replied, placing her empty pitchers in the kitchen and making her way through the cluster of men lingering near the entrance. Gathering her skirts, Brynn jumped over the permanent stagnant puddle in front of the door and scurried in the direction of the nighttime festivities.

As Marek walked toward the tavern, he recalled the last time he'd traveled that very alley. A lump settled in his throat. He'd been taking Brynn to Daman. His fingers wandered up to his neck to feel the weight of the silver.

"Oh, pardon me, sir."

A voluptuous barmaid with long, yellow curls, bumped by him, catching him off guard. His eyes were playing tricks on him again, as they often did. That place haunted him; every female voice sounded like the ghost of his heart. Every golden-haired beauty seemed to resemble the graceful features of his little Engel beauty. Reaching the tavern, Marek slipped through the door and easily found his men laughing while downing ale and rolling dice. "Sorry I'm late, lads." He pushed a man who was passed out from his drink from a nearby chair. The man thumped to floor, and Marek turned the chair to sit with his men.

Ronan greeted his brother with a smile. "Marek, you're just in time. We ordered another round, and there's food. Are you hungry?"

"I could eat," he absently muttered, removing his cloak and draping it over the back of the chair.

"What bothers you?" Ronan pushed a mug toward his brother.

"Nothing — just seeing things, 'tis all."

Allina, a barmaid, returned with a fresh pitcher and plate of cakes. "What can I get for you, love?" she asked Marek, nearly falling in his lap.

"Lager, and leave the pitcher."

"We're refilling the stock. Give me a few moments and I will be right back for you." She touched his chest with a playful finger. "Would you be interested in a little… entertainment while you wait? I catch a fair price."

Marek spied her tousled locks and dirtied face. "Not with you."

Allina scowled and left the area.

Marek told his men what he knew. "There's a wedding. From what I gather, the ceremony will be in the morning. Lord Westmore might show his ugly face then. The trick will be getting him separated from his group so that we don't get ourselves hung in the process. If anyone has any good ideas, feel free to share them now." With no one speaking up, Marek took a swig from a mug and added, *"Bastards,"* before turning his attention to the commotion by the tavern entrance. A pretty barmaid rushed through the door carrying a large basket. She was the same curvy woman who'd bumped into him outside. She tripped over a barstool leg, nearly dropping her things, but the bartender caught her in time. She beamed up at him and planted a big kiss on his cheek before scurrying off behind a closed door.

Marek thought it remarkable how much she looked like his little Engel, except that Brynn was on the smaller side, certainly less endowed, and not as brazen as the barmaid with the basket. This barmaid was quite curvaceous and practically spilling from her bodice — but a welcomed sight none the less. Casting her from his mind, Marek focused on the lads, content to watch them play their games and listen to their comical prattle. Gavin bragged of his equal height to length proportions, while Ronan bet he could last twice as long with the barmaids. Laughing, Marek tilted up his cup until he could see the bottom of it.

"Thank you, Owen. I don't know what I would have done if you hadn't caught me. Where is Godric?"

"He's just left. Is there something I can help you with?" Owen followed Brynn to the kitchen.

"Inform him the lager he asked for is being delivered. Thank you." Brynn hoped that in the bustle of the crowd, no one saw her almost bury her face into the floorboards... again. "Abby, you should step outside. It's a rather gorgeous night. Perhaps you would cool off a bit?" Brynn suggested, noticing Abby's sweaty brow and flushed face.

"No time for gorgeous nights. Ahh, there's my lager. Thank you, gentlemen. Aye, right there is fine. Owen, tap that for me, will you? Thank you, lad. You are such a sweet boy. Brynn, fetch me that pitcher." Abby barked out orders.

Brynn did as she was told and waited for further instruction.

"Well? What are you waiting for? Go keep them occupied while I get the lager ready. Fill their cups until they fall to the floor for all I care. Make us some silver! Those skirts are wearing thin, are they not?" With a thrust, Abby shoved Brynn from the kitchen to fend for herself amidst the ever-growing crowd of drunken men.

As she collected empty mugs in need of refilling, a large man teetered onto a chair and stepped up on top of a table. "Kind friends and companions, come join me!" he bolstered. "Let us drink and be merry, all grief to refrain, for we may and might never all meet here again. A toast to the newlyweds this very pleasant eve — may the gods be with you and bless you. May you see your children's children, and may you know nothing but happiness from this day forward."

The men raised their cups in agreement as Brynn continued her work, surveying the many surrounding faces. From the corner of her eye, she caught the glimpse of a man in the shadows but quickly doubted her eyes. He was no one of consequence, but still, he stirred a memory. The room soon returned to an elevated thrumming of voices as she crossed to the center of the tavern dancing on the tips of her toes, unable to keep up with the demand for more drink. She hummed to herself while winding through the passageways of the tavern floor, lost in her own little world.

I t was the melodic voice that captured his attention — eerily haunting yet calmingly beautiful. He'd heard that voice over and over again in his dreams. Marek stumbled to his feet, shoving his chair back against the wall. Was he that drunk? He couldn't be — he could pick that sweet sound out of a thousand just like it.

Ronan pushed his brother back to his seat. "What ails you? Sit and play with us."

Marek shrugged off Ronan's hold. Just a bit closer and he could put his suspicions to rest. The barmaid worked her way back to the bar. She had just barely skimmed past him, but it was all he needed to justify the racing of his heart. The sweet smell of honeysuckle and lavender combined with that voice could only mean one thing — either Marek had gone raving mad or his Brynn never left the Crossroads. That *woman* was, without a doubt... *Brynn*. The tripping barmaid... every curvy, delectable, seductive part of her. A wave of nausea flooded over him. Gripping the table with his palms, Marek sunk low in his chair and sucked in a long gasp of air, trying to keep from pummeling every man in the place for staring at her.

"The gods be damned. Never have I seen a more desirable woman. That is one you hang on to." Gavin gawked at Brynn. "Apparently I have been searching the wrong countryside. Give me your coins, lads. I *will* be having that tonight."

"Not if I claim her first. I won't be having seconds." Aiden gulped a long swig of his ale.

Did they not recognize her? Jealously crept its way up through Marek as the men continued to comment on who would be doing what to Brynn while she tended to the bar. "She is *mine.*" Marek claimed her. Leaning comfortably back in his chair, he nursed the last of his lager as he waited for his pitcher. He couldn't take his eyes from her. She shined when she smiled. The man behind the bar with the fiery hair leaned in close to her, whispering in her ear. She tossed her head back and laughed, pressing her hands to her chest while the man beamed, besotted. He knew that look. Any man could see another man's lust just by studying the want in his eyes, and oh, how he wanted her. Marek's murderous plans suddenly screeched to a full halt.

"Why do you feel you can always claim whatever *you* want first?" Ronan asked his brother. "We saw her first — we should get her first."

"Because I'm the oldest." Marek smirked, amused his brother still hadn't recognized her.

"*Och,* piss off," Ronan told him, giving up the quarrel as his attentions turned to a refill of ale. Together, the men thumped the bottom of their mugs on the table and pounded back the foaming liquid as fast as they could before it overflowed the mug.

———

"Here, girl, take this and quit your gabbing." Abby set a fresh pitcher of lager on the bar. "Well? What are you waiting for? There's a lad over there waiting for his lager, and he's a mighty handsome one at that!"

"Which table?" Brynn glanced about the room, searching for the area in which Abby had pointed.

Agitated, Abby heaved a sigh in annoyance. She reached over the bar and took hold of Brynn's shoulders, twisting her frame toward the far back corner. "The man on the end near the wall has been waiting for his pitcher. I suggest you get it over there. They are a rowdy bunch, and I would rather see you get the coin than Allina. Now take this and git!"

"Aye, madam!" Brynn snapped with a huff. "Please just let this night end," Brynn muttered as a menacing group of men pushed their way past those still awaiting service. They approached the bar demanding ale in Engel. Westmore's men. Brynn tugged at her sleeve to cover the dark ink etched on her skin.

Owen, tending the bar, blankly stared back at the Engels. "They all want a drink." Brynn translated as she moved from their path. "Lager for them all, Owen, and make haste — they are *not* in a peaceful mood."

"Aye!" he replied, sending a wide, dimpled grin in her direction. "We wouldn't want to upset the darling Engels, now, would we?"

Brynn rolled her eyes. "Call for me if you need anything. I have lager to deliver." So much time had passed since she last heard Engel words. It seemed foreign to her ears. Had she forgotten it that quickly and readily? Placing both hands around the belly of the overflowing pitcher, Brynn started for the awaiting table. As she crossed the bar, her eyes connected with the man waiting for his lager. He lingered on the curvature of her chin, every bend, every arch. Even from across the room their piercing cobalt shot through her heart.

Never, not even in this cruel place or in the best of dreams, had she ever expected to see that shade of blue staring back, etching over her. As if all the world had stopped with her, Brynn froze, unable to move her unyielding frame. She managed to exhale a breathy gasp as she watched the pitcher slip from between her palms. Down it went, floating to the floor below, draining itself of all contents as it careened to one side before exploding into countless jagged pieces against the floorboards. Lager pooled between her boots and a few heads turned to the sound of the breaking pitcher. Feeling her stomach churn, Brynn covered her mouth and whirled on her heels back to the safety of the kitchen. Bursting through the door, Brynn sobbed, a scream hitching in her throat.

"Whatever is the matter, child?" asked one of the older barmaids upon seeing Brynn's wild entrance.

Brynn couldn't seem to keep her hands from trembling, so she twisted them in her skirts, leaning against the wall for support.

"Let me pass, let me pass!" Abby rushed to Brynn's side. "What has come over you, Brynn?"

She couldn't speak even if she wanted to. Her stomach still lurched from her realization. The gods had deceived her once again; her vision couldn't hold true. Brynn closed her eyes and tried to focus her mind. Perhaps she was only mistaken. "Abby…"

"It was only a pitcher, dear, you have broken far worse."

"No, Abby…" she puffed, still trying to gather her composure.

"Yes, what is it?" Abby eagerly answered.

"Tell me, did you happen to hear the name of that man? The one you wanted me to give the lager to?"

"No, why would I bother with names?"

"Please glance out the door… does he head this way?"

Brynn kept her eyes closed, afraid he would be staring back at her if she dared open them.

Abby begrudgingly shuffled her way to the door and poked her head around the corner, surveying the room. "No, there is no one but Owen. Do you owe someone money? Whom should I be searching for?"

"The man, Abby! The man who ordered the lager. Do you see him?"

"He still sits at his table."

"Tell me… what does he look like?"

Allina and a few others gathered beside Abby, curious about the fuss. After a few mutters and a slew of abrupt giggles, Abby responded with, "A rather handsome fellow. *Striking eyes*, that one…"

"He is tall."

"Oh, him? His friends are quite dashing," Allina added.

A barmaid surveyed the room. "Oh, might I serve their table?"

"That one brooding in the corner — he is so handsome!" said another.

Brynn groaned and sank to the floor and hid her head between her knees. "That is what I feared." She whined. "I cannot go back out there."

"I have a strange feeling you know this man, Brynn?" Abby raised an eyebrow.

"No, I do not," Brynn replied, rising to her feet. "He simply unnerves me, 'tis all."

"Well, I have no reason not to serve the man." Allina loosened the ties of her chemise. "Handsome warriors are far and few between these days, and I have found myself a wee bit lonely these long nights."

A burning rage took root at the thought of Allina displaying herself so crudely in front of her warrior. Brynn snatched the pitcher from Allina and held it tight against her chest. "There is no way I am letting a... a... *trollop* like you anywhere near that table! Go find some *Engel* to spread your legs for!"

"How dare you—" Allina hadn't the time to finish before Brynn returned to the bar with Abby at her heels. "Abby, please fill this pitcher as the generously handsome man in the back corner readily awaits it." The pitcher seemed as though it would never fill completely. Did it have some mysterious bottomless pit? Only when Abby pushed it to her did Brynn realize how fast she had been tapping her fingers on the bar. Gathering her wits, Brynn took a steadying breath before taking up the pitcher. She boldly turned toward her warrior. He seemed visually stunned that she approached his table. Were her legs moving? She couldn't tell.

"Your lager. My apologies for the wait." She gave a slight bow, indifferent to whom she served. She couldn't help but smile at the surprising sight of dear Ronan, who sat faithfully next to his brother paying her no mind — after all, she was just another barmaid. "You look well, Ronan," she muttered in a perfect Archaean lilt.

Hearing his name, he looked up. His eyes widened in the middle of a swig at the realization and shortly thereafter commenced in spitting and sputtering his ale across the table, covering the arms of the neighboring men. Before he had a chance to speak in between coughs, Brynn left the pitcher and tended about her business.

"Marek, was that...?"

"Aye, Ronan, it certainly was." Marek raised his mug to his lips. Those Archaean words had rolled off her tongue like fresh cream. She had learned to survive, and that slight lilt of hers was seductive as could be. A bard played his tunes in a corner, and Brynn tapped her feet with the music, ignoring him. It only made her that much more irresistible.

"How the hell is she still here?"

"I don't know, Ronan, but I aim to find out."

"The only thing you'll be aiming is your cock. Just let me know beforehand when you get to murdering people. I gather that barmaid is off-limits, aye? A damn shame."

Marek brushed off his brother's comment but still couldn't shake the uneasy feeling in his gut. He thought it wise to pay his weasel of a friend, Daman, a visit. But for now, he was plenty content watching Brynn circle around the room, swaying those curvy little hips, and waiting for the most opportune time to approach.

That opportune time happened to present itself hours later when most patrons had cleared the tavern in search of a place to plop their drunken selves for the night. Ronan and the others more than willingly left Marek to seek themselves out a woman.

Before leaving, Ronan squeezed Marek's shoulder and drunkenly whispered in his ear, "Bed her well, Marek. Bed her well. I am thoroughly jealous you are the bastard lucky enough to feck that."

If Ronan hadn't been so drunk, Marek would have given him the brotherly thrashing he deserved for his daring brazenness. Instead, Marek chuckled and told Ronan to find his own woman.

---

"Is he still there, Abby?" Brynn had never scrubbed the bar surface with as much fury as she did now.

"Aye," Abby answered, clearing a table. "He is still there."

"What am I to do?" whispered Brynn.

"You do not need me tellin' you what to do, girl."

*"Yes, I do!"* Brynn followed Abby behind the bar to the kitchen, hesitant to be left alone for even a moment.

"Just talk to the man. There isn't any harm in talkin', now is there?"

"Oh, you have no idea. He's the one who sold me to Daman." Brynn untied her apron and tossed it into a corner. "I am so angry with him I fear the words that might leave my mouth. I am afraid to speak with him after what he has done."

"Brynn, the rest of us are wanting to get back. Just get out there and finish your duties so we can leave." One of the other girls spoke, awaiting their departure.

Sighing, Brynn picked up a rag and toed the threshold. Relieved to see Marek had relinquished his corner seat, Brynn let herself breathe a bit easier now that he had at last broken his fixation for the evening. Tugging up the cinches on the sleeves of her chemise, Brynn threw herself into her work scrubbing the woodwork, ignoring the few stragglers conversing quietly near the entrance. How her heart ached. She had wanted more than anything to see his handsome face just once more, and now there he was, sitting, waiting… watching. And what had she done? Waited for him to leave like the scared little child she was, afraid to confront him after their terrible parting. Even after the passing of so much time, she still found herself furious with him.

When the tiny hairs on the back of her neck stood on end, all notions of servitude soared through the roof alongside her very heart. A callused finger traced a line on her nape, following the curvature of her chemise. She gasped at the unexpected touch, and her body went rigid, surprised by sensations she was sure she would never feel again. One little touch and her knees began to tremble. Supporting her wobbling legs, Brynn dug white-knuckled fingertips into the bar top. Fingers dug into her fleshy hips, whirling her around to face those fiery eyes.

Marek stared at her for a few awkward moments, and Brynn bit her bottom lip. Soon she found herself grinning when he hoisted her to sit atop the bar. He wedged in between her legs and her knees spread to accommodate his width. His palms clutched her hips, his unwavering stare tracing her features. Bits of cloth gathered in his fists as he pulled her hem higher.

Brynn had seen that look in his eyes once before and knew exactly what it meant. He wanted nothing more than to touch her, taste her, *lust for her.* "Hello, Marek."

"Brynn, you have… grown." He paused, his eyes drifting to the full breasts pressing against the hem of her chemise with every breath. "You are so beautiful."

Placing a finger under his chin, Brynn raised his eye level from her chest to her face as his palms caressed the milky skin of her thighs. She knew his hunger all too well, and it angered her. "Why are you here, Marek? You made your intentions perfectly clear when you left me to rot."

He didn't respond.

She continued. "Did your wife uncover your shameful little secret?" Brynn raised a wary eyebrow while swatting his wandering hands from her middle. "Did she cast you aside and now you want to settle for what you could not have in the first place?"

Marek's eyes narrowed and his mouth sloped downward. Grabbing her chin, he held her firm. "Do not speak of things you know *nothing* about!"

"Let go of me!" She cried out, pushing his hand from her face. Unable to do so, she raised her palm and swiftly planted it across the side of his jaw. "Do not *ever* grab me like that again!" she warned. "I am not your plaything!"

He tugged her frame closer.

"Nothing else to say, then?"

"I deserved that."

"You deserve a hell of a lot more than that!" Brynn spat, pounding a balled fist against his chest.

"Give me the chance to redeem myself. On my honor, I will never harm you. I only wish…" His voice hushed, and his features relaxed. "I don't know whether I should walk away or just… kiss the hell out of you," he muttered.

Brynn hooked her heels behind his thighs, jerking him forward. All silent apologies accepted, she wrapped her arms around his neck and pulled him close. She kissed his parted lips with such a force her insides tingled. Running her fingers over his shortened hair, Brynn shifted forward slightly, exposing her neck. His lips found the opening and he licked the salt from her skin, nibbling a trail to her breasts.

186

"I must have you, love." His lips fluttered against her skin as he spoke. "By the gods, I must have you now."

"Through the kitchen," she whispered. "There is a place there." She wanted him — wanted him more than she wanted life itself. She could no longer deny her body the pleasures only he could give her. Something twisted inside her belly, yearning for more. Much more.

His muscles flexed beneath her, his grip hard and sturdy as he lifted her from the bar. Brynn fumbled with the ties on his tunic, eager to reciprocate his touches. Marek backed his way through the kitchen door, paying no mind to the women still lingering behind. He muttered suggestively in her ear all the expletives he had planned for her, and a wash of heat crept over her.

"Over there. Up the stairs." Brynn nodded her head toward a steep little stairwell hidden behind ale barrels.

"As you wish." Marek charged at the staircase. "Hang on tight, my lady."

Brynn happily complied as Marek let go of his grip on her and used both arms to heave up the steep steps to the loft. Upon reaching the top, he lowered Brynn to her feet, kicked the loft door closed, then bridged the distance between them to devour her in kisses.

Brynn continued her efforts to rid Marek of his tunic.

He helped her by tugging it over his head. Brynn quickly grabbed it then threw it to the floor with frantic urgency. She placed her palms against his chest then traced the curvature of his pectorals inward to the charm dutifully hanging from his neck. "You kept it."

"Of course. 'Tis all I had left of you."

"Oh, how I have missed you," she murmured, placing her cheek over the steady drumming of his heart.

"You are too kind to me," he replied, kissing her head. "I have done nothing to deserve you." He tangled his fingers in her hair, locking her in his embrace.

"You are here now," she told him, brushing her palm down his chest.

The loft was small and cluttered — more of a storage area than sleeping quarters, but it would offer respite and privacy. Marek scooped her up into his arms and carried her to the undersized bed, placing her on the blanket. "Brynn, I—" She shushed him, placing her thumb to his lips. He took the tip of it in his mouth, gently sucking it in response.

"Just love me," she whispered, the longing and want in her voice thick like an evening fog. "Even if only for tonight." She needed this — she needed him.

"I will." He reassured, taking her lower lip between his and licking it with the tip of his tongue. "I will love you more than any man has ever loved a woman."

Curving her palm around his nape, she lowered his head to hers. She explored his mouth, his neck, and the hard lines of his jaw. His earthy taste filled her senses. His stomach clenched tight when her hands wandered to his middle, leaving no crevice undiscovered. Her innocent kisses didn't seem to satisfy the burning under his skin — he wanted more.

"You have no idea how I have longed for you to touch me, love." Marek played with the ties on her bodice, entwining his fingers in the lacing and loosening them. With no objection from Brynn, he let his lips linger on her collarbone, exploring the newfound wonders around the edging of her chemise.

A blip of hesitance overcame her. Brynn knew the path that followed such actions — but with every cooling kiss upon her smoldering skin, the line she wasn't absolutely sure she wanted him to cross blurred into oblivion. Her body tingled with excitement, craving his next touch. She could only gasp as he grazed a nipple with his thumb before allowing his lips to taste it. Rolling his tongue around the rising bud he caught it between his teeth, curling his lips around it and suckling it taut.

Something inside her clenched and she sucked in a breath, arching beneath him. His calloused fingers brushed over her breastbone, caressing the sensitive underside of her breasts and sending sparks skittering through her belly. "What tortures you bestow upon me." Brynn moaned as he moved to the other eagerly awaiting bud to deliver the same lascivious torture.

"Oh, you know nothing of the tortures I have planned for you." Devilish eyes taunted her, dared her to object. He removed her chemise, and as the cloth boundary slipped from the corner of the fraying bed to the floor below, Marek smoothed his hands up the long length of her thighs, unraveling the ties keeping her on the brink of ecstasy.

Brynn watched as he cupped her calf in his palms and kissed her knee before dragging his tongue up the length of her inner thigh, stopping just short of her womanhood. She closed her eyes and arched toward his touch, a silent plea for more. Sinning against the gods had never felt so good.

Marek reveled in her nakedness, telling her repeatedly how beautiful she was. She shied away, only to have him grab her backside and slide her closer. He gently turned Brynn to her side, and in silence, he traced the scars marring her back. He kissed each one with a tenderness she had never in her life been shown. When Brynn could stand the quiet no longer, she flipped to her back, wriggling her body beneath her lover.

"Such beauty." He adorned, threatening her with empty words when she attempted to move. "You will not run away before I have had my fill of you, and you will take each compliment that I have to give. I have never seen such perfection lying before me in all my days, and I will look upon such beauty for as long as I live, and you will like it."

"Is that so?" She cocked her head to one side. "Such bold words seeing as I am the only one stripped of clothing in this room."

With one hand on his belt, Marek skillfully released the hold on his trousers while kicking off his already loosened boots. Wriggling himself free from his restrictions proved difficult with Brynn creeping across his chest kissing and touching what she could, but as soon as he was free, he wrestled her to her back, pinning her beneath him.

He growled low in her ear, "There is no use in fighting me, woman. I *will* win," before flicking his tongue along the curve of her ear.

"You aim to ravage me then, warrior?" Brynn giggled.

"Aye, I do." He smirked before silencing her laughter with his mouth.

She felt him against her — strong and solid — his need and want as great as her own, and she parted her knees allowing him full access, the ache within her persistent and deep. His hand skimmed across the flat skin of her belly, over her hip, and down to the innermost part of her thigh, tracing incoherent patterns on the tender skin. She cried out, his name parting her lips. The delight of him had her breath coming in uneven pants. Twisting her fingers around his neck, she pulled him to her chest, needing him to release the unrelenting pressure building inside her.

"Please," she begged, writhing beneath him, her hips grinding against his callused palm, seeking the pleasure he so freely gave. "Make this torture end," she pleaded.

She felt him part her, felt him glide and circle his fingers against the most sensitive part of her flesh, felt him kiss the column of her neck, bringing her to the edge of sweet oblivion. Brynn knew he could not deny himself pleasure much longer.

H olding on to the tatters of his self-control, Marek's fingers slipped lower to stroke her, ready her. Her startled cry became a long, rolling moan, and her palms dug into the muscles of his shoulders. Frantic, desperate cries escaped her as he kept up a relentless rhythm; caressing her, teasing her, penetrating her, driving her toward losing all control.

She spread her thighs, lifting her hips to meet him.

Before he allowed her release to peak, he stretched over her arching body and settled in between her awaiting thighs. "Oh, my sweet one..." His words trailed off into a moan as he slid his cock inside her, her warmth slick with her want for him. His eyes rolled back and closed tightly beneath their lids. Briefly, he stretched her, withdrew then pushed a bit further, slowly repeating the torturous movements until he felt the tightening of her barrier. "Oh feck," he groaned, forcing his body to stop — to hover on the threshold of her innocence. His body seized with tension. A breath escaped from between his clenched teeth. Then with one agonizing thrust, he breached her.

Brynn's cry was muffled by his lips, and she froze beneath him. He distracted her with kisses and whispered beautiful endearments in her ears in his thick, husky brogue, diverting her until the pain subsided and was once again replaced with that honeyed heat she craved. He forced himself to breathe, to fight the overwhelming urge to come inside her. She tightened around his shaft in frantic spasms. By the gods, it was too much. Rhythmically he plunged, letting his desire overtake his mind.

Her heart raced and her mouth went dry as she raked her fingers across his glistening back, fervidly trying to pull him in ever closer. She couldn't get close enough. Together, they were one. He leaned in to taste a kiss as his pace quickened, sending waves of sheer bliss throughout her.

Brynn moaned and shuddered beneath him, encouraging him to thrust harder by taking hold of his backside, pushing him deeper. A breath caught in her throat as she dangled perilously close to the edge, and then suddenly without warning, something exquisite exploded inside her and she screamed his name, arching against him. "Oh, Marek!"

He entwined his fingers with hers, stretching her arms above her head as he caught her scream with his mouth. His body tightened and shuddered, and a deep groan escaped him. He finally allowed his own release to come, readily spilling his seed. He wrapped his arms around her and collapsed, breathing in short pants. His lips fluttered against her damp skin, his breath warming a path along the curves of her breasts as he whispered endearments.

Soon, Marek slept soundly with his head on her chest, and she stroked his hair, letting his nakedness warm her. Brynn fought sleep, for she still could not believe even at that very moment he truly was in her arms.

# Chapter Eighteen

## TAKE WHAT IS YOURS

Brynn roused Marek with teasing kisses. He woke with a groan and stretched, and then smiled up at her. She lay on his chest, her hair dangling freely in a cascade of tangles and curls.

"How long have you been awake?"

"For most of the night," she admitted. "I feared that if I fell asleep, when I awoke, you would have been just a very wonderful dream."

"Oh, I am real enough." He rolled his shoulder, stretching the joint.

Noticing his wince, her eyes drifted to the jagged, raised line. "What is this?" She inhaled a sharp breath, taken aback by the lengthy scar she'd somehow missed in the shadows of last eve's darkness. She traced the puckered skin with her finger, concerned he had been in a battle she knew nothing about.

"One of many forms of Engel kindness," he replied. "Dagger," he said, pointing to his shoulder. "Arrow." He pointed to his neck. "I came to the Crossroads in search of an Engel known as Lord Westmore."

Brynn felt sick at the mention of the Engel's name.

"He started these raids, and we have been trying to defeat him ever since. He raided my village and he… killed my family." Marek averted his eyes, the cold chill in his voice hard and evident. "But I know they are well taken care of, away from that Engel. He is the one who gave me these," he said, pointing to his scars. "And then the bastard had the cowardice to steal my horse and leave me for dead."

Brynn's hand trembled. She withdrew her touch, needing to regain her composure.

"Do you know this Engel?" Marek's eyes narrowed.

"I do not," she replied, re-examining his scars. "They have healed nicely." A bird chirped its morning song from behind the small shuttered window. "The sun is rising. I fear I must get back to work before Daman notices I'm missing." Brynn lowered her lips to Marek's for a kiss, but he didn't accept it. His mouth was straight and sullen, visibly upset by her comment. "Have I angered you?" She sat up beside him, pulling the worn woolen blanket around her to ward off the cool morning chill.

Marek simply stared at her. Brynn knew he was contemplating thoughts instead of speaking hastily, but she couldn't read his stone-like features. "Honestly, Brynn, I cannot understand why you are still in the Crossroads. That was not the deal I made."

Brynn bit her lip, uncomfortable with the direction in which the conversation was headed.

"I thought you to be safe in some village far from here with a family and a few children to look after, not slaving away for sex-deprived soldiers in this shit tavern." He raised her lowered chin with his finger. "I'm so sorry. I will spend the rest of my life trying to earn your forgiveness."

He was truly sincere. She could see the hurt in his eyes, how much it pained him still. She paused, not finding words to fit her emotion. "There are plenty of us here. I'm not the only one who was given false promises. Daman, he sells us off like livestock — at least, he used to. With the raids, many cannot afford to purchase slaves, and so here I am — stuck — doing the bidding of Daman, trying to keep myself alive and unnoticed any way that I can, until—" Brynn was too afraid to tell him that Lord Westmore could tear her away or handle her at any time he so deemed appropriate.

"Has anyone ever touched you?"

Brynn had never seen Marek so angered before. "No, I swear it." She shook her head. "There has been no other." On the verge of tears, she hung her head, ashamed at how low her status had become. She wished his intentions for her had been different. Memories of that fateful night swirled in her mind. "There will never be anyone but you."

"Come here." He pulled her close. "You will forever be mine." Marek comforted her, kissing her forehead. "There is no need to worry. I will deal with Daman later, but right now that sun is rising and I am not ready to give you up to it just yet."

Snuggled in his warmth, Brynn relinquished all fear to the safety of his arms, allowing him to taste and caress her body, pleased to be his for a second time. She would let the sun rise to high noon without a care — with him, all the world could wait.

---

"Marek, I must go." Brynn searched for her bodice. "I'm surprised no one has reported me missing at an hour like this." They had made love twice more before Brynn found herself remembering the day that lay before her. Spying the missing garment hiding beneath the bed, she snatched it up and shoved her hands through the armholes while trying to lace it all at once. "Please, help me with this, Marek." Flustered, she wasn't able to tighten the laces as Marek had done a perfectly wonderful job of tangling them the night before. As his fingers set to work fixing the laces to their proper order, he kissed along the ridge of her collarbone.

"Enough." She scolded while plaiting her hair to the side and securing the ends with a tiny strip of twine she found on the floor.

"I don't want you to leave," he confessed, straying to find his own clothing.

"Neither do I, but if they catch me up here with you, it will be my backside to pay." Finished with her clothing, Brynn turned to stare at Marek's figure. He faced away from her while securing his trousers, and she gaped in awe, watching the muscles in his back flex with every movement. Two large inked tattoos stretched across his shoulder blades like wings and rippled like waves blowing across a lake with every effortless move. He was the most handsome man she had ever set eyes on.

Without a doubt, Brynn was more in love with him now than ever before.

"When will I see you again?" he questioned while pulling his tunic over his head.

"The wedding." Brynn tugged on the rope keeping the loft door secure. "You will find me there." She disappeared below.

"Well, well… look who finally decided to join us! A newfound calling as a wench, Brynn? I hear the tips prove better."

"Allina, hush your mouth. Good morning, Brynn." Abby shooed Allina from the area.

Brynn rushed down the last few stairs to engross herself in the food preparation. She grabbed her apron then secured it around her waist before taking her place in the cooking line.

"Late night, last night?" Abby teased Brynn, who snatched a few vegetables from a bowl to chop.

"I do not wish to speak of it," Brynn lashed, feeling her cheeks grow hotter by the moment. Shy little Brynn had become a woman and everyone knew it.

"That good, eh? Be careful — you will chop your fingers off."

Brynn wanted to run and hide. Marek would soon have to exit, and there was only one way down. He was bound to use it at some point… the problem was when.

There wasn't a single soul in the kitchen who did not know what terrible sin she had committed. Instead of taking her frustration out on Abby, Brynn turned her emotions over to her vegetables, hacking away as hard as she could with many of the pieces ending up on the floor instead of the stew pot.

"Who is this mysterious man, Brynn? How much did you charge him for the night?" Another snide comment departed Allina's lips.

"Allina, hush or leave the kitchen! You are nothing more than a jealous and foul woman whose only way of getting a man to look at you is by pulling up your skirts, so it would be best if you keep your hands *and* your eyes off that man if you know what is good for you! Not every woman needs to resort to selling herself for a bit of attention!" Abby wagged a finger at the scowling barmaid.

At the insult, Allina huffed and muttered a curse.

Unaffected by Allina's all-too-common behavior, the others kept up their conversation about the mysterious warrior seen racing up the stairs to the loft with Brynn the night before.

"What was he like?" one young and curious girl asked, anxious for details. "You know... *what was he like?*"

"Does he have any brothers?" teased another.

"Where did he come from?"

"Have ye' known him long?"

"When do the rest of us get a go at him?" an older woman asked. "I'm not getting any younger!"

The questions never seemed to end. Why, suddenly, had she become such an intrigue to them? They spent most days trying their best to ignore her now that she belonged to Lord Westmore, but with just one little incident with a man, they had said more words to her than ever before. Perhaps it was because of the scandal that would ensue if word of her behavior ever left the kitchen. Her entire fate was in their hands.

"He is no one of consequence." Brynn shrugged, trying to end the conversation. "And nothing happened."

"Well, you certainly picked the most handsome man *I* have ever seen to be no one of consequence," retorted Abby with a hearty belly laugh. "If *you* don't want him, I will scoop *him* up and take 'im to the loft for a bit of a toss meself!"

An all too familiar voice replied before Brynn was able to respond to Abby's bold comments. "If only we met under different circumstances, love. The things I would do to you..." Marek had made his way down the stairs while the others were too busy teasing Brynn to notice his descent. With a forceful kiss to Abby's cheek and a playful wink at Brynn, Marek grabbed some food then strolled from the kitchens.

The women stood in awe. Abby's lips made a large oval shape. She tried to speak as her hand touched the still wet kiss on her cheek, but no words would flow. Her face flushed from the affection the handsome warrior gave her. She continued to revel in it for the rest of the afternoon, boasting she had won Brynn's mighty warrior over and how he was going to soon whisk her away to a land of rolling hills and flowers where she'd never have to lift a finger again. He would wait on her hand and foot, all the while worshiping the very ground she trod upon.

Brynn smiled, knowing that he, indeed, would.

They continued the preparations for the wedding, all silliness set aside. All the platters, stews, and foods needed to be transported to the celebration some distance from the tavern. Only then could they enjoy a very rare few hours off to enjoy the festivities. Finished with the meat platter she had been working on, Brynn licked the turkey juice from her finger, wiped her hands on her apron, and hurried to the celebration.

The wedding was in the final stages of the ceremony when she arrived, so Brynn busied herself for the remainder, keeping a wary eye open for a familiar face in the shadows. Instead of finding Marek, she caught the eye of a pale-faced Abby. "Abby," Brynn called, taking her friend by the shoulders. "Whatever is the matter?"

Abby wrung her hands. "He is here, Brynn. Here at the wedding."

"Who?"

"Lord Westmore," she whispered with unease, as if something horrible would happen if she dared say his name aloud.

"But Brute said he would be busy attending to business and would not be here for the ceremony."

"You need to leave, Brynn. Go busy yourself in the kitchens or return to Daman's. I will say you are ill should anyone ask. I fear for your safety amongst all these drunken sods. What if he — he could..."

*Take her.* Brynn forged a smile, ignoring the foreboding thoughts racing through her mind. "I'm sure I will be fine, Abby. Just please, do me a favor and warn me if you see him approach. I'm not about to let him spoil my one night of freedom."

"But he might take you." The fear in Abby's eyes reflected into Brynn's. "Men cannot be trusted. Ever."

"I know, but there is one I *do* trust with my life. He would not let harm befall me."

Abby smoothed her palm over Brynn's and nodded in agreement. "I don't know this man, but I know you speak the truth."

"Abby." Brynn took her friend by the wrist. "He does not know of my connection to Westmore." Only the gods knew what Marek would do if he were to ever learn her secret. He would act the fool and try to kill Lord Westmore for her honor. He almost died battling the Engel once. If he were to try on her behalf and fail, Brynn would no longer have a reason to live. She would take her own life before her heart had time to shatter.

Abby gave Brynn's hand a comforting squeeze before parting ways.

Brynn followed the tune of the musicians, seeking respite. What wonderful music! The tin whistles, pipes, and drums strummed together with joyous singing tugged at her insides, begging for her to dance along. She tapped her toes with the drumbeat, watching as couples joined hands with others, dancing in circles and lines around the joyful newlyweds. How bittersweet their happiness was, for she knew she would never have a life like that of her own. She had aspired for so much more in her short life, but now accepted her fate as a lowly servant. Her restless heart would never be content, but she could still dream — no man could take that from her.

A slight tap to her shoulder brought her spinning about, nearly crashing into the broad chest behind her. She smiled expecting to see her warrior, but instead, a grinning Owen reached for her hand.

"Would you like to learn the steps?" His grip was warm and tender, his eyes expectant.

"I should not." She pulled her hand back to safety.

"What harm is there in a dance celebration?"

"You know, Owen." Anything could be reported to Lord Westmore. His disapproval could have disastrous effects.

"It is a large group of people — a wedding. Come."

"Oh, I don't know," she whined as he led her closer to the group of dancing villagers. She watched the steps at first, wary of anyone noticing her lack of knowledge of the ancient dance, but soon she was surrounded, protected by the crowd of people and forgetting herself in the stirring music. The steps came naturally as if she had somehow always known them. The beating of her heart equaled that of the drums, and her spirits soared like a songbird taken to flight.

He saw her then, twirling about with *him* — the redheaded man from the tavern. The barkeep made her smile, but Brynn was oblivious to the hidden agenda behind those innocent looks. That look of wanting, desiring, owning; except she was his. *His*, damn it. Marek took a deep breath, trying to slow the erratic beat of his heart. That look on her face — happiness. Joy. He could never be enough for her. He couldn't give her all the goodness and hope she deserved in life, but he vowed to try. He wanted to take her away from this hell. She turned his insides to mush and his heart into a massive fire. Could he ever make her smile as such? *Get a hold on yourself. Stop wallowing and go to her. Take what is yours.*

Marek edged his way through the crowd. A jovial tune on the pipes sent a whirlwind of dancers spinning in every direction, but his course didn't waver. Eyes narrowed and determined, a devilish grin curled his lips when the red-head caught sight of him. How menacing he must look — that pleased him. No words were needed — his eyes spoke volumes. Whether it was the rumbling of the sky above them or the look on Marek's unwavering face as he stalked toward his prey he would never know, but the fearful way the man holding his woman looked at him could have been compared to a mighty wolf cowering away with its tail between its legs.

"My lady." Marek took Brynn's hand from Owen's palm. "Dance with me."

"You're here." She stared at him in disbelief. "I didn't think you would come. Marek, this is Owen, my dear friend, and protector of sorts."

Marek gave the man a curt nod. "My thanks. You must be a good man for such praise."

Owen muttered his welcomes but hurriedly left Brynn in his care.

Marek twirled her with the music, always keeping some part of his body in contact with hers — a lingering palm on the small of her back, a finger grazing her inner arm.

"How you tease." She squealed when his hand grazed her breast as he brought her close in an abrupt jerk, dodging another twirling couple.

"I will take whatever I can get my hands on."

"Then take it now," Brynn commanded, wrapping her arms around his middle.

In one swift motion, he swooped in and kissed her. His fingers tangled in her hair, pulling her head back to deepen the kiss.

"Marek," she breathed, pushing him away. "We cannot. Not here, someone will see."

"Let them see." He licked the exposed pulse on her neck.

"Please, you do not know how much I want this... but we cannot."

He released a low growl from deep in his throat but let her go, settling for holding her hand and continuing with the newly formed circle dance. "Where will you be tonight?" he asked, spinning her.

"Working."

"Might I steal you away again?"

"Perhaps." She giggled aloud when a blond eyebrow rose in unison with a wide smirk. The music stopped, the air around them quieting as the dancers left the open field.

"Come with me." Brynn tugged on his arm. "There's no harm in getting a drink. As long as you tip me well, of course," she added. "And this time you can pour your own."

He burst out in laughter. A few swollen raindrops splattered against his flushed cheeks. "We may not have a choice."

The skies opened in full abundance as they approached the road to cross to the shelter of the tavern. Brynn squealed with delight as Marek engulfed her frame with his, shielding her from a full soaking. A slew of Engel soldiers surged by, shoving those escaping the sudden storm to the side. A man scowled from his perch as he trotted by on a familiar black steed. The horse snorted in protest and sidestepped to avoid running them over.

"Is that...?"

"Aye. That is Arran, *my* horse." Fury overtook Marek's playful demeanor. "I will find a way to get him back."

"How, by murder? Thievery? You will be caught and hanged."

"I will find a way." Marek squeezed her hand before letting it drop back to her side. "I have to go, but I will find you later." He jogged down the road, vanishing into a sea of men.

Alone, Brynn returned to the tavern, her bit of fun over.

Abby approached. "So how have you faired this afternoon?"

Brynn couldn't hide her smile or flushed cheeks from Abby. "It was grand. Dancing was glorious. Now I fear 'tis back to work."

"I will do my best to work for you this eve if you so wish it." Abby gave Brynn's shoulder a loving pat.

Brynn spent the better part of the night helping Owen tend the bar, listening to the Engel soldiers brag over how many Archaeans they had slaughtered. It disgusted her how they spoke thinking the Archaean people couldn't understand their taunts and lewd remarks. Archaeans were not as stupid as Engels thought them to be. Many spoke both languages but did not care to divulge such important information to soldiers wanting to kill them. She sighed. "Owen, pour me a drink." He did as she asked and she downed the brew in several gulps. Several more followed over the course of the evening, each one drowning out her frustrations more than the last. Seeking a bit of air, Brynn escaped to the back alley. Leaning against the building, she exhaled a slow breath. Too much ale made her belly ache.

"Are you all right?" Marek spoke from behind her.

"Oh!" She gasped, startled by his intrusion. "I didn't hear you approach." Brynn stood, testing her drunken legs. Her stomach churned. "I... I'm a bit drunk." She swallowed hard.

"I see that."

"Pissed drunk, I think." The taste of ale still lingered in her mouth.

"I don't envy the headache to follow."

"I have a bit of news for you. The Engel soldiers are using the old livery. Arran will be there, but you should claim him soon, while they are still deep within their cups."

"Let us go then."

"No, I cannot. I am watched too closely. Please, just wait with me awhile. I must return soon."

"Who forces you to stay? Is it Daman?"

Brynn turned from his furrowed brow. She mustn't let this conversation continue.

"No, tell me, Brynn. The truth." Marek leaned into her, trapping her frame between his arms, his palms clenching the cool stone behind them.

"Now is not the time."

"Then when is the time, Brynn? When we are old and gray and the children are grown? Will you speak to me then?"

"Marek, please don't say such things." He was furious, but she couldn't reveal her secret. Both of their lives depended on it. How was she supposed to tell the man she loved that she could never be his after he had just spoken of children and growing old? If her heart weren't already shattered, she would have driven a dagger into it.

"Woman, tell me!" A fist pounded the stone next to her. "What is it that you will not tell me?"

"I must go." Brynn inhaled, trapping a sob in her throat. "You won't understand!"

"Then I will find out myself!" His anger seemed to consume him.

He released her, and Brynn scurried back into the tavern. He had scared her. Brynn knew it wasn't at all his intention, but she couldn't give him the answers he wanted.

She wouldn't.

# *Chapter Nineteen*
## DEATH OF A MAN

A single tapered candle flickered fitfully through the slated cracks of the shuttered window. The warrior pursued his target like a hawk stalking its prey — waiting to strike. The front door sat ajar. Marek slipped through undetected. He doubted his target would notice his presence — the almost empty bottle at Daman's side would see to that. "Hello, Daman."

"Who's there?" The man sat stiffly in his chair.

Marek sat across the table from Daman, twirling a small dagger with his fingers. The dim candlelight cast shadows around the small room, enlarging the dagger's size as he played with it.

"Are you here to kill me, Marek?" Daman took a swig from the bottle, leaving his full cup on the table.

"Aye," Marek replied. He took the cup for himself and downed it in one gulp. He set it back in its place.

"Killing me won't get her back, you know. She doesn't belong to me anymore."

"You made a promise to me, Daman. A man is only as good as his word." Daman wouldn't be able to swindle his way out of this lie. Not this time.

"I promised that no harm would come to her and that she would be taken care of. She has clothes, food… shelter. Just not from me."

"Then from who?"

"She hasn't told you?" Daman couldn't contain his pleasure, and a loud belly laugh echoed from wall to wall of the shack.

"You try my patience, Daman."

"I know you, boy." Daman leaned close to the table and whispered as if sharing a secret with an old friend. "You are going to kill me anyway. I know your kind. Murdering is all you know. I could have paid you well. You should have accepted my offer all those years ago. You would be a wealthy man now." Daman's hand shook as he lifted the bottle one last time to his seemingly parched lips. "Let us hurry and get this over with."

Marek shook his head in disappointment. There would be no answers tonight. Daman had no conscience; it was futile to try to convince him otherwise. "You swore, Daman, on your own life. Never swear on your own life." Marek rose to his feet and drove his dagger clean through Daman's neck. Daman's eyes popped open wide as he gurgled and gasped for a breath that wouldn't come. His hands reached for his neck, seeking the wound but not finding it. His eyes flittered to the center just before rolling behind heavy lids.

He fell dead to the floor.

Marek sniffed and wiped a bit of splatter from his cheek then left the shack as silently as he had entered it.

---

"Are you feeling better, love?" Abby felt Brynn's cheek with her palm.

"I'm fine. The bread helped. I just wish the two of you I am seeing would become one again."

Abby stifled a giggle. "You love the man but won't allow yourself to have him. I understand your reasoning, but it hurts to watch you suffer so." Abby caressed Brynn's cheek as a mother would a child.

"Do not fret for me, Abby."

The women made small talk as they walked back to Daman's, relieved that soon things would return to normal. Brynn could only hope that

Westmore wouldn't hear of Marek. Pulling her shawl tight, she squinted, trying to focus in the dark. A slender shadow bolted toward them — running for their life.

"Aye, Rina!" Abby called out, recognizing the figure. "Whatever is the matter?"

The girl slowed to readjust the full satchel she carried.

"'Tis a miracle, Abby." The girl's cheeks were damp from tears. "We are free. Finally free!"

Brynn didn't understand.

"You must hurry, they are taking everything!"

What is happening, Rina?"

"He is dead! The bastard is dead! Someone finally finished the old man off!" Rina laughed, kissed her friends goodbye, and disappeared beneath the cover of darkness.

Abby and Brynn looked at each other in awe before picking up their skirts and sprinting the short distance to Daman's home. They arrived to chaos. Women were cheering, chanting, and looting everything. Several men were enjoying the festivities as well, grabbing sacks of grain, clothing, anything they could carry. Brynn dodged being pummeled to the ground by someone scurrying through the exit as she tried to enter the shack. There in the corner, still oozing on the floor, was Daman's body. A dagger protruded from his neck.

"No!" She gasped, clutching Abby's shoulder for support. This couldn't be happening. Not now.

"Daman is dead! The son of a bitch is dead! Just like that!" Abby clapped her hands in delight. "Dead, dead, dead!"

"Do you know what this means?"

"Aye, it means every single one of us can finally go!" Tears freely dripped from Abby's eyes.

"No... not all of us." Brynn shook her head. "No!"

Daman's death meant she was out of work. There would be no more tavern pay and no reason to work fields that no longer had a proprietor. He would surely take her now. Lord Westmore would come to collect his belongings with the caretaker now lying in a pool of his own blood. "What shall I do?"

"Run. Come, let us get our things before they are taken as well, and you must leave this place."

"No, Abby, I cannot run. If someone were to see me, see his mark on my skin, I would be turned in, and... I will return to the tavern. I will beg Godric to give me shelter. Perhaps he will let me stay. You must go, Abby. This is your chance. Take your things and never look back. I will give you what coin I have. It should buy you safe passage back to Engel."

"Sweet child. I am an old woman now, and I am no longer Engel. That life ended a very long time ago. I will stay with you, whatever your choice may be."

Brynn wrapped her arms around her dear friend. "Please promise me if something should happen to me, please... leave this place."

"Nothing is going to happen to you. Now, let us go below before this pitiful place falls down around us."

The women rushed to the room that felt so much like a prison, only to still be imprisoned by their freedom. Brynn had to wrestle her precious books from a looter, but managed to find her extra clothes and blankets in the madness. Brynn and Abby grabbed what they could from what others had left behind; the linens and clothing would prove useful.

The sun had risen from its nightly slumber when the women trudged through the tavern door with their possessions. Thankfully, Allina had found other sleeping arrangements for the night, and the women were able to rest in the loft before seeking out Godric to inform him of his brother's death.

"We were hoping you would be willing to offer us shelter in return for continued service." Abby smiled at the surly tavern owner. "You have always been more than kind to us. With Daman dead — may he rest in peace — Lord Westmore may offer you some form of compensation for looking after his... property."

It was an appealing offer, despite how it hurt Brynn to hear it. "I *have* brought you a considerable amount of extra income. It would be a shame to lose such an amount so suddenly."

The man stood as stone-faced as ever, his scowl deepening.

"Please, Godric. You need us just as we need you. Come afternoon, your workers will be gone. Please." Brynn made a heavy argument. Without them, Godric's business would surely suffer.

Godric scratched his head and released a heavy sigh. "Fine. You both can have the loft."

"What are they still doing here? I heard you ran for the hills and Daman was dead!" Allina entered from the back door and headed toward the loft entrance, holding a tear in her chemise together with a relaxed fist.

"Allina, the loft is no longer yours. Find another place to whore yourself. You do not make me enough coin — it now belongs to Brynn."

Allina stopped mid-stride. She paused, clenching her free fist by her side. Facing Brynn, she hissed out a warning. "You will pay for this, you conniving little bitch. In the worst of ways, I will make you pay. You will be sorry you ever stepped foot in this place. You will *beg* for your own death!" Allina stormed from the tavern, screaming hateful words.

Brynn rubbed her eyes in a feeble attempt to wake herself. "Abby, would you mind terribly if I were to rest a bit in the loft? I fear I will not be able to work if I do not get some sleep."

Abby gave her an understanding smile. "Rest, girl. I will keep watch."

S leep found her, but so did the nightmares. Brynn pushed up on her elbows. She could not catch her breath. Every bit of her was covered in a cold sweat, and she blinked rapidly in a feeble attempt to clear the visions from her mind. She'd dreamt horrible things. A blade through Marek's heart and her own body riddled with arrows.

She closed her eyes, replaying the dream. They traveled a road together but were not alone. Soldiers surrounded them. So much death.

I n a lavish study, Lord Westmore mulled over various unrolled documents, silently arguing with himself over surrounding territories he had yet to conquer. He bent over a large polished desk, his palms askew on opposite sides of a map. The bright glow from several large candles sent shadows spewing over the desk and on to the painted walls, and they danced together in the corners, creating the illusion of company.

A knock behind the closed door snapped him to attention. "Yes?" he snarled.

A guard appeared, poking his head through the opened door. "My Lord, there is a woman here to see you. She says she must speak with you most urgently about a matter I am sure you shall find rather interesting."

"Send her in."

The guard bowed slightly and exited the room. Moments later he returned with a female in tow. "The woman, my lord."

"Who are you and what could you possibly know that would interest me in the slightest?" Westmore continued to study the maps splayed out on the desk before him.

"I am Allina, my lord, your humble servant. I work in Godric's tavern. His brother, Daman, was recently murdered. Daman was the caretaker of a certain piece of your property, and now that he is dead, I have knowledge that your slave's lover is planning to steal her away. Why, just last eve I saw the two of them wrapped in an embrace, plotting Daman's death and planning their escape."

His lip twitched ever so slightly. "Lover, you say?"

"Aye, my lord. A most... intimate one."

"I must admit, you have me rather intrigued. I have never met a man who has dared defy me." He tilted his eyes from his map to the woman's face.

"He pursues her freely, my lord."

"You seem rather eager to tell me this, woman. Tell me, what is it you are looking for? Money? A reward for being an informant?"

"Nay, no reward, my lord. Just the satisfaction of seeing her dead."

---

"**B**rynn, there is a certain someone waiting for you. How long must you make him wait?"

"Forever, I'm afraid." A small frown puckered her lips.

"Brynn," clucked Abby.

"I'm sorry for my foul mood, Abby, but with Daman dead, I fear Lord Westmore will march through that door at any moment and take me away from you."

"Just go to him. No one is here to see."

"I will go if only to end your incessant nagging." Brynn untied her apron, placed it on the table, and wandered into the bar area to find Marek. She spotted him immediately, seated with his brothers. Sensing her presence in the room, he glanced in her direction. As Brynn shuffled toward the back door, Marek rose to follow.

Within moments she was in an embrace — warm and safe and his. He kissed her soft but deep, eager to taste every part of her. Brynn placed a palm to his chest. Already a fire burned within it. Cradling her body close to his, he held her in one trembling arm while his other fiddled with his belt.

"Marek." She pushed against him, throwing the tiniest bit of effort in with her threat. She hesitated.

"You have tried my patience long enough." He growled as if a playful puppy, teasing her with kisses along the soft curves of her collarbone.

With each touch, it grew more difficult to push him away or refuse his advances. She turned from his kiss, only to have him suckle the tip of her earlobe, sending her careening toward sweet, sinful actions. When he hoisted her skirts and took her possessively about the waist, her body won the battle against good reasoning and rationality.

With a familiar ease, he lifted her against the wall and braced her with his hips while unlatching his belt from the ever-growing restriction of his trousers. She wrapped her legs around his waist and reached for him, feeling his pulsing hardness against her, drawing his frame in close to hers to stroke the sides of his face. He adjusted her to slide into the moistness eagerly awaiting him.

She sighed in delight, clinging to him as he sampled the curve of her jaw, nipping at her pulse. She threaded her fingers around his neck to pull him to her breast, silently begging for more, and matched his rhythm and nearly reached her peak when his tongue brushed along the delicate shell of her ear, sending her into a sweet distraction.

"Don't resist it, love," he muttered. "Take your pleasure."

She let out a soft moan as his mouth found a hardened nipple and rolled his tongue against it. A heartbeat later, Brynn lost all control. Her thighs tightened against his hips, her back arched against the coarse stone holding her secure in a lover's embrace, and a gushing wave of exquisite warmth crashed full force along the edges of her being. She cried out his name, and he covered her lips with his, silencing her.

Marek tightened his grip on her bare buttocks, seeking his own release. He buried his face in the crook of her neck, biting the exposed skin there to keep from shouting out as his body shuddered beneath her, spilling his seed into the warmth of her womanhood.

The moments before Brynn was able to speak seemed like a lifetime, and even longer before she found the courage to look in her lover's eyes. By the gods, she was in love with this man. So truly in love with him and the reason why she must tell him to leave — to keep them both alive. Before her vision came true. Hot tears welled below a thick layer of lashes. A slight fluttering of her eyelids sent them tumbling down her flushed cheeks. How the gods tortured her so. The man of her dreams had just given her the sweetest of all pleasures, and she couldn't even relish in it.

His thumb gently wiped the tears from her skin. "My love, why do you cry?" Marek returned her to the ground, fixing her skirts along the way, and planting a tender kiss atop the golden head. He hastily fixed his trousers and belt, and then she nestled against his chest.

"Tears of joy is all," she said, trying to steady her voice.

"Liar." A boyish smirk revealed his playful mood as he pushed a stray lock of hair back behind her ear. "We must teach our babes to be better liars than their mother, or there will be no saving them." He latched his belt and laughed to himself, his thoughts seemingly lost in future memories.

Brynn choked back a heavy sob and covered her mouth with her palm, forcing the cry to stay concealed. His words were complete torture to her ears. "I must go." She turned to leave.

"Brynn, wait. Please don't go." He snagged her wrist as she turned, twirling her frame about to face him. "Don't go back in there. Come with me. Let us leave, right now."

"You know not what you ask of me," she whispered, trying not to meet his gaze lest she agree to the one thing she wanted most in life. That hadn't been the answer he had been expecting from her. She could tell by the confused look contorting his face.

He took her hands in his. "Come with me. We will leave this very night and no one will be the wiser. By morning's light, we'll be halfway to the horizon. We will find a place to live out our days and grow old... together."

"You would give up everything... for me? Your travels, your quest to hunt down those who have wronged the Archaean people? Your brother — your men?" How could she convince him they could never be, that this was for the best? "You would give up your pursuit to kill Lord Westmore?"

"Everything. All I want is to give my life only to you."

Brynn hung her head to hide her grief.

"I don't understand," he growled. "Do you not want to be with me? Have you not longed to be free of this place? Of this mess I put you in?"

"More than anything."

"Then what troubles you? I cannot look at you. I cannot touch you for fear of someone will see. I cannot make amends with you — you will not allow it. Do you not understand what I have done for you? What I will give up for you?"

"Once again you have condemned me, that is what you have done! Daman is dead and now I have no protection!" Brynn dug her nails into the fleshy part of her palms, trying to keep her mouth from running away from her. "I am sure that Allina has run her mouth about us. No good comes from that woman's lips."

"*I* am your protection! There will be no escape for you — I'm your last chance! I realize you are afraid. I see it in your eyes, but you do not know what you are saying. If I leave, I will not be returning. My people need me. We cannot be together here, so you must come with me."

Brynn didn't look at him in hopes he couldn't see how painful the words were.

"You don't want to escape, is that it? Do you like it here — being a tavern wench for men to wank off to? What is keeping you here?"

"I cannot leave, not now, not ever! I cannot leave Abby here to fend for herself. The gods protect her should they find out I'm missing. I couldn't put a burden like that on her. They know she is my closest, dearest friend, and they would do... just unthinkable things to her to get to me!"

"Then we shall bring her." He shrugged like that was all it took to solve the conflict between them. "Brynn, look at me. *Look* at me." He placed his palm to her cheek, and she pressed it close with her own. "Please forgive me. If this resisting is because of what I have done, please don't think that I haven't suffered dearly. I'm a broken man, Brynn, and I need you to forgive me. I know what I did to you was wrong, but I didn't mean to hurt you so. I had to do it. No — I made myself do it. It hurt so much to hurt you, but things were different then. I am a man of honor, and I could not go against all I had fought for. The gods had put you in my path and I ignored them, and I won't do it again. I cannot live this life without you by my side, Brynn. I need you with me to survive, to be whole once again. Take what is left of this man, and come with me. Just choose to — 'tis that simple."

Her entire world was crashing down around her, and she could do nothing but weep. She suddenly found herself in the sick depths of hell. More than anything she had wanted to hear those words from him, and now, standing before her, he was spouting such beautifully poetic words she couldn't bear to hear. She could only shake her head while she cried, dampening the seam of her chemise and replacing the lingering trace of his kisses with bitter tears.

"Please forgive me, Marek. Heed my words — I cannot be the cause of your death, and you will surely die if I leave here with you. I have seen it. I saw you die. I cannot allow it to come to pass, not when I can stop it. You must leave this place alone. Someday you will forget me." She looked up at him then, measuring the anger in his eyes. "Don't let your duty and honor cloud your judgment. There is no debt to settle. I know where your heart lies, and it is not with me. You will forever yearn for battle, to raise your sword and fight. And although I would give anything just to know you love *me*, I know you never will... not like you do the destiny you were born for. You are a great Archaean warrior, and it is your duty to fulfill that. Without you in this world, there will be no one left to fight for your people."

Marek opened his mouth in protest, but she continued before he could speak. His face grew red at each passing word, but he would listen. She would make him. Brynn placed a palm to his cheek. "I will sleep just to dream of you. My waking moments will be for you, and if I die, know my last thoughts were of you."

"But you are mine!" His hands gripped her shoulders. "You will come with me, whether you like it or not. I know what is best, and *this* is not it!"

"No!" she snapped, pushing herself from his burning touch. "You *had* your chance, and you rid yourself of me! You gave up all your rights the night you left me to rot in Daman's prison! I belong to *Westmore* now!" The words slipped off her tongue before she realized what she was saying. Words breathed out of anger and spite, and now he would know the truth she never meant for him to learn. Brynn watched raw unbridled emotion flood through his body. Shock. Pure terror.

Hate.

Panic.

Grabbing for her in a chaotic frenzy he took hold of her and jerked up her sleeves. There, in black ink was the brand of Westmore. He dropped her arms as if they were poison.

"He was going to kill me if I did not yield to him," she told Marek, tugging down the fabric.

"I would rather see you *dead* than in the arms of another man, especially him!" Marek brought up his fists, pounding them against his forehead.

"You left me, what was I supposed to do? I hoped there was still a chance we would cross paths again, so I kept myself alive!" She placed her palm to his chest, but he backed away. Numbly, she withdrew her hand.

"And here I am, standing before you, and you still will not go!"

"He will kill you, Marek! How do I make you understand? He will hunt us down no matter where we go, and he will kill us both. How do we end a war if we are both dead? He will never let me go. His men watch my every step. I'm never far from some Engel brute ready to step in and crack a man's skull if he should look at me wrong. You left me by myself, Marek. All alone in your country. I did not choose this! We can never be together while that man is alive."

"And does that pain you so, being protected by an Engel?"

"Do not speak to me of pain! I *died* the day you left me!" The words spat from her lips like lighting crashing to the ground. The day he had left her, she'd shattered like broken glass, each little piece splintering in her soul, left to fester.

"There are worse fates than death, Brynn."

She belonged to another man now, his worst enemy. She tried to spare his life the only way she knew how, but he was dead already. "If you go, we at least stand a chance. A life in hiding is no life at all, Marek. We both know this. Do not come back for me. This is how it must be." She turned, unable to withstand the hurt in his eyes.

Marek stumbled from her, finding his way to the corner of the alley and disappeared into the night.

Brynn stood in the alley for moments on end before she allowed herself to accept that she was alone. Marek was gone. He was safe now. She could only hope he would ride from the Crossroads never to return. They would never live in peace for fear Westmore would find them at any moment. That was no life to live. She could at least spare him the pain now before... She couldn't bear to finish the thought. Instead, she returned to the shadows of the tavern to cry herself to sleep.

# Chapter Twenty

## ALL FOR NAUGHT

Brynn awoke with a start, sitting up in the small bed she shared with Abby.

"Whatever is the matter, child?" Abby yawned, rubbing the sleep from her eyes. She pushed open the shutters — just barely sunrise.

"I thought I heard something below." The eerie feeling growing in her stomach made her feel ill at ease, and its lingering effects didn't sit well. "It gave me a fright."

"'Tis probably just Godric readying for the day. No need to worry yourself."

Abby lowered her head to her pillow and continued to rest her eyes, but Brynn was unable to settle herself. She had dreamed a terrible dream of ravens and it still haunted her, fresh in her thoughts. Her heart fluttered as if a new bird taken to flight.

Perhaps it was Marek, returning for her, but all hopes of being rescued were quickly stamped out when the door to the loft burst open and three soldiers from Lord Westmore's army rushed at her and forced her to the floor. She crumbled beneath their strength.

Brynn hears Abby's screams and pleas and wanted desperately to calm her, to reassure her everything would be all right, but she couldn't get the words out. When she didn't rise quickly enough, another man yanked her to her feet and thrust her toward the stairs.

Brynn just barely caught the edging on the floor, saving herself from tumbling down the steep stairwell while the men trudged behind her. Her arms were forced behind her back while another checked for the branding mark.

"This is the one." The tall one laughed, bringing his palm to her breast and squeezing it between his fingers, roughly rubbing a thumb over the nub under her chemise. "I can see why he is upset."

Brynn bit his arm, unable to defend herself in any other manner.

The man scowled, backhanded her, then ripped the ties to the front of her chemise open, exposing flesh to his greedy eyes.

"We have not the time, Bruce. We must deliver her to the square at once."

"I shall be quick." Bruce sneered, tracing her collarbone.

"Later," the other replied. "We will all have our turn."

"I will be all right," she mouthed to Abby. She was towed from the tavern, unsure of her fate and unsure of the punishment, but one thing she did know, Allina had been behind it. Her tryst with Marek had been revealed.

A large crowd gathered in the square at her arrival. Lord Westmore stood tall and regal against the others — very much Engel in his features against a sea of Archaean heads — as he addressed the people. The soldiers brought her to him, using her body to push a path through the gathering of townspeople. "Do you all see this?" Westmore asked in Archaean while fingering the torn fabric of her chemise. "This is my property." He held up Brynn's arm so that her brand was exposed. "My brand claims her, which means she belongs to me and only me. *Someone...* has spoiled my property!"

Brynn gasped. Her life had come to an end.

T hey were to head out before daybreak, but Marek had drunken himself into such a stupor that Ronan had been unable to wake him. When the effects of the drink finally wore off, they hustled to pack their gear and head into town to purchase a few supplies before moving on to regroup and plan. The blacksmith's shop was their last stop. Ronan tapped his brother's shoulder before entering. Marek paused at the threshold, curious as to what commotion lay just beyond the marketplace at the square.

"Perhaps it is another damsel in distress." Gavin let out a chuckle before Marek's fist found its way to the center of his belly.

Marek continued his way into the shop, not interested in the gathering. His head pounded to the beat of a silent drum, his very being was crushed to the core, and he wanted nothing more than to leave the cursed place.

"Let us have a look, shall we, lads? Oh, I do love a good hanging." A morbid glint lit up Gavin's eyes.

"The gods damn you, Gavin," Marek cursed, reluctantly following his men into the crowd. As he reached his men near the middle of the crowd, Roman thrust out his arm, blocking Marek from proceeding further.

"What?" growled Marek, pushing against Ronan.

"You won't like what you see, brother. I give you fair warning."

Marek elbowed himself to a viewing point. There before him under a tree was his Brynn, battered and bleeding, her head lowered in defeat as Lord Westmore confronted the crowd.

"*Someone*... has spoiled my property!" Lord Westmore accused. "And I want to know who dares to defy my ruling!"

"No, my lord! You have been misinformed! No one has touched your property, no one!"

Westmore paused, searching the crowd. There were no confessors, only confused faces searching for the guilty. He nodded to the soldier at his side and caught the long rope the man tossed to him, swung one end over a low branch, and slipped the other end — a noose — over Brynn's head. "Very well," he calmly told his audience, "she will die instead." With one swift pull, Brynn was on the tips of her toes, clawing at the rope tightening around her neck.

Marek lunged forward, only to be restrained by his men. He tore at their grasps, fighting every step of the way as they dragged him into the depths of the crowd. His roars went unanswered as the cheers from the townspeople smothered any hope of his cries reaching her precious ears.

"No, Marek, it is too dangerous. We are greatly outnumbered here!" Ronan used all his strength to keep his frantic brother away from the girl.

"That Engel is going to kill her for my deeds, and she will let him, the stupid girl she is! Let me pass!"

"Marek!" Gavin shouted. "*Listen!*"

From the crowd there came a voice — a steady, unfaltering confession of guilt. "Please do not harm her, my lord. 'Tis I who have betrayed you and touched her against her will. My lust for her has taken over my mind, and I cannot deny it any longer."

"Owen, no!" Brynn sputtered against the rope. "He lies, my lord! There has been no man! He only tries to protect me. Do not believe him."

Marek watched the interaction between the two in horror. Owen stared at Brynn, searching her eyes for some sign of hope. A sign she had loved him just as much as he loved her. Only Marek saw a different love — the love that belonged to him alone — the one who couldn't save her now. Brynn's life rested in the hands of another. Owen wouldn't let her die.

Westmore paused between the two accused. With the flick of a finger, two soldiers were upon the Archaean, taking the noose from Brynn's neck and securing it around Owen's.

He did not struggle.

With a swift jerk, Owen's feet were dangling above the ground, left to die a slow and agonizing death in front of the woman he sought to protect.

"No!" Brynn sobbed, uselessly beating the chest of the soldier confining her. In desperation, she searched the crowds, seeking absolution for her friend. Her eyes fluttered over faces, searching to no avail.

"Aiden," Marek sighed, watching the man hanging in the tree struggle. He took his brother-in-arms by the shirt collar and muttered low in his ear, "Strike fast. Strike true." He knew what must be done. Aiden was, by far, the best bow in the Archaean highlands, and if one were to want their life ended, an arrow to the heart would be the swiftest way to die.

Marek had some compassion in him for the man. Owen had protected his woman when he didn't. He owed Owen a swift death, at least. There was nothing more he could offer. Engel soldiers guarded every corner.

Aiden darted to the outcropping of buildings beside the crowd. Bursting through the front door of the closest building, he removed a single arrow from his quiver and nocked it in his bow. He bound up the stairs two at a time to find an opening facing the makeshift gallows. Squaring himself with the window, Aiden drew his bow, bringing the bowstring level to the corner of his mouth, steady and focused. He took a breath and held it, aimed, then released the arrow. It struck true, piercing Owen's heart. The target went limp, and his struggle ceased. As silently as he had entered, Aiden ducked out of sight and escaped into the shadows of a back alley.

O wen was dead. Her sweet, dear friend had given his life for hers, all for naught. Marek was gone, Owen's death the proof. She stood and watched in a clouded daze as the crowd dissipated in all directions, taking Owen's body away with it.

And then all was quiet.

# Chapter Twenty-One

## REBORN

rynn wiped her brow with the corner of her apron, dabbing at the fine beads of sweat gathered there. Her stomach churned, tying itself into twisted knots, and she covered the pang with her palm. For days on end, she hadn't been well. A sickness had found its way inside her body and wouldn't offer respite. Perhaps it was her undying grief eating away at her insides and finally working itself to the surface. Maybe if it wretched itself from her body she might know a bit of relief.

Owen had been dead for more than two moons but still, the shadow of him haunted her every thought. She visited his ailing father almost daily. The death of his son wore on him like a sickness. The guilt would torture her if she didn't pay him some small token of condolence.

"Are you not well?" A concerned voice interrupted her thoughts.

"I'm fine. 'Tis just my grief that pains me, Abby," Brynn told her friend while returning to her cooking station.

"Are you sure, love? You haven't been yourself for quite some time."

Brynn could understand Abby's concern, but there was no use in coddling her. Her heart would heal in time. "Let us please just finish this meal so that I might take it to him and get it over with all the sooner." Brynn had been called into Lord Westmore's service the day after Owen had died for her. She saw to his meals twice daily, ran errands for him, and sometimes helped his maids dress him when he made her stay. He had not bedded her yet, thank the gods, but had kissed her and roamed his hands freely over her body, exploring her curves and staking claim to what he thought was rightfully his. She didn't return his favors — it shamed her to let him do so, but she had no choice. Her lack of interest seemed to keep him at bay, and no longer being pure curbed his fascination with her. Now she was just like any other slave, and lucky to still be alive. Brynn learned very quickly to let another one of his servants see to him when he was well within his cups.

Abby raised a wary eyebrow. "Very well, then." From a pail beneath the table, Abby withdrew a dead duck, plucked and ready for roasting.

Brynn took one look at it, covered her mouth with her fingers, and ran to the corner to vomit into the rubbish bucket.

The women in the kitchen clucked their tongues. Abby let out a hearty laugh.

Brynn spat into the bucket and wiped her mouth with her apron before taking a small sip from the water ladle to rinse the foul taste from her mouth. "Stop looking at me like that."

"Sit down, love, and catch your breath."

"I'm fine!"

"And I'm the bonny Queen of Engel! Might I ask you a question?" Abby reached for a butcher's knife and raised it high over the head of the dead duck.

Brynn nodded, looking away from her friend as the knife found its mark and the duck's head went flying off the counter, bouncing to the corner of the room.

"When was your last woman's course?"

"My what?" Brynn sputtered.

"Your last bleed, Brynn."

"I... do not recall."

"Think, Brynn. Think *hard*." Abby grinned, placing her arms on her hips. "Was it before or after you opened your legs to your lover?"

Brynn could only stare, astonished. "I... umm..." Her eyes widened at the startling revelation, and her heart raced. Her hands flew to her belly in a panic. "No..."

Although weary from a long days' work, Brynn couldn't settle her mind and allow herself to sleep. The evening events still rapidly swam nervously through her thoughts. She turned toward the edge of the bed she shared with Abby.

"Does the babe pain you still?" A groggy voice croaked.

"'Tis asleep, I think," Brynn replied.

"Something else troubles you then?"

"Aye. Lord Westmore has been taking more… liberties. He placed his hands on me this eve when I served his meal. He laughed at me and told me I had been eating very well. I fear I cannot hide my growing belly for much longer. I have no more skirts to let out, and if anyone were ever to learn of my… condition, I'm scared of what he might do to me… or the babe."

Abby murmured her agreement.

"I've been thinking for a while, Abby, about what I might do, and I think we should leave." With no response from Abby, Brynn continued. "I've seen Lord Westmore's maps. In a few days' time, he marches toward the Southlands. I think he intends on bringing me with him. He mentioned I would like my accommodations at his future fortifications. I cannot let that happen, so if we are to slip away unnoticed, this would be our one chance." It would be no easy feat, but possible. The Engel soldiers were used to Brynn's presence and she could easily take supplies and food without causing a stir. They would need money and horses but she fully believed it possible. "What say you?" Brynn whispered to Abby.

Abby's breathing staggered. "I love you like my own child, Brynn, and that babe growing in your womb. I cannot fathom the evil that Westmore will bestow upon you both if he were to learn his prized Archaean girl carried another man's seed. We have no other choice. I know where we can get the needed coin, but it might be there no longer. Tomorrow night we shall see."

The women planned their escape while they worked. Every so often one would hide a hunk of dried meat or a loaf of bread, or stow away a water bladder where it could be later taken to the loft in secrecy. Brynn was excited, and it showed on her face. She smiled and laughed, things she hadn't done since Owen died. The guilt had been overwhelming at times; she still had to face the tavern on a daily basis. She would find herself mindlessly turning to speak to him — only Owen wasn't there. A shadow of where he had once been was all that was left. Her life needed a new course. A change was on the horizon — she only had to get there.

With the paper tucked securely in her satchel along with a fire starting kit, some food, and extra clothing, Brynn could barely hold in her excitement as she raced back to the tavern loft to show Abby her discoveries. The map had been tossed aside, simply forgotten about. A drunken soldier left his pack out in the open for all to see, and when Brynn tidied up the mess, she covertly snuck the fire kit and the map under her full skirts. The extra clothes she took were to be mended — what luck she had stumbled on! Abby would be sure to scold her for being so late, but when shown the prize, hopefully all would be forgiven.

Brynn couldn't have been more right. Abby was thrilled with the detailed map graphing the highlands, the midlands, and most of the western section of the Engel territories. Lord Westmore's camps and strongholds were marked on the map, so the women would easily be able to avoid those areas during their trek toward a new life.

"Where do we go?" Abby smiled. All was falling into place easily.

"Why, Dunlogh, of course!" Brynn's smile warmed the room. "You have spoken of its beauty and homeward shores. I can think of no better place." She placed her palm on her rounded belly.

Abby wrapped her arms around Brynn's shoulders. "Oh, my child, you are truly a blessing for this old woman."

They laughed together with their treasures spread around them on the bed. They spoke of new beginnings and of the adventures they would have running from the dirty Engels — which made them both laugh so hard they wept. They were running deep into Archaean lands when just a short time ago Brynn would have given anything to return to Engel.

"All we need now is a fat purse of silver and a few fine mounts to get us through our journey."

"That seems to be where our luck runs out, Abby. I wasn't able to locate any spare horses or purses of money just lying about for the taking. I hope you have a plan for that part."

"Of course, I do." The laughter quickly faded from Abby's voice. "But it won't be easy. We must return to Daman's."

A thick blanket of clouds covered the moon when the women left the safety of their loft. They hadn't returned to Daman's since the night of his murder. Brynn took great care in avoiding places reminding her of Marek. She knew without a doubt that he killed Daman as some sort of justification for what happened to her. Punished by death, when Marek was just as much at fault as Daman was for what had happened — but she had to put it behind her and focus on her new life. She had all the memories she could ever want of Marek growing inside of her.

What was left of the shack was dark and quiet. The front door had been ripped from its hinges and now sat propped against the outer wall. The two women cautiously slipped inside. The stench within immediately made them gag. Brynn held up the lantern, determined to continue on, and covered her nose and mouth with her apron.

"Follow me," Abby whispered. She led Brynn to the back of the shack toward the kitchen. "I cooked for Daman many a time over the years here. He grew accustomed to my presence and foolishly believed I wouldn't remember his secrets — like where he hid his coin." As they rounded the corner to the kitchen, there in the corner seeped into the wooden floor were the bloodstains of Daman where Marek had struck him dead. "'Tis just over there." Abby pointed to the opposite corner while rushing past the bloody patch on the floor. A rat scurried over her boots, and both women shouted out before ending with nervous laughter. Abby knelt down to the threshold of a doorway and pried at the rickety board with her fingers. "I would often see him hide things under here, and it looks as though it has been left undiscovered. I assumed it would have been the first of his things to be taken. I wish I had taken the time to look."

"Here, let me help you." With Brynn on one side and Abby tugging on the other, the board popped free, sending the women reeling to their backsides. Both righted themselves, anxious to peer into the dark hole. Brynn held the lantern high and a soft glow fell onto the many pouches of coin, jewelry, and other valuables stowed safely under the floorboards.

"'Tis there, Abby, look! Quickly, take it!" Brynn held open her satchel and eagerly awaited the retrieval. Pouch after pouch, Abby emptied the hidden treasure trove. "Why, there's enough here to buy a stable ten times over! We don't need to steal horses; we can simply buy them!" Brynn laughed while wiping a tear from her cheek.

A matching tear rolled down the old woman's cheek, settling into a fine wrinkle at the corner of her mouth. "Come, we mustn't tarry. We have much work to do."

T heir bags fully packed, the women headed to the stables to procure horses. "Wait here," Brynn told Abby as she set her bags down. "I'll be back shortly." She pulled her arisaid over her shoulders, hiding her features, and for the first time in a long time, she had Marek's boot knife strapped to her inner thigh.

The stable was crowded, as she had expected it to be. Lord Westmore's men were preparing to leave. If she were to be recognized, they would think nothing more of it — after all, she was to prepare to depart with them in the early hours of the morning. Taking horses to ready her things wouldn't be out of sorts. Putting all thoughts of deceit and doubt from her mind, Brynn entered the stable, found the three horses she wanted, then sought out the groom. He was busy with his nose buried in his accounting book, so she silently retreated before she revealed her presence and decided at the last moment to just take them. He wouldn't notice. She made quick work of the tack, and with two horses fully tacked and one loaded for a packhorse, she led them toward the exit.

"Oy, you there!"

She stopped in her tracks, the horses almost pushing her down. Slowly, she turned to face the groom. "Aye?"

"What do you think you are doing?" He snapped, approaching her.

A sly smile curled her lips as she looked up from beneath sooty lashes. "Why, I'm taking these horses."

"No, you are not. Those belong to Lord Westmore."

She beckoned him closer with her finger.

He stepped forward, but hesitated.

Once more, she urged him closer. Then closer. Finally, he was near enough that she could step on his boots if he were to move any further. She leaned into him and whispered, "And who do you think I belong to?"

The groom pulled away. "I'm terribly sorry. I didn't know 'twas you. Forgive me."

Brynn reached into her satchel, pulled out a small leather pouch, and placed it in the groom's hand. "For your silence."

The groom jingled the pouch. His eyes grew wide, and his jaw dropped before tucking it securely to the inside of his tunic and smiled.

Silence, indeed.

Brynn turned on her heels and exited the stable. With one hand supporting her belly and another leading the horses, Brynn crested the hill returning to Abby. "We must hurry. They are readying to leave, and someone will notice when I'm not where I'm supposed to be."

"I cannot believe this is happening." Abby giggled as she helped Brynn stow their belongings on the packhorse. "Ready?"

"As I shall ever be."

---

"**A**bby, we must rest. Please." The long trip to Dunlogh had not been kind to Brynn.

"But we must cover more ground today. We are sorely behind schedule." Abby carefully refolded the worn map and tucked it away in her bodice. "Once we're past the hills of Slorn, we'll be deep into Northern Archaean territory where they fiercely protect their own. No Engel will dare follow us there." They had managed to elude Lord Westmore's men for months, thanks to Abby's knowledge of the land and the map Brynn had stolen.

Brynn pulled her mount to a halt. "If we go any further, I will be birthing this babe on horseback."

"Why did you not say something? We must find an inn."

Brynn clenched her eyes tight and waited for the tightening of her womb to slow. "How much further?"

"There's a small village just over the next rise. We shall seek shelter there. Besides, the sky looks as though a storm in the heavens is about to wretch down upon us."

By the time the women found the inn, they were soaked through and Brynn was writhing in labor pains. She nearly fell dismounting as a contraction rendered her helpless. Thankfully, a young stable boy broke her fall.

Abby sought out the innkeeper, towing Brynn behind her. "Sir, we need a room, and quickly. My... daughter is about to give birth."

"This is no place to be birthing babes. Perhaps you should just travel a bit farther home?" the innkeeper replied, eyeing the distraught, soaking mess of fabric and dirt.

"Please, sir, there is no time. I was visiting a nearby village, and I cannot make it home. I'm afraid my husband has been caught in the storm and cannot fetch me. Please, just allow me a bed and some clean water. We can pay you very well for your trouble, sir." Another wave of pain hit her, sending a gush of fluid to the floor between her legs. Brynn screamed out and clutched Abby's arm to stay upright.

The innkeeper looked down at the mess and sighed. "I will fetch my wife to assist you. She is a rather good midwife. Colleen, please show them the back room and give them anything they might need."

"Thank you." Abby gave the innkeeper a warm smile and placed a handful of coins on the table next to him. "For your troubles, good sir. You are most generous."

They were shown a back room away from the other guests where they made quick work of preparing the room for Brynn to give birth. She labored for hours as the rain pummeled the roof, drowning out most of her screams.

"Just one more time, love."

"I cannot!" Brynn cried out. "I cannot do this anymore!"

"You have to, Brynn. Now, the next time the pain comes, I want you to push with all your might. The end is near."

Brynn nodded and laid her head back on the pillow, seeking some shred of relief while Abby wiped her forehead with a damp cloth. Tears clung to her flushed cheeks. "I wish he was here," she muttered, choking back a sob.

"Who?" The innkeeper's wife questioned Abby.

"Oh... her husband. They are very much in love. 'Tis a shame he cannot be here for the arrival of his firstborn."

Brynn's grip on Abby's hand tightened, signaling the rise of another impending labor pain.

There was a knock on the door, and the innkeeper's wife left Brynn's side to answer it. "Just the maid," she stated, but behind the door stood her husband with two Engel soldiers.

"I'm sorry, my wife, but they insisted on seeing the travelers."

His wife placed both hands on her hips and frowned at them. "What ails you men? Can you not see that a child is being born here? By all means, come and look," she clucked, "but let me do my work!" She rushed back to Brynn as she let out a gut-wrenching moan that would scare even the brawniest of men away.

One man edged forward, glanced back at his partner, then took a step backward.

"*Get out!*" Brynn screeched at him as she wrapped her arms around her knees, hunching over her belly.

"It couldn't possibly be them," the soldier muttered to the other. "We must have followed the wrong trail." The Engels disappeared, shutting the door behind them.

"Just one more push!" The midwife urged Brynn, a wide grin gracing her aging face. "The babe is almost out!"

Brynn pushed once more, and the tiny being slid into the midwife's arms.

Brynn slumped backward with relief. She had done it.

"A boy!" The nursemaid laughed. "And a right strapping lad he is, too!"

Brynn pushed herself up. "What?" She had prayed to the gods the babe would be a girl.

"Ohh," cooed Abby, helping the innkeeper's wife clean off the newborn. "He looks just like his da."

Brynn groaned, returning to the bed. All fears, regrets, and resentments were thrown aside when the tiny little boy was placed in her arms. She held a precious miracle, a piece of the greatest love she had ever known. How he had grabbed her heart in just a few short moments. With eyes the bluest of blue and soft fuzzy curls, he was a perfect sculpture of his father. Her life would never be the same.

· · ·

"Oh, 'tis perfect, Abby! I love it already." Brynn stood at the top of a winding willow-lined entranceway to the most beautiful home she could ever have imagined. It overlooked the pebbled ocean shore on one side and was flanked by rolling fields of heathery pastures on the other for as far as the eye could see. A sturdy stable rested quietly in a nook of the glen by a slow-moving river with a bubbling spring near the tree line. The entire property was hidden in a secluded valley — the perfect spot to live out the rest of her days and watch her son grow. "You were right, Abby. Dunlogh must be in the heavens, for this is the most wonderful place we could be. I have officially whisked you away, Abby," Brynn teased.

They hugged each other and wept tears of joy. They had done it. They had escaped their prison. No longer were they held captive. Just like the babe she held in her arms, Brynn had been given a new life. All that was left to do was secure it.

The women headed in the village of Dunlogh to secure their future.

"Hello?" A bell above the door jingled as they entered the tiny, dark shop on the main thoroughfare of Dunlogh.

"Hello," a man called from the corner. "Yes, can I help you?" The man limped from the darkness toward the counter of the shop. His clothes were worn and damp; a musty odor permeated the air as he shuffled by.

"I was told you're the man I must speak with in order to inquire about a piece of property." Brynn bounced the babe in one arm as she dug through her satchel for the piece of parchment detailing the property.

"Yes, yes..." he grumbled, muttering indistinct words.

"Well, I wish to inquire about this one." Brynn placed the description of the glen on the counter in front of him.

He took it in his crooked fingers, placed it close to his face, and slowly withdrew it, trying to focus his failing vision on the words. When he recognized the property, he looked at the two women, back at the parchment, and then back at the women. A confused look washed over his face. "You wish to rent a piece of this croft? Is there a man present? Edenshire is quite expensive, my dear."

"Rent it?" For a brief moment, Brynn didn't understand. Then a soft laugh echoed through the room. "No, good sir, I wish to *buy* it!"

Abby clunked a heavy purse onto the wooden counter. "That should cover it."

"Eh, which part of it?" the clerk inquired.

"The whole lot of it!" Abby burst out in a hearty laugh.

"We will also be needing a list of local merchants that may be interested in helping us furnish it as well. The best woodworkers, blacksmiths… and I shall need to find someone I can purchase a few horses from. Good breeding stock, you see," added Brynn.

"I will get right on that, madam — err, I shall need to know what name to put on the deed."

Abby and Brynn quickly exchanged glances before Brynn replied with, "Brynn — Coinnich of Cinn Tàile." She gave the name of her babe's father.

"Well, Mistress Coinnich, welcome to Dunlogh." The old man smiled a toothless grin and handed Brynn the deed to her new home.

# Chapter Twenty-Two

## I HAVE MISSED YOU

*Dunlogh*
*Archaean Highlands*
*Summer*

"Stupid, stupid hare! If I ever get my hands on you I... I will turn you into stew!" Brynn grumbled, trying to salvage what was left of the new herbs she'd planted. All attempts thus far to keep the wildlife out of her garden had failed miserably. Inspecting the half-eaten shoots of bannowick only left her more frustrated and defeated. The seeds had cost her a small fortune to have them sent from Engel, and now the pesky hare was liberally enjoying its many healing properties.

She stood, stretching her arms toward the bright summer sun, taking in its rare beauty and warmth. It rained far too often in the Archaean highlands for her taste. A bug flew past her cheek, and she swatted it with the back of her hand. Warm breezes ruffled her hair, and she pushed the annoyance from her face. A hound's excited bark mingled with a child's laughter and floated along contentedly with the summer air. She paused from her gardening to watch her son, Talon, play with the large wolfhound he called Rufus.

The two were inseparable. The boy mock-attacked the hound with a wooden sword, pretending to slay the evil monster invading his castle. Rufus would rise up on his hind legs, towering well above his playmate to "attack" back. She sighed and smiled when the boy pushed unruly golden curls from his forehead and beamed a beautiful wide grin at her. It was remarkable how much he reminded her of his father; his smile, his deep azure eyes, his brazen boyish mannerisms, and especially his unyielding spirit for all things warrior. He wanted nothing more in life than to grow up and be a fierce warrior like his da was.

Rufus caught the scent of an animal, distracted from his mock battle. The boy lowered his sword and wiped his sweaty brow on the sleeve of his little brown tunic. "May I see if Deven can come and practice with me, Mum? I promise I shall rush right home!"

"All right," she replied as he bolted for the drive. "Talon!" she called out after him. "Stay away from the river, and I expect you washed up and on time for supper! And take Rufus with you!"

"Aye, Mum!" he answered, trotting down the rocky drive. Talon let out a shrill whistle for his companion to follow, and the giant beast closed the gap between the house and his master in just a few long leaps.

"Oh, that boy." She sighed, returning to her herb salvaging. Brynn hummed a pleasant tune while she worked, thankful the end of day was near. Soon the sun would set — only then could she relax. Between the horses, the bit of healing she dabbled in for the local villagers and raising her spirited son, she was lucky if she had enough energy left to crawl into bed.

She shouldn't complain, though — her life was brilliant. She was blessed with a wonderful son, her closest friend, and the home of her dreams where she ran a rather successful horse breeding business, and she had accomplished it all by herself without the presence of a man in the home. The villagers were apprehensive of her at first, but Brynn tempted them with paid work, mostly to the men seeking extra coin. They helped her till the fields or complete any job that might have required the finishing touches of a stronger, more agile man, and she paid them well. When questioned about a husband, she simply stated she was a widow and left it at that. With the many wars raging across the country, no one seemed to question her starting over.

"*Mum!*" The frightened scream broke her scattered thoughts.

"Talon?" Frantic, she called out to the breezes surrounding her.

"*Mother!*"

A gasp caught in her throat. Brynn picked up her skirts and moved further from the cottage, searching the valley for her son. "Talon?" she yelled, almost commanding him to show himself over the indentation of the drive.

"Mum! Hide! A rider approaches!"

She saw him then, pale as snow and bolting toward the shelter of her arms with his hound at his heels. She knelt and reached out for him. The boy crashed into her at full speed. Brynn scanned the horizon for a rider, elbowing Rufus from her visual path. She saw no one.

"I ran as fast as I could, Mum, to tell you. He looked mean, with all sorts of weapons and a horse that looked like hell itself spat it out. I have never seen him before, Mum." Talon was terrified. It reverberated from his entire body like a strong river current.

"Get inside and tell Aunt Abby," she told him in a hushed tone, placing her palms on his cheeks and kissing the top of his head. "And stay there." As the boy nodded and rushed through the open door and disappeared inside, Brynn took another quick glance behind her and hurried to the threshold.

In the corner sat a bow and quiver of arrows at the ready. She had no need for weapons while living in Dunlogh, but there was always that resonating feeling deep in her chest telling her she could never be too careful. That gut feeling was why she had one of her farmhands teach her how to use them. She'd learned as a child, but she was older now, stronger. Wiser.

She slung the quiver over her shoulder and drew an arrow. Taking a deep breath, she tried to steady her trembling hand. Hooves pounded up the dirt drive. She counted the paces — a steady canter. Raising the bow, she nocked the arrow and pulled the bowstring taut... and waited. She would put as many arrows as possible into her target before he had the time to reach her family. Brynn had to remind herself to breathe as the pounding of hooves grew closer.

*Thump thump thump.*
*Thump thump thump.*

Soon the horse would show its head above the rise, and show, it did. A larger than life black charger with a brilliant white blaze reared to a halt mere feet from her. Brynn held her ground for what seemed like an eternity until the face staring back at her spoke.

His voice cracked. "Brynn?" It rolled off the warrior's tongue like a foreign word.

She lowered the bow, although still wary of the stranger. Could it be? *No.* She forced such foolishness from her thoughts.

His eyes scanned over her, the bow, the cottage, and the two heads peeking from the threshold. Only when Brynn fully lowered her bow and allowed the bowstring to slack did he attempt to dismount. He dropped to the ground, never taking his eyes from her.

"Hello…" The word was forced out of her on a breath she'd been holding, barely audible to even her own ears.

Something crashed into her back and grabbed her about the waist. Talon had left the shelter of the cottage and now hid behind her, eager as always to be near.

Her eyes flickered to the man standing before her and then to her son. The man was flustered, confused, and certainly not prepared to be staring back into his own eyes.

"Who's boy is this?" Marek questioned, his voice gruff and raspy as if trying very hard to make the words come out at all. He stood as still as stone except for the constant tightening and loosening of his fists at his sides.

Brynn was at a loss for words. Never had she thought this situation would arise — not in a thousand years. She glanced back at Abby, who cautiously watched from inside the door. Abby only shrugged. Brynn's lips drew together in a thin tight line. Taking her son by the arm, she moved the boy to stand in front of her and placed her hands on both of his shoulders. The boy protectively curled his palms around the leather cuffs she wore around her wrists. "Talon," she muttered low and soft into the boy's ear, "Say hello to your da."

The boy's eyes grew wild with wonder. Brynn managed a weak smile. Long ago she'd told her son that his father had perished in one of the highland wars, as he was a great warrior hellbent on giving the Archaean people back their freedom from the Engel Lord who sought to conquer and enslave them. Now here he was standing before them, very much alive.

Talon rushed forward and grabbed Marek about the thighs, tightly ensnaring his father in a crooked twist of limbs.

Marek stood there, awestruck with his arms slightly splayed to the sides.

Once again Brynn turned toward Abby, wide-eyed, looking for some sort of reassurance.

Abby could only wring her hands. "I will go put on some tea," she mouthed. She disappeared from the doorway, leaving Brynn stranded with her love-struck son and a man who awkwardly seemed like a stranger to her — or perhaps a walking, breathing ghost.

Brynn found herself watching her son, who would not remove his arms from the stranger, and the father who would not touch his son. Realizing his mind couldn't seem to grasp the concept of the shocking information, Brynn removed Talon's arms from Marek's legs. "Talon." She faked a smile. "Please go wash up for supper."

The boy slung his arm around her neck in a swift hug and laughed his way behind the house to wash, his unruly curls bouncing in stride with his steps.

Brynn toed the dirt. The silence was unnerving. Something had changed between them, and it twisted her insides. She had changed him, forever scarred him; their last words hadn't been on the best of terms. At last, she spoke. Her lips quivered. "Hello, Marek." She glanced up at him, not knowing what else to say.

"Hello, Brynn."

She searched his eyes, looking for some sort of answer as to what he was thinking, what he thought of her and of his new-found son, but she couldn't get past the pain residing there. His face was rigid — tired. A scruffy yellow beard lined the chiseled jaw she had admired so long ago. A thin strip of yellow lined his upper lip as well, almost hiding that remarkable mouth she had dreamed of countless times over. His hair was cropped shorter — his youthful curls had fallen into flowing waves but still hinted at the playfulness lurking beneath them. He was a man now. Time and battle had transformed him. "Will you be joining us for dinner, then?"

He hesitated but nodded his acceptance to the wary invite.

"Very well. Come in."

Marek tied his horse to a nearby hitching post and followed her inside. He ducked through the door and entered the spacious cottage.

Perfectly placed windows let in the sun's rays during all times of daylight so that the rooms would stay bright. Freshly polished wood lined the floors. A remarkably made table and chairs set was tucked into a corner opposite the open kitchen. A large stone hearth sat on the opposing side of the cottage, surrounded by tapestries, two rocking chairs, and a child-size bench. A large wolfhound dozed on a rug near the fireplace with one watchful eye still open. A ladder to the loft was securely tied to a post near the center of the cottage. The spacious ceilings rose high, keeping the lower level cool.

"Please come in." Abby fussed with her apron. "The stew is nearly ready." Behind her, the back door burst open, nearly knocking the teapot from Abby's hands.

Talon squirmed by her only to rush to his mother and father, who sat at the table across from one another, not speaking.

"By the gods, child, you gave me a fright!" Abby huffed, recovering her steps and moving to the table to pour the tea. Brynn took a sip and returned the cup to the table, content to listen to Talon talk faster than the wind could blow. He could barely contain the exciting stories and details about everything and anything he could think of, and many of his words were jumbled and indistinct. The stew arrived shortly after, and the four of them ate in silence with the exception of Talon, who continued with his bombardment of talk in between slurps and bites.

When he finished, Abby herded the boy out-of-doors to play. "I can see you two have much to say," she quipped, following the boy. "I will be in the back if you need me." She eyed Marek with guarded suspicion but nodded and disappeared.

Brynn sighed and rose from the table with her dishes.

She set them aside, not wanting to deal with them. She had too many other more important thoughts running full speed through her mind. "There are pastures in the back you may turn your mount out in if you like," she told Marek, keeping the talk light. She pressed her palm to her forehead, rubbing away the pain gathering there.

"That would be helpful, thank you."

"And there is grain in the eastern barn if you need feed."

"Again, my thanks."

Neither continued the conversation, just awkwardly stood in the kitchen staring at everything else except each other. After a painful silence, Marek spoke. "Brynn, I-I…"

"The stable is this way."

They both spoke at once.

With purpose, Brynn turned and exited through the back door, too nervous to have *that* conversation with Marek. She had hurt him terribly, she knew that. She regretted it every moment she breathed and wished things could have been different, but the past could not be changed. What was done was done.

Marek followed. A smile broke through his placid demeanor. He stopped mid-step, taking in the vast array of barns, fences, and the greenest of pastures littered with some of the most amazing mounts in the highlands. "Is this all yours?"

"Aye," she replied, walking toward his horse.

"Is this how you pay the rent on the croft?"

Brynn turned to him and smiled, the pride radiating from her chest. "I do not rent it, I *own* it. All of it."

Marek raised an eyebrow. "Do ye now?"

"Aye." She stopped beside his mount and gathered up the reigns.

"Marry a rich man, did ye?" he pressed.

"*No.*" The word was cutting and short.

"So you married a poor one and then found yourself rich?" He leaned casually against a wooden fence post, watching her. He looked about the property as if expecting a man to appear from thin air to chase him away.

"I'm not married, Marek, if that is what you are getting at," she huffed, yanking the last rein free, and heading to a nearby paddock. Marek stumbled after her like a puppy whose paws were too big for its body. "And no, I have never been married, nor will I ever marry, so I will answer before you even ask it."

"Then what in hell did you do to acquire this pretty piece of land?" he blurted, trotting alongside his horse as it followed Brynn all too willingly.

"*You*... killed a man."

Marek's brow narrowed.

Brynn rolled her eyes and removed the bridle as Marek slid the saddle from his mount. "The money belonged to Daman, and when Abby and I decided to leave, we took it. We figured we deserved most of it anyway." She gave the horse a friendly pat to its backside and it entered the paddock. "Abby knew where it was hidden, and there was... a lot of it."

"Ahh," Marek replied, seemingly deep in thought.

"There were stolen jewels and heirlooms mixed with many a purse that surely belonged to Godric, but we took it all. No one else knew where it was hidden besides Abby, so it wouldn't have been missed anyhow." They both watched in silence as Marek's horse trotted out to the middle of the paddock, promptly lowered itself to the ground, and rolled in the grass, scratching its back where the saddle had been.

"He is a fine horse, Marek," she told him, breaking the heavy silence.

"Aye, he takes after his father in many ways."

Brynn must have said those very words a hundred times over... only they were about her son.

He turned toward her. "The boy?"

"Mmm." A frown marred her face. "He is nearly five now."

Marek exhaled a long breath through pursed lips and ran his fingers across his matted hair and down across his brow. "I'm sorry. Had I known, Brynn — I am just so, so sorry. I don't know what else I can say."

Talon's infectious laugh floated to her ears, caught on a breeze. "Don't fret yourself." A soft smile briefly formed on her lips before fading away just as fast. "He is the reason I breathe."

Marek watched Talon pick up a wooden sword and swing it fiercely at his hound, completely mesmerized by the boy.

Brynn laughed when Talon jumped on Rufus's back and rode him as he would his pony during a romp around the pasture. When Talon heard the laugh, he paused, pushed the hair from his eyes then waved. "I know that this may come as a shock to you — to learn you have a son after all this time — and I never once tried to seek you out to tell you about him. I know he cannot replace your firstborn, but Talon *is* your son. Could you find it in your heart to love him as one? Please do not deny him." She looked at Marek. "I couldn't bear it."

Marek's palm lightly cupped her cheek, and he wiped a falling tear with the pad of his thumb. "If you declare it as such, then he is my son. I ask no questions."

He searched her eyes, seeking absolution. Marek had been gone from her life, end of story. Now everything had changed within the course of just a day. One single day and her entire life had been turned on its backside once again.

---

Marek pulled her to his chest, wrapping his arm around her neck, closing the gap between them. He inhaled the fresh smells of her body, burying his face into her long, untamed tresses. Her hair was longer; the end curls curved playfully around her buttocks. She was more of a woman now than she had ever been. He had only wished that the past five years had been as kind to him as they had been to her. He had thought her beautiful then, but now, he had never seen her equal.

He'd seen more than he cared to over the years traveling during his hunt for Engels to kill. He'd always assumed if he found Lord Westmore, he would find Brynn as well. After years of the Engel just barely slipping through his fingers, Marek changed course and returned to where it had all started, the Crossroads. It was there he learned from the blacksmith that Brynn had escaped and eluded the Engel forces, vanishing into oblivion. Many thought she had returned to her homeland. The older woman, the Engel Abby, was said to be with her. That information led him to searching the Engel countryside for nearly two years before getting caught in the middle of the greatest Archaean and Engel war, the battle at Kirkwood. He fought alongside his countrymen, driving the Engels deeper into their own territory and further away from Archaean lands. He had narrowly escaped with his life. It was there, on that battlefield, surrounded by death and despair, he had decided he'd finally had enough. He had given up his will to live — tried with all his might to be cut down in battle — and still, death wouldn't claim him.

The gods showed him a different journey.

Searching the depths of his soul in solitude, he had wandered without purpose, without the passion he'd once had for life. Without his little Archaean girl, he had no meaning, no reason to live. And then, in a tavern near Kirkwood, he learned Abby once resided there. She had run away with an Archaean merchant when she was just a girl and the stories of her daring escape were still told. In hopes they would return to the only place Abby still held fond memories of, he forged on to Dunlogh.

It didn't take long after arriving in Dunlogh to hear word of the beautiful healer who lived on the hillside down in the valley. And here she was — alive and well — and in his arms of all places. Finally, in his arms.

---

"Aye, just like that! Good, lad. Now, when you are blocking a strike, hold your ground. Look your attacker in the eye and never lose your concentration. Not even for a pretty girl." Marek teased Talon. "They will only bring you trouble."

"Like this, Da?" Talon swung his practice sword at Marek, narrowly missing his arm.

"Aye, now quickly come in for the kill. The first rule of fighting is to spill as much blood as possible. Aim for an arm or leg — incapacitate your enemy the quickest way you can." Marek borrowed the sword and demonstrated to the eager young boy. "See, if I attack you here," he said, gently slashing the inside of the boy's thigh with the tip of the wooden sword, "you will no longer be able to stand. The kill will be easy once your enemy is on the ground. The second rule — never hesitate. It will only show weakness."

"How do you know so much, Da?" The boy looked up at him in awe.

Marek chuckled. "Well, my da taught me when I was about your age. He taught my brother and me how to stand, how to walk, and how to hold and swing a sword, how to attack and defend. You try to outsmart your opponent and be the victor. It is a very difficult skill. It takes discipline to learn. I practiced and found it to come easily to me, and I have great suspicion it will to you as well."

"Will you teach me, Da? I wish to be a great warrior, just like you.

Mum has told me all the stories. When I am big enough, I am going to defeat the Engels, too."

Marek knelt on the ground near his son, to search his eyes. "All the stories, eh? I have also learned there is more to this one life we have been given. There is more than the blade — than death. There is also life. Choosing to kill another is a heavy burden. The rains wash away the stains of war but those battles will forever stay in your mind. Each and every strike will haunt you for the rest of your days."

Talon stared at Marek, his skin pale and eyes wide. He swallowed hard and tightened his grip on the wooden sword between his palms.

Marek ruffled the boy's hair. "Forgive me, Talon, I didn't mean to frighten you. Would you like to battle me? I would bet you have a fair amount of good skills to take me down. What say you? Want to give it a go?"

"You think I can best you?"

"The gods willing, I think you can." He winked and flashed the boy a devilish grin. "Let me fetch my sword."

Jogging to his things nearby, Marek retrieved the long sword, keeping it sheathed.

"Well, I'll be buggered!" Talon whispered as he eyed the blade. "Might I hold it?"

Marek couldn't deny the boy's eager face. He handed Talon the hilt and watched as it sunk quickly to the ground, tugging the boy down with it under the heavy weight of the steel. A full laugh escaped Marek as he retrieved the sword. "I think you should stick to wood for just a bit longer, son."

"Will you be coming with us to Kaius, Da?" Talon traded Marek's sword for his wooden one and raised it over his shoulder, at the ready.

"What is in Kaius?" Marek lightly parried with his sheathed sword, letting Talon try his best to beat him.

"The games. Mum has a job there, and she promised this season she would take me. I'm to compete with my sword."

"Is that so?"

"Aye. Will you come? You could best any man there!"

"I don't think I'm invited," Marek replied, eyeing Abby near the cottage. She leaned against the wall with her arms crossed, watching —

no, guarding — the boy. Talon burst into another one of his verbal eruptions, but Marek ignored him. The look on Abby's face bothered his insides. It told him he hadn't been invited, nor was he wanted. "I think we should go inside now." The sun had set below the tree line of the gently sloping valley. The last few beams of amber light clung to the treetops like spindly fingers reaching for a last hope at life.

Talon agreed, gathered up his sword and trotted off toward the cottage, while Marek took his time ambling in, the angry stares of Abby following his every move. "Abby." His nod was polite. Her wariness was justified. More than once, he had disrupted their lives. He had hurt them both. She only had the best of intentions for Brynn and the boy — he could see that.

"I knew this day would come," she began, looking over her shoulder to make sure there weren't any other ears listening. "I know she would never say it to you, but I must. Your arrival won't go unnoticed. We have been living here quite peacefully and undetected for many years now with the notion that you are dead. Brynn is — in all respects — a widow, to the people of Dunlogh. We have raised Talon in a loving, merciful home, and I cannot have you unsettling that and filling his head with all that noble warrior nonsense only to leave again and break more than one heart this time."

"Abby…"

"No, you listen to me. I will not see her hurt again. I do not know what your intentions are, or why you are even here for that matter… but wherever you seem to be, the fighting follows you. Now sooner or later, *that Engel* will find us, and your vicious game of cat and mouse will continue! We have managed to keep our past lives a secret. We have managed to keep the scars a secret. Of course, she will welcome you back — I have no doubt in the matter, for she loves you, even after everything that has transpired between the two of you. But my arms will not be as open to the idea as they once were."

Marek pressed his fingers against the deep crease in his brow. "Dearest, sweet Abby. I don't know what I can say to you to make you trust me. I don't know what Brynn has told you of our parting, but I'm not the only one at fault. She pushed *me* away, and I stupidly did as I was told. All I can offer you is the truth of my heart. I have given up that life. I'm no longer

248

the man I once was. I'm sure you've heard the story of what a fool I was in my younger days. For years I wandered like a drunken sod, seeking my own death for what I'd done. I should never have left. I should never have let her go in the first place. Please believe me when I tell you that I mean no harm. I have given up the ways of the warrior. I seek only to live out the rest of my days with my family if they will have me. I have a son, Abby. *A son!*" He took her by the shoulders and gave her a gentle shake. "I sought death but it would not come for me, no matter how hard I fought for it. And now I know why. If only I had known then. I have been given a great gift this day."

"Very well. I will not interfere but please, I beg of you... don't break her heart. I fear she wouldn't survive it. She has had to endure seeing *you* in that beautiful little boy every day... watch him grow up without his father."

Marek placed his lips to Abby's forehead and kissed away the worry line. "I'm here now."

"All right, off to bed with you." Brynn stood from her chair to stretch.

"But, Mum!" Talon wrinkled his face tightly in protest. "I haven't finished telling Da my story!" He sat at his father's feet, leaning back against his hound while it slept next to the warming fire. Marek had listened patiently to the many stories Talon spouted about various things that happened — or rather, how he remembered them happening.

"I'm sure he would be happy to hear the rest tomorrow. We have a busy day in the morn, and the hour is late. Come and give me a kiss."

Talon rose, reluctant, and stood upon the tips of his toes to reach his mother's cheek. After planting a quick peck he threw his arms around her, squeezing her tight. He whispered, "Thank you for my present, Mum, I love him." As he climbed the ladder to the loft, he paused. "Goodnight, Da."

"Goodnight, Talon." Marek turned toward Brynn. "I should be going. I didn't realize how far from the inn you live."

Talon jumped off the third rung to the floor. "Mum, don't make him go! He can stay in the loft with me! Please, Mum?"

"No, Talon, 'tis all right," replied Marek, halting the boy's pleads.

"He may stay if he wishes. There is but a sliver of moonlight tonight. A trip to town wouldn't be the wisest of ideas at this late hour." Brynn placed a hand to her hip. So much had changed this day. It was all a bit much to take in at once. Her son had simply accepted his father without question or second thought. It was as if he had known him his entire young life and tonight had been no different than any other. If only she could feel the same. There was a familiar tightening in her stomach — it was disconcerting.

---

"Da?" The voice was barely a whisper.

"Hmm?" Marek murmured, surprised the boy was still awake. He had taken Talon up on his offer to share the loft. The space was tight, but he was able to lay out a few blankets and make himself comfortable enough on the floor next to Talon's bed. The open window allowed a comforting breeze to flow, cooling his skin and stirring up wonderful odors from the rooms below.

"What happens when we die?"

"Well, we become part of the earth, part of new life."

"Mum says the gods take us, if we pray to them. Do you pray to the gods, Da?"

"Aye, I do, if I remember."

The boy paused. "What gods do you pray to?"

Marek couldn't help but chuckle. "Whatever one suits me best at the time, I suppose. Why are you asking all these questions about the gods?"

"I hear my Mum pray. Each night it is to a different god, some I don't know. Perhaps she cannot pick the right one, so maybe she needs to pray to the same gods you do."

"What does she pray for to these different gods?"

"It is always the same thing — she prays for her prayers to be answered."

"Oh?"

"Aye — but this night she prayed to them all at the same time. I heard her in her room. She was crying and saying thank you over and over and over, for answering her prayers. Do you think, perhaps, she finally found the right one?"

Marek smiled in the darkness. "Perhaps she did."

After patiently waiting for silence, Marek rose to his knees and checked on his son; Talon's chest rose with each rhythmic breath. His eyes were closed — finally asleep. He descended the ladder in three strides and waited for his eyes to adjust to the darkness before turning the corner toward Brynn's back bedchamber. Rufus huffed out a warning but soon calmed and resumed his guard by the front door when Marek hushed him. A tapestry nailed over the entrance served as a door to her room. Looping a finger around the edge of the worn fabric, he pulled it back, peering into the shadows. In the corner was the milky white glimmer of her skin, a beautiful contrast to the deep darkness encompassing her.

She slept like an angel with her golden mane spread about her pillow, shimmering like waves when the slivered moonlight from the window touched it. Without a sound, he slipped past the tapestry and crossed the room. A curl lingered atop her cheek, and he brushed it to the side with his thumb, leaving a gentle kiss in its place.

A breath escaped her lips. "I have missed you."

# Chapter Twenty-Three
## GAMES

Three black ravens circled above her, eagerly awaiting her death. Crimson spilled from her nose and mouth, cascading to the powdery blanket of snow below. It pooled around her toes, congealing into pale red clumps on her boots and carelessly staining the front of her pretty gown. Her breath crystallized in the air before her, but yet, she felt no cold.

A great sense of foreboding overtook her body then, paining her insides, and she reached up toward the ravens, searching the heavens for strength. She had been there before. She paused to twirl her palm in the air and watched it intensely as it slowly rotated. It felt disjointed from her body as if it didn't belong to her. She felt no immediate pain from the deep laceration on her palm. She gaped at the gash as it wept bloody tears — watched as they dripped in steady rhythmic beats to the perfect white earth. There were others surrounding her — faceless, lifeless beings standing where hearts once beat to the tune of life. Blood trickled from their burning eyes and spouted from their fingers in a strange death spell which had been cast over their unmoving bodies. It kept them erect but frozen in time as swirls of white and crimson danced around their corpses in victory.

So much death.

Had she caused this? No, the death swirl surrounded her as well.

It wanted her.

It took her.

Brynn shot upright, hot tears scorching her flushed cheeks. Fine beads of sweat gleamed over her pallid skin. Darkness surrounded her. Just a dream. *Just a dream.* She drew in a ragged breath, forcing her lungs to accept it. With a trembling finger, she pushed a lock of matted hair from her brow and swallowed hard. She had dreamt of this before. It seemed to come more frequently as of late, each time growing worse.

More death.

More destruction. More war. In her dreams, she held a bow. In her dreams, she brought peace, but each one always ended in her death.

And she had no idea the meaning behind it. All her life she'd dreamed of these ravens and despite her studies, she could not find the reasoning as to why they haunted her so. What were they trying to tell her? If she had the time, she would devote herself to her books in search of respite. The dream had grown more frequent and she needed to know why. She shuffled from her bed, donned relatively clean clothes, and plunged her toes into a pair of worn shoes, eager to free her mind from the night terror.

"Good morning." Abby greeted her with an obligatory smile.

The dark circles under her eyes told Brynn it had been a restless night for her friend. "Good morning," Brynn muttered in return, her thoughts elsewhere. "Where is Talon? I'm surprised to not find him engrossed in deep conversation with you by now."

Abby shrugged her shoulders. "I have not seen him. I assumed he was with you and Marek." His name seemed forced from her lips.

"No, I have just risen. They are not with you?" Brynn yawned, stretching tall in the morning sun. Then the realization hit her. "Abby!" she breathed, clutching her chest.

She darted toward the door without bothering to search the cottage. Could he have taken him during the night? Had he been so angry that he would punish her by taking the one thing her life depended on? "Talon!" she screamed, reaching the top of the drive. Her voice echoed between the hills and disappeared into the tree line.

The rocks dug into the tender soles of her feet through her shoes, but she wouldn't stop running as she sped to the back of the property. She must search the river. Talon knew better than to play near it, but that hadn't stopped him countless times before. Instruction seemed to flitter through his head like butterflies upon a breeze. "Talon, where are you?"

"I'm here, Mum!" The voice sounded like the tinkling of bells to her ears.

A yellow head bobbed just below the horizon of a hilly incline. Before long, Marek came into full view, toting Talon playfully over his shoulders. The boy clung to Marek's neck and let his slight frame dangle down the great length of his father's back. Both smiled and laughed like nothing was wrong while Rufus trotted along beside them, tongue lolling.

"Talon!" she fumed, overcome with relief. "Where have you been?" She placed both hands upon her hips and glared at Marek.

Talon slid from his ride and beamed up at her. "Catching breakfast!" From across his chest, he lifted a rope snare. Dangling from it was an all too familiar fuzzy brown hare. "I killed it meself, Mum!"

His proud, silly grin melted the anger from her heart. "Oh did ye now?" Foolish thoughts ran through her mind. Brynn knelt down beside the boy and brushed the hair from his face. "Well, the next time you decide to go and catch breakfast, please tell me first. You had me very worried. I didn't know where you were. I thought you had fallen into the river."

"I was with Da, Mum..." Talon rolled his eyes as if that made everything perfectly all right.

"And safe as could be." She kissed his forehead. "That is a fine hare, Talon. I bet he will taste delicious in the stew I have been meaning to make out of him." The critter had eaten so many of her herbs it probably would season itself in the pot.

The boy giggled. "I *knew* you would like it, Mum."

"Do I get one?" Marek goaded, pointing to his cheek. "I set the snare."

"When you decide to rid yourself of *this*." Brynn returned the tease, lightly running her finger along his hair-covered jaw.

"What, you do not like it?" He feigned a shocked expression and smoothed the hair on his chin.

"It makes you look old," she replied truthfully. In her dreams she still pictured him as the never-changing boy — she hadn't yet adjusted to his change to all-man.

"I *am* old," he snickered, "but if it makes my lady happy, I will do as she wishes."

"It is wonderful how well he has taken to his father, is it not?" Brynn prepared the ingredients for the stew she would make once Marek finished showing Talon how to skin the hare.

"Let's not be too hasty," Abby replied, sweeping the floor in circles, distracted.

"I just still cannot believe it... that he is here." Brynn smiled, recalling some distant memory that had pushed its way to the present. "He had a little boy before, did you know? He was killed with his mother by—" She paused; she couldn't say the name. "By the Engels," she finished.

"Marek was married?" Abby stopped her sweeping mid-stride. "You have never spoken of his past before. I didn't think of Marek as the marrying type of man, but more as a rover."

"Aye, and his faithfulness to his wife was what landed me in that hell-hole to begin with. He saved my life, Abby, but couldn't bear to hurt the woman he loved."

"So instead he hurt the *other* woman he loved." Abby chuckled, the hint of sarcasm still hanging on her words. She resumed her cleaning after shrugging off the thought.

"To have him here now, to be with his son, is a gift from the gods. He is whole again. I can see it in his eyes. And Talon just adores him. In a way, I guess I have saved his life as well." Brynn paused to listen to their laughter as it wafted through the open window.

"You *do* realize the danger him being here puts us in?"

"Aye, I know." Brynn heaved a heavy sigh. The thought had been a never waning constant in the back of her mind. "If word spread that a rebel high-lander was here, that bounty on his head would lead to temptation in some. But I cannot deny my heart. I don't want to hurt anymore, Abby. A few thousand tears I have cried over that man, and now the gods have finally given me the chance to make it right. I hurt him deeply, telling myself it was for the best. And right now Marek being here with his son is for the best. Please try to understand." Brynn looked at her dear friend, seeking acknowledgment and perhaps even a tiny bit of permission to allow her heart a chance to heal.

"All I am asking is to be careful, 'tis all." Abby continued her grumbling into the next room while she swept.

"We have skinned the hare!" Talon cheered, carrying the battered and headless body into the kitchen.

"And we managed to keep most of it," his father added, shaking his head disgracefully at the badly butchered pieces of meat barely clinging to the bone in some places.

"Wonderful job, Talon." Brynn praised, taking the dismembered hare from the boy's outstretched arms. "Now go wash up — you are covered in filth."

"He learns fast," Marek commented while watching the boy disappear behind a door. He washed his own hands in the washbasin on the table. "He wants to know… *everything.*"

"Talon is a very curious boy. He thirsts for knowledge. He has never had someone to show him how to do these things. I usually pay the help to do the hunting and… skinning."

"You have farmhands?"

"Aye, five regulars. You don't think I could run this homestead by myself, do you?"

Marek whistled in a low tune and raised an eyebrow. "A beautiful woman with a deep purse… the men must be lining up at the door to work for you, fumbling around like idiots to tend to your every need."

She liked his light teasing. Why, she didn't know. If the truth were to be told, she hadn't had a man show her any sort of affection in a long while. When word had spread that she was a widow whose husband had suffered a terrible death in the wars, most let her be out of respect for the dead. The people in Dunlogh were very spiritual, and most honored her late husband's position. And that hadn't bothered her one bit. His flattery, no matter how undeserved, was welcome. "They come every few days to help, and most barter with me. They help me, and I in turn help with injuries, healing herbs, or help their wives with the birthing of their babes."

"You seem very happy here." Marek took a piece of the hare and helped her add the chunks of meat to the already simmering stew.

"I am happy." *Now that you're here.* She looked up at him, at those piercing eyes, already lost in their depths.

"I want to be what makes you happy," he whispered, cupping her chin with his palm.

She closed her eyes and tilted her mouth toward his but pulled back when Talon returned with Rufus at his heels.

"Is it ready yet?" the boy chirped, peeking into the pot. "I'm half starved!"

L unch had been a welcome rarity, although Brynn couldn't help but feel a tinge of guilt with eating the hare she had despised for so long. She was sad to see his antics come to an abrupt end but grateful her herbs might now have a starting chance at life. A few hired hands arrived shortly thereafter to see to her needs — the stables needed cleaning and the horses readied for her journey with Talon to Kaius.

Abby was to stay behind to manage the property in her absence. Niall, the huntsman, would be accompanying them on the day's journey to the games and act as escort. Brynn stood in the entrance to the drive, watching the flurry of people scurry about the cottage. "Remember, Miss Claire should be stopping by to pick up the basket of lavender and oats for her daughter. I placed them on the shelf in the garden room. Oh, and don't forget to pay Murray when he drops off the chickens."

"Stop this fretting, child, I have everything under control. Enjoy yourself at the games." Abby squeezed Brynn's shoulders tightly. "Ask him to go," she whispered while hugging Brynn close. "He doesn't have the courage to ask."

"Neither do I," Brynn mumbled in reply, hoping Abby didn't hear the words. Would this awkwardness ever come to an end?

"Mum, I'm set to go! I gave Niall my satchel, and my horse is ready." A towering brown mare followed the small boy, reluctantly allowing herself to be tugged from the comfort of the stable. Rufus obediently trotted next to his master.

"Talon, I told you Rufus cannot come. The journey is too far and he might get hurt or lost."

The boy crossed his arms and pouted his bottom lip.

"You might ask your da if he would like to go instead." An easy escape from a torturous position.

The boy's eyes lit. "May I?"

"Mmm-hmm. He's by the spring, I believe. Hurry now, we haven't much time." Brynn took hold of Talon's mount and fussed with the bags, triple checking that the straps were secure on the saddle and that the bridle was clean and the horse's feet were clear of stones, trying to think of anything to keep her mind from worrying about the decision.

A horse snorted from behind, and she turned toward it. Marek sat with Talon on his stunning mount, loping toward the traveling party in long beautiful strides. Envy swelled in her chest. She would pay nearly anything to have a stallion of that quality in her breeding herd.

"I hear we are to compete in some games?" Marek flashed a wide — hairless — grin.

"Only if you so wish to." Brynn fumbled with a bag that needed no attention, returning to the horse in front of her. She hoped he couldn't see the fire burning her cheeks.

"Who is this?" Niall questioned, suddenly appearing. His gaze wary, he took a protective stance in front of Brynn.

Niall was a large man, strong and thick. He was tall, older, but pleasing enough to the eyes. His yellow hair, peppered with flecks of white, caught the light under the brightness of the morning sun.

"Niall, this is my da!" Talon answered as Marek lowered him to the ground.

The man's eyes narrowed and flashed to Brynn. Confusion seeped from his body. "Mistress Coinnich, how can this be? You yourself said your husband is dead and left ye a widow."

"Niall, let me explain—" she muttered, but was interrupted by a hearty belly laugh. "You find this amusing, do you?" She scowled at Marek.

"I am very much alive, despite the rumors of my tragic death. It was very surprising, was it not, *Mistress Coinnich*?"

"Very surprising, indeed," she said between clenched teeth.

"He will be joining us, then?" Niall asked, still eyeing the disrupter.

"I wouldn't miss this, even if you bound me to a pig pole."

"I could arrange it," Niall sneered before helping Brynn to mount.

"Give it a go, old man."

"Let us not fight like children," Brynn scolded, giving them both a warning glance. "You are grown men — act like it." She reined in her mount, made sure Talon was set, then turned her horse in the direction of travel.

"Would you like me to ride beside you?" Niall asked her, clearly concerned for her safety.

"That won't be necessary, Niall, I will ride beside my *wife*. I'm sure Talon would love to tell you all about my arrival, right, Talon?" Marek urged his horse closer to Brynn's.

She sighed, annoyed by his blatant jealousy. It dripped from his tongue like a dog hungry for meat. "Be nice. He is only looking out for my wellbeing."

"It is not required."

She glanced back at Niall, who was listening to Talon spew long sentences several paces behind, before continuing, "Just because you show up here unannounced and force yourself back into our lives does not give you allowance to behave like that. We have been living quite contentedly without you — you don't have the right to just... take over."

His jaw twitched, but Marek didn't reply.

"Please," she whispered, her eyes pleading. "Please do not ruin this for me." Visions of the truth revealed flashed through her mind — her bastard child's father arriving to lay claim to her fortune, which was based solely on lies. That wouldn't sit well with the people of Dunlogh.

"You haven't exactly told me to leave, have you? We will talk about it later," he grumbled.

They rode for hours without so much as a word. The silence ate at her insides. Talon happily chatted with Niall about every possible story his young mind could recollect about his father. Most were misconstrued and intertwined within one another, but Marek seemed content to listen to them from a child's perspective. Apparently, Marek had felled seventeen men with one solid swoop of his sword, saving his mother from the death grip of a giant ready to eat her alive. Brynn asked Marek how he fared during that particular battle, as it sounded as though it would have been quite entertaining to participate in.

"What was I supposed to tell them?" she told him, unable to withstand the awkwardness between them any longer. "Hello, I'm Brynn from the Engel manor of Galhaven and this is my bastard Archaean child and we would like to buy this property with this stolen money I'm giving you. Or how about... I have just escaped from an Engel encampment ruled by Lord Westmore, and I was his favorite you know, but I am ripe with my Archaean lover's child, so I need to lie about my identity so I don't bring on the downfall of the Archaean highlands. I'm sorry if it upsets you, Marek, that I told such a terrible lie to protect your child."

"Well, when you word it like that..." A small smirk formed on his mouth. "But why *my* name? Why did not you just... give a false one? Cut all ties with your past and start anew?"

"Well..." She paused. "Yours was the only one I knew. And every day I would have had to live knowing my son would never have known his father's real name. How could I look at my boy and lie when I saw his father staring back at me?

He smiled that amazingly beautiful boyish lopsided grin at her then, the one she had always dreamed about. "I don't mind. Honestly, it's quite satisfying you would choose my name."

"So I became the widowed mistress Brynn Coinnich of Cinn Tàile, whose husband left her a rather *large* sum of money when he died in battle."

"A widow no longer," he added, his thoughts quickly moving on. "Who is this Niall fellow? He seems quite... fond of you."

"Oh, stop. He is not. He is my huntsman only."

"He has eyes for you, Brynn. Any man with a cock between his legs can see that."

"Why, I believe you are jealous, Marek. Is it not possible someone other than you could possibly show affection toward me? He does not, mind you. He is married and leaves his children with their mother in order to provide an escort for me."

"Do not play the fool and think just because a man is married he doesn't want your body. We both know the truth of that. You could have just asked me to escort you."

"You weren't exactly here then, Marek," she replied, her voice soft. The conversation had quickly become uncomfortable.

"Well, if he should as much as lay a hand on you, I'm ripping him in two."

Marek's words left her plenty to ponder during the remainder of the trip south. She hadn't given much thought to the men she employed. After Marek, no one had ever again held her heart, so she'd foolishly thought the days of men doting on her had come to an end. She hadn't stepped foot in a tavern in years and no longer needed to flaunt her body to earn a night's meal. Had she been blindly overlooking such things? Did Niall now feel threatened with Marek's sudden appearance as her husband? No, Marek was just playing the rival fool. He had always been the jealous kind. That trait hadn't faded one bit during her absence. Perhaps it had only intensified it.

K aius was crowded and the inn overflowing as the hour was late when they finally arrived. Joyous festivities still flooded the streets well into the night with dancing, loud music, and intoxicated visitors. With so much war surrounding the country, the chance to celebrate was a welcome relief. Brynn waited outside the inn while Marek saw to the rooms. Talon slept peacefully in her arms, unaware of the chaos surrounding him.

"There are no rooms here." Marek returned, a deep frown creasing his jawline. "The innkeeper said to try the Stoneclave just up the way." He mounted his horse and reined him away from the bustle of the Kaius Inn, clearing a path for the others to follow. They found the next inn easily enough — it was just as crowded as the first one and filled with drunkards as well. "I'll be but a moment," he told Brynn when she covered a yawn.

She readjusted Talon in her arms and feigned a smile.

S eeking out the innkeeper, Marek elbowed his way through the entrance, feeling ill at ease. Armed guards lined the walls and corners. Whores all but fornicating with the players smothered crowded gambling tables.

"Can I offer you a drink, handsome?" cooed a seductive female from behind the bar.

He turned to face the woman. She was tall and willowy with hair like fire and eyes like liquid emeralds. The woman leaned over the bar and propped herself up on an elbow, enhancing the plummeting neckline of her bodice.

"No, I need a room."

"Mmm, so bold," she purred, slightly parting her lips with her tongue. She reached toward him, removed a curly lock from his eyes, and tucked it gently behind his ear, letting her fingers linger against his skin as they made their way down to his chin.

Marek clenched his fists, trying his damnedest to keep his temper under control. He wasn't in the mood for this game. "Do you have any available rooms?" he growled.

"For a handsome man like you, I would give you my own, if you don't mind sharing." The woman pressed her palm against his chest, tracing the outline of his muscles with the tip of her finger. "So delicious. I could do amazing things for you. All you need to do is lie there."

"Woman..." he threatened, his voice sharp and clear. "If you touch me one more time, I swear to the gods I will carve you in two right here on this bar."

The redhead pouted. "The last room upstairs at the end of the hall — you should find it... adequate. 'Tis three silver a night."

He dug through his pouch, found the coins, and clunked them to the bar. "Thank you." He could barely spit at her, for his jaw clenched just as tight as his fists. Marek ducked back through the doorway to Brynn.

"Are you all right?" she asked him.

"There is one room available, but it's not the best of places." He took the sleeping Talon from Brynn's arms. "We will have to share and find another place to stay tomorrow."

"I shall stay in the stable with the horses, if that is all right with my mistress," Niall replied. "With this many people, there are bound to be thieves lurking in every corner."

"Thank you, Niall." Brynn smiled, dismounting. "If you could help with the supplies, I would be forever grateful."

"Of course."

"The room is upstairs, the last one at the end of the hall. Come, Brynn." Marek adjusted Talon so his head cradled in the crook of his neck. He grabbed one of his saddlebags with a free hand and braved the entrance to the inn once again.

He kept to the wall as they passed through, pressing the boy firmly against his chest. It seemed though every cutthroat, thieving, kill-you-for-your-boots highlander chose the Stoneclave to philander in. No sooner had he made it to the stairs when Niall appeared, protecting them from behind. He carried several saddlebags over his shoulders and glared, intimidating anyone they happened to encounter by sheer size alone.

Marek kicked open the door, startling the mostly naked man and the bar wench he was trying unsuccessfully to debauch.

"What in hell?" The man cursed, rising from the bed in a flurry of skirts, blankets, and bed linens.

"*Out.*"

"Just who do you—?"

Marek's eyes tunneled and his fingers noticeably flexed over the handle of his dagger.

"Was just on me way out now," the man muttered, pulling up his trousers while teetering toward the door.

"Don't forget your whore."

"Oh, certainly. Margaret," the evicted squatter snapped. The woman covered her exposed breasts with her arm and scampered after him.

Marek shooed Brynn inside. He dug through a bag for blankets, using them to fashion a makeshift bed in the corner for Talon. "Well, you can have the bed, and I will take the floor. Are you hungry? Can I get you anything?" He clasped his hands together. "You need your privacy. Right. I shall leave. I... oh, hell." Marek rubbed his nape and turned on his heels, exiting the room.

S he watched him leave, puzzled by his sudden act of propriety. She remembered a time when he teased her with his tunic, hoping for a chance to see her without clothes. Did he no longer find her attractive? They had made love — conceived a child together. Perhaps those days were no more.

Taking the least amount of the grimy bed linens possible in her fingers she inched them from the bed and dragged them across the floor, leaving them in a heap behind the door. She had been spoiled these past few years living quietly in her cottage and away from the bawdy lifestyle of the typical tavern. She had almost forgotten how crude and vile they were. And dirty. Disgustingly dirty. She was ever so thankful Abby had ordered she bring clean blankets with her for the trip. Unfolding a few from her bag, she spread them on the bed and changed into her nightclothes. She paced the floor, unsure as to whether or not she should climb into the bed or wait for Marek to return. She brought her palm to her lips to stifle a yawn. Honestly, why should she wait up for him? She wasn't his keeper. He was a grown man. He could do as he pleased. Confused and tired, she put out the oil lamp and climbed into the bed.

Her eyes were closed for only a few moments before the hinges creaked and the lock bolted in place across the door. She heard the clunk of boots being kicked into a corner and the shuffling of cloth on the floor. He exhaled, long and slow, breaking the monotony of the silence that seemed to smother her in the tiny, humid room. She focused on his breathing, praying the rhythmic tune would lull her to sleep.

They had the opposite effect. Those long, slow breaths made her wish they were against her skin, caressing her in a way only he could. She longed for his touch, the comfort of his presence next to her. Her skin turned to goose flesh beneath her nightclothes. She had been alone for far too long.

M arek rid the blanket from his body, kicking it aside with his feet. The room was hotter than hell and suffocating. She was still awake, and he guessed she found sleep as elusive as he did. She was so close but so untouchable. He could smell the sweet perfume of her sun-drenched hair, hear the crispness of her nightgown crinkle as her chest rose and fell with each forced breath drawn. A war between good and evil battled in silent waves inside him. Curse the gods — what he wouldn't give to slide in beside her and remove that gown from her luscious skin and taste every inch of it. Every fecking inch of it.

His erection grew hard beneath his pants, and he forced himself to think of anything else.

Swords. Staffs.

War. *Women.*

Lips. *Nipples.*

*Sex.*

"B rynn, wake up." He shook her shoulder, but she wouldn't break from the fretful dream keeping her locked in its grasp. "Brynn." Marek shook her again, and a small cry left her lips. Her eyes were wet from tears unknowingly wept, and he smoothed them from her cheeks.

"Please, no, don't take him from me," she murmured as her face wrinkled in pain. "No!" She shot upright, nearly knocking Marek to the floor.

He took her by the arms and searched her vacant eyes. "Brynn?"

She trembled beneath his hands. Her eyes fluttered, returning to consciousness. "Just a dream," she whispered. "Just a dream, just a dream, just a dream."

"Shh," Marek soothed, pushing the hair from her face. "Aye, just a dream. I'm here — no harm will befall you, love."

"Where is Talon?" Brynn scanned the room in a frantic flail of limbs.

"He is still sleeping. I checked on him just moments ago."

"Oh."

"What was your dream?"

266

"Ravens," she muttered. "It was about ravens. I must get ready." She pushed his hands away.

Marek grabbed her shoulders. "Brynn. Talk to me. Tell me about these dreams. Are they... visions?"

She hesitated, but answered. "Yes. The ravens, they deliver messages to me in my dreams. They..." She closed her eyes momentarily. "Please do not think me mad."

"Why would I ever think that? I do not know how, or why, but you were given to me for a reason, and I trust you like no other."

"Marek, I believe I know how to stop this war. It's my destiny, and solely the reason why I was born. My mother was killed for it, and I will die for it. I see no other way. The ravens, they are trying to tell me what to do, but I just don't understand. My books, the ancients spoke of a prophecy, and I... I think that prophecy is—"

"Is you."

She raised her eyes to meet his. "Yes."

He nodded. "The winter child." Marek pulled her in close and nestled her head under his chin.

Brynn dressed, gathered her supplies, and made her way to the stables to ready Talon for the day's events while Marek sought out Niall. He returned shortly thereafter, food in one hand and towing Niall with the other.

"Niall?" Brynn questioned upon seeing a rather ragged-looking version of her huntsman.

"Shh, don't speak too loudly, Brynn, your sweetums is still mostly drunk." Marek snickered, clearly enjoying the headache Niall was sure to have.

"How do you expect to compete like that, Niall? You will find yourself in my tent with both of your arms cut off, and what will that accomplish? You cannot compete with nubs." Brynn shook her head in disgust and thrust her bags toward the swaying man. "Do you think you can manage to stay atop your horse and accompany me as my escort, or would you rather sleep off your drink here?"

"I'll be fine with a bit of fresh air, mistress," Niall reassured. "I will wait outside if that pleases you."

"Aye, go." She dismissed him with a wave before pressing a palm to her forehead.

Marek's scowl morphed into a wide grin when Talon rounded the threshold of an empty stall door. He knelt beside the boy and offered him the package he'd been carrying. "I brought you a bit to eat. A champion needs a fine breakfast to keep his body fit for fighting. Do you remember what I taught you?"

"Aye." The boy nodded, picking a stray piece of straw from his tunic. "I shall make you proud, Da."

"I would never doubt it, Talon." Marek gave the boy a playful cuff and handed over breakfast.

"Will you compete today, Da?" Talon shoved a roll into his mouth, biting off more than he could possibly chew.

"I would be most content just watching you today, I think."

Brynn found her medical tent easily enough — men formed a line by the entrance with injuries needing attention, and the games had yet to begin. Both ends of the tent were open, allowing a cool breeze to flow through. Three strategically placed examination tables circled a supply table on which she set her herbalist kit, fresh bandages, and needles and thread should the need for them arise.

The men in line paid their coin, and she saw to their minor injuries — all of them from the previous night's tavern brawl. The rules of the games stated each contestant must be fit to compete, so all prior injuries must be tended. She mended a few gashes, set a dislocated shoulder with the help of a brawny lad, and sent them all on their way.

Curious to know which events her son had entered and hoping to watch a few, Brynn cleaned up the remnants of a few unused bandages and then ventured from the tent. She wandered through the crowds, content to hum along with the familiar tunes of the pipers playing in the distance. The scent of a roasting pig nearby teased her insides, and she realized she had skipped breakfast. With the coin from her pocket, she paid the nearest vendor for mulled wine and a meat pie to munch on while she searched for Talon. Brynn found him shortly thereafter, waiting for his chance to compete in the sword arena. Talon paced the ground, tossing his wooden sword from palm to palm.

"He's nervous." The familiar smooth lilt made her heart skip, just for a moment.

Brynn turned from the split rail fence she leaned against to greet Marek with a smile. "He has waited so long for this. I would hate to see him fail because of his nerves."

Marek made himself comfortable against the fence beside Brynn and chuckled as Talon tossed his sword, missed, and stumbled into the boy behind him. "I'm beginning to think he gets his clumsiness from you though, aye? He certainly doesn't get it from me."

"That boy has been training for the games since he could pick up a practice sword. Granted, he spars mostly against the hound..."

"He hasn't tossed himself from any cliffs yet, so I think he will be all right." Marek took a jab at Brynn's own unfortunate blunder.

She slapped his arm in playful protest. "I don't see you out there competing, so leave the boy be."

"I would much rather be at your side, if it pleases you." Marek tucked a stray curl behind her ear.

The slight touch of his finger brushing the shell of her ear sent her heart aflutter. "It would please me very much."

The crowd soon hushed so the competitors could hear the rules. The young lads' competition would be until first strike to the lower body only. The prize — a real sword. The presenter then went on to explain the rules for the men's sword competition. Matches would be won by submission, or the inability to defend one's self. Swords were to be blunted and any blows to the head would result in immediate disqualification. "Those wishing to compete should go to the entry tent as the competition is about to begin," the presenter told the crowd.

"And the prize?" someone questioned.

"Ahh," crooned the presenter. "The best prize of all. The last man standing will win a kiss from any eligible maiden here at the games!"

A gasp erupted from the crowd, most of the noise originating from the mouths of the women.

Marek turned toward Brynn and cocked an eyebrow.

An all-out protest from the women around her made her smile. "Now don't you be getting any silly ideas in your head." Brynn bit her bottom lip to keep from laughing.

"I suppose I *have* to enter now, aye?" Marek let out an unusually long sigh and brushed his palm over his hair as if it were the most difficult decision he would ever make. "It seems to be the only way I'm ever going to be able to taste those sweet lips."

"Marek… don't be a fool."

"Don't chide me, woman. I'll do whatever it takes."

"Then why will you not just kiss me now?"

"Ahh, but then it would be stolen, and not earned. A pity kiss."

Brynn rolled her eyes and planted her hands on her hips. "You don't even have armor."

"Well then, my love, I suppose that means I mustn't lose." He winked, slapped her backside, then left with pure determination set in his eyes.

Marek jogged off toward the entry tent, leaving Brynn to ponder what had transpired between them. Had she somehow just accepted she would be his prize should he win? He had gone mad. She had seen the damage even a blunted sword could do to unprotected flesh. One hard hit and Marek's ribs would shatter. She forced the thought from her mind and turned her focus to her son.

Talon patiently waited his turn, cheering on his friends and promptly covering his eyes when the loser of the present match connected with the winner's fist, his lip cracking and blood splattering in the direction of the crowd. Talon's eyes grew wide and his little fingers moved to cover his mouth. Marek would soon return to coach him through his first-ever match — the boy would fare well. She shouldn't worry — but she couldn't watch, either. She could only pray he wouldn't need her healing ministrations.

Brynn returned to her tent, a line of injuries surprisingly absent. Without patients to tend, she prepared her things for the afternoon that lay ahead. The sword competition would be starting soon — the line would be sure to grow. Archaeans were brutal, even during matches for sport. They had everything to prove to those around them. Position, strength, honor — all things Marek held to the highest regard. He would die trying to prove himself, and that scared Brynn to her very core.

Her thoughts of Marek were pushed aside when a ragtag group of beaten competitors tumbled into her tent, many with significant bruising and bleeding head wounds.

"It seems we're all playing by the rules then?" Brynn muttered, applying a fresh bandage to a gash along a man's temple.

"Gah. No one ever follows the rules. 'Tis the big one, mistress — the one with the inking on his back. Try as we might, no man can best him. He has the look of the devil in his eyes, that one. Determined to win."

"Or die trying. Press here." Brynn motioned for her patient to hold the bandage while she gathered linens to dress the wound. She ripped them into strips and tied one securely around the man's forehead. "All set. Now go get yourself a drink, and you can pay Gràinne on your way out." Brynn gave the man a parting smile before turning her attention to the next examination table. The assistant assigned to Brynn, Gràinne, took the payment and showed the man out, only to usher in the next in line to take his place.

"Hello, Mum."

A discouraged voice filled her ears. Talon had returned. "So soon?" Brynn stuck out her bottom lip in a playful pout.

"I won my first match, but I lost in the second. I think I need to work on growing first. I was smaller than the other lads."

"Are you hurt, son?"

"Just me pride, 'tis all."

"It was your first time, Talon. There will be other games to compete in."

"Aye, I know. I just wish Da could have been there to guide me." Talon plopped to the ground near the center of the tent and helped himself to the few morsels leftover from Brynn's noontime meal.

"Was he not there?"

"No, he is too busy beating the men, Mum. You should see him!" The boy jumped to his feet with a sudden vigor and swung his wooden sword in wild arcs around the tent, battling imaginary enemies. "He is the greatest warrior I have ever seen!"

"Gràinne, do you think you shall be all right here for a few moments? I need some fresh air." Brynn finished inspecting a bruise on her current patient, decided nothing was broken, and shooed him from the tent.

"Just fine, mistress. Take all the time you need." Gràinne formed a smile. "It seems to be slowing down now."

"Thank you," Brynn replied, dodging Talon's swinging sword before grasping him by the arm. "Let us go watch your da for a while, shall we?"

"Aye, Mum! I want to see him beat that man to a bloody—"

"Talon, that is quite enough."

Seeing a group of young lads, Talon slipped away, leaving her to push her way to the front of the crowd.

Finding Marek was simple enough — Brynn only had to follow the line of ogling women lining the arena fence.

Strangers scowled when she elbowed them from her path, but she was determined to see how he fared. At last, she broke through the sea of bodies and took up residence against a fence rail.

Marek hunched over a stool near the far corner of the arena, clutching a dirty rag to the back of his skull. His head hung between his knees. Patches of gritty dirt mingled with a fine coat of sweat, creating a mud-caked layer of grime. It covered his bare chest, back, and arms. He must have taken his fair share of falls, perhaps even a few too many blows, and he had done it for her. And for what — to prove himself worthy? She should have just given him a kiss and been done with it. As if he'd heard her thoughts, his head ascended from its defeated position and turned toward her. He smiled that devious smile, bringing to the forefront of her mind the many sinful things he could do with that mouth.

---

B roken and bleeding, Marek found the strength to continue. She was there now, his pain wouldn't be all for naught. He suppressed the aching in his skull and downed a gulp of ale before tossing the rag aside to stretch his sword arm. The gods shined upon him — if he won the next two matches, he would be the victor. The amount of ale the men consumed beforehand might help his chances, as well. The current match was won by a mere submission, so Marek prepared the best he could. His opponent was nearly a boot-length taller and twice as big around the middle. Marek had watched the man carefully during previous matches; the way he moved, how he swung his sword. He was slow but powerful.

Marek stepped into the arena. "We can do this two ways, friend. My way or the easy way. The choice is yours." He circled his opponent with wide strides, adjusting the grip on the hilt of his sword. The large man standing in front of him wore leather-plated armor and carried a wooden shield over his forearm... two things Marek wished he had thought to bring. Had he known this was what he must do to gain favor with his lady, he might not have come at all.

"And what might your way be?" the man sneered, countering Marek's steps.

"You withdraw, and I will not beat you into submission."

"And why should I do that?"

"Because I'm tired," Marek answered honestly.

The man laughed and swung a testing strike in Marek's direction.

He easily dodged the blow. "I give you fair warning. You will feel the pain."

"Do your worst, highlander."

Marek shrugged. "We don't have time for my worst." He brought about his sword with a flick of his wrist and dodged an oncoming swing by tucking up his knees and rolling under the unrestrained arc of his opponent's blade. Marek jumped to his feet behind the burly man and brought a boot up to his backside, knocking him to his knees.

Making quick use of his opponent's vulnerable state, Marek stepped to the side, balled his fist, and connected it with the man's jaw. He watched two eyelids flutter, the jaw slacken, and shoulders drop in defeat. The opponent slumped to the ground, unconscious. "I told you I was tired." Marek wiped the perspiration from his brow and returned to his stool to await his next match.

The following battle droned on. Both men were equally matched and Marek would battle the victor. He studied each carefully, marking their movements in his mind. It had been many years since Marek had tested his worthiness on a battlefield against such experienced warriors. He could only pray those skills ingrained as a boy wouldn't fail him — not today.

Without so much as a warning, the winning blow was delivered when the victor spotted a vulnerability on his opponent's side and swung full force against the loser's chest, knocking the breath from his lungs. The man submitted in defeat. The victor tossed up his arms and let out a ferocious roar to the crowd. They cheered in response.

"Would ye like to use my shield, lad?" A stranger approached, offering a simple wooden shield that had seen better days.

Marek released a long, slow breath. He certainly could use the protection. *No*, he must do this by himself, with no shield nor armor. He'd made it this far — he could finish it on his own. "Thank you, my friend, but I have everything to prove. You understand?"

The aging man grinned. "Aye, I do. And when he beats the piss out of ye, you can take a visit to the healer's tent. She fixed me up good, you see?" He held up his limb to show off a clean bandage wrapped around his upper arm. "She's quite the pretty little thing, too. Nice to look at."

"So I've heard."

M arek entered the arena, his head held high. He radiated confidence. The sun glinted off his chest, slick with perspiration from the afternoon heat. His movements were an intricate dance, choreographed by instinct alone. A flame ignited inside her. Many nights she had welcomed sleep and the dreams that followed. The image of his nakedness pressed against her own still lived vividly in her mind. Brynn stared at the god-like statue before her, securing the bindings around his blade. His lips formed inaudible words. He brought the weapon to his lips and gave it's center a gentle kiss. A breath caught in her throat.

Marek outstretched his sword, holding it horizontal to the ground. He pointed the tip of the blade at his intended prize — her. By the gods, he had to fight — he must win. She wanted to be claimed... be his.

T he men circled, nipping at one another's heels — testing, each sizing up the other man. Marek's opponent, Donnell, showed no hesitation and attacked within moments of their fetid dance. Marek rolled his shoulder back, turning his body away from the strike in one fluid motion, and countered with his blade. He narrowly missed his intended target, striking a shield instead.

Donnell rebounded with the strength of a bear.

Marek lost his footing while blocking the ferocious swing and tumbled to the ground. The vibrations of steel hitting steel still echoed throughout Marek.

Donnell let out a ferocious yell, bringing his boot to Marek's chest. Marek rolled, but Donnell caught a bit of flesh on Marek's side. A trickle of warmth crept along his skin.

Marek shook off his nervousness. Donnell's presence was intimidating, but he couldn't let that best him. He could beat the halfwit — he only needed to find his thoughts. He had battled far greater enemies and slaughtered more men than he cared to think about. Winning this mock battle should be the easiest fight of his life.

Marek returned to his feet, adjusted his grip on the hilt of his sword, and focused his thoughts on his opponent. When Donnell moved, Marek anticipated the attack and executed a string of unwavering blows. A fury of raw power flowed through his veins — Marek only needed to unleash it.

B rynn dug her nails into the rail — her heart beat in an unsteady rhythm as she watched the battle unfold before her. The beginning of the match had been questionable, but Marek seemed to have found his stride. His movements powerful, his muscles fully flexed — he looked magnificent.

A woman standing next to Brynn licked her lips. "Mmm... delicious."

"Which one? The fat one or the piece of meat I want to rip my teeth into?" another woman replied, elbowing her companion in the ribs.

"I wonder if the rest of him is as tasty as the top half."

The women giggled and continued their gawking while the match continued, and Brynn did her best to ignore them.

"Has he won yet?" A golden-haired head popped up between the fence rails.

Brynn ruffled the unruly locks of yellow curls as Talon contorted his body through the rails to get a better view. "No, not yet. He's still fighting but doing a fine job in the arena."

Again, the women chimed in with their lustful comments. "Aye, and I bet he would do a fine job in my bed, too!"

"Perhaps he will pick you as the prize?" one said.

Talon beamed a toothy grin at the women. "That's me da. He will pick my mum." He pointed a finger at Brynn as though no other option existed.

Brynn watched two sets of eyes widen and two sets of cheeks flush a deep, rosy hue. She turned her back on the women, biting the inside of her cheek to keep them from seeing her own color of blush. A smug smile contorted her mouth as she concentrated her thoughts on the battle raging on before her.

Brynn didn't quite catch the sequence of events that brought the match to an abrupt halt, but Donnell was sprawled with his face smashed into the boot-trodden dirt. The victor, Marek, fell to his knees in relief. The hilt of his sword rolled from his fingers to the ground.

"He's done it. He's won." Brynn muttered the words into the palm she pressed against her lips.

The crowd roared in celebration. A few eliminated competitors rushed the arena to help Marek to his feet, and several attended to the defeated Donnell.

"The new champion of the sword!" The presenter of the games raised Marek's arm in triumph. "You, sir, may now pick your much-deserved prize." The man grinned, wide and toothy, insinuating more than his words implied.

Marek strolled around the arena, calm and casual as if surveying a herd of farm animals for purchase, toying with the women. They pressed their bodies against one another in hopes of being chosen, but soon realized he played them as fools — the man had eyes for only one. He stopped his saunter near the center of the arena and motioned the presenter to his side. "I have chosen."

"And who might the lucky lass be?"

Brynn stood on the lowest rail of the fence, her arms clinging to one of the longer vertical support beams. A tepid wind swirled her curls with each little gust, and a soft smile formed on the lips he had waited years to kiss. Marek raised a finger and pointed to the beauty in the blue dress.

"The widow?"

"She is no widow… she is my wife." His steps fell with purpose.

"What is this nonsense you speak of?" Brynn gazed down at him, her eyes searing a hole through the very heart she held.

"Do not contradict me, woman." His lips twitched, exposing the beginnings of a grin. She would be his, whether she agreed to it or not.

"You speak the truth?" Her breathless whisper barely audible.

"Aye, if you'll have me." Marek met her bewildered gaze. Brynn stared back at him. She opened her mouth to speak, but no words left her lips. The silence was almost unbearable.

"Well?" she questioned, raising an eyebrow. "Are ye goin' to kiss me, or not, husband?"

In one fluid burst of movement, Marek planted a boot on the fence, hoisting himself level with her. The kiss that followed nearly knocked him to his backside. Her fingers laced through his hair — rough and wanting. She pulled his lips to hers and kissed him like she meant it… every heavy breath, every flick of her tongue against his. The crowd cheered.

His need for her grew to a feverish pitch.

Without the slightest warning, Brynn broke the kiss.

Marek sucked in a ragged breath, willing himself to suppress his urge to ravish her on the very fence keeping them apart. He pressed his forehead to hers. The sweet smell of her breath on his lips intoxicated his mind.

"I must go." The words escaped her lips on a restrained pant.

"Damn it, not again." Marek refused to loosen his grip on her.

"I must return to my tent. I have been away far too long. Poor Gràinne, I left her alone to clean up your mess." Brynn turned her face from Marek, a sudden shyness consuming her. "Besides, I fear we shall produce quite the show for our audience if I continue to kiss you like that."

Marek chuckled. "Very true."

# *Chapter Twenty-Four*

## LIE TO ME

"Y ou will be fine." Brynn rolled her eyes. "Go. Drink. Dance. Leave my tent."

"But, but... I think I am losing too much blood," the patient stammered, searching for an excuse to stay in the medical tent.

"*Maurice*. You are *not* bleeding. 'Tis but a scratch, honestly. The way you are carrying on, one would think you were at death's door. Now off with you." Taking him by the arm, Brynn led him to the exit, urging him to use it.

"Are you sure, mistress?" Maurice paused. "I can come back later so you might redress it."

"Maurice, if I see you back in my tent this day, rest assured you *will* be bleeding by the time you leave it."

The man's eyes bulged, and he promptly left.

Gràinne giggled from across the tent. "Methinks you have a few admirers, mistress."

"Aye, such foolishness. If I didn't know any better, I would swear these men are injuring themselves on purpose." A frown tugged at her mouth as Brynn tinkered with her supplies, entertaining the thought.

"Would you like me to gather the supplies?"

"I can manage this, Gràinne. Take your wages for today and go enjoy yourself. I will see you in the morning."

The girl, tall and willowy, thanked Brynn for the coin, tidied her workstation, and scurried from the tent.

"Do you have time for one more, mistress?" Marek stood just outside the entrance, waiting.

The smooth tone of his voice tickled her insides. She finished rearranging her tools then sauntered in his direction. Placing her hand on her hip, she said, "I suppose I could make time for the champion of the sword. Do you have injuries that need tending?"

"Hmm." He strolled into the depths of the tent.

"Perhaps I could find a few."

Brynn bit her bottom lip to keep from grinning like a child.

"But then again," he added, taking a step closer, "I believe that is your task, is it not?"

She waved him closer. "Come, let me take a look."

Marek closed the gap between them in two long strides. Standing in front of the examination table, he placed his hands behind him on the flat wooden surface and hoisted himself up to a sitting position. He removed his tunic in one fluid motion, discarding it on the table next to him. "You are welcome to look, my love. I believe we've had this conversation before."

Brynn filled a bowl with water and found a few clean rags. Even from a distance, she could feel Marek's gaze burning into her backside. She found the courage to return to him and did her best to push the impure thoughts bubbling to the surface from her mind. She wet a rag, wrung out the excess, and gingerly pressed it to his chest. A trickle of water etched a path across his ribcage and arched around the sharp edges of his abdomen before being devoured by the hem of his trousers. She dragged the cloth down the length of his torso, methodically washing away the smears of mud and sweat.

She stopped mid-swipe when his arms encircled her. His hands settled on the small of her back, pressing her closer. Fingers clenched the thin cloth of her dress, their tips digging into her flesh. Brynn sucked in a breath and held it when his legs spread, encouraging her to fall against him. A small cry escaped her lips. The cloth slipped from her fingers, all but forgotten.

His embrace wandered, caressing her with a brazen desire. Up her back, to her shoulders — his hands carved a path, settling along the roundness of her bottom. He squeezed, drew her to him, and pressed ever closer. His lips found the pulse on her neck and he flicked his tongue over it. His breath, warm and wet, lingered on her cheek.

Her thoughts spiraled into madness.

He tasted her, the salt from his skin clinging to her lips. His mouth explored the slight indentation of her collarbone, and he traced the delicate lines with his lips, murmuring incoherent words in his lyrical lilt. A thumb brushed over her nipple, leaving a tantalizing hardness in its wake. Marek gave the shell of Brynn's ear a playful nip before finding her lips. He parted them with his tongue, coaxing her, tempting her. Slow, deep kisses, his mouth reclaimed every part of her.

Brynn turned her face up to his, her palms aimlessly wandering in half-felt protest. She trembled beneath him — every deliberate touch set her insides on fire. Feelings she hadn't realized she was still capable of having only added to the sweet torture. Brynn buried her hands in his hair, urging him to continue his welcomed seduction. "More…" The word escaped on a whisper.

"I had forgotten just how delicious you are."

In a deliberate disruption, a stranger made his presence known by clearing his throat.

Marek's touch of pleasure turned protective in an instant. He stood, shielding his woman with his body. The sun cast a shadow over the imposing figure making it impossible to identify the man at first glance.

"Is this the healer's tent?" The man asked.

The grip on Brynn's arms tightened. Engel words. The words seemed so foreign — an echo of her past she'd nearly forgotten. Every ounce of pain, every night terror, every thought of death suddenly consumed her. The world slowly collapsed, constricting every breath. Hot tears stung her eyes.

Brynn peeked from behind her protector.

"*Michael?*"

"Is it truly you, my dear sister?" Michael let out a laugh. "I thought my eyes played cruel tricks at the arena, but yet, here you are, standing before me. All this time, I thought you dead."

"What are you doing this far north? Do you travel alone? Did you bring Marcus with you? How long have you been in the Highlands?" The Archaean words spewed from her mouth in excited tones until she realized Michael's contorted face was one of confusion.

Michael shuffled closer, his stance awkward and uncomfortable. "I'm sorry, I… I don't know the Archaean words you speak."

Marek brushed a fallen tear from Brynn's cheek. "I don't know why he's here," he whispered, "but we must be cautious. My instincts tell me this is wrong."

"Please, Marek. Help me speak to him." Brynn locked eyes with her warrior and didn't waver until she won the silent battle between them. She struggled for a translation. Had it really been that long? Had she forgotten the tongue of her birth so quickly — and so willingly? "Why is it that I cannot speak the words I learned as a child?"

"Just focus your mind and you will remember them."

Brynn took a deep breath, closed her eyes, and forced herself to remember. Memories she had suppressed long ago intruded her thoughts. A smiling, laughing, happy little girl chased boys in a field of green. Satin the color of the summer sky. A man crouching in a stable. Broken promises. Pain. Lies. A betrayal like no other.

Her eyes flashed open.

"Why are you here, Michael?" She stumbled over the words, but they were there. Brynn swallowed hard, forcing the lump in her throat to recede.

"I'm just passing through… a courier." He explained. "I heard of the games and thought I would enjoy the day. And then I saw you. I thought you were a ghost, standing there next to the arena. I had to see for myself if you were indeed… alive."

"Indeed I am."

"How — how are you? Are you well?"

"I'm well enough." *No thanks to you.*

"We should go, Brynn." Marek's voice cut the tension in the air like a freshly sharpened blade. "Talon."

"It was good to see you, Michael." Brynn managed a weak smile and gathered her things, a sickening feeling settling in her belly.

"Wait."

Brynn paused, even though Marek tugged at her hand.

"I have rented a cottage for the night not far from here. Join me for dinner. Stay the night if you like — there is plenty of room."

Brynn turned to Marek. "We do need a place to stay tonight. It would be safer than returning to the tavern," she told him.

After a silent deliberation, Marek tipped his head in approval.

"I will need to find Talon first." Brynn smiled at her brother, a glint of happiness shining through.

"Who is Talon?"

"He is my son." She answered with a pride only a mother could have.

Michael's brow narrowed, visibly stirred. "You have a child?" His reaction seemed more like a declaration than a question.

"Does this news upset you?"

"*No.*" Michael was quick to reply, perhaps with a bit too much haste. "I didn't know you were alive, let alone married." Michael's eyes drifted to Brynn's hand tightly engulfed by Marek's. "To *this* Archaean."

"Many things have changed, Michael." *Since you abandoned me and left me to die.*

"It isn't much, but there is a bed in the back and a loft for the boy, and it is quiet." Michael ushered Brynn into the modest cottage.

"And where will you be?" she questioned.

"I will take the cot next to the fireplace. I haven't been successful in the ways of sleep as of late."

Brynn chuckled. "I would have to say the same."

"The room is back here." Michael crossed the cottage to the single door and opened it. "You should find it comfortable enough. The boy—"

"Talon." Brynn corrected. "His name is Talon."

Something deep inside told her that Michael hadn't been expecting to learn she had a child.

"He will be all right in the loft?"

"He will stay with me." Marek appeared at the threshold, cradling his sleeping son. "He hasn't even stirred."

"He has had quite enough excitement today, with the tournament and meeting his uncle. Tuck him into bed, and I will see to him later." Brynn pulled back the coverlet before allowing Marek to place the armful of dangling limbs safely in bed.

Marek removed Talon's boots, kissed him on the forehead, and drew up the blanket tight under his chin.

"If you don't mind, Marek, I wish to speak to my brother alone. You're exhausted and need your rest. I'll be in shortly. You need not wait up for me." Brynn placed a palm on his cheek.

He took it, brought it to his lips, and kissed the tender skin just above the leather cuff she wore to cover the Engel mark etched in her skin. "Wake me when you return, my love."

Brynn met Michael out of doors. She wrapped her shawl around her shoulders to ward off the night's chill. "They are beautiful, are they not — the heavens?" She stared at the sky, dark as velvet, mesmerized by the stars flickering like tiny, shimmering gems.

Michael tilted his head to the darkness. "He truly loves you."

"Aye, he does."

"And do you love him?" Michael lowered his gaze to his sister. The moon cast harsh reflections on his skin, its paleness turning an ashen shade of gray.

Brynn inhaled a long, slow breath, held it, and then released it through her nose. "We both know you fill the time with frivolous words, Michael."

"I only seek conversation."

"You have never been a good liar."

Michael's sudden interest in the fraying fabric on the sleeve of his tunic gave him enough pause to choose his words carefully. "You know why I must do it, then?"

She spoke with a soft calm, her eyes never wavering from the night sky. "I do. I have seen it in my dreams. There is still time to choose a different path, 'tis why I'm here."

"You were always different, Brynn. You were never on the same path as the rest. There is a certain quality about you that mystifies, and it breaks my heart to have to do this. But I have no other choice. Had I known there would be a boy involved…" His words faded into the silence.

"I knew you would come. I just didn't realize how soon. I was hoping for a few more years before… How much longer do I have?" Wiping away the tears with her fingers, she pressed her palms to her face to cool her burning cheeks.

"They will be here soon."

A panic started to manifest itself inside her chest. Her heart beat in her throat, making each breath a strain. She wasn't ready. She hadn't had enough time to prepare. She hadn't foreseen this in her visions. Brynn shoved her fingers in her mouth and bit down just to keep from screaming. *Stay strong.* "Promise me this — promise me you will not harm my son." Brynn moved closer to Michael and forced him to meet her eyes. "*Michael.* Promise me this.*"

He couldn't ignore her insistent plea. "What would you have me do?"

"Hide him. Steal him away. Let his father take him home. You are obviously a man of great importance now — think of *something*. I would have expected this sort of thing from Father, but you… *you*, Michael? Never in my life would I have thought you—" She couldn't go on. Saying the words out loud would only intensify the pain. "I… I must go."

Michael hooked her arm with his as she walked past, sending her spinning about. "Brynn, don't act the fool."

"Do not fret, Michael. I have seen your death, and I will trust you no more."

T he paper in front of her was nearly impossible to see under the dim light of the single tapered candle sitting faithfully next to her on the desk. She feared she might set her hair on fire should she venture any closer. Brynn paused her fervid writing to rub the sleep from her eyes. Oblivion threatened to consume her, but she fought it, pushing her writing to the forefront of her mind. She must finish before dawn.

Checking her pages for the last time, Brynn sent up a silent prayer to the gods and wrapped the binding around the pages, securing the knowledge inside. She rose from the desk, found her satchel, and added the book to its contents. The ravens had finally come for her. Harbingers of death. Three would die before this war would end.

Brynn allowed her eyes to linger on the rise and fall of Marek's chest, her breaths falling in stride with his. Steady and rhythmic, it calmed her. The once-sharp edges of his mouth and jaw now lay slack and soft, lost in peaceful slumber. Removing her gown, Brynn crawled into the bed and settled in, cradled between her warrior and her son.

She kissed the back of Talon's head when he nuzzled in close. She breathed in his scent, the smell of soap still lingering in his hair from days gone by. Salty wetness rolled over her lips and down to her chin. It remained there long enough for another tear to join then plopped to the linen below.

Marek stirred behind her, his fingers finding a new resting place on the curve of her hip. He caressed the flatness of her belly before wrapping his arms around her torso and engulfing her with his warmth. He kissed the crook of her neck in a slumberous wake then soon drifted back to his dreams.

Her head fit perfectly under his chin, and she snuggled close, the thump of his heart beating a steady song in her ear. Brynn closed her eyes.

# Chapter Twenty-Five

## BETRAY ME

B rynn woke before dawn. She dressed in the dark, checked the position of her boot knife, and carefully removed Marek's weapons from the bedroom. Michael's absence was noted, his cot empty.

Trusting Michael wouldn't harm an unarmed man, she hid Marek's swords and daggers in the cluster of bushes lining the back of the cottage. Brynn knew full well the ramifications of Marek's temper and allowing him a weapon would only add to the chaos. A few small rolls of bread from the evening meal still sat on the small table, and Brynn took them, placing them in her satchel. Talon would need them.

She decided he would need to leave with her when the Engels arrived. Weighing the options, it seemed the lesser of two evils. Marek would need to ride on the wind to reach his brothers in time, and having Talon would only slow him down. Time was of the essence.

With the letter she had written tucked safely in the bodice of her chemise, Brynn slung the satchel containing her writings and precious books over her shoulder. She took a deep breath, gathering her strength and courage. She would need to rely on both when the Engels arrived.

**M**arek burst through the door, his trousers hanging loose about his hips, unfastened. He gripped the threshold like an imprisoned madman — spouting slanderous words at the band of horsemen surrounding his family. "You fecking son of a whore! I will kill you! Even if I have to do it with my bare hands, I will tear your beating heart from your chest!" His hands balled into tight fists, the knuckles turning a ghostly white against the redness of rage.

Brynn's wrist cuffs lay untied next to her feet, the mark of Westmore clearly visible. "Marek, please, calm yourself! It is your turn to trust me!" Her attempts to calm the situation were slowly turning against her. Brynn hugged Talon close to her side, keeping him away from the Engel soldiers encircling her. The boy couldn't understand the harsh Engel words and his frightened stance drew the mercenaries closer.

"He brought soldiers to kill us and you want me to fecking calm down?" Marek narrowed his glare on Michael. "Tell me, how much? What amount of silver could possibly tempt a brother enough to carry out his own sister's death warrant?"

Michael wouldn't meet Marek's eyes, nor would he answer the question.

"There will be no more killing!" Brynn huffed. "No one needs to die! Michael, bring me to Lord Westmore. I know that is what he truly desires, and I will go with you — willingly — if you promise me you will not harm my husband. You are a man of honor, Michael. There is no honor in slaying an unarmed man. He carries no weapon and therefore is of no threat. The bounty for my return will outweigh the price of his head by tenfold. Leave him be, take me and the boy with you, and no one, including your own men, will have to die here today."

Michael's jaw twitched — he contemplated her proposal.

"Brynn, what the *hell* are you doing?" Marek said.

"Keeping us alive," she answered.

"And if he follows?" Michael questioned.

"He will not follow," reassured Brynn, locking eyes with her warrior. "He will go home to his brothers."

The silence seemed to suck the breath from her chest. She prayed Michael would not make another foolish decision.

"Very well." Michael decided.

Brynn turned up her eyes to Michael, a slight pout curving her full lips. A single tear rolled down her cheek. "Allow me to say goodbye?"

Michael nodded, granting her temporary freedom from the Engel confinement. Taking Talon by the hand, she raced to her husband and wrapped her arms around his chest. She pressed her cheek against his skin, the pounding of his heart echoing in her ear. "Take the parchment from my hand," she whispered.

Marek brought his hands to meet hers, removed the small, rolled parcel from Brynn's fingers and cupped it securely in his palm. He grasped her wrists, brought them around to his chest and hugged her frame before kneeling low to say goodbye to Talon. "Take care of your mother while you are gone. You are going on an adventure, but I will meet up with you soon, aye?"

Talon nodded. "I will, Da."

"Such a good boy." Marek pulled his son in close and slipped the piece of parchment under the cuff of his own boot before standing to embrace his wife one final time.

Brynn drank in the color of his eyes. "Say you will come for me?"

"I will always come for you," he reassured, pressing his lips to her ear. "Even in death."

"Your swords are behind the cottage... in the bushes. You will need them after I am gone."

He brought his mouth to hers, bidding her farewell with one last kiss. With the salt from her tears still fresh on his tongue, he backed away, releasing his woman and son into the arms of his enemy.

Brynn mounted her horse, secured Talon in the saddle, and gathered up the reins. Four Engel soldiers closed in around her, leading her away.

Michael lingered behind with two of his men, blocking Marek's vision of her. "See that he does not follow." Michael instructed, circling his horse around Marek. "And be quick about it."

When Michael cantered away, Marek retreated into the cottage, barred the door and bolted to the back bedroom where he donned his tunic, fastened his trousers, and pulled the parchment from his boot. He tugged at the binding twine and unrolled the letter while the Engels rammed the barricaded door. The cottage shuddered beneath the assault.

. . .

*My Love,*

      *Do not fret for me. I have foreseen the coming events, and you must put your trust in the gods that all will be well. Do not follow me. Gather your brothers in arms. You haven't much time. You will find us in the White Forest. Once I'm gone, everything you need will be in the book.*

*Kill him.*

*Forever yours,*

*Brynn, your loving wife*


Confused, he returned the parchment to his boot. The cottage shook once more as the Engels broke through the entrance. Marek unlatched the window shutters and promptly dove through the opening, landing in the bushes below. His fingers touched leather, and he scooped up the weapons, slinging a scabbard over each arm as he leaped to his feet and rounded the cottage. He found both soldiers waiting for him near the broken door.

Marek paused, catching his breath. He crossed his arms behind his head, each fist grabbing a sword and pulling them free from their sheaths. He swung them in a great arc, waiting for his opponents to strike. Marek tilted his head from side to side, the vertebrae popping under the pressure. "Who wants to die first?"

The Engels charged at once, their swords drawn for battle. Marek let loose his rage in a fury of steel and with a strength so powerful he cleaved his closest attacker in two with the first strike.

The second Engel saw his companion fall in a heap of blood and guts and stopped mid-swing. The color drained from his face, and the soldier turned his back to run. His escape came to an abrupt halt when the blade of Marek's dagger lodged securely in the man's upper thigh. The Engel fell to the ground.

"Please don't kill me, please don't kill me." The man wept like a child, raising his hands above his face in a defensive stance. "I have a family."

Marek pressed the tip of his sword to the Engel's throat and cocked his head to the side in disbelief. "Really, Engel? *That* is the plea you give me? You have a family? Well, your captain just stole mine." A half-crazed laugh spewed from Marek's throat.

"I was only following orders, Archaean."

"And I act of my own free will." With one quick thrust, the sword penetrated its intended target, nearly severing the man's head.

Marek gathered his weapons, packed his gear, and tacked his horse. If he didn't tarry, he would reach his home by the sea in three days' time. He could only hope his men would still be near — and alive.

M ichael shifted in the saddle, the leather groaning under his weight. He twisted and scanned the hills behind them, searching the tree line.

Brynn couldn't help but notice his fidgeting. Michael never could hide his emotions well. Her father had once told him during an argument that it would be his downfall, and she was beginning to think he was right.

Michael motioned to a nearby soldier, and the man dutifully urged his mount forward. "Go and see what is keeping them."

"There's no need for that, Michael," Brynn told him. "Your men are already dead."

Michael's menacing stare fixed on her. "And what makes you think that?"

"Because Marek is what legends are made of. He is the greatest of warriors, and his love will conquer all. The only reason you are still alive is because I made it so."

"I don't wish to kill you, Brynn, for I have loved you as a sister since the day you were born. I accepted you even though your mother proved to be a whore. My orders were to kill you, and I will if I must."

"It will not be here, nor will it be this day, but you must know you are going to die, Michael. We all are going to die." Brynn ended the Engel conversation then and returned her focus to the path in front of her. Her thoughts turned to her dreams, wishing she could open her book and unscramble what was left of the puzzle. The images were still scattered in incoherent pieces. She had seen faces, heard familiar voices, but she couldn't define the significance of them. Brynn had an inkling of where they now traveled. Judging by the position of the afternoon sun, they journeyed south. Each passing hour brought her closer to the Engel border… and to the ravens. The journey was unforgiving and relentless. Talon tired easily, and the Engel soldiers grew increasingly agitated with the frequent stops and the whines of a child, who just wanted to go home.

"Brynn, you need to quiet him. My men will silence him otherwise."

"Do you have children, Michael?"

"No, I do not."

"Then you must realize the strain of travel on a child is of great excess. He's tired and hungry, and he doesn't understand what is happening. He's scared." Brynn was scared. She couldn't make excuses much longer.

"There is an Engel stronghold only a few hours distance away. We'll be stopping there. Just keep him quiet." Michael returned to his position at the head of the traveling party.

Brynn managed to keep Talon quiet by singing to him, and telling him stories of his father, and of great battles from the past until they stopped at the Engel post. "This is your Engel stronghold?" Brynn stifled a laugh. The fortifications before her were nothing but a ransacked Archaean fortress long ago abandoned by its inhabitants. The outer walls crumbled from age. Thick vines threatened to constrict the inner beams keeping the ceiling intact.

"It's more of an outpost."

"I would hardly call it that. I would call it desperate."

"Since when did your tongue become so bold, sister? You best hold it and do as you're told, or you will find yourself in confinement."

"Like you?" She followed her guards through the front double doors and into the dim entry hall, seemingly empty of life. Talon clung to her leg, his face buried in her skirts.

"Someone will take you to your chamber. Father will want to know you're here." Michael disappeared into the shadows, leaving Brynn to ponder his last words alone.

*Father?* She and Talon were shoved into a back room and left for what seemed like hours. Guards were posted outside. There were no windows, no hidden doors, no escape routes.

Michael returned for her soon after she sang Talon to sleep. "Brynn, come." When she went to stir Talon from his restless slumber, Michael stopped her. "Leave him." When Brynn showed signs of protest, he explained, "He will be safer here. Father has a temper."

They walked through a damp hallway and down a set of jagged stairs. The moisture clung to her skin, dampening her gown. It clung to her lower back and legs as she walked. "What has Father gotten you into, Michael?"

Michael didn't have time to reply. He opened the door to the study, an argument already in commencement when they entered. Her father, Bertram, the Earl of Galhaven, sat at a solid desk strewn with parchment and towering books ready to topple to the floor. Engels, tall and thin, surrounded him, pointing to various fixtures on a large map. The voices silenced — all heads turned in her direction.

Brynn stepped back a few paces, but Michael took her arm, pulling her to his side.

"What is the meaning of this?" Bertram staggered to his feet. Age had ravaged his body. He was no longer the fat, greasy man she remembered. His body was frail, his skin yellowed, and his once brown hair had turned white as winter's snow.

"I have found her, Father." Michael pushed her forward presenting the man with a prize.

"Why is she not dead?" The venomous words spit from the old man's mouth like poison.

"I told you he wouldn't be able to do it." The voice, calm and familiar, echoed from the corner of the room. The man continued to peer out the window he stood near.

"She belongs to Lord Westmore. She bears his mark, and by law, we must return her to him." Michael clasped Brynn's palm and uncovered the symbol on her wrist to show his proof.

Brynn slapped his hand away and tugged at her sleeve. "Don't touch me."

"I do not care *who* she belongs to… she is a traitor to her country and she must die for it!" Bertram pounded his fist, nearly knocking himself over in his rage. He lowered to the chair, swiping the desk clean with his arm during his descent.

"I'm not a traitor, you stupid old fool! I would have been married to an Engel and you would have had the land you wanted if it hadn't been for your ignorance!"

"Indeed, you would have." The smooth voice slipped from the shadows like ripples on water. "Just as beautiful as the day you were taken from me." Julian, once her betrothed, was suddenly next to her. "Michael is right, Bertram. We must return her to Westmore. The bounty we will receive will fill the coffers of our cause. Well done, Michael." Julian gave Michael's shoulder a pat before returning to his perch near the window.

Bertram paused for thought. "Send out a dispatch. Inquire as to the amount of silver we can procure for her return. Until we receive word, keep her out of sight."

"And what of the boy?" Michael inquired.

Brynn shot him a look of pure hatred.

"What... *boy*?" Bertram articulated the words with a click of his tongue, rising from his seat. He leaned over the space of the desk, awaiting the answer.

"She has a son, Father. He is here with her."

"You have a child?" Bertram rounded the desk, hobbling closer to the center of the room where Brynn stood.

"Aye, I do."

"And who sired this boy?"

Brynn rolled her eyes. "His father, of course."

"Do not play games with me, girl. Who is the boy's father?"

"My husband is his father." Brynn took delight in watching the feeble man squirm.

"Oh, you are married now, are you?"

Brynn thought she could see Bertram's blood begin to boil beneath the paper-like skin hanging loose around his features. She nodded with a mocking enthusiasm. "To an Archaean, even. The same Archaean who rescued me from *you* all those years ago. I expect him to do the same this time, as soon as he finds me. I have a suspicion he will not be so generous with your life this time... *Father*."

"Get her out of my sight." The command was followed by a sputtering spasm of coughing and a deep inhale.

Brynn was escorted from the room before she could diagnose the sickness eating at his insides. She would let it kill him for all she cared.

The passing of days left her in utter turmoil. Brynn was kept in confinement. A servant brought her food and emptied her chamber pot, and she was given an ill-fitting Engel gown to wear. It was a silky blue and matched her eyes but would soon be stained red with blood — she had seen it in her dreams. The very gown she now wore. She filled her time going over every passage she had written in her books, making sure all of the instructions for Marek were legible and clear. She checked her herbs and concoctions twice over and lined them up just so at the bottom of her satchel. The most torturous part of her captivity — they had taken Talon from her. She hadn't seen him in days. She would ask of him whenever anyone would enter her chamber, but no one would give her information. She hadn't the slightest idea if he even lived. She had made the right decision by bringing him with her — her dreams had shown her so, and she dared not alter the course of the foreseen. She couldn't trust Talon's life in the hands of another, nor leave him with Marek, as he had his own life to fret over. But still, the unsurety ate at her insides like a festering wound.

She paced the floor like a caged animal, testing her boundaries for weaknesses — she found none. She slept only when exhaustion overtook her, and ate only when she thought she would wretch from the pains of hunger. Planning an escape seemed futile. She would have to wait on word of Lord Westmore. From what she knew of him, he would bite at the bait. He wasn't a man that took being outsmarted by a woman lightly.

A slight rapping on the door interrupted her thoughts.

Julian entered, carrying a plate of food.

"Julian. Where is Michael?"

"He has been called to his duties. I will be overseeing your stay now." Julian closed the door behind him and crossed the small room to the desk, setting down the plate.

"Eat."

"I'm not hungry." Brynn clasped her arms around her waist and returned to her pacing, trying to focus her thoughts on the task at hand.

"You need your strength… we leave in the morning."

Her pacing stopped. "Where are we going?" She didn't dare face him again, for fear he would see the panic in her eyes.

"Lord Westmore has requested you be returned. We ride for Braemir at dawn."

"And what of my son? Where is he? Why has he been taken from me?" Brynn approached him then, falling to her knees at his feet. If his absence was to break her defenses, it had worked. "Please, Julian. Tell me he is well."

"The boy is fine. He plays with the hounds in the courtyard. Michael was looking after him." Julian helped her stand.

Perhaps her brother still had some semblance of a soul. "He is unharmed?"

"He will travel with us, and upon your return, will also become the property of Westmore."

Brynn clasped her palm over her mouth to keep a sob from slipping out. "No."

"It is the law. All nobles shall claim ownership of all property and possessions acquired or belonging to said property. Talon is your son, and therefore, belongs to Lord Westmore to do with as he pleases."

"I would love to hear what his father has to say about that." Brynn chuckled, knowing Marek would have killed Julian for even speaking the words.

Julian plopped in the desk chair, crossing his legs at the ankles. "We could have had a family, you know. If that heathen hadn't ruined everything."

"You could have defended me, Julian. You chose not to. That 'heathen' is twice the man you will ever be."

"And where is that man now?" Julian placed his hands behind his head, relaxing against the wall. "I haven't seen anyone fighting their way in to rescue you."

"He will come for me."

"Are you so sure?" Julian rose from his chair, meandering closer to her with every slow step. His boots scuffed across the stone floor, sending fine dust particles into the stagnant air.

"He loves me. He will come." Her chin tilted up — just a little — in defiance.

"And just what is it that he loves so much about you? Perhaps you will easily spread your legs for him? Or perhaps your womanhood is so tight that he comes upon entry? Hmm?" Julian was nearly on her, so close she could smell the wine on his breath.

"If you touch me, Julian, you will seal your fate. Marek will kill you for it." She held her ground. She would play the mouse no longer.

"Your husband is surprisingly absent. Who would stop me from taking my pleasure? Something I should have done all those years ago. I was foolish to think marriage was the only way to have you." His fingers wrapped around a lock of her hair, and he rubbed it between his thumb and finger. A sinister grin contorted his once handsome face. "I should have just taken you as my whore, with you being Archaean and all."

"Did *you* marry, Julian?"

"I did, years ago." His breathing came in quick pants and his hands rose to her shoulders, pushing her flat to the bed.

Brynn's fingers crept ever closer to the small dagger strapped to the inside of her thigh. "And you would dishonor her so now?"

"My wife was a bitch." His mood pitched sharply, and he brought a clenched fist to his forehead as if trying to beat out the memory. Then, in an emotional turn, he dropped his hand and soothed the side of her cheek. "She told me what she did to you, how she destroyed our happy engagement. I couldn't forgive her for that."

Brynn gasped. "Meredith?" She thought back on Julian's words. *Was. My wife* was *a bitch.* "Julian, what happened to Meredith?"

"She died."

"How did she die, Julian?" Terror was quickly overtaking her, and Brynn began to quiver beneath his grasp.

Julian leaned in close, so close his lips touched her ear when he whispered to her. "I pushed her down the stairs."

"*Guards!*" Brynn's scream released Julian from whatever trance he was in. The door opened, and two Engel soldiers appeared with swords drawn. "Remove him from my chamber! He's trying to lay claim to Westmore's property!" Brynn hoped the accusation would extinguish Julian's fire.

# Chapter Twenty-Six

## DEATH BECOMES US ALL

M arek tucked the parchment away after reading it for what seemed the hundredth time. He still couldn't decipher its cryptic code. Frustrated, he tossed the remains of the wild hare he gnawed on into the coals of the campfire. He buried his hands in his hair and hung his head between his knees. He needed to think.

Mindless chatter clouded his thoughts. He had somehow persuaded a handful of men to join his cause — most simply anxious for battle. His brother, Ronan, had insisted he accompany him, even though Marek had screamed and yelled that Ronan must stay with his own family. They made camp not far from the bordering wagon road, a popular traveling route to the deepest Archaean territories. Marek hadn't received word from his wife, and the worry pained him. He would do as her note instructed — wait for her in the White Forest — and hope she was still alive to carry out whatever plan she had forthcoming.

"What troubles you this night, my friend?" asked Gavin. With a groan, his childhood friend settled next to him.

"'Tis nothing, really." Marek stared into the fire, watching the flames lick at a fresh piece of kindling.

"We are here to help, aye? So out with it. How am I supposed to utilize my greatness if you won't talk to me?" Gavin cocked an eyebrow, flashing a grin.

Marek sighed. Gavin was right. He couldn't do it alone. The only way he was going to get his family back alive was if they all worked together. He retrieved the wrinkled piece of parchment and handed it to Gavin. "Brynn gave this to me just before she was taken. It's her plan, but I don't know what to make of it."

"Let me have a go at it." Gavin carefully unfolded the crumpled paper and read the first line aloud. "My love," he spouted in his best effort at a female voice. "Well, I believe you should take that part meaning she loves you. 'Tis obvious, aye?"

Marek rolled his eyes. "If you think this is a joke, Gavin, give it back."

"No, no, I said I would help, now let me read it." He turned from Marek, continuing to read the letter by the light of the flames. "I have foreseen the coming events… what does that mean?" Gavin stroked the blond whiskers on his chin.

"Brynn has foreseeing dreams. I can only assume she knew this was going to happen."

"Do not follow me. Gather your brothers in arms — that's us—" Gavin pointed a finger to his chest. "You will find us in the White Forest." Gavin stopped reading, but his eyes were still fixed on the words. "She doesn't mean *that* White Forest?"

"Aye, she does, but I don't think she understands what peril she's leading us into." Marek released a long, slow breath and took the paper from Gavin.

"The White Forest will be certain death. Only evil lives there. Wraiths — the death walkers, they will kill us all."

"The death walkers are a legend. Who is to say they even exist?"

Gavin rose to his feet. "I do! I say they exist, and I say we are not going! No, not happening, Marek!" His outburst caught the attention of the others. "Fighting for a cause is one thing, but walking into the White Forest with my arms raised high shouting, 'Kill me!' is not high on my list of priorities!"

"They say the White Forest is blanketed in snow, even during the summer seasons — that Death himself resides there," spoke another.

Ronan approached, snatching the parchment from his brother. He glanced over the words, his lips moving in silence as he read. "What is this about?"

"He intends to send us into the White Forest," Gavin blurted.

"Then that is where we will go." Ronan's firm tone put a stop to Gavin's outburst. "Where is this book she mentions? Perhaps the key lies within."

"She didn't give me a book, only the parchment," Marek replied.

"And who are you to kill?"

"I know not."

"Well, at least we get to kill somebody." Ronan handed the letter to his brother and addressed the men before fear overcame them. "Listen, lads. Tomorrow we face a great challenge. We fight together or die together. Marek needs us. Our brother... needs us. We will do as he commands, and if that means we face the wraiths in the White Forest, then so be it."

"Where are my scouts?" Marek called to his men. Two stepped forward. "Which road do they travel?"

"They travel the high road to Braemir."

Marek's face contorted into a deep scowl. "That will take them completely around the forest." Pressing his fingers to his temple, he pictured the road in his mind. In his younger years, he once fulfilled a bounty near there. A deep ravine curved alongside the wagon road. There was also a bridge. Destroying the bridge would leave Brynn's captors no choice but to turn around, or detour through the forest.

Marek picked up a nearby stick and drew a map in the dirt. "At first light, we will take out the bridge, here." He placed a rock where the bridge was located on his map and filled in a few other key elements of the surroundings. "The White Forest is here," he pointed out, "and we will intercept them *here*." Marek stabbed the soil with the stick to mark the spot where the battle would take place, deep inside the forest.

"Why not wait until they clear the forest?" someone questioned.

"Who is to say they will even make it out?" Marek looked at his men, at their expectant faces. "I won't lie to you; it will be dangerous. I won't hold it against any man who does not wish to continue. This is my family, my fight."

Two men withdrew, and Marek wished them safe travels back to their homeland. Their departure left him with a mere fifteen men. They spent the night gathering supplies by torchlight and preparing to meet the Engels. Weapons were sharpened, armor double-checked, and arrows well stocked.

S unlight warmed Marek's cheeks as he knotted a length of rope then tied it securely to the saddle on his mount. The morning held the promise of a beautiful day — not one cloud disrupted the clear summer sky. The Engels would make good time... he must hurry. His attention turned to several more of his men who were diligently securing the other ends of the lengths of rope to the support beams of the wooden bridge. "You lads almost done down there?"

The men dangled precariously over the edge of the bridge, trusting completely in the grip of their comrades to keep them from plummeting to the ravine below. "Nearly finished!" one called back as he swayed slightly in the breeze.

"We must get this bridge down... we are running out of time." Marek directed others to line up the horses, ready to pull when given the signal. The dangling men finished their work and motioned to be brought up. They cleared the bridge, and Marek gave the subsequent signal to move. "Go!" he shouted, slapping the rump of his horse.

Four steeds pulled in unison at the command of their owners. Snorts and grunts mingled with excited cheers, infusing together to make a joyful praise as the beams started to moan. Marek gripped the rope and dug his heels into the soft earth, tugging with his horse. "Again!"

The beams let out a cry, giving way to the strain.

"Come on lads, pull!"

Men scrambled to their horses, doing whatever possible to join in the effort, grasping on to whatever they could in the combined effort to destroy the bridge. The wood groaned as the planks loosened. With a few more heaves, the rope frayed and the wood gave way. Planks fell into the void of the ravine as beams swayed freely, bound by the twisting of the ropes. A swift sawing with a blade freed the wood, and they, too, disappeared into the nothingness below.

Marek allowed a brief celebratory round of hand clasps and shoulder slaps with his men before refocusing on the task at hand. The bridge was down, but the hardest part was still to come. He now had to lead his brave and seasoned — but perhaps too few — band of brothers into death's own territory, where superstition and fear were additional but unseen enemies. Keeping them all alive would prove to be his greatest challenge, one he knew he was unlikely to accomplish.

The edge of the White Forest stood steadfast, just a stone's throw before Marek. He pulled his horse to a sudden halt. The animal tossed his head, rearing slightly at the unexpected jerk. His surroundings were eerily quiet, and he motioned his men forward with caution. "Stay focused, we know not what evil lurks before us."

A frigid dusting of snow coated the narrow path leading into the depths of the forest. The beauties of the once lush terrain dwindled into an unbearable solitude. The horses picked their way over rocks and gaps with an uneasy carefulness. Skulls from those who had succumbed to the perils of the forest dangled from barren branches. Splintered bones crunched under the weight of the horses as they dutifully pressed forward.

A terrifying screech from an unknown being echoed through the trees, and Marek's mount let out a snort, his ears flattening against its head. Marek reassured the animal by rubbing his palm along the gelding's neck. "Easy, Cyran, I need you strong now."

The men followed one another deeper into the bowels of the wood, making an easy escape less than likely. A cold panic seeped amidst the group. Marek shut out the whispers and the unsteady breaths of his comrades, closed his eyes, and listened. A stoic silence blanketed the air like a wall of stone, heavy and thick. Leather creaked and bits of metal clinked as the horses moved, but no natural sounds were heard. No birds, no wind rustling in the pines — no life at all. An unnatural quiet loomed over them.

A shadow darted across Marek's path, and he stopped short, the rider behind him nearly crashing into the backside of his mount. "Did you see that?" He spoke the words so quietly he might as well have been talking to himself. Blackness flitted in the corner of his eye, and Marek turned toward it, only to find nothing. The little hairs on the back of his neck stood on end and a shiver crept up his spine when a presence grazed his shoulder. He swallowed the lump in his throat and gave Cyran a nudge with his heels, but the horse wouldn't move forward. Rather, it took several steps backward. Marek reined him in, turning the horse full circle. Cyran pawed at the ground, tossing his head, and violently strained against the bit as the forest began to stir.

Inaudible whispers ricocheted through the trees, and the horses pranced precariously on the thin walking path. Unexplainable children giggled in the distance. More shadows appeared amongst the men but vanished when touched by the tiny slivers of sunlight flitting across the forest floor.

Gaining control of Cyran, Marek redirected his eyes to his men. They were no longer in a tight formation. Some had dismounted, others strayed into the forest with dumbfounded looks on their faces, oblivious to the surroundings. Something was amiss — they were being lured into the darkness. The whispers, the shadows, the faint sounds of children — Marek and his men were walking straight into some kind of unearthly trap.

A scream in the distance set Marek galloping from the footpath and into the thickness of the wood. *Brynn.* He and his mount moved as one, dodging branches and weaving through the endless maze of impassable thickets. It was as if the forest knew he was coming and purposely blocked his path. When he finally reached the scream, it was not Brynn, but one of his own men. Marek rushed to his side, only to find him dead. A look of sheer terror still masked the man's face.

Marek drew his sword. In a bout of panic, Cyran tugged the reins from his master's grasp and cantered from sight. "Damned horse," spat Marek, gathering his wits. His boots sank in the fresh layer of powder as he pressed onward, retracing his steps to the trail and, hopefully, his men. The sweet smell of summer flowers overtook his senses. He inhaled deeply, veering from his path to follow the intoxicating aura. No smell was greater than the fragrance of a woman. He rounded a tree, clearing a path with a swing of his blade. He stopped mid-stride, overwhelmed. "Nya?" He called out to the figure, his voice cracking. She stood in the distance, her smile beaming her love for him. "Is it truly you?"

"Hello, my love!" The figure waved excitedly at him, beckoning him closer. "Come! Play with us!"

Marek took a few steps forward. His chest rose and fell heavily. His own eyes deceived him. His beautiful wife stood before him, her essence radiating light. "It cannot be," he gasped. His sword arm went limp, the steel falling to the snow.

"Well? What are you waiting for? Aren't you joining us, Marek? Supper is ready." She giggled, her attention focused on the emptiness beside her. She knelt to the ground and held out her arms, waiting. A swirl of snow appeared at the tips of her fingers and in an instant, a boy formed from the fragments of ice and earth.

Marek dropped to his knees. His boy, his little Ewan, was wrapped in his mother's arms only paces away. Tears dampened his cheeks as Marek regained his footing and started toward the pair.

"Da!" the little boy greeted, his auburn curls bouncing atop his head. "Wait till you see the fish I caught! Will you not come home?"

"I'm on my way, son!" Marek choked on a sob. His family stood before him, awaiting his return. He would give everything just to hold them again. He would go to them and never let them go. He almost reached happiness when a force from behind knocked him to the ground. Marek wrestled with the beast, attempting to claw his way free, but the figure locked its strength around his middle, pinning his arms to his sides.

Ronan shoved his brother against a nearby tree, his grip unwavering. "They are death walkers, Marek! Do not believe your mind, they are not real!"

"Release me, Ronan, before I kill you!" Marek hissed, his rage boiling to the surface.

"They are *dead*, Marek! You need to remember!" Marek kicked back against the hold, but Ronan only tightened the cage of his arms. "They take the shape of your greatest anguish to use it against you. Listen to me, Marek!"

"No! You cannot keep me from them!"

Without hesitation, Ronan released him, pulled back his fist, and punched Marek square in the face.

The blow jarred Marek enough that it took a moment for him to recover. He rubbed his jaw and blinked, confused. "Why the hell did you hit me?"

"You were walking to your death, and it was the only way I knew how to stop you." Ronan backed away from Marek with caution.

"I saw Nya and Ewan," Marek told Ronan. "They were here."

"I know." Ronan cast his brother a sympathetic glance. "In this forest lies a realm between the living and the dead. It will try to overcome your soul — you must not let it. Look." Ronan pointed to the two figures evaporating before their very eyes. The figure that had once been Marek's love grew dark and lanky. The shape hovered above the ground as it formed into a hazy mist. It paused over his sword for a moment, released a shrill scream, and then disappeared into the forest. "Remember why we are here." Ronan gave Marek's shoulder a tight squeeze before fetching the discarded sword. "You are going to need this, aye? To save your *current* wife, if I recall correctly?"

Marek managed a lopsided grin. "You are an ass."

Ronan nodded, accompanied by a slight bow. "With pride."

S hadows lurked in every corner. It was as if they could read her thoughts, so Brynn focused her mind on only the happiest of memories. The horses were spooked by the noises of the forest, forcing many soldiers to walk beside their mounts. Trudging through the snow made for a slow journey, but the party came to a complete stop when they reached a ridge.

Julian peered over the edge. "We will have to circle back around and find a way down. I see a clearing." He pointed below, kicked the snow with his boot, and turned just as an arrow hissed by his ear. Startled, Julian blamed one of the soldiers next to him, but when the Engel stammered that it had come from afar, Julian dropped to a defensive position, barking out orders to his men. "Secure this ridge! Find out where that arrow came from!"

The Archaean ambush seemed to materialize before her very eyes. Her horse reared, and Brynn could no longer steady herself in the saddle. She tumbled backward and landed in a windswept drift of snow, narrowly missing the plummeting hooves of her mount. She rolled to the side, rising to her feet before the confusion could engulf her, too.

Michael seemed too preoccupied with engaging the warriors than keeping a watchful eye on her, so, in the midst of Engel soldiers, Brynn searched for Talon. The confusion of the White Forest and its mysteries was proving to be the perfect distraction for their escape. She found Talon still mounted and rushed to his side, pulling him from the saddle. "Come, Talon, we must hide."

"Where is Da?" he whined, tired and disoriented. "You said he would come for us."

"He is waiting for us on the other side of the forest, so we must hurry and go to him," Brynn reassured him while urging him closer to the trees.

"I don't want to go in there, it frightens me." Talon refused to follow.

Brynn knew his instincts were correct. Only danger awaited them, but they had no choice. They couldn't turn back. "I know you're scared, I am as well, but we must go."

Talon nodded and placed his hand in hers. "Don't let go of me." Together they raced for the tree line but were spotted before they could conceal themselves in the shadows of the forest.

"There they are, milord!"

"Get them!" Julian ordered, trying to regroup his men.

"Don't lose them, you imbecile!"

Within moments, two horses were upon them. "Stay out of the forest, Engel. Don't let them get you," she warned one of the soldiers, positioning herself in direct line with her escape route should an opening occur.

"Don't let who get me?" the soldier questioned.

"The death walkers." Brynn added a little laugh, hoping her warning would further the madness ensuing amongst the Engels. "They will eat your soul. You should leave now before it's too late. Everyone is going to die."

The soldier eyed her precariously but pushed her words aside. Reaching down, he pulled her into his lap. Talon was secured by another soldier, and both were returned to the Engel party.

A firm grip locked around Brynn's waist, pulling her to the ground. She struggled to free herself but was no match for the strength of Julian. "Release me," she ordered through gritted teeth.

"The only way you are leaving my side is by death. I will not disappoint my master." Julian's shouts to his soldiers only added to the chaos surrounding the ridge. Men scrambled for shelter, while others tried to calm the horses. Some wandered off in unknown directions, straight into the line of fire.

Several more arrows cleared the ridge, sinking into the snow inches from Brynn's feet. She drew Talon to her side and pushed closer to the edge. Excited shouts echoed through the forest, and Brynn recognized several of the voices. He had come for her. She must make herself known. "Marek!" she screamed, emptying her lungs of air. "Marek, up here!"

A gloved palm circled around her throat. "Make another sound, bitch, and I will slit your throat." Julian pulled a dagger from his side, waving it in front of her face.

"Hurt me, and he will hunt you down."

"Not if he is dead. I will pick the arrow myself."

Brynn stared into Julian's dark eyes, at the man he had become. She searched for the man he once was, the charmer, but all that remained was evil and hate. She took in a mouthful of air and called out to Marek once more. Her voice reverberated through her body. The dagger dipped close to her face, but Brynn drew up her hand, snaring it. Her fingers curled around the blade, and she pushed back, countering the blow. Blood circled her wrist and ran down her forearm, the lace cuff of her gown staining red from the flow of the gash. She fought against her attacker, straining to reach the hem of her dress.

Julian's grip on her throat tightened.

Her fingers found the hem, and she tugged it upward until she felt the cold metal of her boot knife. It slipped easily from its sheath, and she swung it wildly at Julian. Steel met flesh, and Julian released her. She kicked at him with the fury of an untamed stallion until he retreated to cover the wound. Crimson poured from the deep laceration on his cheek. Her blade marred the handsome face she once admired.

Without hesitation, Brynn rose to her feet and rushed to the cowering Talon. She seized his palm, snatching up a discarded bow and quiver along the route, and searched for a way down the ravine. She didn't have to look long. An abandoned horse marked the way. She followed in its tracks, reaching the forest floor with ease.

Hiding behind a tree, Brynn opened her satchel and pulled out a well-worn book. Blood smeared across the binding from her palm. She flipped it open to a marked page and read the passage written on it. Her lips quivered beneath the words as she fumbled over them.

"Ma, you're bleeding," Talon told her, his voice trailed behind a cry.

"Quiet, Talon, I must get this right." While she recited the words, Brynn removed a vial from the bag. She pulled the cork free, drank its contents, and replaced both the book and the empty vial in the satchel, finishing her chant. Within moments, warmth spread throughout her body. The aching of her wound ceased to pain her, and for a moment, she sighed in relief.

The moment ended when she heard the order for her death from the ridge. Keeping to the trees, Brynn tried her best to stay hidden. Julian and his men held the advantage, however — she was visible through the thickets from the high vantage point of the bluff. An assault of arrows showered above her, raining death upon impact should they find their marks. The Archaeans were close — Brynn could hear their voices clearly. They would counter-fire to protect her position, but two Archaean warriors fell in the crossfire.

"Brynn, stay covered!" Marek and his men took up a defensive position across the clearing from her, firing off arrows at the Engel archers.

She did as she was told and hunkered low. Her lungs burned as she tried to catch her breath. The Archaeans would be slaughtered while trying to save her — they fought a losing battle. They would never get close enough to use their swords. She knew what must be done, but summoning up the courage to do so was proving to be more difficult than she thought.

"Stay where you are and I will come to you!" Marek called to her.

"Do not!" she commanded. "He is waiting for such a move, and he will kill you!"

"I'll take my chances!"

"Marek, don't reveal your position! I know what I must do — it is *my* destiny! 'Tis the only way we will ever be free! I alone must end this war!" She took a deep breath to calm herself and turned to Talon. She managed a bittersweet smile, caressing his dirty cheek with the back of her palm. "I love you, my son."

The boy looked at her with expectant eyes. "I love you, too."

"I need you to do something for me, aye?" Talon nodded. "No matter what you hear, no matter what you see, I need you to run. And do not look back." The boy wanted to object, but Brynn put her finger to his lips. "You must run as fast and far as you can until your da comes for you, do you understand?"

"But why will you not come with me?"

"I need to take care of these bad men first. Stay in the trees and follow the path, all right? And don't stop until your da finds you." She kissed her son and wrapped her arms around him for one last hug before slinging the quiver over her shoulder and readying the bow. "Now go. I'll see you soon." Brynn pointed him in the right direction and watched as her little boy vanished from her line of sight.

Arrows flitted through the forest, some finding their mark in Archaean bodies. Marek's men were being picked off one by one, defenseless against the high advantage point of the Engels.

"Courage, Brynn." She rose to her feet, slid an arrow from the quiver, and stepped into the light of the clearing. Despite the trembling of her hands, she managed to nock the arrow and pull the bowstring. She found her intended target — an Engel soldier aiming his bow at Marek — and released the bowstring. The arrow flew like a bird on wings, plummeting into the belly of the man. He keeled forward and tumbled over the edge of the bluff.

She reached over her shoulder for another arrow.

"Brynn, what in hell are you doing?" Sheer terror resonated from Marek. "Get back behind the tree!"

She ignored him, once again drawing the bow, hitting another soldier. Julian appeared at the edge of the ridge then, yelling words she couldn't understand.

The first arrow struck her in the thigh, sending her staggering to regain her footing. A red circle formed on her gown where the arrow hit, but Brynn pushed it from her thoughts. It brought her no pain. She was fidgeting with the bowstring when the second arrow hit. The sharpened point crashed into her chest, cracking her ribs on impact. The blow knocked her to her knees. She struggled for breath but didn't give up. She would put an arrow through his heart. If she must die, Julian would first.

The world swirled around her. Brynn willed herself to stand. She glanced to her side. "I'm sorry," she mouthed, watching Marek scream against the restraints of his men.

She lowered her bow and tilted her head to the sky. Three black ravens circled above her, eagerly awaiting her death.

She was dying. Blood pooled in her mouth, and she spat it to the ground. It dripped from her nose, cascading to the powdery blanket of snow below. It congealed around her toes, forming steaming balls of red clumps on her boots and carelessly staining the front of her pretty gown. Her breath crystallized in the air before her, but yet, she felt no cold.

Death was a strange thing.

Brynn reached up toward the ravens, searching the heavens for strength. Her dreams had proven to be true. The ruse of her death would, at last, give her people freedom from Westmore. With his death, they would rise up and reclaim what was once theirs. She prayed Marek would find the writings she had left for him in time before death could claim her. She would die this day — her dreams had shown her so — but with the proper planning, and a bit of luck, it wouldn't be so for long. She did not know the reason why, but the gods had chosen her for this task, and she would see it through. She alone would free the Archaean people. Her people.

She twirled her palm in the air and watched it intensely as it rotated. It felt disjointed from her body like it did not belong to her. The potion she made had served its purpose. She gaped at the gash on her palm as it wept bloody tears — watched as they dripped in steady rhythmic beats to the perfect white earth.

There were others surrounding her — faceless, lifeless beings standing where hearts once beat to the tune of life. Blood trickled from their burning eyes and spouted from their fingers. Swirls of white and crimson danced around the corpses of the fallen in victory. The death walkers beckoned her to join them.

Blood filled her mouth, and she spat it to the ground. Breathing had become a task she had to concentrate on as her lungs filled with fluid. Her eyes fluttered, but she continued her attack, drawing her last arrow. She took her time aiming — it was imperative her shot find its mark. Her fingers released and the arrow cut through the air.

At the same time her shot lodged itself in Julian's chest, a barrage of arrows flew from behind her. The Archaeans joined in her battle against the Engels. She watched as Julian stumbled forward, lost his footing, and slipped from the bluff. His limbs tangled in the vines protruding from the ridge wall, and his bones cracked in perverted ways, leaving him hanging precariously.

The third arrow sent her careening to the bloodstained snow. She attempted to crawl to safety, but her arms couldn't support her. She fell to her back and sucked in a breath that wouldn't come.

Arms gathered her limp body, carrying her from the clearing. Marek propped her up against the trunk of a tree, mumbling incoherent words. He wiped the blood from her mouth and kissed her lips with the tenderness of an angel.

"Ronan, help me with these arrows." Marek searched her body for exit wounds, finding two. He let them be.

Brynn attempted to speak but only blood flowed from her lips. She brought her hand to Marek's face and placed a stained palm to his cheek. He closed his eyes and cradled it with his own, while hot tears streamed between their entwined fingers.

"I will take you home, love, I promise it. We will watch our children play in the fields under the summer sun. We will grow old together, you and I, and I will love you all the days of my life." When her eyelids began to flutter, Marek pulled her close. "Stay with me, Brynn." She fought against her body for a breath, arching violently in his arms. His tears splattered on her face as he cradled her head. "Damn it, Brynn, breathe!" His hands wandered aimlessly over her body, unsure of how to help her. "Please don't leave me," he whispered, a cry shattering his words.

"Kill him." She focused on the ocean waves crashing in his eyes and inhaled sharply, then breathed no more.

## Chapter Twenty-Seven

### RETURN TO ME

"Ronan, help me!" Marek begged for assistance as his wife's lifeless body hung limp in his arms. Gripping an arrow, he pulled it from her flesh, tossing it to the side. "I need bandages. Hurry!" Marek pressed his palm to the wound to stanch the flow of blood. "Return to me, Brynn. *Please.*" He lowered her to the ground, oblivious to the battle still raging around him. Pressing his ear to her chest, he listened for a heartbeat.

"Marek," Ronan muttered, his voice soft — sympathetic.

"*No.*"

"Marek." He placed a firm hand on Marek's shoulder. "She is gone."

Marek ignored the words. "Why are you standing there? Ronan!"

"She is gone, Marek. Let her be."

His body felt numb and no longer his own. "Where is my son?"

"I sent Aiden and Gavin to find him. They should return soon."

"They will not find him," said a voice from the shadows. "He is in the hands of Westmore."

Recognizing it, Marek jumped to his feet and charged into the darkness, rage spewing from his mouth in a violent scream. He lunged for Michael, pummeling him to the ground. When Marek realized Michael didn't fight back, he hesitated, fist still poised for attack.

"It wasn't supposed to happen like this." Michael stared at Brynn's body. "She finally found happiness, and I destroyed her. She is dead because of my own greed." Grief for his sister contorted his face into a deep scowl.

Grabbing a fistful of clothing, Marek hauled Michael to his feet. Anger and frustration seethed throughout his body, his chest rising and falling with each painful breath. "Twice now, this Westmore has killed a woman I loved. Twice, he has taken what matters most from me. It will not happen a third time. You will take me to him — you will take me to my son!"

"I'm sorry. I cannot help you, for I do not know the way."

"Give me one good reason why I shouldn't kill you."

"I cannot."

Marek stared at the Engel and all he saw was pity and a saddened heart. They both mourned the same woman. "There has been enough death this day." Marek released Michael, shoving a distance between them before he changed his mind. "Let's get the hell out of here."

Marek wrapped Brynn in a blanket and draped her over his horse while the others regrouped. Michael followed behind Marek and his men at a safe distance as they cleared the White Forest. The battered warriors marched in solemn silence, leaving Marek to ponder over just who had won the battle.

The Archaeans made camp under the setting summer sun, its rays illuminating their souls and restoring hope to the world. Marek sorted through his supplies, but it was more of an aimless wandering to make his actions seem as though they had purpose. Instead, he found his eyes drifting to the shape of the beautiful woman now resting in eternal peace. He couldn't stand the thought that underneath the woolen blanket she lay torn apart like a practice target. He would never again hear a sweet melody leave her lips or taste the delicate skin only he knew. Never again would she say his name. Dampness settled on Marek's cheek, and he brushed it with a finger, clearing his throat. "What is the count?" He turned his attentions to Ronan.

"Nine."

A curse slipped from Marek's mouth as he exhaled. "That is all? Tell them all to go home."

"What is your plan?"

"Promise me you will look after the lads." Marek checked his blades before securing them to his mount.

Ronan gripped Marek's forearm. "What are you going to do?"

"Something stupid."

"Don't go getting yourself killed now, aye? Your son is out there, and he needs his da."

"Just promise me you will look after them. They will go getting into a heap of trouble without someone keeping eyes on them. Keep Gavin away from the forest. I'm sure he'll see every woman he has fornicated with and run off to find his death." He paused, unsure of how to approach the subject of Brynn's ceremonial burial. "If I'm not back in three days, you can proceed." Marek turned to meet Ronan's gaze. "A proper Archaean burial. Take her home, Ronan, as I promised."

"I give you my word, brother."

Marek clasped Ronan in a tight embrace, knowing it might be the last time he would see him in the worldly realm. "Three days, Ronan, or I will find you in hell."

The White Forest proved just as formidable the second time through as it was the first. Marek retraced his trail through the trees, searching for any signs that might lead him to the Engels and his boy. The wraiths lingered in the shadows keeping their distance, but Marek still heeded their silent warning to make haste. If he were to be sucked into their spell again, he would never recover.

Passing the blood trail from Brynn's death nearly sent him over the edge. Breathing in a heavy gulp of air, Marek somehow kept from vomiting at the sight. He closed his eyes as Cyran walked through the crimson-stained snow, unable to withstand the coloration. Blood had never bothered him before, but now it had new meaning. He pressed onward, breaching the depths of the trees. The bluff on which the Engels had attacked edged ever closer. A dark shadow dangled near the middle of the ridge, tangled in the tree roots jetting from the dirt. Marek recognized the body of Julian as he approached, looking for the path leading to the top of the bluff. "Burn in hell." He spat at the body as he passed, satisfied Brynn had been the one to kill the monster. Sweet revenge.

"Kill me…"

Marek jerked the reins, pulling Cyran to a stop. The voice sounded real enough.

"Please…" Julian coughed, struggling for a breath.

Marek approached the bottom of the cliff, sword at the ready. "Where is my son?" he asked, dismounting.

"Please, kill me, Archaean."

"*Where is my son?*" Marek screamed the words.

"They head to Braemir. Kill me!"

Marek sheathed his sword. He gripped a nearby root and heaved himself up to eye level with Julian, who hung helpless. "No. You are going to take me there." He curled his arms under Julian's then pulled the broken man to the forest floor. Julian landed in a heap. Marek rolled Julian with his foot until his bloodied face was visible. "What should we do, drag you? No, that won't do. Can you walk?" Marek rammed his boot into Julian's ribcage. "Get up, Engel."

Julian coughed, gagging on his own blood. "My legs are broken, please just kill me. I beg you."

Marek knelt beside the Engel. "Oh, you will die eventually, and when you do, I shall be standing at the gallows of hell to tighten the noose around your neck, making my face the last thing you see on your journey to the underworld. I will never give you the satisfaction of a warrior's death." Marek left Julian in the snow, twisted in an unnatural position, while he looked for a forgotten horse. He found one nervously awaiting the return of its owner at the top of the ridge — spooked but travel-worthy. With reins secured to a tree, Marek returned to the forest floor to drag Julian back up the footpath.

A whimper left the Engel's mouth when Marek hoisted him to the horse. "Will you shut the hell up? I have seen maimed children die braver than you." Marek secured Julian to the saddle.

"I'm going to die anyway, Archaean, why should I give you what you desire?"

"Would you rather I turn you over to Westmore? I'm sure he would take great pleasure in a torturous death for you, especially now that you have failed him."

Julian didn't reply.

"I will offer you this — take me to Braemir, and I will kill you before Westmore has the opportunity to tarnish your Engel nobility, or whatever it is you fools like to believe."

Julian curtly nodded in agreement.

Marek took the reins to Julian's horse before ascending into his own saddle and turned toward the road to Braemir. He cut across the forest since the bridge was at the bottom of a ravine, but at the pace he was keeping, Marek would arrive soon. Several times, he noticed Julian hunched over in the saddle, and Marek would tap Julian's backside with the flat edge of a sword, exclaiming there would be no dying yet.

As abruptly as it began, the White Forest and its ice-covered enchantments dissipated and the road to Braemir emerged under the cool breeze of night. The moon kept watch in the midnight sky, illuminating each crack and crevice as Marek came to a divide in the road.

"Which way?"

"Left. It will take you to Braemir." Julian titled his head to the sky to gaze at the twinkling stars. "Think my gods will welcome me?"

"Your gods do not exist." Marek recalled the time he had spoken those words to Brynn.

"There is a bend just ahead of where the river meets the bank. Take me there, if you don't mind, Archaean. I wish to see the heavens when I take my last breath."

Marek complied, following the split in the road until he came upon the river. He dismounted, untied Julian, and pulled him from the saddle. Marek dragged the Engel down the grassy embankment and set him near the river's edge. The quiet babbling of the water reminded Marek of a child's voice, rekindling his purpose. "Would you rather do it yourself or have me get it over with, Engel?" Marek drew his sword, waiting on the decision.

"I fear I do not have the courage to dispatch myself, Archaean, so I give you leave to take pleasure in completing the task for me." Julian, positioned flat on his back, focused on the sky above.

"A great pleasure, indeed." Grasping the hilt with both hands, Marek placed the tip of the blade over Julian's heart.

"He will no longer seek your death… Westmore, with her now dead. Her betrayal to him is what fueled him. He will seek other amusements now."

"'Tis his turn to die."

"I thought I could love her, you know, long ago," Julian spouted, his voice ripe with wasted melancholy.

"Not nearly as much as I." Marek took a breath — said a silent prayer for Brynn — then thrust downward. Blood spurt from the wound and Julian's eyes rolled behind his eyelids. Marek withdrew his sword, wiped the blade clean, and returned to the horses. He removed the tack from the extra horse and left it piled near the road, releasing the steed to roam.

The hours upon hours he traveled had neither beginning nor end. When his horse demanded they stop, Marek would dismount, but only long enough to rest Cyran. Marek wouldn't rest until he held Talon in his arms. Just before daybreak, Marek breached the walls of Braemir. The Archaean stronghold reeked of an off-putting Engel stench. Highland colors had been removed and replaced with fat, sleeping guards in ill-fitting armor. Crops sat unattended and left to wither, while wagons loaded to near capacity with ale and mead lined the inner walls of the crumbling fortification. Shards crunched beneath Cyran's hooves as Marek pressed deeper into the courtyard.

Two solid doors towered above him, locked from the inside, he supposed. No guards secured the gate to the stronghold — Westmore must have felt secure enough to leave his walls unattended. Walls that were, unfortunately, too high and slick for Marek to climb. He would have to find another way in. He loped his horse along the length of the wall looking for inconsistencies, stairs, or crumbling stone, anything that would allow him entry, but he couldn't find a single crack to slink through. Annoyed, Marek returned to the stronghold doors. "Well, it looks as if there is only one way in, my friend." Giving the horse an appreciative pat on the neck, he dismounted. Cyran nickered, tossing his head. Marek clasped the bridle on both sides of Cyran's muzzle, quieting the horse with the soothing words of an Archaean lullaby. Pressing his forehead to

Cyran's forelock, Marek whispered, "You go on now. 'Tis safer if you do not come with me this time, brother."

Cyran rested his head on Marek's shoulder in a final goodbye. A burst of warm air ticked the back of Marek's neck, and he reached up to scratch the horse's forehead. "All right, no more crying, beast, off with you now. Go find the others." Marek removed his weapons from the horse, gathered a few items from the saddlebag and slapped the animal on the rump. Cyran trotted away, returning to the Braemir Road.

Adjacent to the stronghold wall stood a crumbling watchtower. Large stones barricaded the entrance, and several dead vines twisted throughout pieces of charred wood and broken foundation. He stashed his weapons behind the overgrown mess, knowing he would lose them the moment the Engels were made aware of his presence. He would need them later.

Satisfied with the covering, Marek sauntered to the middle of the courtyard before the massive entry door. He drew in a long, slow breath, finding the Engel words in his mind. "Oy! You there, you fat bastard..." Marek picked up a small rock and flung it at the guard, who was busy snoring on the overpass of the inner curtain wall. The rock ricocheted off the man's metal armor, and he woke with a start, drawing his sword in dazed confusion. "Aye, down here, you piece of Engel shit! Is your master at home? Enjoying his morning cup of tea, is he?" The guard rushed to the wall and peered over the edge, mouth agape. "Don't just stand there, you idiot, go and wake his royal ass up! How in hell were you ever put on security detail? Do you even know how to use that sword? I bet your mother was a whore, was she not? A big fat one with tits so big even *she* could suckle them!" Marek continued with his taunting until the guard disappeared.

Moments later, several dark heads appeared in full battle regalia, just as stunned as the sleeping guard was to see him standing below. They muttered between themselves and pointed at him obscurely, almost ignoring him altogether. Marek rolled his eyes. "Who does a man have to kill to get some attention around here?"

Lord Westmore stepped forward into the morning sun, shielding his eyes against the harsh light in order to see who caused such a commotion below.

"You will do!" Marek shouted up at the Engel. "Good morning, your lordship!" He gave a small courtesy in jest then splayed out his arms to show he carried no weapon. Marek grinned at Westmore, cocking an eyebrow. "Miss me?"

———

"It has been two days, Ronan. I don't think he's coming back."

"He told us three days, Aiden." Ronan pushed his wavy hair from his eyes and kicked at a fallen tree branch. He did as instructed; he waited. And waited. Two full days had come and gone with no sign of his brother.

Aiden shrugged and returned to his puttering — whittling arrow shafts with a small knife.

"I cannot take this waiting anymore. 'Tis driving me mad." Gavin rose to his feet to pace the campsite.

Michael, separated from the group, spoke. "Perhaps we should start with the burial rituals then? I don't know anything about Archaean burials, but—"

"You." Gavin pointed a finger at Michael. "Shut your mouth. Count your blessings that I don't have you hogtied and on a spit for my dinner."

"We have three days." Ronan reassured the men. "We still have time."

"Three days, Ronan, and she's gonna' start to smell, aye?" Gavin stopped his pacing next to Brynn's body. A thin blanket covered her form, stained red by the seepage of her wounds. The fine details of her features were still visible, from the slight curvature of her lips to the fair definition of her calves. Beside her, Brynn's satchel lay discarded. Gavin picked it up and returned to his seat by the fire to peruse through its contents.

"Gavin, what are you doing?" Ronan shook his head in disgust.

"Don't nag me, Ronan. You sound like your wife. 'Tis not like she needs it now anyway." He continued to dig through the bag, pulling out various papers, bottles, and books. He placed them to the side and opened the biggest book. "Bah, it's in fecking Engel," he scoffed, tossing it toward the fire.

Ronan sighed, crossing the campsite toward Brynn's body while Gavin flipped through the pages of another book. Taking the corners of the blanket in his fingers, Ronan pulled it away from Brynn's face. With eyes closed and lips gently parted, she looked like a fallen angel, except Ronan couldn't stand to see how her blood flawed her delicate features. He returned to his gear to grab a spare tunic and his water bladder.

Nearby, Gavin munched on a piece of summer fruit. "Ronan, look at this. She wrote notes all over the pages on this one. From Engel to Archaean."

"Since when have you ever liked to read, Gavin?" Ronan returned to the body to wash the first bit of blood from her face.

"Since when I was bloody bored out of my skull, that's when. We should be killing Engels, not sitting here watching a body decompose." Gavin bit into the fruit, its juice dribbling from his lips. A drop clung to the whiskers on his chin before gathering enough strength to fall to the pages below. "Damn the gods," he cursed, wiping away the residue with a grime-covered finger.

Ronan ignored his friend, tuning out Gavin's rant. He washed the dirt and blood from Brynn's cheeks, revealing a soft rosy hue as if she had just woken from an afternoon sleep. If it weren't for the gaping wounds in her chest, he would have sworn she only now slept. He continued to clean her by washing her neck and hands but still couldn't shake the vision of her. She simply didn't look like every other dead body he'd seen, especially days later. Ronan placed a gentle hand to her breastbone, almost expecting to feel her heart beating beneath his palm. "It doesn't make any sense," he mumbled.

"What doesn't?" Aiden questioned, looking up from his busywork.

Ronan pushed the thought from his mind. It simply wasn't possible. He wet the cloth again, but his hand hesitated over her body.

"What's wrong, Ronan?" Aiden rose to his feet and took a step closer.

"It's just that… she seems… she still feels… *warm.*" A nervous laugh parted Ronan's mouth.

"How can that be?" Michael stood, edging his way closer to the Archaeans.

"It's 'cause she ain't feckin' dead." Gavin hurled the book from his hands as if it contained fire and stumbled backward, crawling from the object.

Aiden darted forward to retrieve it before the fire claimed its secrets. "You speak like a mad man, Gavin. We all saw her die."

325

"Look at it, look at the pages."

Uninterested in the commotion, Aiden handed the book to Ronan and returned to his whittling.

"Show me." Ronan set it on a rock. Gavin pointed to the spot he had been reading, and Ronan's brow narrowed. "Well, interesting, to be sure. You, Engel, come here. I have trouble with your words, so you will help me read this." He motioned for Michael to approach. "What does this say? Here, you read it to me." Ronan shoved the small book to Michael's chest and waited expectantly for a translation.

Michael read silently, turning page after page, referencing descriptions, illustrations, and mumbled in riddles. "It looks to be some sort of incantation. From what I gather... an ancient resurrection spell."

Aiden chuckled. "You cannot be serious. Incantations are legend. It is said the gods deemed us unworthy and so removed the power ages before us."

"I do not lie. She translated the entire book and wrote her own notes over every passage. She knew what this was."

"This." Ronan pointed to a symbol hand drawn repeatedly throughout the book, covering page after page. His eyes narrowed. "I've seen that before. Marek wore it about his neck. Our mother said it was some.... birth charm of some sort. From the ancients."

Michael smiled. "What a conniving, manipulative, *smart* thing to do."

"What do you mean?" Ronan asked, puzzled.

Michael perused a few more pages, following a passage with his finger. "Brynn knew all along this was going to happen. She knew she was going to die. I remember this from when we were children. People spoke about it, some superstitious prophecy of some sort. That the winter child had been born. They were afraid of her. Her fulfilling this prophecy, her dying, it was the only way Westmore would give up his search for her if he thought her dead. They *needed* to see her die."

"It would leave him unsuspecting enough for Marek to catch him unawares." Ronan toyed with the thought.

"Aye, and now she *is* dead, so what good is this book going to do?" Gavin scoffed, once more picking up the satchel and its contents. "The bag is full of items... vials, more books, herbal supplies, a medical kit. What good is any of it if she is already dead?"

Michael closed the book. "She left us directions. We are to perform the incantation." His brow dampened with fine beads of sweat.

"You mean we are to bring her... back to life?" Ronan choked on the words. He paced the ground, crossing his arms tightly around his chest. "'Tis impossible."

"We can at least try, we owe her that." Michael opened the book, finding the passage with the instructions and the incantation. "She has written the instructions in her own hand. Perhaps, she's caught between life and death."

"All right, Engel. Tell us what to do."

"If she rises up as some undead creature who wants to eat me, I am taking her head off. Just want to make that clear." Gavin raised his hands and returned to his own bit of ground near the fire.

Michael read from the book, jotting down his own notes on a piece of parchment from Brynn's satchel. He matched the potions and vials to those described in the book, placing them neatly beside the body. He read aloud from the book. "This potion will bring one back from the dead, provided they have been dead for less than three days and the body and spirit are both present when the incantation is cast. It will not restore lost limbs or heal wounds, poisons, or curses. Any wounds inflicted before death must be treated and healed once the intended has risen. Failure to heal will result in death. There is a note here. She writes that the healing herbs are in the medical kit. Its vial is blue in color."

Ronan searched the kit, finding the vial. He placed it with the others.

Michael continued to read. "The dead must be willing to return to life and may choose to decline the energy. Persons revived from the dead will not recall their time as a spirit. Within the safety of a fire circle, only the chosen one must repeat the words of the incantation."

"We need to enlarge the fire." Ronan gathered kindling and dry grasses, creating a ring of fire around the perimeter of Brynn's body. "What's next, Engel?"

Michael hesitated. His eyes focused on the book, but his thoughts seemed to be elsewhere.

"Are there no more instructions?"

"There is more, just one more." Michael sighed, looking up at the sky. "The sun is setting, we must hurry."

"Just tell me what to do and I will do it."

"Hand me your dagger." Michael reached out to Ronan, his palm facing upward.

Ronan's eyes narrowed. "Why do you need a dagger?"

"Only the giver of life may perform this incantation, as the giver freely gives his own life so the spirit may once again join its earthly body. One must die for the other to live," he said.

"You… intend to kill yourself then, Engel?"

"Brynn has already seen my death. I have caused enough pain, ruined too many lives. If I can save just one, one meant to live, one that would put an end to this war, I will do what I must. And if that means dying, then so be it. I will have served a purpose. Perhaps this has been *my* destiny all along."

Ronan nodded and slipped his dagger from his belt. He handed the hilt to Michael. "Your courage will be remembered."

"Once I am dead, you will need to combine the ingredients. My blood will be the last you will add. The mixture must be given to Brynn before her spirit fully enters the body, just when the sun gives way to moon. If you do not, the spirit will leave and return to the underworld forever. Once she breathes, you must treat the wounds. Give her the healing potion and sew her up. Do you think you can handle that?"

"Aye." Ronan sighed. "This is mad. This is witch's work. We should not be doing this."

"Tell my sister I never stopped loving her." Michael grasped the dagger and stepped into the ring of fire. Taking a deep breath, he began the incantation. "*Adun et nar shudet. Medu et ban ordon. Jestu dar mordak. Adun et nar shudet. Adun et nar shudet.*" He pulled the covering from Brynn's body and tossed it from the circle. Leaning over, Michael placed a kiss on her forehead. "Return to him, dear sister." He thrust the dagger inward, gasping as the life faded from his eyes. Within moments, his body slumped forward. The book of incantations slid from his hand.

When the shock abated, Ronan hurried to finish the spell. Believe in it or not, it was happening. He gathered every ingredient needed, including blood from the giver of life, Michael. While Gavin and Aiden tended to Michael's body, Ronan assembled the concoction, careful to get it right. There would be no second chances. When the sun met the early evening moon, Ronan opened Brynn's mouth and dribbled in the mixture. Then, with heavy skepticism, he waited.

She began to twitch. Her body contorted into unnatural positions, flailing about as the potion coursed through her. She drew in a long, deep breath and her lungs filled, her chest rising with the breath. Her back arched and her eyelids fluttered open. Her eyes rolled, not focusing. She struggled for a breath, one that would not readily come. She clutched her chest, trying to force air into her lungs. She was dying, again.

Using his shoulder to hold her still, Ronan pulled the cork free with his teeth and tipped the vial containing the healing potion into Brynn's mouth. She choked on the liquid but managed to swallow most of it. Ronan released her and waited.

The next few breaths were ragged and shallow, but soon her body relaxed and her breathing steadied. Ronan placed his head to her chest. A slow, rhythmic beating filled his ears. He backed away, too stunned to touch her. "Feck the gods — it worked."

"*Well.*" Gavin crossed his arms and smiled. "'Tis a good thing we didn't burn her then, eh?"

# Chapter Twenty-Eight

## FLESH AND BONE

B rynn winced as the needle poked through her skin. A small cry escaped on a breath.

"You're doing it wrong, give it here!" Gavin pushed Ronan to the side, snatching the needle and thread.

"It's going to hurt no matter which way we do it, Gavin."

Gavin knelt next to Brynn, surveying the wound on her thigh. The working space was tight. "Maybe we should take off the gown."

Ronan slapped the back of Gavin's head. "I don't think Brynn would appreciate that nearly as much as you would."

"Where is Michael?" whispered Brynn.

"He... completed the incantation," answered Ronan.

"And Marek?" She choked on the word, her voice raspy and coarse.

Ronan retrieved a water bladder and helped her to drink. "He's gone to fetch Talon. We expect him to return shortly."

Brynn shook her head. "No. I must go to him. He will die."

Ronan placed her hand in his. He motioned to Gavin to continue sewing, while he comforted her. "Did you see his death? You are not well enough to travel."

"The healing potion will continue its work, but I must go to him. The three ravens — one must not be Marek."

Confused, Ronan pressed for more information. "What do you mean?"

"The ravens, they are death. Three must die. The third must not be Marek." Brynn closed her eyes, silently fighting against the pain. "It must be Westmore."

"Hurry, Gavin," Ronan urged.

"I'm sewing as fast as I bloody well can. These hands were not made for woman's work. They were made for working a woman's ass." Gavin snickered at his own crude humor. He finished closing the first wound and set to work on the second, fishing out pieces of splintered wood from the arrow shaft. "She has a broken rib, but it seems as though it will heal," he commented, pinching the skin to add a stitch.

"Just sew."

"Really, this would be so much easier without clothing in the way," Gavin grumbled but shut his mouth and finished piecing the wound together when Ronan balled his fist.

Ronan monitored the sewing of the final wound as it was located precariously close to Brynn's breast, but Gavin behaved and stitched the wound closed with minimal tearing of the bodice. A tunic was slipped over her gown and a broth made for her dinner.

Propped against a saddle and covered with a blanket, she slept, dozing in and out of consciousness. Ronan roused her throughout the night to help her drink and check her wounds. Little by little, Brynn regained her strength as the healing potion worked its magic.

---

A gentle hand shook her shoulder. "Brynn, 'tis time to go, aye?" She pushed herself to a sitting position, testing her mobility. "How do you fare?"

"I'm better." She forced a smile and tried to stand.

Ronan slung his arm around her middle to steady her. "You shall ride with me." He walked her to his horse, transferred her weight to Gavin, then mounted.

"Up you go," said Gavin, hoisting Brynn to Ronan. "Let us fetch your husband, shall we?"

"By all means, let's." Ronan nickered to his horse, nudging it forward with his heels.

"And back to the death walkers we go." Gavin sighed, following.

They traveled the path through the forest, keeping watch for Engels, but found no resistance. Several wraiths materialized in the distance, hissing whispers between the trees, but ventured no further than the shadows. Ronan stiffened in the saddle at their appearance, but Brynn reassured him. "Show no fear and they will not harm you."

"Did you see anyone before you... died?" Ronan asked.

"I saw my mother."

"Was she as you remembered?"

"I do not remember my mother. She was murdered shortly after my birth." Brynn sucked in a breath and blinked to keep tears from filling her eyes. "But, aye, she was beautiful."

"I must tell you, Brynn, I find this all... a bit hard to understand. I do not know what you are, but my brother needs you and I will do what it takes to keep him alive."

"One day, Ronan, I will tell you." Brynn sighed softly, the words a breathy whisper.

Soon the snow dissipated, and the road to Braemir was within sight. A cool breeze greeted them, welcoming them from the shadows. The pace quickened once on the road and talk of their plan took form. No one knew what to expect, not even Brynn. She could only hope that she would find Marek and Talon alive.

As they traveled, the men took a verbal inventory of what weapons they carried, who would search the stronghold, and who would protect Brynn. It was agreed upon that Ronan would take most of the duties pertaining to her safety. Aiden, being the stealthiest, would stay to the shadows and find the boy. Gavin would cause the biggest disturbance outside the walls as possible to draw the Engels away from the stronghold if need be.

"I will lure their whores to the courtyard and put on a show for their masters. Tell me, how could they resist this?" Gavin gestured his hand over his chest, beaming.

"The words escape me," replied Ronan. A branch snapped in the trees lining the road and he stopped, turning his ear toward the sound.

"What is it?" whispered Brynn.

"An animal," Ronan replied. "I think."

Cyran appeared from the trees, riderless. "That's Marek's horse." She clutched Ronan's forearm.

Aiden approached the horse, checking for signs of combat, blood, or a message from Marek. "His weapons are missing, but the horse is unharmed. There are no signs of struggle."

Ronan pondered the split in the road before them.

"Which way do we go?"

Aiden chuckled, pulling himself up into the saddle.

"Left."

"How are you so sure?" asked Ronan.

"Just follow the hoof prints."

---

"There are Engels everywhere." Hunkered out of sight near the stronghold of Braemir, Ronan and Gavin surveyed the area. "Marek must have alerted them to his presence." Ronan took note of the guard placement.

"We cannot ride in with swords drawn, they will be expecting that."

"Two men guard the gate. Five watch from the inner curtain." Ronan pointed to the area, spotting several more patrolling the courtyard below. "We need a plan."

Gavin grinned. "You are in luck, my friend, for I have one. Follow me."

The men left Brynn with the horses while they procured disguises of farmer's cloaks and stole an unattended wagon full of molding hay. Finding several discarded barrels near an outer wall, they placed them in the back of the wagon. They hid the horses near the road and tucked Brynn under the hay. Ronan took up the reins with Gavin at his side, while Aiden rode in the back next to a barrel, imbibing on a flagon of ale beneath his newly acquired poor-man's cloak.

Ronan approached the gate, bringing the wagon to a stop before the Engel gate guards.

"Halt!" The guard blocked the entrance to the stronghold courtyard. "State your purpose."

"Wine, my friend." Ronan nodded toward the barrels in the back of the wagon. "For his lordship. Only the best. A gift from our clansmen."

The two guards conversed about their entry before replying, "Visitors must leave their weapons at the gate. Do you carry weapons, Archaeans?"

Ronan's brow narrowed. Looking to Gavin he asked, "Gavin, do we carry any weapons?"

Gavin rubbed his chin in feigned thought. "I might have a blade here somewhere." He rose from the bench seat and jumped down. Searching the inside of his cloak he produced a dagger. "Ah, here it is." Gavin tossed it to the ground in front of the guards.

Ronan descended from the wagon and dropped his own daggers. "It seems I carry some as well."

Gavin pat his arms, searching for the small knife he kept hidden beneath his armguard. "Oh! Here's another." He relinquished it to the growing pile. "Almost forgot about that one," he told the guard closest to him.

Ronan pulled a short sword from its hiding place — behind his back — hidden by the ragged cloak. It, too, joined its companions in the increasing pile of weapons. "Any more I may have forgotten?" he asked Gavin.

"I have one more, I believe." Gavin also withdrew a short sword and handed it to one of the guards. "Hold this for me, would you?"

The dumbfounded guard took the outstretched sword by the hilt.

Gavin removed his cloak, revealing his broadsword. He withdrew its great length from the scabbard and gave it to the other guard. "Last one, I'm pretty sure of it. Say, Aiden, you have any weapons back there?"

Aiden procured a dagger from his side and tossed it to Gavin.

He caught it with ease. "Cheers, mate." Gavin raised the dagger in thanks. Aiden hoisted his flagon in return before taking a long swig. "Oh, this one's a beauty. Have a look." In a split second, the blade sliced through the air, slashing the throat of the closest guard.

With yet another hidden weapon, Ronan dispatched the remaining guard. The Engel's bewildered face stared up at him from the ground.

"Nicely done," Gavin complimented, retrieving his weapons.

"Aye, well played." Ronan tossed Aiden his dagger.

"That was good fun, aye?"

"The most fun I've had all day." Securing the last of his weapons, Gavin donned his cloak and climbed up into the wagon.

"Much more fun than a bloody resurrection, I'll say. Aiden, give me a hand, would you?" With Aiden's help, the Engel guards were heaved into the back of the wagon and covered with hay. "Sorry about the mess, Brynn." Ronan apologized, climbing back into the driver's seat.

"Quite all right," she told him.

The wagon rolled to a stop in an abandoned corner of the courtyard. Commoners went about their daily business, ignoring the seemingly ordinary cart of ale. Ronan and Gavin jumped from the seat, conversing of their plan while Aiden tossed the flagon and helped Brynn from the hay. He covered her with his own cloak, hiding her face with the hood.

"You should stay out of sight, my lady," Aiden spoke, picking a stray piece of straw from her hair. "I will find a safe place for you to hide."

"You need not speak so formally, Aiden, and I'm coming with you." Brynn held firm.

His fierce blue eyes flickered over her features. "You are the wife of my clan brother. I am sworn to protect you at all costs."

Brynn managed a weak smile. "I will be the safest with you, then, aye?"

"I am to find your boy." Aiden protested.

"Talon won't know you. He will not go with you, but he will come with me."

"You are in no shape to be running through the stronghold."

"And I am sure you will keep me safe." The corners of her mouth twitched. Brynn knew she had won the argument.

Aiden's mouth formed a slight frown, and he bit his bottom lip. "Stay close." He clasped her forearm, keeping her steady.

When they were sure no one was watching, Ronan and Gavin approached the doors in a contrived panic, telling the guards they had seen a man with a weapon near the wall. The guards followed willingly… to their deaths. The bodies were dumped in a nearby building, leaving the Archaeans free to enter the stronghold undetected. Brynn and Aiden slipped inside, while Gavin set to work in the courtyard confusing its occupants.

"Are you all right, Brynn?" Aiden paused on the staircase, waiting for her to catch up.

She let out a breath and removed her palm from her side. A smear of blood covered her skin. "I'm fine." She wiped her hands on her gown and continued up the stairs. They entered a long corridor with doors lining each side. "Which door do we try?"

Aiden peeked around a corner. "He is not here," he told her. "No guards. Let us try the next one." They snuck down the corridor only to find another staircase leading to the next level of the stronghold. Halfway up, Aiden pushed Brynn against the wall with his arm. "Listen," he whispered. "Engels." He removed his bow from his shoulder before making his way up the stairs. In the middle of the corridor, two Engels guarded a single door. They argued over something incoherent before one left his post and exited to the stairs opposite Aiden.

Crouching to one side, Aiden drew his bow, releasing an arrow. The guard clutched his chest before crumpling to the floor, dead. Aiden motioned for Brynn to follow as he made his way. He tested the handle — locked.

"The guard," Brynn suggested.

Aiden searched the man's belt, finding a set of keys.

With the very first key, the lock clicked. Bow ready, he nodded at Brynn to open the door. She turned the latch then moved to allow Aiden entry. He burst through the door, searching for resistance, but instead found a startled nursemaid.

The old woman rose from her chair, steadying herself on the armrest. She didn't move, only stared at the warrior before her. Aiden stepped further into the room, seeking Talon. "Brynn, ask her if your boy is here. I do not speak the Engel words as well as you."

Brynn entered the room.

The woman's eyes narrowed and she took a shaky step forward. "My girl, is that you?"

Brynn eyed the white hair and the frail frame of the woman, trying to place her in memory. And then it dawned on her, the woman she remembered was of dark coloration then with a hearty laugh and a mother's warmth. "Magda?"

"Oh, it is you, my sweet girl. Come and give this old woman one last happy memory before she dies. Come closer so that I may see you."

Brynn rushed to her Magda's side, cradling her face in her hands. "Have you seen my son, Magda?"

"He is there." She pointed to a bed tucked in the corner of the room. "He sleeps."

Brynn rushed to the bed, dropping to her knees. Snuggled deep in blankets, Talon slept peacefully. She kissed his forehead, rousing him. The boy rubbed the sleep from his eyes.

"You must stay for a visit, my girl. We have so much to talk about." Magda lowered herself to her chair and resumed her mending.

"I'm so sorry, Magda, but I cannot stay." Brynn hugged Talon to her chest, not wanting to release him.

"Brynn, we must go. The absent guards are bound to be noticed." Aiden kept watch in the threshold.

"Where is Da?" Talon asked, squirming from his mother's arms.

"He is here, Talon, and I'm going to find him. You need to go with my friend, Aiden, all right? He is going to take you to safety." Brynn kissed him once more before ushering him to Aiden. "Please make sure you get him out. I need to find Marek."

"I must go with you," Aiden told her.

"I need to find him, Aiden. They will not be expecting me, as they believe me dead. They *will* be searching for you. Take him." Brynn thrust Talon's hand into Aiden's.

"Very well, but take this." Aiden drew his dagger and handed her the hilt. "You know how to use it?"

"Aye, the pointed end goes first. Now go!" Aiden slung Talon over his shoulder and on to his back before exiting to the corridor. Brynn turned to Magda. "I must leave. They hold my husband, and I must find him. I will die without him." Her thoughts briefly turned to her seeping wounds.

"The warrior from the north? He is your husband?"

Brynn nodded.

"They keep a man chained below. I have heard his screams. Go find your warrior, girl. There is a passage behind the red tapestry on the lower floor. It will take you to him, but I must warn you. The lord's council meets in the study in the very same corridor."

"Your mother would be so proud of you. You've grown into a fine woman, my child."

Brynn returned to the woman to give her one final hug goodbye. "Thank you, Magda."

R onan cleared the first floor without finding a trace of Marek. He encountered several Archaean slave girls who didn't bat an eyelash at seeing an Archaean warrior in the stronghold, but he didn't see a single Engel worth exposing himself for. He headed to the stairwell, intent on searching the second level. Hearing footsteps, Ronan pressed his back against the wall, keeping to the shadows. His fingers wrapped around his sword, ready for attack. A familiar face rounded the corner. Gavin. Grabbing him by his armor, Ronan hauled him into the shadows. "What the hell are you doing in here? You were supposed to be in the courtyard. I could have been an Engel and you would be dead right now!"

"They show no interest in us outside the walls, and you need me in here, to find Marek." Gavin removed Ronan's grip from his brigantine. "Two sword arms are better than one."

"I hate it when you're right, Gavin."

"Be thankful 'tis not that often." Gavin approached the stairwell first, sword drawn. His feet fell soft on the stone steps as he ventured up two at a time. Nearing the top, he spotted the dark shadow of a woman hiding in the threshold.

She turned to face him. She gripped a weapon, poised for attack. "Brynn?"

She sighed in relief. "There is a passage behind that tapestry," she told him, pointing down the corridor. "Marek might be at the bottom of it. However, the Engels gather in the study just across the way. I cannot reach it without being seen."

Gavin and Ronan conversed in hushed tones, devising a quick plan. When finished, Ronan placed his palm on Brynn's shoulder. "No worries, Brynn. When the timing is right, get to the passage. Under no circumstances do you enter the study."

The two Archaean warriors hesitated just outside the open study door. Inside, several Engels conversed over battle strategies and war tactics. They counted at least five voices, but wouldn't be sure of the count until they entered the room, Ronan first.

"Good afternoon, gentlemen!" he greeted, sauntering into the study.

The voices hushed at the unexpected interruption.

"I'm terribly sorry to disturb you, but I seem to be missing one of my men. Have any of you seen him, by chance? Tall like me, golden hair... foul mouth when angry?"

The Engels looked at one another, unwilling to answer.

Gavin paced the room, eyeing the furniture and decorations, feigning interest in the Engel fabrications that covered the previous Archaean tapestries. "I think we have enough to work with in here," he told Ronan in his native tongue.

Ronan insisted again. "One of you must tell me where he is, or you will all die."

"The gods piss on you!" spat one of the Engels, rising from his chair near a desk.

"Gavin, kill him."

Before the others could take in what was happening, Gavin singled out the man and tore a gaping wound through his abdomen with his sword. The Engel slumped to the floor, landing in a pile of guts and blood. The others backed away, seeking escape through the door, but the Archaeans had them cornered. Gavin surveyed the ceiling. "Get me that rope if you wouldn't mind, Ronan."

"My pleasure," Ronan replied, using his blade to free the ceiling chandelier. It crashed to the floor below, and Ronan severed the binding rope to toss the length to Gavin.

"Come on, all together now." Gavin clapped his hands rapidly. "Do not fear, Engels, all you need to do is tell me where my man is and you can all go about your merry way." After tossing one end of the rope to Ronan, he cinched the thick binds around the remaining men, twisting it around each of their arms, lining them up back to back. When the rope was secure, Gavin perused the documents on the desk. There were maps, detailed outlines, and descriptions of the Archaean territories, and more importantly, correspondence letters from Lord Westmore to his Engel benefactors. "Where is this Lord Westmore?" Gavin asked the restrained men.

"Probably killing your friend right now," one of them answered.

Gavin frowned, turning to Ronan. "We cannot have that now, can we?"

"Certainly not," Ronan answered. "Pass me that lamp, would you?"

"This?" Gavin picked up the table lamp but dropped it on the desk. The oil spilled from the round pot, seeping into the documents on the desk. "My apologies, take this one."

Gavin picked up another lamp from the desk and tossed it to Ronan, who backed away from the throw, letting the lamp crash to the floor near the group of Engels.

"Ahh, there is another lamp, just over there." Ronan crossed the room to a small table, picking up the lit lamp. The radiant heat burned his palms and he flung it to the floor, cursing it.

"Well, damn it, Ronan, we seem to be running out of lamps. Light a few candles, would you?"

"Pass me that torch, dear brother?" Ronan pointed at the wall behind Gavin. It burned with a steady flame.

Gavin removed the torch from the sconce and flung it at the oil-soaked desk. It landed among the papers and books, setting them ablaze. "There."

"You idiot," scolded Ronan. "You were supposed to throw it over there!" Picking up the torch by its handle, Ronan pitched it at the wooden floor, slick with oil. The fire spread the length of the spill, licking at the wooden legs of chairs, steadily making its way to the bound Engels. They shuffled together in a panic, backing away from the fire, but couldn't escape its clutches. "Goodbye, gentlemen." Ronan waved before bolting to the door on Gavin's heels. "Sorry we couldn't stay for tea." Ronan heaved the door closed.

---

Darkness surrounded her, but Brynn found her way one step at a time, ever closer to Marek. She dragged her fingers over the moist walls of the stairwell, steadying herself. The dank smell of mildew and stale blood filled her nostrils. She was heading to the prison cells. A muffled scream made her heart race, and she stumbled on the stair, falling to her backside. She slid down several steps before recovering. Righting herself, she followed the sound of the scream.

Rounding a corner, light from a wall sconce flooded her eyes and she shaded them until she adjusted to the brightness. Muffled voices echoed off the walls as she pressed onward. A dull pain from her side radiated across her middle, and she covered the area with her palm. She needed to hurry; she didn't have much time left. He must not die.

A threatening voice rumbled through the corridor, followed by a laugh and a grunt. She continued until the voices were clear. She stopped before a door. Peeking through the crack, she spied the back of a large Engel man.

"Is that the best you can do?" said a slurred voice from within.

*Marek!* Frantic, she searched for a shield, anything she could use to protect herself while entering. She found nothing, not even a scrap of wood. Deciding to rely on the element of surprise, she clutched her dagger, practicing a few thrusts. Saying a quick prayer to the first god she could think of, Brynn tiptoed to the door and widened the crack just enough to slip through.

The Engel's back faced her, protected by a thick leather vest. She would never have the strength to penetrate it, so she took aim for his neck. But as she raised the dagger to strike, the Engel moved, revealing her form to Marek.

His bloodied face sunk to an ashen shade of pale and his eyes grew wide. Marek choked back a scream, alerting the Engel to a presence within the cell. The Engel turned.

She shoved the dagger upward, striking the man just below the neck.

The hilt of the dagger protruded from the area at an odd angle, but she'd hit her intended target. The Engel stomped in her direction, swinging a fist, but Brynn dodged the blow. Retreating from the cell, the Engel stumbled through the door, collapsing in the corridor.

Brynn lunged at Marek. He hung from a beam, his wrists clasped in irons. His feet dangled above the floor. His chest was bare and mottled with dirt, bruises, and oozing wounds. Fresh blood was smeared over dried blood. A gash just above his temple flowed down his chin.

"Are you a spirit that stands before me?"

"No," she said, stepping closer. "I stand before you flesh and bone."

Marek shook his head. "It cannot be. You are dead. I held you in my arms when you took your last breath."

"We do not have the time for me to explain, but you must believe me. I am alive."

"I don't know what kind of enchantment this is, but you are *not* my wife."

"Dead or alive, it does not matter. I am still your wife. We must hurry." Brynn glanced at the ceiling. A thin, velvety smoke flowed through the cracks of the wooden floorboards above. "How do I get you down?"

"The key — the guard carries it. Are you a death walker, then? A wraith come to take me?"

"No, 'tis just me." She left his side, returning to the Engel. Searching his belt, she found a key ring and unhooked it. With hands that shook too much, she fumbled with the mass of different keys. "Which one is it?"

"Just try them all."

Smoke continued to fill the small cell. Brynn stretched toward the beam but could not reach the lock. A short sob followed a whimper as a cold fear consumed her. She wasn't tall enough to free him. "I cannot reach it," she cried. In the midst of her effort, she lost her grip on the iron ring and it fell to the rushes below.

"Calm down, love, we have plenty of time." A few hot ashes trickled from above, settling on his shoulders and he sucked in a breath.

Brynn fell to her knees, feeling for the keys. Her fingers touched the cool metal, and she snatched them up. "I must find something to stand on."

"Brynn, behind you!"

She turned in time to see the guard reach for her, dagger still protruding from his neck. Tumbling backward, she avoided most of his assault, but his elbow caught her shoulder, sending her spinning to the floor.

Marek managed to swing his legs enough to wrap his thighs around the guard's neck and pin him. The more than man struggled, the tighter Marek squeezed. "Brynn, climb."

She hesitated, not fully understanding. "You mean climb the guard?"

"Yes, Brynn, just like you would a tree." Marek locked his ankles together, trapping the Engel.

"We both know I am no good with trees, Marek." Placing the key ring between her teeth, Brynn hiked her gown and placed her foot on the man's thigh then grabbed his chest armor, pulling herself upward, finally high enough to reach the locks. The first key she tried wasn't a match. She tried the second. No luck.

Marek grunted as the man shook beneath him. "A bit faster, Brynn." Smoke seeped between the wooden slats, filling the air around them. A steady heat bore down on them from above.

"I'm going as fast as I can. I've been mostly dead all day," she chided, trying the third key. The lock clicked and the iron ring released Marek's wrist. He grasped the loose chain to keep his balance. Using the same key, Brynn unlocked the other cuff. The three of them tumbled to the floor in a heap.

Marek scuffled with the guard but managed to grip the dagger. He pulled it free for only a moment before readjusting its position, this time through the Engel's vertebrae, finishing him.

Brynn collapsed, clutching her middle.

Crawling to Brynn's side, Marek lay beside her. "Am I in hell?"

"I would hope not," she wheezed.

His palm hovered above her, hesitating.

Brynn grasped his hand, bringing it to her heart. "Feel how it beats."

"I don't know what sort of trickery this is, but you are alive."

"Aye, and you would have made better choices had you just read the damn book."

Marek took her in his arms, pulling her close. "You are alive." He kissed her lips, her eyes, her cheeks with a fervid purpose.

"Aye." She glanced up at him, her smile weak. "But not for long, I fear." Marek shifted his gaze to the patch of red under Brynn's palm. Her stitches had torn through. "Do not fret for me."

Rolling to her side, Marek let out a cynical laugh.

"What a sordid pair we make, wife. Look at us. You were dead, but have risen to rescue me, only to be trapped in a fire together." Taking in a smoke-filled breath, he found the strength to rise. "I believe it's time we leave this place. There is no need to die twice." Kneeling beside her, he lifted Brynn to his chest.

She wrapped her arms around him, burying her head in the crook of his neck, content to breathe in his scent. "Westmore," she whispered. "We must find him before the potion fades."

"And why is that?" he questioned, leaving the cell and heading to the stairs.

"He must die for me to live." Her voice hitched and she coughed. A spurt of blood splattered against Marek's skin, mixing with his sweat. "The longer he lives, the sooner I die. My wounds need tending, and that cannot happen in this place. This war will never end while he lives."

Reaching the main stairwell, Marek wrenched open the door with great urgency. Thick, black smoke gushed into the corridor, clouding his vision. He turned, shutting the door with his hip. "The fire has reached the exit," he told Brynn. Searching each cell, he looked for another way out. Instead, he found a ladder and a few pieces of a broken sword. After returning Brynn to her feet, he placed the ladder against a wall and climbed it, testing the damaged ceiling for heat. Finding it cool, he rammed the jagged blade against the wood. It splintered but not enough to break it. Marek rotated the sword and assaulted the barricade with the hilt. Letting out a fierce scream, he thrust his shoulder against it, cracking the board. He hacked at the pieces with the blade, managing to create a hole large enough to fit his fist through by pulling at the edge of the boards until he could squeeze through the hole. The splinters grated his skin as he wiggled his way to freedom. "All right, your turn," he told Brynn, reaching his arm back through the hole.

She scaled the ladder, taking his hand. Marek pulled her through the opening. Fire roared above them, rippling from beam to beam, consuming anything within reach. He lifted Brynn in his arms before working his way to the front of the stronghold. Dodging a piece of burning wood as it fell from above, he ducked into an alcove to catch his breath. "Which way, love?" he panted, wiping his brow on his arm.

"The main hall is through one of those corridors," she told him, pointing him in the right direction. "We must find him soon."

Braving the smoke and fire once more, Marek worked his way over the falling rubble. Choosing the first corridor he saw, he jetted through the exit, freeing them from the fire. "We are almost out, love," he muttered, planting a kiss to her forehead. Rounding a corner, Marek nearly tottered to the floor when he unexpectedly collided with Westmore.

The Engel drew his sword, circling the pair. Confusion settled in his brow. "Well, if it is not my whore and her mongrel. You… are supposed to be *dead*. My men killed you… they saw you die."

Marek lowered Brynn to her feet.

"You are the third raven, Westmore. It is you who must die," she said.

"Am I supposed to know what that means?" Westmore spoke through his gritted teeth.

Marek pulled Brynn behind him, positioning himself between her and Westmore. "Brynn, you need to leave now. Let me do what needs to be done."

"But you do not have—"

"*Now*, Brynn." Marek circled the Engel in a twisted battle dance.

Hiking up her skirts, Brynn found the strength to leave. She clutched her middle as she staggered down the corridor.

"Are we dead, Archaean?" Westmore surveyed his surroundings.

"Not yet," answered Marek.

"Then how is it she lives?"

"That is for the gods to answer."

"It looks as though you are sadly unarmed, Archaean." Westmore swung wide, testing Marek.

"Looks that way," Marek replied, dodging the swing. "I don't suppose you will throw down your blade and fight me like a man, Engel?"

Westmore shook his head.

"You Engels never could fight fair."

"Where is the fun in fair?" Taking a long stride forward, Westmore stabbed his sword frontward, following the movement with a blow meant to strike.

Marek leaped out of the way, spiraling around the Engel. Seizing the opportunity, Marek shoved his foot between Westmore's legs, tripping him. Balling his fist, Marek planted a solid blow to the Engel's jaw.

Westmore swung wildly, the tip of his sword connecting with Marek's chest. "Another mark to add to your list of injuries, Archaean, if only to help you bleed a bit quicker."

"I will fight you until the very last drop is shed, Westmore."

"Then I fear this battle will not last very long."

"Then drop your sword and best me as a man, not some sniveling Engel that needs to hide behind a blade."

Marek held up his fists, planting his feet.

"Very well, Archaean." Westmore tossed his sword to the side and removed his overcoat. He circled Marek then stepped to the side, delivering a punch to Marek's ribs.

Marek hunched forward. His body near submission, his recovery was slow. Westmore delivered two more strikes before Marek could retaliate. The Engel backed away, emitting a sinister laugh. He held out his arms gesturing toward the burning embers and blood splatters. "All this… for a *woman?*"

"*My* woman. She is my constant, the reason my heart beats. I will die to protect her. Without her, I am nothing." Marek charged Westmore, locking his arm around the Engel's neck. They scuffled, each trying to best the other in a never-ending battle of blows.

Westmore freed himself from the grappling and took a step back, sucking in a breath. "You are never going to best me, Archaean. Give up now, and I promise you a swift death."

"I must kill you, Westmore." Marek wiped the sweat from his eyes. "Her life depends on it."

"She is already dead! They *killed* her in the forest!" the Engel argued. "Three arrows, Archaean — you were there! That *thing* cannot be mortal!"

"We shall end this now."

Westmore bent over his sword, picking it up. "Well, seeing as I'm the only one with a weapon… let us get this over with, shall we? I've become rather bored."

Marek dodged Westmore's assault using what he could to defend himself — pieces of broken timber, hanging tapestries, and the occasional wall torch. Without a weapon, he stood little chance of becoming the victor. Making the decision to rid Westmore of his sword, Marek charged him, intending to knock him to the ground. Instead, his face met with the pommel of Westmore's sword, sending him careening to the floor.

Westmore tossed his head back in a wicked laugh. "That was too easy, Archaean! What a delight it will be to watch the life leave your eyes. My men did a fine job on you below, it seems. This has been too easy." The Engel raised his sword high, ready to plunge it into Marek's chest.

"I will see you in hell," Marek said.

Westmore took a breath, gripped the hilt of his sword, and plunged. His death blow came to an abrupt halt inches from Marek's heart. Eyes wide, they traveled to his chest, and to the bloodied blade protruding from it.

From behind, Brynn released her grip on the sword.

Westmore floundered from his stance over Marek, lurching violently against the corridor wall. A sickening gurgle caught in his throat as he slid to the floor, leaving a bloody smear on the gray stone as he fell, dead.

Marek let out a long breath and chuckled, which developed into a full belly laugh.

"Are you all right?" Brynn towered over him.

He smiled up at her. "I thought that was it… that I was going to die. You, my love, are my angel. My saviour."

From the end of the corridor, battle cries cut through the heat of the fire. Gavin and Ronan charged, swords fully drawn. When they reached the scene, their attack slowed, morphing into visible disappointment. Gavin turned to the body of Westmore, nudging it with his boot. After casting his sword to the floor, he threw his hands up in disgust. "I missed it? What the hell, Marek?"

"It is finished." Brynn slumped against the wall. She surveyed her wounds. "Does anyone have a needle and thread? It would be a shame for me to bleed out here next to him." She cast a glance at Westmore's body, then up at Marek. "We did it."

Marek rose to his feet and wrapped his arms around his wife. "No, *you* did it. You succeeded where I could not. You returned for me."

"I will always come for you," she told him, tightening her grip on him.

Pushing a lock of matted hair behind her ear, he kissed her, full and unyielding. "Let us go home, aye?" he told her, his breath hot on her skin. "Let me show you what a husband can do for his wife."

Brynn's lips brushed against Marek's. "Take me home, husband."

"Ask me nicely," he replied, completing the kiss.

### The End

# Epilogue

Marek pulled the wagon to a stop just over the crest of the gentle slope of a hill. Below, nestled quietly in the valley, his family awaited his return. His heart raced at the simple thought of holding them again. His horses grazed in the meadow, lush and green from the summer rain. Nearby, the frame of an unfinished house stood tall against the tree line.

He was home.

Beside him, Gavin trotted next to the wagon, peering below. "Are we here?"

Marek nodded.

"*Och*. What a right proper homesteader you are, Marek!" Gavin laughed. "And is that monstrous beast of wood the project you enlisted our services for?"

"Aye, need it finished before the winter."

"Ambitious, Marek?" Ronan snickered, joining his brother.

"Do not complain, brother, for when it's finished, you and your brood get the croft."

"Truly?" asked Ronan's wife, Ireni, from the back of the wagon.

"Aye. Your lads are big enough to help now, and they will stay out of trouble here in Dunlogh with me putting them to work."

Ronan couldn't hide his astonishment. "Thank you. You are too kind."

"You are welcome." Marek clicked at the horses and flicked the reigns.

The sweet sounds of giggles wafted on the breeze, greeting him at the top of the drive. Three golden-haired children chased after a hound, running barefoot through the grass. The smallest, a little girl with rosy cheeks and curls bouncing with each step, beamed a smile when she saw him.

"Da!" she shrieked with delight, leaving her two older brothers to race to the wagon. Marek had barely descended from the bench seat when she leaped into his arms, placing her tiny little hands on his cheeks. She planted a kiss on the tip of his nose. "I missed you so much!"

Wrapping his arms around her frame, Marek twirled her in a long hug. "Oh, my little Brienne, I missed you more than anything."

"More than Mum?" she remarked, coy and cute.

Marek laughed. "Almost. Did you terrorize your brothers like I told you to?"

"Excessively so." A devilish grin curled one side of her perfect little mouth.

"That's my girl. Brienne, say hello to your Uncle Ronan, your Aunt Ireni, and your cousins, Phinn and Cameron." Marek gave her one more squeeze before returning her to her feet. Gavin cleared his throat. "And your uncle, Gavin," Marek added.

Brienne bowed her head in greeting. "Welcome." She flashed a wide smile before whirling in the opposite direction and racing away, giggling.

"Sharp as a whip, that one, and her tongue even sharper." Marek laughed. "The gods help me when the courters come calling. Takes after her ma, I suppose. Lads!" he called to his boys, beckoning them to his side. The two boys dropped their wooden swords and jogged over to their father. Marek ruffled Talon's hair. "Swords are more important than greeting your da now?"

"Sorry, Da. I was winning," Talon replied.

"Talon, Owen, show your cousins to their room and take some bags with you."

"Hello, Da," said Owen, giving his father a slight hug.

Talon hoisted himself into the back of the wagon, grabbing a bag with each hand. "You could help, you know." Talon glared at Gavin, who leaned on the wooden rail, watching.

"I will duel you with that little twig you call a sword and loser empties the wagon. Deal?" Gavin offered.

"Deal."

"You had better be careful, Gavin, Talon is a mighty fine swordsman. Where is your mum?" asked Marek, scanning the grounds for Brynn.

"She is resting in her room. Want me to fetch her for you?"

"No, I shall find her. You best beat your uncle or you have a lot of work in your future." The back of the wagon was loaded down with Ronan's household goods. Marek left the two to argue over who was better with a sword, heading toward the croft at a quickened pace.

Familiar sounds and smells greeted him as he opened the door. Freshly baked bread cooled next to the hearth, and his stomach growled just looking at it. Cut flowers in delicate vases lined the windows, and Brienne's doll lay on the dining table — turned operating table — with a freshly stitched arm and a tiny bandage wrapped around its threadbare head. How he'd missed the womanly touches during his absence.

As he rounded the corner to the back bedroom, her scent flooded his nostrils, consuming his thoughts. Sweet like honey with a lingering hint of her precious milled soap. Marek kicked off his boots, not bothering to unbuckle them. Grasping his tunic by the neckline, he tugged it over his head and discarded it to the floorboards as he walked. Pulling back the corner of the light linen covering her frame, Marek slipped into the bed and curled up next to his wife.

Brynn stirred, stretching beneath his warmth. She sighed, nuzzling her backside against him. "Do I dream?"

"No, love, I am home, and eager to taste your sweetness on my lips." He brushed away her hair with the tip of his finger, exposing her neck. Placing a gentle kiss on her skin, he wrapped his arms around her, pulling her even closer to him. His palm traced the curves of her hip and down her thigh until he found the hem of her chemise. He slid his hand beneath it. Her skin was silk beneath his calloused fingers, and he molded it to fit in his palms, kneading it with his fingers, eager to sample it with his tongue. He gravitated toward her middle, taking his time to trace every curve, every line. When he cupped her belly, he slowed his exploration of her.

"What is this?" he murmured, caressing the fullness of the new life within her.

Brynn rolled to face him. Wrapping her arms around his neck, she kissed his slackened mouth. "You left before I was sure the seed had taken. You have been gone many months, husband."

"Mmm." He pouted. "My apologies for being gone so long. It took forever to track Gavin down. We found him losing a game of dice in a pub, and he was about to be pummeled by the bastard he cheated. And then Ireni couldn't decide what she wanted to bring with her, and the boys, well… I'm sorry. I should have sent a courier."

"You mean they're all here?"

"Aye. Ronan's croft was in disrepair. Even with my help, he wouldn't have been able to fix it. So I brought them all instead of just Ronan. I am truly sorry I didn't tell you, my love."

"It matters not. You are home now and in my arms again."

"What have I done to deserve such a gift as this life?" Marek kissed her with a heated passion, unrestrained and hungry for more.

Brynn returned the kiss but pulled away from his advances.

"I cannot enjoy the pleasure of my wife?" he growled, nibbling on the shell of her ear.

Brynn let out a small laugh, pushing him from her. "Not until you take a bath." She wrinkled her nose. "You smell."

"Oh, that's how 'tis going to be then, eh?" Grabbing two handfuls of buttocks, he tugged Brynn against his hips, gliding his knee between her legs.

"Until you wash the stink away and shave that stubble from your face, aye." Taking his chin in her fingers, she shook it gently before rolling away from him. "Besides, I have plans to visit Abby this afternoon."

Marek fell to his back, placing his hands beneath his head to watch her rise from the bed. The sun cut through her chemise, her perfect silhouette swaying with her hips.

"Bring her some flowers from the garden for me then, would you?"

"Aye, I will," she replied, slipping into her skirt. After securing it about her waist, she stepped into her shoes then crossed the room to give Marek one last kiss. "Scrub well," she teased, "and I will show you just how much I have missed you."

"Anything for you, love." He watched her saunter from the room and smiled. Perhaps the gods did shine upon him after all.

---

The ocean waves crashed against the sea wall, spraying her with a fine, salty mist. Upon reaching the rock, Brynn knelt in front of it, placing the bouquet of wildflowers at its base. "These are from Marek," she told the rock. "He would never admit to it, but I know he misses you. I miss you, too, Abby." Brynn kissed her palm then transferred the kiss to the gravestone. "May the gods bless you, my dear friend, as they have blessed me."

# Acknowledgments

This book is my baby, and my baby it will always be.
I've been writing since I was a child. It was my escape, and I could do anything I wanted in the pages. RETURN TO ME is the first "serious" book I wrote. It took me eight years to write it, because it had always just been a hobby for me. Write what you know, right? And I adored fantasy. It was my husband who encouraged me to finish it, and to publish it, and to republish it under my own when the small press who had it first closed its doors. He has been my rock, and my stories wouldn't be here if it wasn't for him cheering me on from the sidelines. He's supported me and writing in more ways that I ever imagined. And I love him for that.

# About the Author

Melissa spent her childhood exploring the coast of down east Maine without parental supervision and immersing herself in any book she could get her scrappy little hands on. Although she pursued a career in theater, the written word is her true calling. She leads a full life with her husband and six children traveling the country to wherever the Army sends them in her very large twelve passenger van, in what she lovingly deems "organized chaos". She finds time to write in her "spare time", somewhere in between soccer practices and nap time with coffee. Lots and lots of coffee. She loves creating unforgettable romance, and enjoys writing and reading everything from sexy, sword-toting heroes to spit-out-your-coffee funny romantic comedies... as long as she doesn't get the book wet. She leaves that up to the characters.

# Also by Melissa Mackinnon

The Archer's Daughter

Immortal Magic

The Do-Over

Cupid Wore Dog Tags - A Military Romance Anthology

Songs of the Deep - A Mermaid Box Set

Rituals & Runes - A Paranormal Anthology

Gilded Pages - coming 2023

Star Struck - coming 2023

Made in the USA
Middletown, DE
06 July 2022

68633066R00220